Baby for the Tycoon

EMILY McKAY
KAREN ROSE SMITH
EMILY FORBES

D1386741

MILLS &
BOON

Published in Great Britain 2015
by Mills & Boon, an imprint of Harlequin (UK) Limited,
Eton House, 18-24 Paradise Road, Richmond, Surrey, TW9 1SR

BABY FOR THE TYCOON © 2015 Harlequin Books S.A.

The Tycoon's Temporary Baby, The Texas Billionaire's Baby and *Navy Officer to Family Man* were first published in Great Britain by Harlequin (UK) Limited.

The Tycoon's Temporary Baby © 2011 Emily McKaskle
The Texas Billionaire's Baby © 2010 Karen Rose Smith
Navy Officer to Family Man © 2011 Emily Forbes

ISBN: 978-0-263-25218-7
eBook ISBN: 978-1-474-00397-1

05-0615

Harlequin (UK) Limited's policy is to use papers that are natural, renewable and recyclable products and made from wood grown in sustainable forests. The logging and manufacturing processes conform to the legal environmental regulations of the country of origin.

Printed and bound in Spain
by CPI, Barcelona

THE TYCOON'S TEMPORARY BABY

BY
EMILY McKAY

Emily McKay has been reading romance novels since she was eleven years old. Her first romance book came free. She has been reading and loving romance novels ever since. She lives in Texas with her geeky husband, her two kids and too many pets. Her debut novel, *Baby, Be Mine*, was a RITA® Award finalist for Best First Book and Best Short Contemporary. She was also a 2009 *RT Book Reviews* Career Achievement nominee for Series Romance. To learn more, visit her website at www. EmilyMcKay.com.

For Tracy and Shellee, two great friends and phenomenal writers. Ladies, thanks for making this so much fun. And to Ivy Adams, 'cause…well, you know.

One

Jonathon Bagdon just wanted his assistant to come home, damn it.

Wendy Leland had left seven days ago to attend a family funeral. In the time she'd been gone, his whole company had started falling apart. A major deal she'd been finessing had fallen through. He'd missed an important deadline because the first temp had erased his online calendar. The second temp had accidentally sent R&D's latest prototype to Beijing instead of Bangalore. The head of HR had threatened to quit twice. And no fewer than five women had run out of his office in tears.

As if all of that wasn't bad enough, the fourth temp had deep-fried the coffee maker. So he hadn't had a decent cup of coffee in three days. All in all, this was not his best moment.

Was it really too much to ask that at this particular time—when both of his business partners were out of town and when he was putting the finishing touches on the proposal for a crucial contract—that his assistant just come home?

Jonathon stared into his mug of instant coffee, contemplating whether he could ask Jeanell—the head of HR—to go out and buy a coffee maker, or if that would send her over the edge. Not that Jeanell was at the office yet. Most of the staff wandered in sometime around nine. It was barely seven.

Yes, he could have just gone out to buy himself a cup o' joe—or better yet, a new coffee maker—but with one deadline after another piling up, he just didn't have time for this crap. If Wendy had been here, a new coffee maker would have magically appeared. The same way the deal with Olson Inc. would have gone through without a hitch. When Wendy was here, things just worked. How was it that in the short five years she'd been the executive assistant here she'd become as crucial to the running of the company as he himself was?

Hell, if this past week was any indication, she was actually more important than he was. A sobering thought for a man who'd helped to build an empire out of nothing.

He knew only one thing, when Wendy did get back, he was going to do his damnedest to make sure she never left again.

Wendy Leland crept into the executive office of FMJ headquarters a little after seven. The motion sensor brought the lights up as she entered and she reached down to extend the canopy on the infant car seat she carried. Peyton, the tiny baby inside, frowned but remained asleep. She made a soft gurgling sound as Wendy lowered the car seat to a darkened corner behind her desk.

She rocked the seat gently until Peyton stilled, then Wendy dropped into her own swivel chair. Swallowing past the knot of dread in her throat, Wendy studied the office.

For five years, this had been the seat from which she'd surveyed her domain. She'd served as executive assistant for the three men who ran FMJ: Ford Langley, Matt Ballard and Jonathon Bagdon.

Her five years of Ivy League education made her perhaps a tad over-educated for the job. Or maybe not, since she hadn't procured an actual degree in any of her seven majors. Her family still thought she was wasting her talents. But the work was challenging and varied. She'd loved every minute of it. Nothing could have convinced her to leave FMJ.

Nothing, except the little bundle of joy asleep in the car seat.

When she'd left Palo Alto for Texas to attend her cousin Bitsy's funeral, she'd had no idea what awaited her. From the moment her mother called her to tell her that Bitsy had died in a motorcycle crash, the week had been one shock after another. She hadn't even known that Bitsy had a child. No one in the family had. Yet, now here Wendy was, guardian to an orphaned four-month-old baby. And gearing up for a custody battle of epic proportions. Peyton Morgan might as well have been dipped in gold the way the family was fighting over her. If Wendy wanted any chance of winning, she'd have to do the one thing she'd sworn she'd never do: move back to Texas. And that meant resigning from FMJ.

Only Bitsy could create this many problems from the grave.

Wendy gave a snort of laughter at the thought. Grief welled up in the wake of the humor. Squeezing her eyes shut, she pressed the heels of her hands against her eye sockets. Exhaustion had made her punchy, and if she gave in to her sorrow now, she might not stop crying for a month.

There would be time to grieve later. Right now, she had other things to take care of.

Wendy flicked on the desktop computer. Last night, she'd drafted the letter of resignation and then emailed it to herself. Of course, she could have sent it straight to Ford, Matt and Jonathon. She'd even spoken to Ford last night on the phone when he called to offer his condolences. Physically handing in the letter was a formality, but she wanted the closure that would come with printing it out, signing it and hand delivering it to Jonathon.

She owed him—or rather FMJ—that much at least. Before

her life became chaotic, she wanted to take this one moment to say goodbye to the Wendy she had been and to the life she'd lived in Palo Alto.

Beside her, the computer hummed to life with a familiarity that soothed her nerves. A few clicks later, she'd opened the letter and routed it to the printer. The buzz of the printer seemed to echo through the otherwise quiet office. No one else was here this early. No one but Jonathon, who worked a grueling schedule.

After signing the letter, she left it on her desk and crossed to the closed door that separated her office from theirs. A wave of regret washed over her. She pressed her palm flat to the door, and then with a sigh, dropped her forehead onto the wood just above her hand. The door was solid beneath her head. Sturdy. Dependable. And she felt herself leaning against it, needing all the strength she could borrow.

"You can hardly blame Wendy," Matt Ballard pointed out, a note of censure in his voice. At the moment, Matt was in the Caribbean, on his honeymoon. It was why they'd scheduled this conference call for so early. Matt's new wife, Claire, allowed him exactly one business call a day. "It's the first time in five years she's taken personal leave."

"I didn't say I blamed her—" Jonathon said into the phone, now sorry he'd called Matt at all. He'd had a legitimate reason for calling, but now it sounded as though he was just whining.

"When is she supposed to be back?" Matt asked.

"She was supposed to be back four days ago." She'd said she'd be in Texas two to three days, tops. After the funeral, she'd called from Texas to say she'd have to stay "a little longer." The lack of specificity made him nervous.

"Stop worrying," Matt told him. "We'll have plenty of time after Ford and I get back." As if it wasn't bad enough that Matt was on his honeymoon during this crisis, Ford and his family were also away, at their second home in New York City. "The proposal isn't due for nearly a month."

Yes. That was what bothered him. "Nearly a month" and "plenty of time" were about as imprecise as "a little longer." Jonathon was a man who liked precise numbers. If he was putting together an offer for a company worth millions, it mattered if the company was worth ten million or a hundred million. And even if he had nearly a month to work on the proposal, he wanted to know how long a little longer was.

Rather than take out his frustrations on his partner, Jonathon ended the phone call. This government contract was driving him crazy. Worse still was the fact that no one else seemed to be worried about it. For the past several years, research and development at FMJ had been perfecting smart grid meters, devices that could monitor and regulate a building's energy use. FMJ's system was more efficient and better designed than anything else on the market. Since they'd been using them at headquarters, they'd cut their electricity bills by thirty percent. This government contract would put FMJ's smart grid meters in every federal building in the country. The private sector would follow. Plus the meters would boost sales of other FMJ products. How could he not be excited about something that was going to cut energy consumption and make FMJ so much money?

Everything he'd been working for and planning for the past decade hinged on this one deal. It was the stepping-stone to FMJ's future. But first they had to actually get the contract.

Once he snapped his laptop closed, he heard a faint thump at the door. He wasn't optimistic enough to imagine the temp might come in this early. But did he even dare hope that Wendy had finally returned?

He pushed back his chair and strode across the oversize office he normally shared with Matt and Ford. When he opened the door, Wendy fell right into his arms.

Though unexpectedly falling through an open door seemed an apt metaphor for her life at the moment, nevertheless Wendy was surprised to find herself actually falling through the doorway. Jonathon's arms instantly wrapped around her, cradling her safely against his strong chest. One shoulder was pressed against him and her free hand automatically came up to the lapel of his suit jacket.

Suddenly she was aware of several things. The sharply crisp scent of his soap. The sheer breadth of his chest. And the clean, just-shaven line of his jaw, which was the first thing she saw when she looked up.

Normally, she did a decent job of ignoring it, but Jonathon Bagdon was the stuff of pure, girlish fantasies. He always looked on the verge of frowning, which lent his expression an air of thoughtful intensity. Though he rarely smiled, when he did, deep dimples creased his cheeks.

At just shy of six feet, he wasn't too tall, but his physique more than made up for what he lacked in height. He had a build more suited to barroom brawls than boardroom negotiations. He was strong and muscular. She'd never seen his naked chest, but he had a habit of shucking his suit jacket and rolling up the sleeves of his white dress shirt when he worked. Obviously she spent too much time looking at him. But until this moment, she'd never noticed he had a single mole on the underside of his perfectly square jaw.

Staring up into his green-brown eyes, she felt something unexpected pass between them. An awareness maybe. Some tension she'd never felt before. Or perhaps something she was too smart to let herself feel.

He swallowed. Fascinated, she watched the muscles of his throat shift mere inches from her face. She flattened her palm and pushed herself out of his arms.

She was all too aware of Jonathon's gaze following her every move. And even more aware that her outfit was inappropriate for work. He'd never seen her in jeans before. Certainly not topped with her favorite T-shirt, a retro Replacements concert T-shirt she'd bought online as her twenty-first birthday present to herself. It was old and ratty and she'd cut the neck out of it years ago. But somehow the shirt was all comfort. And today, she needed comfort more than she needed professionalism.

But, dang it, she wished he would stop looking at her with that hungry look.

It wasn't the first time in the five years they'd worked together that she'd seen him look at her like that. As if she was a temptation he had to resist. But it was the first time she'd allowed herself to feel even the faintest bit of need in return. Jonathon may be the stuff of feminine fantasies, but he was hell on women. She'd watched up close and personal as he'd trampled countless female hearts. She'd promised herself long ago that she'd never join the legions of women crushed by Jonathon Bagdon.

She could only hope that this new awareness she felt for him was the result of her exhaustion. Or perhaps her emotional vulnerability. Or maybe some bizarre hormone malfunction. At any rate, she wouldn't be around long enough for it to matter.

Jonathon wanted to pull her back into his arms. He didn't, of course. But he wanted to.

Instead, he held open the office door with one hand and shoved the other deep into his pants pocket, hoping to hide the effect her nearness had had on his body. As ridiculous as it was, in the few seconds he'd held his tempting little assistant against his chest, his body had responded. Only her shoulder and her palm had touched him and he'd still gone rock hard.

Of course, he'd felt that punch of desire for Wendy before. But normally he was better at schooling his response to her. Then again, she was usually dressed in blandly professional, business casual clothes. Not today. Her faded jeans were skintight and her T-shirt hung loose on her, its wide neck baring a tempting swath of collarbones, part of one shoulder and a hot pink bra strap.

He swallowed again, forcing his gaze back up to her face,

searching for something to say. Something other than "Lose the shirt."

"I trust your trip went well," he finally ventured.

She frowned and took another step back.

Then he remembered she'd been to a funeral. Hardly the kind of trip that would go *well*. "I'm sorry for your loss," he added. Her frown deepened. Were those tears in her eyes? "However, I am very glad to have you back."

He sounded like an idiot. Which was not wholly unexpected. He didn't deal well with emotional women.

"I—" she started.

Then she broke off again. She turned away from him and pressed her hands to her face. If the tension in her shoulders was any indication, she was about two seconds away from bursting into tears.

In five years, Wendy had been nothing but completely professional. If she was going to break into tears, why couldn't she have done it when Ford was here to deal with her? Ford had three sisters, a mother, a stepmother, a wife and a daughter. Surely all of those women in his life had better prepared him for dealing with this sort of thing.

Jonathon followed her into the front office and placed a hand on her back. He meant it to be comforting, but he was instantly aware that he'd placed it on the shoulder bared by her shirt. She twisted to look at him, her eyes wide and surprised, damp with unshed tears, but lit with something else as well. Beneath his hand her skin was hot, the strap of her bra silky and tempting.

She bit her lip again before pulling free of his touch.

And then he heard it. The unmistakable sound of crying. But not a woman crying. And it wasn't coming from Wendy.

Confused, he walked in and scanned the room for the source of the sound. It wasn't all-out screaming. More of a soft, mewling noise. Like a puppy might make. The room appeared empty. He moved toward the sound as Wendy rushed up behind him and practically threw herself in his path.

"I can explain!" She held up her hands in front of her as if warding off an attack.

"Explain what?" He dodged around her to look behind the desk. Her chair had been shifted to the side and where Wendy normally sat was an infant's car seat. And in that was a pale pink bundle.

He turned back to Wendy. "What is that?"

"That's a baby."

Jonathon's shock was palpable.

If she didn't know better, Wendy would have thought he'd never even seen a baby before. Though she imagined they were rare in his life, surely he had encountered at least one. After all, Ford had one himself. Jonathon must have been in the same room as his best friend's child at some point.

She dashed around him and squatted beside the car seat. She gave the back of it a gentle nudge but Peyton continued to fuss. Peyton's sleepy eyes flickered open, blinked and then focused on Wendy.

Something inside of Wendy tightened into a knot. A gut-level reaction to those bright blue eyes. Perhaps the only thing she'd ever felt that was actually stronger than that burst of attraction she'd felt for Jonathon just now.

Of course, she couldn't *have* Jonathon. She wasn't stupid enough to try. But for now, she did have Peyton. And she'd do anything in her power to keep her.

She unfastened the buckle strapping Peyton in and picked up the pink cotton bundle. Snuggling the baby close to her chest, she pressed her lips near Peyton's ear and made shushing noises. Then she drew in a breath scented like tear-free shampoo and pure love.

Suddenly feeling self-conscious, she looked up to find Jonathon watching her, a frown on his face.

She tried to smile but felt it wavering under the weight of her shifting emotions. "Jonathon, meet Peyton."

"Right," he said bracingly and he looked from her to the baby and then all around the room as if searching for the spaceship that must have dropped off this strange creature. "What is it doing in our office?"

"*She's* here because I brought her here." Which maybe hadn't been the smartest move, but she and Peyton had only gotten in the previous evening, after driving from Boulder, Colorado. With less than seventy-two hours of parenting experience under her belt, Wendy hadn't known what else to do with Peyton. "I didn't have anyone to watch her. And I don't think she's ready to be left with a stranger yet anyway. I mean, I'm strange enough, right? And—"

Jonathon cut her off. "Wendy, why do you have a baby?" His gaze dropped to her belly, suspicion lighting his gaze. "She's not…yours, is she?"

She was glad he'd cut her off, because she'd been babbling, but at the same time dreading the conversation to come, because he was not going to like what she had to say. Still, when she glanced down at the sixteen-pound baby, she had to laugh.

"No, I didn't go away for seven days and miraculously get pregnant, gestate and deliver a four-month-old. She's—" Her throat closed over the words, but she forced herself to say them. "She was my cousin's. Bitsy named me guardian. So she is mine now."

There was a long moment of silence during which Jonathon's expression was so blank, so unchanging she thought he might have suffered a stroke.

"I—" he began. Then he looked down at Peyton, his frown deepening. "Well—" He looked back at her and cocked his head to the side. "It turns out Jeanell was right. On-site childcare was a good idea. I'm sure she'll be just fine there."

Dread settled in Wendy's belly. As well as something else. Sorrow. Nostalgia maybe. She didn't want to leave FMJ. Even though she was just an assistant here, she'd never felt more at home anywhere else. Professionally or personally. Working at FMJ had given her purpose and direction. Something her family had never understood.

"I'm not going to bring Peyton to work," she began. And then decided there was no point in pussyfooting around this. "I'm not coming to work anymore. I came in today to resign."

Two

"Don't be ridiculous," Jonathon barked, too shocked to temper the edge of his words. "Nobody quits a job because they have a baby, much less because they inherited one."

Wendy rolled her eyes in exasperation. "That's not—" she started, but he held up a hand to cut her off.

"I know how stupid that sounded." This was why he needed Wendy. Why she was irreplaceable. Most of the time, he was too outspoken. Too blunt. Too brash. He had a long history of pissing off people who were easily offended. But not Wendy. Somehow, she managed to see past his mistakes and overlook his blunders.

The thought of trying to function without her here as his buffer made him panic. He wasn't about to lose her over a baby.

"FMJ has one of the highest-rated on-site child-care facilities in the area. There's no reason why you can't continue to work here."

"I can't work here because I have to move back to Texas."

As she spoke, she crossed to the supply closet in the corner. She moved a few things around inside and pulled out an empty cardboard box.

"Why on earth would you want to move to Texas?"

She shot him another one of those looks. "You know I'm from Texas, right?"

"Which is why I don't know why you'd want to move back there. I've never once heard you say anything nice about living there."

She bobbed her head as if in concession of the point. Then she shrugged. Rounding to the far side of the desk, she sank into the chair and opened her drawer. "It's complicated."

"I think I can keep up."

"There's a chance members of my family won't want me to raise Peyton. Unless I can convince them I'm the best mother for her, there'll be a custody battle."

"So? You don't think you can win the battle from here?"

"I don't think I can afford to fight it." Sifting through things in the drawer, she answered without looking up. She pulled out a handful of personal belongings and dropped them into the open box.

He watched her for a moment, barely comprehending her words and not understanding her actions at all. "What are you doing?"

She paused, glancing up. "Packing," she said as if stating the obvious. Then she looked back into the drawer and riffled through a few more things. "Ford called yesterday to offer his condolences. When I explained, he said not to worry about giving two-weeks' notice. That if I needed to just pack up and go, I should."

Forget twenty-two years of friendship. He was going to kill Ford.

The baby squirmed. Wendy jostled her knee to calm the little girl, all the while still digging in the drawer. "I swear I had another tube of lip gloss in here."

"Lip gloss?" She'd just pulled the rug out from under him.

If he'd had two weeks, maybe he could talk some sense into her. But no. His idiot of a partner had ripped that away too. And she was worried about lip gloss?

She must have heard the outrage in his voice, because her head snapped up. "It was my favorite color and they don't even make it anymore. And—" She slammed the drawer shut and yanked open another. "Oh, forget it."

"You can't quit."

She stood up, abandoning her task. "You think I want this? You think I want to move? Back to Texas? You think I want to leave a job I love? So that I can move home? I don't! But it's my only option."

"How will being unemployed in Texas solve anything?" he demanded.

"I…" Peyton squirmed again in her arms and let out a howl of protest. Wendy sighed, sank back into the chair and set it rocking with a pump of her leg. "I may not have mentioned it before, but my family has money."

She hadn't mentioned it. She'd never needed to.

People who grew up with money had an air about them. It wasn't snobbery. Not precisely. It was more a sense of confidence that came from always having the best of everything. It was the kind of thing you only noticed if you'd never had money and had spent your life trying to replicate that air of entitlement.

Besides, there was an innate elegance to Wendy that was in direct contrast to her elfin appearance and plucky verve. Yet somehow she pulled it off.

"From money?" he said dryly. "I never would have guessed."

Wendy seemed too distracted to notice his sarcasm. "My grandfather set up a trust for me. For all the grandkids, actually. I never claimed mine. The requirements seemed too ridiculous."

"And the requirements are?"

"I have to work for the family company and live within fifteen miles of my parents." She narrowed her eyes as if glaring at some unseen relative. Peyton let out another shriek of frustration and Wendy snapped back to the present. "So if I move home now—"

"You can claim the trust," he summed up. "You'd have enough money to hire a lawyer if it does come down to a custody battle."

"I'm hoping it won't come to that. My grandmother still controls the purse strings. The rest of the family will follow her wishes. Once she sees what a great mother I'm going to be, she'll back off and just let me raise Peyton." Wendy's jaw jutted forward in determination. "But if it does come to a custody battle, I want to be sure I have enough money to put up a good fight."

"I don't get it. You're doing all this for a cousin you barely knew? Someone you hadn't seen in years?"

Wendy's eyes misted over and for a second he thought that—dear God—she might actually start crying. She squeezed the baby close to her chest and planted a kiss on top of her head. Then she pinned him with a steady gaze brimming with resolution. "If something happened to Ford and Kitty, and they wanted you to take Ilsa, wouldn't you do whatever it took to honor their wishes?"

All he could do in response was shove his hands deep into his pockets and swallow a curse. Damn it, she was right.

He stared at the adorable tot on Wendy's lap, summing up his competition. He wasn't about to lose the best assistant he'd ever had. He didn't care how cute and helpless that baby was.

Peyton undoubtedly needed Wendy. But he needed her too.

Fighting the feeling of complete and utter doom—which, frankly, was a fight she'd been losing ever since the nanny had first handed her Peyton—Wendy glanced from the baby, to the open desk drawer and then to Jonathon.

She had so much to do, her mind couldn't focus on a single task. Or maybe it was lack of sleep. Or maybe just an attack of nerves brought on by the way Jonathon kept pacing from one side of the room to the other, pausing occasionally to glower in her direction.

When she'd first started work at FMJ, Jonathon had made her distinctly nervous. There was something about his combination of magnetic good looks, keen intelligence and ruthless ambition that made her overly aware of every molecule of her body. And every molecule of his body for that matter. She'd spent the first six months on edge, jumping every time he came in the room, nearly trembling under his gaze. It wasn't nerves precisely. More a kind of tingling anticipation. As if she were a gazelle who wanted to be eaten by the lion.

She'd forced herself to get over it.

And she'd thought she'd been successful. Only now that feeling was back. Either she could chalk it up to exhaustion and emotional vulnerability. Or she could be completely honest with herself. It *wasn't* nerves. It was sexual awareness. And now that she was about to walk out of his life forever, she wished she'd acted on it when she'd had the chance.

Forcing her mind away from that thought, she stared at the open desk drawer. The lip gloss was gone forever, just like any opportunity she might have had to explore a different kind of relationship with Jonathon. The best she could hope for now was to gather her few remaining possessions and make a run for it.

She had a Voldemort for President coffee mug in the bottom drawer, her Bose iPod dock, a tub of Just Fruit strawberries and in the very back, a bag of Ghirardelli chocolate caramels. Precious few possessions to be walking away with after five years, and the cardboard box dwarfed them. On the bright side, at least she'd only have to make one trip out to the car.

Balancing Peyton on her hip, she wedged the box under her arm only to find Jonathon blocking her route to the door.

"You can't go."

"Right. The car seat. I can't believe I forgot that." She turned back around, only to notice the diaper bag as well.

She blew out a breath. Okay. More than one trip after all.

"No," Jonathon said. "I'm not letting you quit."

Turning back around, she stared at him. "Not letting me? How can you not let me? If I quit, I quit."

"You're the best assistant I've ever had. I'm not going to lose you over something this…" He seemed to be searching for the least offensive word. "Frivolous."

She raised an eyebrow. "She's a child, not a frivolity. It's not like I'm running off to join the circus."

There was something unsettling about the quiet, assessing way he studied her. Then he said, "If keeping this baby is really so important to you, we'll hire a lawyer. We'll find the best lawyer in the country. We'll take care of it."

She felt her throat tighten, but refused to let the tears out of the floodgate. Oh, how tempting it was to accept his help. But the poor man had no idea what he was getting into.

"You should know, my family is extremely wealthy. If they fight this, they'll put considerable financial and political weight behind it."

"So?"

She blew out a long breath. The moment of reckoning. She always dreaded this. "Leland is my mother's maiden name. I legally took her name when I left college."

Jonathon didn't look impatient, the way some people did when she explained. That was one of the things she liked best about Jonathon. He reached conclusions quickly, but never judgments.

"My father's name—" Then she corrected herself. "My *real* last name is Morgan."

Most people, it took a couple of minutes for them to put together the name Morgan with wealth and political connections. She figured as smart as he was, it would take Jonathon about twenty seconds. It took him three.

"As far as I know, none of the banking Morgans live in Texas. That means you must be one of the Texas oil Morgans."

He didn't phrase it as a question. His tone had gone flat, his gaze distant.

"I am." She bit her lip, not bothering to hide her cringe. "I should have told you."

"No. Why would you have?" His expression was so blank, so unsurprised, so completely disinterested, that it was obvious, at least to her, that he cared deeply that she'd kept her true identity to herself. His calm, direct gaze met hers. "Then Senator Henry Morgan is…"

"My uncle." In the interest of full disclosure, she nodded to the baby gurgling happily on her hip. "Peyton's grandfather."

"Okay then." He stood with his hands propped on his hips, the jacket of his suit pushed back behind his hands. He often stood in that way and it always made her heart kick up a beat. The posture somehow emphasized the breadth of his shoulders and the narrowness of his waist all at the same time.

Despite his obvious disappointment, he immediately went into problem-solving mode. He stared at her blankly, then left the room abruptly. A moment later he returned with a copy of the *Wall Street Journal*. He flipped the paper open, folded it in half and held it out to her. "So, Elizabeth Morgan is your cousin. The baby's mother."

It was an article about her death. The first Wendy had seen. She didn't need to read it to know what it would say. It would be carefully crafted. Devoid of scandal. Bitsy may have been an embarrassment but Uncle Hank would have called in favors to make sure the article met with his approval. That was the way her uncle did business, whether he was running the country or running his family.

Jonathon frowned as he scanned the article. His eyes crinkled at the edges as his face settled into what she thought of as his problem-solving expression. But if he could figure a way out of this one, then he was smarter than even she thought he was.

"It says here she is survived by a brother and sister-in-law. Why don't they take the baby?"

"Exactly," she said grimly. "Why not? It's what every conservative in the country will be thinking. Those conservative voters made up a huge portion of Uncle Hank's constituents." And they weren't the only ones who had that question. It was no secret that their grandmother, Mema, didn't approve of modern families. In her mind, a family comprised a mother and a father. And possibly a dog. Mema would want Hank Jr. to take Peyton. And what Mema wanted was generally what the family did.

She may have been in her late eighties, but she was a wily old dame. More importantly, she still controlled the money.

"It's so frustrating," she admitted. "This wouldn't even be an issue if I had a husband I could trot out to appease my grandmother and Uncle Hank's constituents."

"You really think that's all you need?"

"For my family to see me as the perfect mother?" She gave a fake, trilling laugh. "Oh, yes, a husband is the must-have accessory of the season. The richer, the better. Optional add-ons are the enormous gas-guzzling SUV, the Junior League membership and the golden Lab."

"And it's really that simple?"

"Oh, sure. *That* simple. I'll just head over to the laboratory and whip up a successful husband out of spare computer parts. You run out to the morgue and steal a dead body I can reanimate and we'll be good."

His lips quirked in a smile, his eyes crinkling at the corners, just a hint of cockiness. The expression gave her pause, because he wasn't laughing at her joke. No, she knew this look too. It was his I've-solved-the-problem look. "I think we can do a little better than that."

"Excuse me?"

"You said it yourself. All you need is a rich, successful husband."

For a moment she just stared blankly at him, unable to follow the abrupt twist the conversation had taken. "Right. A rich, successful husband. Which I don't have."

"But you could." He smiled fully now. Full smiles were rare for him. Usually they made her feel a little breathless. This one just made her nervous. "All you have to do is marry me. I'll even buy you a dog."

Three

Having never before asked a woman to marry him, Jonathon wasn't quite sure what reaction he expected, but it wasn't Wendy's blank-faced confusion. Or maybe that was a perfectly normal reaction under the circumstances. After all, it wasn't every day a man proposed to his assistant for such transparently selfish reasons.

For a long moment, she merely stared at him, her blue-violet eyes wide, her perfect bow mouth gaping open in surprise.

She wasn't just surprised. She was disconcerted. His proposal had shocked her. Maybe even offended her. On some deeply intimate level, the thought of marriage to him horrified her.

Not that he could really blame her. Despite his wealth, he was no prize.

She was going to say no, and he couldn't let her do it.

He needed her. Quite desperately, if the past seven days had been any indication.

"I'm not proposing a romantic relationship," he reassured her, hoping to make his proposal seem as benign as possible.

"Obviously," she muttered. Still holding the baby in her arms, she sank to the edge of the desk. She dipped her head, nuzzling the tuft of dark hair on Peyton's head.

"This would be strictly a business arrangement." He argued more vehemently as he felt her slipping away. "We'll stay married as long as it takes to convince your family that we're suitable parents. We won't even have to live together. I'll grant you an annulment as soon as we've convinced them."

"No," she said softly.

He felt a pang in his chest at her response. Then he saw it. Her letter of resignation. Signed, dated and ready to be handed over. As official as an order for his execution.

This past week had been a premonition of his future without her. He could envision an endless parade of incompetent temps. Countless hours of interviewing assistants, all of whom would fail to live up to the precedent set by Wendy. This government contract would slip through his fingers, just as the Olson deal had. FMJ had lost millions on that one. Which was nothing compared to what they'd miss if they didn't secure this contract. He could feel the stepping-stone slipping out from under him, the future he'd planned out for the company dissolving before his very eyes.

Panic mounting, he kept talking. "If you're worried about sex, don't be. I certainly wouldn't expect to sleep with you."

Her gaze darted to his as she bolted to her feet. "No." Then she squeezed her eyes closed for an instant. "What I meant was…" She drew in a deep breath. "…a fast annulment wouldn't work."

Just as quickly, her eyes shifted away from his. In that moment, a powerful, unspoken message passed between them.

Not once in all the years they'd worked together had they talked about sex. They had shared countless other intimacies. Eaten meals late at night. Sat beside each other on long plane flights. He'd had her fall asleep with her head on his shoulder somewhere over the Atlantic Ocean. They had slept in hotel rooms with walls so thin he'd heard the sound of her rolling over in her bed. And yet despite all that, neither of them had ever broached the subject of sex.

But now that the word had been said aloud, it was there between them. The image of her, sprawled naked on a bed before him, was permanently lodged in his brain.

He found himself oddly pleased by the faint blush that crept into her cheeks as she couldn't quite meet his gaze.

"If we're going to do this—" she shot him a look from under her lashes as if she were trying to assess his commitment "—then we have to go all in."

He raised his eyebrows, speculatively. She wasn't saying no. She was making a counteroffer. He felt a grin split his face. Just when he thought he knew her, she always managed to surprise him.

"We can't get an annulment in three or even six months," she said. "My family will see right through that. In a year, maybe two, we'll have to get divorced. Simply pretend the marriage didn't work out."

"I see."

She shook her head. "I don't think you do. I'm committed to fighting for Peyton. I'll do whatever I have to. But I can't ask you to do the same."

"You're not asking," he pointed out. "I'm offering. And just so we're clear, I'm not doing this out of the goodness of my heart." The last thing he needed right now was her developing some starry-eyed notion about his motives. "I'm doing this to keep you working for FMJ. You're the best damn assistant I've ever had."

She threw up her hand to interrupt him. "This is ridiculous. Just hire another assistant. I'll even help you find one. There are plenty of other competent people in the city."

"But none of them are you. I need you," he argued. "None of them know the company the way you do. None of them would care about what FMJ does the way you do."

She seemed to be considering for a moment, then admitted, "Well, that's true."

"Besides. I don't have the time or energy to train someone new. My motives are very selfish."

"Trust me, I wasn't about to swoon from the romanticism of the moment." Her lips twisted in a wry smile. "I just want to make sure you know what you're getting into. If my family suspects what we're up to—"

"Then we'll convince them that our marriage has nothing to do with Peyton."

Her eyebrows shot up. "Convince them we're in love?"

"Exactly."

Wendy gave a snort of laughter. Baby Peyton squirmed in response. She turned her head and gave Jonathon a look of annoyance. If a baby could be annoyed. Obviously she wasn't going back to sleep. Pressing her tiny palms to Wendy's chest, she pushed away as if she wanted to be set free.

Wendy crossed to a diaper bag sitting on her desk. He hadn't even noticed it before, but when Wendy tried to unzip it with one hand, he moved to help her. He brushed her fingers aside and unzipped the bag. "What do you need?"

"The blanket. That pink one there. Spread it out on the floor."

Once the blanket was out, she situated the baby on her belly in the center of it.

The sight of a baby in the middle of FMJ's executive offices was so incongruous he could barely remember what they'd been talking about. Oh, right. She'd been snorting with laughter over the idea of them being in love. Nice to know he'd amused her.

"So you don't think we can convince your family we're romantically involved?"

Wendy was back at the diaper bag now, pulling out an array of brightly colored toys. "No offense, Jonathon, but in the five years I've been here, I don't think I've ever seen you romantically involved."

"That's ridiculous. I—"

She held up her hands to ward off his protests. "With anyone. Oh, I know you've dated *plenty* of women." She stressed "plenty" as if it was an insult. "But romance is not your strong suit."

Dropping to her knees, she strategically placed the toys in an arc in front of the baby. By now, Peyton had wedged herself up on her elbows.

"You think I can't be romantic?" he asked.

"I think you approach your love life with all the warmth and spontaneity of a long-term strategic planning committee."

"You're saying…what? That I'm a cold fish?" His voice came out tight and strained.

There was something very matter-of-fact about her tone. As if she were stating the obvious. As if it hadn't even occurred to her that this might insult him.

"Not really." She tilted her head to the side, her attention focused on Peyton. She nudged a stuffed elephant closer to the baby. He didn't know if the topic made her uncomfortable or if infant toys were really just that fascinating. "More that you keep your emotions tightly under control." Apparently satisfied with the arrangement of toys, she stood, dusting her hands off. "You're a dispassionate man. There's nothing wrong with—"

Okay, he'd had enough. He strode toward her, pulled her into his arms and kissed her.

He didn't know what pushed him over the edge. Whether it was her unending lecture about how dispassionate he was. Or the fact that ever since he'd said the word "sex" aloud a few minutes ago he hadn't been able to get it out of his head. Or maybe it was that tempting bit of shoulder her shirt kept exposing. Or hell, maybe it was even the hot-pink strap.

Whatever it was, his restraint snapped and he had to kiss her. And then, he couldn't stop.

Wendy had not seen it coming. One minute, she was trying to calm Peyton down, keep her distracted enough so she could keep talking to Jonathon. Because frankly, Wendy was having enough trouble concentrating on the logistics of the conversation without Peyton breaking out into all-out fussiness.

And then, a second later, her body was pressed against Jonathon's and his mouth was moving over hers in a kiss heaven made to knock her socks off.

One hand cradled her jaw, his fingertips rough against the sensitive skin of her cheek. The other was wrapped firmly around her waist, his hand strong against her back, pressing her so close to him she could feel the buttons of his shirt through the thin cotton of her T-shirt.

His kiss was completely unexpected. When he had crossed the room to her, the lines of his face taut, his expression so full of intent, it had never occurred to her that he was going kiss her.

Sure, in the past, she'd imagined what it might be like to kiss him. After all, they'd worked side by side for years. Just because she had a modicum of restraint didn't mean she was dead. Despite the pure perfection of his exterior, she'd always imagined that in the bedroom Jonathon was very much how he was in the boardroom. Analytical. Logical. In control. Dispassionate.

Holy guacamole, had she been wrong.

His lips didn't just kiss hers. They devoured her.

She felt his tongue in her mouth, stroking hers, coaxing a response, all but demanding she participate, until she found herself rising up onto her toes and wrapping her arms around his neck, brushing her palm against the bristle of soft hair on the back of his head.

The kiss was hot and endless. He tasted faintly of coffee and fresh minty toothpaste and deeply buried longing. He stirred feelings within her that she'd never even imagined. And she could just not get close enough to him.

He backed her up a step. And then another. She felt the

edge of her desk bump against the back of her legs. And still he pressed into her, bending her so her back arched.

An image flashed through her mind of him sweeping the desk clear, pressing her down onto her desk and taking her right there. The idea came to her so completely, it was as though it had been right there in the back of her mind for years. Just waiting for his kiss to pull it out of her.

There was no one else in the building. Why shouldn't they give in to this thing between them? She couldn't think of a single reason not to.

She still hadn't thought of one a moment later when he pulled his mouth from hers and stepped away. He cleared his throat, then tugged down the hem of his jacket to straighten it.

He left her aching for him. Missing the warmth of his body, even though he was only a foot away. Wishing she had some idea of why he'd kissed her. Why he'd stopped…

Peyton.

Oh, crap. Peyton!

Wendy looked past Jonathon to where Peyton still lay on her belly on the floor.

Holy guacamole, indeed! She'd been a mother for less than four days and she'd already abandoned her daughter on the floor to make out with her boss. Maybe her family was right. Maybe she really was unfit to be Peyton's mother.

Her gaze sought Jonathon. He'd crossed to the other side of the room so that Peyton lay between them like a landmine.

He ran a hand across his jaw, then shoved his hand deep in his pocket. She'd never seen him look quite so disconcerted. Though he still looked less shaken than she felt.

"Well," he began, then swallowed visibly. "I think we can both agree that if I need to I can convince your family that I am more than your boss."

"Yeah. I think so." Then she paused for a beat while his words sank in. "*That's* what this was about?" For a second, confusion swirled through her, muddling her thoughts even further. "You kissed me merely to make a point?"

"I—" He shrugged, apparently at a loss for words.

Indignation pushed past her embarrassment. "I was seconds away from dropping my panties to the floor and you were making a point?"

For an instant, his gaze fell to her feet as if imagining her panties lying there. He swallowed again as he dragged his gaze back to hers, then ran a hand down his face.

Well, at least she wasn't the only one whose world had been rocked.

"It seemed a prudent move," he said stiffly.

She nearly snorted her derision. Prudent? The kiss that had curled her toes all the way up to her kneecaps had seemed *prudent* to him?

"Oh, that is wrong in so many ways, I don't even know where to start."

He tried to interrupt her. "Actually—"

But she cut him off with a wag of her finger. "No, wait a second. I *do* know where to start. If you think offering to marry me for Peyton's sake gives you an all-access pass to this—" she waved her hand in front of her body "—then you have another think coming." He looked as if he might say something in protest, but she didn't give him a chance. "And secondly, you have no business kissing me merely to make a point."

And then—because she realized that was practically an invitation to kiss her for other reasons—she added, "In fact you have no business kissing me at all. If we're going to do this pretend-marriage thing, we need to set some boundaries. And thirdly…well, I have no idea what thirdly is yet, but I'm sure it will come to me eventually."

For a long moment, Jonathon merely stared at her, one eyebrow slightly arched, his lips curved to just hint at his amusement. "Are you done?"

She clamped her lips together, painfully aware of how cool

and collected he seemed when she'd just been rambling like an idiot. A surefire sign that her emotional state was neither cool nor calm.

Maybe she was wrong about the kiss affecting him as much as it did her. And wouldn't that just suck. Didn't she have enough on her plate just now? This was so not the time for her to be nursing a crush on her boss. Or her husband.

When had her life gotten so complicated?

On the floor between them, Peyton wedged her tiny hands under her to push up onto her forearms. She let out an excited squeal of pride.

Right. This was when her life had gotten complicated. Approximately five days ago in her grandfather's study when the lawyer dropped Bitsy's will on her like a bomb.

Wendy let loose a sigh of frustration. "I'm sorry," she said. "None of this is your fault. I shouldn't take it out on you. I just—"

"I agree we need boundaries," he said abruptly, cutting her off before she could bumble further into the apology. His tone was stiff, as if he was searching for the most diplomatic way to broach the subject. "Keeping sex out of this is a good idea. However, kissing you now seemed prudent because we will have to kiss again at some point."

"We will?" she asked weakly, her gaze dropping to his mouth.

"Naturally."

She felt a curious heat stirring deep inside at the idea. He was going to kiss her again. Soon? She hoped so. Even if it was a very bad idea, she hoped so.

"If we're going to convince people we're in love and getting married, people will expect certain displays of affection."

"Oh, I hadn't thought…" Obviously, there was a lot she hadn't considered about this idea. She didn't know whether or not to be thankful that Jonathon's brain worked so much faster than her own. Was it a good thing he was around to consider things she hadn't? Or was it merely annoying to always be one step behind?

"The people who know us best will be hardest to convince. Luckily Ford and Matt will both be out of town for another few weeks. We'll have to get used to the idea ourselves before see them."

"Ford and Matt? Surely we don't need to lie to them?" Jonathon had been best friends with Ford and Matt since they were kids.

He leveled a steady gaze at her. There was no hesitation. No doubt. "Yes, we do. If your family decides to fight us on this, it could mean a court battle. I can't ask either of them to lie for us."

"Oh." Feeling suddenly weak, she sank back to the edge of the desk.

Of course they couldn't ask Ford and Matt to lie for them. In the five years she'd worked with FMJ, she'd served as executive assistant for all three men equally.

They worked so closely together they'd decided long ago it was easier to share one assistant among the three of them. Undoubtedly that was why they'd gone through so many assistants before she'd come along. Managing the schedules and needs of three such disparate men was no easy task. In short, she was a miracle worker.

If the thought of lying to them was this difficult for her, then how must Jonathon feel about the matter?

She propelled herself away from the desk and crossed to stand in front of him. Gazing up into his mossy-green eyes, she studied him. "This is a crazy and ridiculous plan. Are you sure you want to do this?"

His lips curved into a slight smile. His eyes lit with a reckless gleam as they crinkled at the corners, giving her the distinct impression that he was enjoying this. "Yeah. I'm sure. If there's one thing I know, it's how to make the strategic risk pay off."

The resolve in his gaze was as clear as the doubt probably

was in her own. Then she looked down at where Peyton lay on the floor. She scooped up the precious little girl and held her close. This moment felt profound. As though she and Jonathon were striking a bargain that was going to change all of their lives. It seemed only right that Peyton be a part of it as well.

"Okay," she said. "Let's do this."

Jonathon's face broke into a full grin. He gave a brisk nod then spun on his heel, moving toward his office as he started barking orders, back into full boss mode.

"First off, email Ford and Matt and schedule another teleconference for later in the day. Then call Judge Eckhart and see if he has time in his schedule to perform the ceremony next Friday. Clear my schedule and yours for the following two weeks."

Wendy was used to having Jonathon rattle off a to-do list like this. Even trying to juggle Peyton, she kept up pretty well. Until he got to the last item on the list.

"Wait a second. Clear our schedules? What are we going to be doing? And what about the government contract?"

"We'll work on that this week. And we'll have another couple of weeks after we get back. It'll be tight, but I have no doubt we'll get it done."

"Get back? Get back from where?"

He paused by his desk and looked up at her, that cocky smile still on his face. "From our honeymoon."

"Our honeymoon?" Surprise pitched her voice high.

"Don't get too excited. We're just going to Texas. If we're going to win this battle with your family, we need to go on the offensive. That means taking the fight to them."

Four

When Jonathon called her into the conference room the next morning, she was surprised to see Randy Zwack there. Randy had gone to college with Jonathon, Matt and Ford before going on to law school. He'd occasionally done work for FMJ, before they'd hired an intellectual property legal department, but that had been long before her time. She was more confused than surprised when she walked into the conference room and saw him there—looking more harried than usual.

Jonathon stood at the far end of the room, back to the door, staring out at the view of Palo Alto sprawling below. Randy sat dead in the center of the table, stacks of paper spread out before him. The lawyer looked up when she entered. He half stood and offered her a strained smile.

"Oh, good. You're here," he said as if he'd been waiting for her. "We can get started."

"Hi, Randy." She looked past him to Jonathon. When he turned around, she raised her eyebrows in question. "What's up?"

He frowned and with unusual hesitancy said, "I asked Randy here to draw up a prenuptial agreement for us." He held out a hand to ward off some protest he imagined she might make. "Don't worry. I trust his discretion."

"I'm not worried." In fact, delighted was more like it. "Calm down. I think a prenup is a fantastic idea."

"You do?" Randy looked surprised.

"Why wouldn't I?" She sat down in the chair opposite Randy. "I assume Jonathon told you why he's helping me?"

Randy gave a little nod, still looking suspicious.

"This is a marriage custom-made for a prenup."

"In the interest of full disclosure…" Randy ran a hand over his hair, which today looked disheveled, though it was normally meticulously styled to hide his growing bald spot. "This is not my area of expertise. I told Jonathon he should hire a good family lawyer, but—" Randy winced.

"But Jonathon can be very pig-headed."

"I was going to say determined."

No wonder the poor guy looked so disconcerted. Jonathon had obviously browbeat him into drawing up the prenup. And doing it on a very tight schedule, since Jonathon had proposed less than twenty-four hours ago.

"Don't worry." Wendy reached across the table and patted Randy's hand. "I'm sure you did great. It's all pretty cut-and-dry."

Jonathon took a few steps closer to loom over them from the end of the table. He'd shoved his hands into his pockets in that way she found so distracting.

This was the man who was going to be her husband. In less than a week. Her stomach tightened at the thought.

"Okay, let's see this puppy. It's just your standard prenup, right?"

Reaching for the stack of papers in front of Randy, she clapped her hands in a way that was overly cheerful, as if this was a big fake check from Publishers Clearinghouse. But neither man noticed. Randy was too busy sending Jonathon a pointed glance and Jonathon was too busy glaring Randy into intimidated silence. She looked from one man to the other.

"This *is* a standard prenup? Right?"

Jonathon cleared his throat and loomed some more.

"You have nothing to worry about. Any assets you bring to the marriage or inherit while married revert to you upon the absolution of the union." Randy flushed bright as he spoke. Just in case she'd seen through his obfuscation.

Ignoring Jonathon, she looked pointedly at Randy, waiting for him to cave. "That's not what I asked, now, is it?"

He cleared his throat. "You…um…have nothing to worry about."

"Yes, you said that already. What about him?" She nodded in Jonathon's direction.

"The prenup was written to my specification," Jonathon said tightly. "I'm satisfied."

Which was not the same thing at all.

Randy blushed all the way to his receding hairline, but refused to look at her. Jonathon, on the other hand, met her gaze without even flinching, which actually made her more nervous.

"Give me a minute." Neither man budged. "Alone. With the prenup." Still no movement from the united front. "Either you give me time to read it or you—" she pointed at Randy "—tell me what it is he doesn't want me to see."

Randy looked to Jonathon, who glowered at her for a second before granting a tight nod. Randy pulled her copy closer and flipped to a page midway through.

She scanned the paragraph, then read it aloud to give voice to her exasperation. "In the event of separation, annulment or divorce, the following premarital assets belonging to Jonathon Bagdon shall transfer to Gwendolyn Leland—the monetary value of twenty percent of all real property, tangible property, securities and cash owed by—"

She broke off in frustration, too stunned to continue. She glared at them both. "Whose idea was this ridiculous clause?"

Randy held up his hands. "Not mine." He sounded as offended as she was.

"But you *let* him include this? Are you insane?" She clenched and unclenched her fingers around the pen Randy had handed her as he gave a what-could-I-do shrug. She smiled tightly at him and said through clenched teeth, "Will you please give me a minute alone with my future husband?"

Randy skittered away like a death-row inmate given a pardon. She didn't blame him. Someone was going down. She wouldn't want to get caught in the crossfire either.

The second they were alone she asked, "Twenty percent? Twenty? Are you crazy?"

Jonathon at least had the good sense to try to sound placating. "Now, Wendy…"

"You know I'm not taking twenty percent!"

"After two years being married to me, you may think you've earned it."

She blew out a breath of exasperation. "I'm not taking. A penny. Of your money."

"Don't forget, California is a community property state. If you don't sign the prenup, you're entitled to half of anything I earn while we're together. For all you know that could be more than this twenty percent."

"What? Because you haven't been meeting your full potential before now?" He just scowled at her. "You know that has nothing to do with why I'm marrying you."

"I also know exactly how much money you make and that you'll have trouble supporting yourself and a child on that income."

"Lots of single-parent families get by on what I make," she pointed out.

"Maybe they do," he countered. "But you don't have to."

"So what? You're just going to give me all of that money? Did you somehow miss the conversation yesterday where I mentioned that I'm a Morgan? Trust me when I tell you, Jonathon, I will be fine."

His lips curved into the barest hint of a smile. "No. I didn't miss that, but I also know how damn stubborn you are. And I know that you're not going to ask your family for money. If you were the kind of person who would do that, you wouldn't be in this position to begin with."

Hmm. Good point. "But," she countered, "you thought you'd talk me into taking twenty percent of your assets?"

"No. I rather hoped you'd sign the prenup without noticing that part."

Well, that she could believe. He was just arrogant enough to think he could get away with a stunt like that.

"Even if I *had* signed the papers, I still wouldn't have taken the money. That's almost—" She struggled to do the math. Jonathon, no doubt, knew exactly how much that was, to the dime, at any given moment. "That's…tens of millions of dollars." Certainly more than the trust she'd never bothered to claim, which was a measly eight million. "I'm not taking that kind of money from you."

He shrugged dismissively. "It's a drop in the bucket."

"It's a fifth of the bucket. That's a lot of drops." She forced out a long, slow breath. Why was she angry? Why exactly?

She put voice to her thoughts as they came to her, not willing to give herself time to soften them. "Look, you've always been arrogant and controlling."

He raised his eyebrows. Probably in surprise that she'd say it aloud to him. He certainly couldn't be shocked by the idea.

"At work, it's fine," she continued. "You're my boss. But if we're going to get married, then the second we walk out that door each day—" she jabbed a finger toward the door "—you have to stop trying to control everything. Even if this isn't a real marriage."

"Wendy, I'm not—"

"But you are," she said, cutting him off. "Don't you get it? If I wanted to sit back and be taken care of for the rest of my life, I never would have left Texas. I *like* having to work for a living. I've been rich. I know that money alone won't make me happy. And I also know that being with someone who's always trying to control me will make me miserable. So either you back off, or we walk away from this now."

He stared at her a long time, his gaze hard-edged and steely. She didn't back down. She couldn't. Her gut told her that if she lost her foothold now, she wouldn't recover. Besides, she was far too used to intimidating glares from her father or uncle to do that. Eventually, she even smiled. "See. Your Jedi mind tricks don't work on me."

His lips twitched at her comment and finally, he gave a terse, reluctant nod, as if agreeing to keep his own money was an affront to his personal honor.

"There's something else you should know."

"Okay, hit me."

"In the event of my death, you and Peyton get it all." She opened her mouth to protest, but he raised a hand to cut her off. "I'm not budging on that one."

"What about your family?" As familiar as she was with his schedule, she knew he didn't see them often, but they did exist. "Surely you want them to have your fortune."

His eyes were dark and shuttered. His face nearly expressionless. "There are certain charitable organizations that I've already provided for. If I die while we're married, I want you to have the rest."

She studied him for a moment. Since this was the most she'd ever heard him say about his family—precisely nothing—she had to assume he was serious. Boy, and she thought her relationship with her family was screwed up. "Okay," she said softly. "Then we'll just have to take very good care of you for the next two years. Make sure you take your vitamins." She smiled at her own joke, but he didn't return the smile. "Now that that's settled, I'll go tell Randy he can do his job and protect his client."

She'd almost made it out the door when Jonathon's words stopped her.

"I don't want you to fall in love with me."

Hand already on the doorknob, she turned to face him, eyebrows raised. "Excuse me?"

His expression was so strained as to be nearly comical. "If we're going to be together a year or maybe two, I don't want you imagining that you've fallen in love with me."

Fighting back a chuckle, she searched his face, but saw no signs that he was joking. In fact, he looked so serious, it made her heart catch in her chest. She had to force a teasing smile. "Why? Because you're so charming and charismatic that I won't be able to be constantly in your company without falling in love?" He didn't smile at her, so she asked, "Is this a separate issue from the money or are the millions of dollars supposed to ease my heartache if I did fall in love with you?"

His lips twitched again, but she wasn't sure if it was with suppressed humor or irritation. "Separate issue. But I'm serious."

She could certainly see that. It made her uneasy, but she couldn't say why. It wasn't arrogance—his fear that she might fall in love with him. No, despite his natural confidence, she didn't see that in his gaze now. Instead, she saw only concern. For her.

"Let me guess. You're not the type of man who believes in love." She could imagine that all too easily. Jonathon may feel physical passion—he'd proven that clearly enough when he'd kissed her yesterday—but love was something else entirely.

But to her surprise, he shook his head. "Oh, I believe in love. I know exactly how crippling it can be. That's why I don't want you to imagine you've fallen in love with me."

"Okay," she said, torn between wanting to reassure him, without telling him outright that she had absolutely no intention of risking her heart. Finally, she made the only counteroffer she could think of. "Then don't fall in love with me either."

He studied her for a moment, slowly smiling.

Her chin bumped up a notch. "What? You think you're above falling in love with me? I'll have you know I'm very loveable." Arching an eyebrow, she said, "I'm cute. And plucky. Greater men than you have fallen in love with me."

"I'm sure they have."

"You think I'm joking?" she demanded, all fake belligerence.

"Not for a minute," Jonathon conceded. And the really pathetic things was, he was being honest. In this moment, watching her trying to cajole him into laughing, it was all too easy to imagine falling in love with her. Smart, funny, never taking herself too seriously. Wendy was the whole package. Men who wanted things like a wife and family were probably waiting in line for a woman like her. Too bad he wasn't one of them.

"Just don't forget why I'm doing this. This isn't a favor to you. This isn't because I'm a nice guy. Don't romanticize me. Don't forget, not even for a minute, why I'm here. Why I'm doing this."

She looked up at him, her eyes wide, her expression suddenly serious but a little bemused, as if she had no idea where he was going with this. "Remind me then. Why are you doing this?"

He was struck—not for the first time—that she wasn't merely cute, but truly beautiful. With her swoopy little button nose and her pixie dimples, her face had more than its share of cuteness. But she was also lovely, with her dark—almost violet—blue eyes and her luminous skin. Her beauty had an ephemeral quality to it. Like a woman in a Maxfield Parrish painting.

He was so struck by her beauty that for a second, he forgot her question. Forgot that he was trying to direct this conversation. To remind her that he wasn't some hero.

"I'm doing this for the same reason I've done everything else since I was eleven. I'm doing this because it serves my own goals. It serves FMJ."

She gave me an odd look, as something almost like pity flickered across her expression. "If you didn't want me to romanticize you, then maybe you shouldn't have tried to give me a big nasty chunk of your fortune. So I'm going to reserve the right to think you're not the heartless bastard you pretend to be."

"You have to believe me when I tell you that everything I've done for you was for my own benefit. Keeping you in California was the best thing for FMJ. Marrying you is the best thing for FMJ. That's the only reason I'm doing it."

Finally she nodded. "Okay. If you want to keep insisting you're so coldhearted, then I'll try to remind myself as often as possible. We'll start with the prenup, okay? We'll ask Randy to rewrite it so I have to pay you twenty percent of my money. How does that sound?" She smiled as she asked, but it looked strained.

"Wendy—" he started.

"At the very least, we'll put Randy out of his misery. We'll go with the bare-bones prenup. Everyone walks away with what they had when they came into the marriage."

He sighed. It wasn't what he wanted. Not by a long shot. But he was starting to realize that when it came to Wendy, he wasn't ever going to get what he wanted.

She paused at the door and looked over her shoulder, her forehead furrowed in thought. "The thing is, Jonathon, if you really were a heartless bastard, you wouldn't have warned me off."

Five

The next few days passed in a blur of planning and activity. Wendy often felt as if her life was moving at double time while she was stuck at half speed. She'd felt like that ever since she'd gotten that fateful call about Bitsy, less than two weeks before. Her shock and grief were finally beginning to recede into the background. Though she no longer faced the daunting challenge of moving back to Texas, agreeing to marry Jonathon had created even more turmoil in her life.

True to his word, Jonathon managed to cram in considerable work on the proposal for the government contract, delegating things he normally would have handled himself. Ford and Kitty flew home immediately with their daughter, Ilsa. Matt and Claire arrived a few days later, having cut short their honeymoon, something Wendy still felt bad about. Claire insisted that seventeen days in a tropical paradise was enough for anyone and that she wouldn't miss the wedding for anything. Her reassurances didn't make Wendy feel any less guilty.

The Sunday before the wedding, she was still half-asleep watching a rerun of *Dharma & Greg* wishing Peyton seemed half as drowsy. Jonathon had eventually convinced her that she should move into his house. Since they were planning on being married for a year or more, he pointed out that people were unlikely to believe they were truly in love if they weren't living together. The night before she'd pulled out her trusty suitcase and hoped to pack the bare essentials once Peyton fell asleep. If she could stay awake herself. She'd leave her other belongings for some later date.

She hadn't slept well since…well, since taking Peyton, and her exhaustion was creeping up on her. Frankly, it had been all she could do to drag herself out of bed this morning. The middle-of-the-night feedings were just not her thing. She was sitting on the sofa, blearily rocking back and forth, wondering if she could get Babies "R" Us to deliver a rocking chair by the end of the day, when the doorbell rang.

It was a bad sign that it took her so long to identify the noise.

She set the bottle down on the side table, stumbled to her feet and pried the door open, praying that no one on the other side would expect coherent conversation.

She frowned at the sight of Kitty and Claire. She'd only known Claire for seven months, but the concern lining the other woman's face was obvious in the crinkle between her brows. As if to distract from her frown, she thrust forward a pink bakery box with the Cutie Pies logo stamped on the top.

"We brought food!" Claire announced, her tone overly chipper. "We just flew in from Palo Verde this morning. I made this batch just before I left."

Claire owned a diner in the small town of Palo Verde, a couple of hours away. Jonathon, Ford and Matt had grown up in Palo Verde. If Claire had baked whatever was in the box, she couldn't wait to dive in. And if fate was kind at all, the box would be filled with the spicy, dark chocolate doughnuts that the diner was known for.

Kitty gave Wendy a once-over, then announced, "Since you're obviously too tired to invite us in, why not just step aside." She held out her hands. "Here, hand me the baby. You take the doughnuts. Please, eat some before I fight you for them."

Mutely, Wendy handed the fussy Peyton over to Kitty.

Kitty Langley was the kind of woman who looked as if she didn't have a maternal bone in her body. The jewelry-store-heiress-turned-jewelry-designer had lived in New York until falling in love with and marrying Ford the previous year. How that woman could look glamorous while cradling a baby in her arms, Wendy didn't know. But she did envy the skill, since she was pretty sure she herself looked as if she was recovering from the flu.

Wendy happily traded baby for doughnuts.

Though her arms ached from the hours of holding Peyton, the bone-deep weariness melted a bit as she sank her teeth into the dense buttermilk doughnut.

"I'm not sure why you came," she muttered past a mouthful of heaven. "But, frankly, I no longer care. You can hold me at gunpoint. Rob me. Even take the baby. Just leave the doughnuts and I'll be happy."

Kitty stifled a smile as she pressed her bright red lips to the crown of Peyton's head. "You're in that too-exhausted-to-be-tired stage, aren't you?"

After a few minutes of being held by Kitty, Peyton stopped fussing long enough to put her head down on Kitty's shoulder. And then there was silence. Peyton's eyes drifted closed and she exhaled a slow, shaky breath. Then her back settled into the gentle rhythm of sleep.

Tension seeped out of every pore in Wendy's body.

"Oh, thank goodness," she muttered.

Claire smiled wryly. "Did you get any sleep at all last night?"

"A couple of hours here and there," she admitted. "This caring for a baby gig is way harder than I expected."

"Oh, honey, you said a mouthful there." Kitty gave a low whistle, no doubt remembering her own new-to-mothering days. Walking with an exaggerated sway, Kitty crossed to the bassinet, so she could lay the baby down. "And at least I had seven months to get used to the idea."

The room fell silent as Kitty eased the sleeping Peyton down. Claire trotted off to the kitchen and returned a few minutes later with a steaming cup of coffee. "With cream and sugar," she said as she handed it over. "I assume all sane people take it that way."

Wendy took a grateful sip as Kitty asked, "Can we get you anything else? Something to eat maybe? I can't cook worth a damn, but Claire could McGyver a feast out of the barest cupboard."

Wendy didn't doubt it. "I think I'll save room for another doughnut."

"You sure?" Claire asked, in hushed tones so as not to wake the baby. "I could whip up an omelet. Or something else? I saw some nice Gouda in the fridge when I was foraging for cream." With a smile she added, "I could make you a grilled cheese sandwich so good you'll cry."

"No, thank you."

"You should try the grilled cheese," Kitty urged. "It's amazing."

"No, really. I'm okay." Wendy looked from Kitty to Claire, suddenly suspicious. "Why do I get the feeling I'm being plied with food for nefarious reasons?"

Kitty and Claire exchanged a look.

Wendy raised an eyebrow. "Come on, spill. What's up?"

Claire's cheeks reddened with what Wendy could only assume was guilt. Kitty played her cards closer to her chest. Her expression revealed nothing.

"Okay, obviously you have some bad news for me. Either that or you're going to try to get me to join a cult. Which is it?"

Claire bit down on her lip, her chin jutting out at a rebellious angle.

Kitty gave a little eye roll and sighed with obvious exasperation. "Fine," Kitty said, managing to flounce a bit while sitting almost perfectly still. "We're worried about Jonathon."

Wendy gave a little grunt of surprise and sat back against the sofa. "Worried? About Jonathon?"

"Whatever is going on between you and Jonathon," Claire began, "obviously has something to do with Peyton."

Wendy opened her mouth to protest, but Kitty didn't give her a chance.

"Jonathon wouldn't talk about it, so I assume you won't either. That's fine. But we're not idiots. Don't forget, you told Ford why you were resigning just twenty-four hours before you and Jonathon announced you were getting married. If I had to guess, I'd say you're pretending to be some happily married couple so your family will let you keep Peyton."

Well, so much for hiding the truth from their friends.

"As convoluted and bizarre as that seems," Kitty continued. "We're not going to try to stop you."

"We'll even play along," Claire added in. "Anything you need from us, you've got."

"But when you're off playing house together, just be very careful."

For a long moment, Wendy had no idea what to say. She turned away from their careful scrutiny and walked over to the bassinet where Peyton lay sleeping.

She thought about the conversation she'd had with Jonathon before they'd signed the prenup. Apparently, he wasn't the only one who thought she was in danger of falling in love with him. And here she'd thought she'd hid her attraction to him so well over the years. Was she really so transparent?

Glancing back at Kitty and Claire, she forced a perky smile. "Look, I admit Jonathon is a great guy. I've always thought so. But I know his dating history probably better than either one of you. I know he doesn't open up easily. I'm not going to make the mistake of falling in love with him."

Claire and Kitty exchanged nervous glances, seeming to have an entire conversation with just their eyebrows.

"What?" Wendy demanded after a second, crossing back to the sofa to get a better view of their unspoken exchange.

Claire kept her mouth shut.

But it was Kitty who admitted, "Actually, it's him we're worried about."

Wendy sank back to the sofa. "You're worried about Jonathon? Falling in love with me?"

Claire nodded.

"Not me falling in love with him, but him. Falling in love. With me."

Kitty gave an elegant wave of her hand. "Obviously we don't want to see you left brokenhearted either. But you're a smart woman. Very practical. We just assumed you can look out for yourself."

"But you're worried that Jonathon, the brilliant, analytical CFO is going to get his feelings hurt?" Wendy fought back a giggle.

"Well," Claire hedged. "Yes."

Wendy looked from one woman to the other, her amusement fading. "You're serious?"

They nodded.

"I know that Jonathon seems…" Claire trailed off, searching for the right word.

"Detached," Kitty provided. "Ruthless."

Claire glared her into silence. "You're not helping."

"Like a heartless bastard," Wendy offered quietly.

"Yes!" Kitty agreed.

"But he really isn't," Claire said quickly. "Don't forget, I've known him longer than you have."

Which was technically true. Claire had grown up in the same small town as Matt, Ford and Jonathon. "But you're younger than he is. You didn't even go to school together."

"We overlapped some," Claire argued. "And I've seen him in love. Senior year, he was…" she trailed off, apparently struggling to convey the full force of his emotion. "He was just head over heels in love. Crazy in love with this girl. He would have done anything for her."

"Who was she?" Wendy found herself asking.

Claire hesitated. "Just a girl at school. Kristi hadn't grown up in Palo Verde. Her parents were divorced and she moved there to live with her dad her sophomore year."

"And they dated?"

"A little." Then Claire shrugged. "I think mostly he just chased her. She flirted a lot. He was completely determined to win her over. Any grand gesture you can imagine an eighteen-year-old guy making, he made it. Flowers, jewelry. The whole nine yards."

Flowers and jewelry? She knew he didn't have a lot of money growing up. He'd once told her he'd started saving money for college when he was twelve. She couldn't even imagine the man she knew taking money out of his precious college fund to buy gifts. For a girlfriend.

"Once," Claire said, leaning forward and warming up to the story, "she told him that her mother always bought her birthday cake from the same bakery. She'd grown up in San Francisco. So for her birthday, the guys made a road trip out to San Francisco to buy her a cake. On a school day. They got in so much trouble." Claire chuckled for a second. Then seemed to realize how much she'd revealed about herself. Her blush returned as she sank back against the sofa.

"You were a little bit of a stalker, weren't you?" Kitty asked, grinning.

"I had a crush on Matt. That's all." Then she smiled smugly. "Besides, he eventually came around."

"I'll say." Kitty bumped her shoulder against Claire's in easy camaraderie.

"So what happened?" Wendy asked, unwilling to leave the thread of Jonathon's story dangling. "Why did they break up?"

"That's the thing." Claire gave a little shrug. "I'm not sure they were ever really together. And not long after the birthday cake thing, she moved back in with her mother. Jonathon was…"

"Heartbroken," Kitty supplied.

"No." Claire frowned thoughtfully. "He was just never the same." She gave her head a little shake, as if she was returning to the present. "But I know it's still there, buried inside of him. The capacity to love like that."

Claire and Kitty exchanged another one of those pointed glances and Wendy felt a stab of envy. This girl he'd loved, Kristi… Wendy had never been loved like that. Kitty and Claire, that's what they had with their husbands. But no one had ever felt that way about Wendy.

She pushed herself to her feet. "I don't think you have to worry. He doesn't love me. I'm sure of it." She forced a bright smile. "You can go home and rest assured that I'm not going to crush his delicate heart beneath my boot heel."

"It's not just you we're worried about." Kitty stood also and looked across the room to the bassinet. "What about Peyton?"

"What about Peyton?"

"Have you ever seen Jonathon with Ilsa?" Kitty asked.

"I—" Then she broke off. Remembering that she had, once, seen him holding Ilsa. Right after she'd been born, Wendy had brought flowers by and Jonathon had been there, an expression of pure wonder on his face as he held the baby.

She nodded, rubbing at her temple, trying to dispel the tension headache that was spiking through her head. When had this all gotten so complicated?

"He's fantastic with kids," Kitty was saying. "He adores Ilsa. He's been bugging us to have another one in fact."

"And if you are getting married just to fool your family," Claire said. "And he falls in love with you or that darling little girl, how do you think he's going to feel when you end the marriage?"

"I—" What could she say to that? She'd never imagined Jonathon might fall in love with her. The idea was preposterous. But Peyton? Yeah. She could imagine that. And if they

really were married for two years—it might take that long—
then he'd have plenty of time for Peyton to wrap him around
her tiny finger. She looked up at Kitty and Claire and found
them watching her expectantly. "All I can say, is that when…*if*
we get divorced, I wouldn't dream of keeping him away from
Peyton. If he wants to see her, that is. From this moment on,
I'll think of him as her father. Just as I think of myself as her
mother."

Jonathon as a father. The idea was…so foreign. So odd.
Yet, she knew in her heart that Kitty and Claire were right
to warn her. He was doing this amazing thing for her. She
didn't want him to get hurt because of it and she would do
everything in her power to make sure he didn't. She only
wished she was half as confident in her ability to protect
herself.

After a long moment, Kitty stood and gave a dramatic sigh.

"Very well, then. I suppose there's only one thing left to
do."

"What's that?" Wendy asked, hesitantly.

Kitty's face broke into a smile. "Welcome you to the family."

Six

The wedding itself went off with all the precision of a well-planned military maneuver. And it was just about as romantic. A small ceremony performed in a drab municipal office in downtown Palo Alto, it was over so quickly that Jonathon felt sure Claire and Matt wished they had stayed in Curaçao instead of making the trip back.

After that first kiss in her office had gotten so out of control, he didn't even dare cement the ceremony with more than a quick peck. So much for convincing their friends that they were in love. But no one in the office that day seemed surprised, least of all Wendy.

That evening, they swung by Wendy's apartment to pick up her suitcase and Peyton's few possessions before heading over to his house. They'd decided to keep her apartment for now. Her lease wasn't up for another few months, which would give her plenty of time to decide when she wanted to move into his house and what she wanted to keep in storage. When they arrived at his house, they discovered that Claire had made them dinner, and they found it waiting for them in the warming drawer of his kitchen.

He stood beside Wendy in the doorway to the kitchen, staring at the table with a fist clenching his heart. The table had been set with two of the elegant place settings his interior designer had bought seven years ago and which he'd never used. Long, thin tapers sat in the center of the table, a book of matches propped against the candle holder. In between the two chairs sat the new Svan high chair he'd had delivered. A bottle of unopened champagne sat chilling in a bucket opposite the high chair.

Wendy cleared her throat. "Um…" She hitched Peyton up on her hip. "I think I'll just…um…unpack a few of the bags first." Her gaze looked from the wine to him. "I'm not really hungry yet."

Before he could muster a response, she took the final suitcase from him and made a dash for the door. Probably a wise decision. Neither of them was ready yet for a intimate dinner. Let alone wine.

Three hours later, she still hadn't made it back down to eat. He'd sat at the table himself, eating in front of his laptop. Finally, he shut his laptop and went in search of Wendy. He found her upstairs in the room he'd set aside as a nursery.

He paused just outside the door. Leaning his shoulder against the doorjamb, for a long moment he simply watched her. The room had been painted pale pink. Butterflies fluttered across the walls and bunnies frolicked in the grass painted along the trim. A white crib sat in the corner under a mobile of more butterflies and flowers. Overall, the décor of the room was a little cloying in its sweetness, but the decorator had assured him that it was perfect for the new addition to his life. This evening, he barely noticed the butterflies, but rather focused his attention on the woman sitting in the rocking chair in the corner and the baby she held in her arms.

At some point, Wendy had changed out of the dress and into a pair of jeans and a white V-neck T-shirt. Peyton was asleep in her arms. Her eyes were closed, her head tilted back against the headrest of the rocking chair. Only the faint tensing of her calf as she occasionally nudged the chair into movement indicated that she wasn't asleep too.

He cleared his throat to let her know he was there.

Her head bobbed up. "Oh," she said, wiggling in the chair to reposition Peyton in her arms without waking her. "How long have you been there?"

"I just walked up."

She glanced down at the baby in her arms as Peyton stirred but didn't wake. "I suppose I should put her down," she whispered. "But I hate to do it. If she wakes up again…"

If the smudges of exhaustion under her eyes were any indication, Peyton wasn't the easiest of babies. No wonder given the upheaval in her young life.

"If she wakes back up," he found himself saying, "then I'll take over and you can get some sleep. You should go eat."

Wendy shook her head. "I can't ask you to do that. That's not why we got married."

There was almost a hint of accusation in her voice.

"Maybe not," he hedged. "But we are married now. And you obviously could use the sleep. At this point, I'm more rested than you are. A sleepless night won't hurt me, but a good night's sleep could do you a world of good."

"If she needs a bottle in the night—"

"Then I'll give it to her."

Wendy looked skeptical. "The bottles are downstairs. You just—"

"I saw you mixing the formula. I've got it."

"But—"

"Wendy, I'm one of five kids. I had a niece and two nephews before I graduated from high school. Peyton won't be the first baby I've ever fed."

"Oh." After a moment of hesitation, she stood and crossed to the crib.

As he'd told her, he knew his way around an infant. It

was so obvious to him that she did not. There was a sort of fearful hesitancy to the way she moved. As if she were afraid of breaking Peyton.

She lowered the baby into the crib then stood there for a long moment, her hand resting on Peyton before she moved back a step. She cringed as she raised the side of the bed and the hardware clattered. But Peyton slept on and Wendy slowly backed away.

She paused as she closed the door to unclip the baby monitor from her hip and turn it on, as if Peyton might start crying any second and Wendy would miss it now that she was out of sight. He couldn't help chuckling when she raised the monitor to her ear to listen more closely.

She shot him an annoyed look. "What?"

"You know you're only one room away. You could probably hear her cry without the monitor." When she looked as if she might comment, he reached out and carefully extracted it from her fingers. "Not that you're going to need this tonight anyway."

"I really don't mind staying up with her."

"The discussion is over."

She opened her mouth to respond, then snapped it shut, her lips twisting into a smile. "I guess I know you well enough to recognize that I'm-the-boss-and-what-I-say-goes tone."

"I have a tone that says all that?"

She snorted her derision. "Yeah. And don't pretend you don't know it." She took a step in the direction of the room at the end of the hall—the guest room she'd claimed for her own—then she paused. "You didn't have to do this, you know."

"Wendy, let's not have another discussion about my motives."

She took another step toward him, closing the distance between them and lowering her voice. "No. I'm not talking about the wedding. I'm talking about all this." She nodded her head in the direction of Peyton's room. "I mean the nursery. The crib. The rocking chair. It's all—"

"It's nothing."

She quirked an eyebrow. "Like the twenty percent nothing? Unless you were up all night hand-painting butterflies and daisies last night, I'm guessing you hired an interior decorator to come in and do this. In less than a week. That's not nothing."

"Kitty mentioned that all you had was a bassinet."

She smiled a slow, teasing smile. "And you knew that wasn't enough. Being such an expert on babies and everything."

He was struck once again by the idea that this was their wedding night. That if there wasn't a baby asleep in the next room, he might now be slowly lifting that sweater up over her head. He might be unhooking that hot-pink bra of hers and stripping her naked.

But of course, if there wasn't a baby asleep in the next room, then there wouldn't have been a wedding to begin with. Let alone a wedding night.

Suddenly she reached up and cupped his jaw in her hand. Her gaze was soft, her touch gentle. "Thanks for taking such good care of us."

For a solid heartbeat—maybe longer—his brain seemed to completely stop working. He couldn't remember all the reasons why touching her was such a bad idea. All he knew was how much he wanted her. Not just in bed, but here. Like this. Looking up at him as if he was a decent guy who deserved a woman like her.

Before he could give in to the temptation to let her go on thinking that, he grabbed her hand in his and gently pulled it away from his face. Backing up a step, he said, "You should go to bed. Catch up on that sleep you've been missing."

He even used his I'm-the-boss tone.

"Right." She gave a chipper little salute. "Got it, boss."

* * *

Wendy had been so sure she wouldn't be able to sleep. She'd been positive she'd find herself waking at every sound coming from Peyton's room. She feared that she'd lie awake in bed thinking about the moment in the hall. But instead of the sleepless night she expected, she woke ten hours later to sun streaming in her bedroom window, feeling more rested than she had in weeks. Then she bolted upright in bed as panic clogged her heart. She'd slept through the night. Which meant she'd slept through Peyton waking and needing her God only knew how many times.

Wendy dashed down the hall and into Peyton's room, skidding to a halt beside the crib. It was empty. Her heart doubled its already accelerated rate. Where could—

"Morning."

She spun around to see Jonathon seated in the rocking chair, Peyton nestled on his lap as he fed her a bottle. Wendy pressed a hand to her chest, blowing out a whoosh of air, willing her heart rate to slow.

"You have her," she muttered. "She's fine."

Jonathon gave her a once-over, his gaze lingering on the tank top and boxers she always slept in. Finally his eyes returned to hers. "What did you think had happened to her?"

Wendy tugged at the hem of the thin white cotton, resisting the urge to glance down to verify just how thin the tank top was. She doubted knowing would bring her comfort. Instead she crossed her arms over her chest. "I don't know," she admitted. "It's the first morning in…what, almost three weeks now, that she hasn't been the one to wake me. For all I knew, she'd been abducted by aliens. I panicked."

His lips curved in an amused smile. "Obviously."

For a second she was entranced by the transformation of his face. He had a smooth, charming smile he used at work. She thought of it as his client-wooing smile. He also had a wolfish grin. That was his I'm-about-to-devour-some-innocent-company expression.

Neither of those reached his eyes. Neither held any warmth.

But this slight, amused twist of his lips wrinkled the corners of his eyes, and it nearly took her breath away.

Before she could respond, or do something really stupid, like melt into a puddle at his feet, he continued. "Peyton and I have been up for hours now."

"I'm—"

"Don't apologize. I'd have woken you if she'd been any trouble."

Wendy's eyebrows shot up. When was Peyton not trouble? She fussed a lot. Wanted to be held constantly. Screamed anytime Wendy put her down. In general, made Wendy feel like a real winner as a parent.

"We got up a couple of hours ago," Jonathon was saying. He continued rocking as he spoke, looking down at Peyton the whole time. "She had her morning bottle. Then we made me some oatmeal. She sat on my lap while I read through some emails. She spit up a little on the office floor. Thank God for the plastic mat my chair sits on, right, Peyton?"

Ooookay. Maybe that explained why his smile looked so different than his normal grin. Obviously, it was Jonathon who'd been abducted by aliens and replaced by some sort of pod person. The man before her bore no resemblance to the cold and calculating businessman she'd dealt with for the past five years.

Unfortunately, this new guy was way more appealing, which was so annoying.

Jonathon looked up at her, his expression clouding with concern. "Anything wrong?"

"No, I… Why?"

"You looked a little, faint or something."

"No. I'm…great. Fantastic. But hungry. That's it. I must be hungry."

"Okay." The concern lining his brow had taken on a decidedly skeptical gleam. As though he suspected she might need to spend a little time in a padded room. "Why not get dressed and grab yourself some breakfast. Peyton and I will be fine here."

As if to signal her assent, Peyton blinked up at him with wide blue eyes, then gave the bottle a particularly vigorous suck before sighing and allowing her eyes to drift closed. She looked for all the world like a baby completely happy and at peace.

Emotion choked Wendy's throat, something that felt unpleasantly like envy. She'd worked her butt off for that baby over the past few weeks, turned her life upside down, prepared to battle her family to the end. And yet Peyton had never once looked up at her with dreamy contentment. Then again, Jonathon always had been quick to win over the ladies.

Wendy sighed. "I wish she was half as peaceful in my arms as she is with you."

"Why do you say that?"

Because if growing up a Morgan had taught her anything, it was that the best way to deal with negative emotions was to voice them aloud. Get them out into the open rather than letting them simmer. Still, admitting such a feeling was unpleasant, so she softened her words with a diffident shrug. "She seems to fight me constantly. Makes me wonder if—" Wendy blew out a breath. "I don't know, if she knows something I don't. If she knows I don't have what it takes to be a good mother."

When she looked back at Jonathon, his smile was still there, but the humor in his eyes had dimmed to understanding.

"The thing about dealing with babies—" he gently pulled the bottle nipple from Peyton's mouth, then maneuvered her so her belly rested against his shoulder "—it's about five percent instinct and ninety-five percent experience. Plus, they're very intuitive—that's all they've got. So if you're nervous, she'll pick up on it and she'll be nervous too."

Jonathon gave Peyton's back several thumps. After about the tenth, she burped without even opening her eyes.

"How'd you do that? I can never get her to burp."

"Like I said. It's experience. If she's been a difficult baby so far, it's not because she has you pegged as a bad parent. You just don't know all the tricks yet. Besides, she's been through a lot in her short life."

Was it really that simple? Time would heal all wounds? Watching Peyton sleep on Jonathon's shoulder, Wendy certainly hoped so. But she couldn't help worrying if there was more to it than that. That there were deficiencies no amount of experience could compensate for. After all, she'd never be Peyton's real mother.

Almost as if he could read her mind, Jonathon added, "Give her some time. Give yourself some time too." Then Jonathon let out a bark of laughter. "Jeez, I sound like Dr. Phil."

She laughed along with him, despite the lump of sorrow burrowing into her chest. "Don't worry. I won't tell anyone at work."

"Thanks."

A moment of silence stretched between them. She should leave. Take advantage of Peyton's sleep to go shower or something. Yet she found her feet rooted to the ground as she watched him rocking the tiny infant.

"Why aren't you a father?" she asked, almost before she realized she meant to say it.

He arched an eyebrow.

Heat crept into her cheeks. "I mean, clearly you're great with kids. It seems like a no-brainer that you should have some of your own."

"I get frustrated enough trying to get Matt to clean up his third of the office."

"I'm serious."

"So am I. I've never had any desire to be a father." His tone was harsh, leaving no room for doubt. The touchy-feely portion of their discussion was over. "She should be asleep for a couple of hours at least. You should take advantage of it and get some breakfast."

"Thanks. I will."

She left the room without looking back, but with his words still echoing in her mind. He'd never wanted to be a father. Yet he'd just signed up for a two-year gig. She'd assumed when he asked her to marry him that he wouldn't be playing an active role in raising Peyton. But less than twenty-four hours in and he'd cared for Peyton more than she had.

He was going to an awful lot of trouble to keep her around. She could only hope she was half as good an assistant as he thought she was. Because she was certainly going to need to earn her keep.

Since he'd insisted repeatedly that he didn't need her, she wandered down to the kitchen for breakfast. She'd never even stepped into his house before last night. It wasn't quite what she'd expected. Like Matt, a few years before, Jonathon had bought one of the ridiculously expensive craftsman houses in Old Palo Alto. Though the homes were aging and modest, the neighborhood was one of the more expensive in the country. The interior of Jonathon's house had been renovated to its early-20th-century glory with meticulous detail. The furniture was a collection of authentic Mission antiques and clean-lined Japanese pieces that complemented them. She found the kitchen surprisingly well stocked. Not in the mood to cook anything, she rummaged through his pantry until she found a box of Pop-Tarts. She eyed them warily for a second—because Jonathon so did not seem like the Frosted Strawberry Pop-Tart type—then snagged a package and headed back upstairs.

She took a leisurely shower, nibbling on the pastry as she dressed. Jonathon had never been one of those men who didn't know how to ask for help. If he'd needed her before now, he would have woken her up. She'd gotten enough phone calls at six o'clock in the morning over the years to know that. Whatever he was doing with Peyton, he didn't need her immediately. Confident that Peyton must still be asleep, she took the time to linger over her grooming in a way she hadn't in the past couple of weeks. She did things like brush her hair. Floss her teeth. And put on ChapStick.

The rest had done wonders for her. Not only had she finally gotten a decent night's sleep, but obviously Jonathon had handled Peyton with perfect competence. Just as he'd said he would. That one small thing renewed her faith in this whole endeavor.

They had a week before they left for Texas. Which was more than enough time for them to settle into enough of a routine to fool her parents and family about their relationship. Jonathon obviously knew enough about babies that he'd be able to help her over the rough spots she was sure to encounter.

They'd spend a quick weekend in Texas convincing her family that they were Peyton's perfect guardians. Then they'd head back to Palo Alto and their lives would return to normal. Or as normal as they could be since she and Jonathon were now married and living together. All in all, life seemed damn good.

Once she'd verified that Peyton wasn't asleep in the nursery, she headed downstairs. She was about halfway down the stairs when she heard voices. Trepidation tripped along her nerves as she paused, head tilted to better hear the conversation coming from the kitchen.

Heart pounding, she made her way there. It could be Ford or Matt. Or a neighbor. Or… Then she heard it. Just outside the swinging door leading into the kitchen. A deep Texas twang.

"We would have come earlier if you'd given us more warning that y'all were fixin' to get married."

She squeezed her eyes closed, fighting back a burst of panic as she blew out a long breath. Then she shoved open the door and walked into the kitchen. To face her family.

Seven

Having lived his entire life in the northern half of California, Jonathon had weathered his share of earthquakes. He'd long ago gotten over whatever fear he might have had of them. But there were plenty of other act-of-God weather systems that scared the crap out of him. Tornadoes. Hurricanes. Tsunamis.

Anything that would swoop in and level an entire coastal plain deserved a healthy dose of respectful fear.

Clearly, Wendy's family fell into that category.

About ten minutes after Wendy had disappeared to take a shower, her family had arrived on his doorstep in a tidal wave of hearty handshakes, welcoming slaps and tearful hugs. It was a bit overwhelming, given that he'd never met any of them and would have had no idea who they were if he hadn't recognized her uncle, Big Hank, from the news clips he'd seen of the senator. And before Jonathon knew it, Wendy's parents, Tim and Marion, had swept into the house, followed by Big Hank, carefully lending an arm to the infamous Mema.

Jonathon had barely recovered from the stinging clap on

the arm from Big Hank, when he faced down Mema. After Wendy's description, he'd half expected an old battleship of a woman. Instead, Mema was thin and stooped, fragile in appearance despite the strength of will that seemed to radiate from her.

A hush fell over the other members of the family as she shook his hand and appraised him. She had the wizened appearance of a woman who had lived hard and buried too many loved ones, but who was not yet ready to release her control over the rest of her clan.

She eyed him up and down. "Well, at least you're real."

"You doubted it?" he asked.

She sniffed indignantly. "I wouldn't put it past Gwen to invent a husband just to defy me."

"I assure you, ma'am. I'm real."

"As for what kind of father you'll be for my great-granddaughter, that we'll have to see about." Then her steely gaze narrowed with sharp perception and raked over Jonathon a second time. Finally she gave a little nod. "I've never had much use for overly handsome men. But then, neither has my Gwen, so I suppose there must be more to you than good looks."

He offered a wry smile. "I should hope so."

It was almost thirty minutes later when Wendy came down. The guarded look on her face as she walked through the door told him she'd heard them before entering the kitchen.

She was greeted with hugs that lasted longer and more joyful tears than he would have expected, given the way she'd described the strained relationship she shared with her family. Throughout it all, she kept a careful eye on Peyton, who was currently being held by Wendy's mother, as if Wendy expected that any moment the family might escape with the baby.

"What are y'all doing here?" she asked when she was finally able to get a word in edgewise.

He suppressed a smile. In five years, he'd never heard a

hint of the Texas accent her family all sported. But three minutes in their company and she was slipping into *y'alls*.

"Oh, honey," her mother cooed, her voice all sugary sweet. "Of course we would come for your wedding. If we'd had enough warning, we would have been here." She shook her head, tears brimming in her eyes. "I can't believe I missed the wedding of my only daughter."

"I did tell you a week ago we were getting married. If you'd really wanted to come, you could have."

"But Big Hank had the jet in D.C.," her mother bemoaned, "and we had to wait until he could fit the trip into his schedule."

Jonathon felt a pang of regret, but Wendy muttered, "I'm glad to know you found the idea of flying commercial more repugnant than the prospect of missing my wedding."

Tim's head snapped up. "Young lady, you'll speak respectfully to your mother."

"Or what?" Wendy asked, anger creeping into her voice. "You'll cut off my allowance? The woman has missed almost every major event in my life since I was ten. And those that she showed up for, she criticized endlessly. I think she'll live."

"Gwen—" her mother started to protest.

Then Mema cleared her throat and both Wendy and her mother fell silent. Their heads swiveled to face her.

"In the wake of our Bitsy's recent and tragic death, it is time for you to put aside your past differences." She stared them both down. Mother and daughter both dropped their gazes. "Now, the flight from Texas was long and I'd like to clean up before resting a bit before lunch." She turned to Jonathon. "I assume all the bedrooms are on the second floor?"

"They are," he said, not sure what she was getting at.

"Very well, then. I noticed an office just off the foyer. I'll sleep there. I don't do stairs well. Big Hank, please arrange for a bed to be delivered before evening. In the meantime, I'll rest on the sofa there."

Jonathon watched in amazement as a senior U.S. senator practically leaped to help his mother out of the kitchen. A moment later, Wendy's father had been sent out to the limo to instruct the driver where to bring the bags, and her mother had retreated to the nursery "to get reacquainted with her great-niece."

The second Jonathon and Wendy were all alone, she practically threw up her hands. "Why didn't you come get me the second they arrived?"

"You were dressing. I told them they could wait until you came down."

She tilted her head, studying him as if he were some foreign life form she'd never seen before. "You stood up to them?"

Ah. So that's what had her so puzzled. "Yes. I stood up to them. Do people not normally do that?"

She gave a bemused chuckle. "No. People don't normally do that." Shaking her head, she started carrying coffee cups from the kitchen table to the sink. Almost under her breath, she said, "I once dated a guy whose parents were lifelong members of Greenpeace. He'd spent every summer since he was ten on boats protesting whaling in Japan. He'd marched on Washington forty-four times before he was twenty. He'd been a vegan since he was three. Within thirty minutes of meeting my family, he was eating barbeque and smoking cigars out on the back porch with Big Hank." Shaking her head, she started rinsing out coffee cups and loading them into the dishwasher. "Within a week, he'd accepted a job working for my dad."

Jonathon studied the tense lines of her back. Her tone had been sad, but resigned. "The guy sounds like an idiot."

"No. He was very smart. The last I heard, Jed was VP of marketing for Morgan Oil. And Daddy would never promote anyone that high up who wasn't brilliant."

Jonathon gently turned her away from the sink and tipped

her chin up to look at him. "That's not the kind of idiot I mean."

Her gaze met his, confusion in her eyes for a minute. Then her gaze cleared as she realized his meaning. Pink tinged her cheeks and pulled away from his touch. Tucking her hair back behind her ear she swallowed. "Thank you. For standing up to them, I mean. For everything."

"You're welcome."

She gave a bitter laugh. "You say that now. But you don't actually know what you've gotten yourself into." She looked pointedly at the kitchen door through which her family had left not long before. "This nonsense with them sweeping down on us unannounced? Inviting themselves to stay here? Ordering a bed for Mema to sleep on? This is all just the beginning. It'll only get worse."

"Of course it will," he stated as blandly as he could. "You think I didn't know that the second I opened the door?"

"I…I don't know. I guess… Most people don't see them for what they are."

"Try to have a little faith in me," he chided.

"I'm just warning you. My dad and Uncle Hank will woo you with their good ol' boy charm. And just when you think that you're their buddy and they're nothing more than simple roughnecks, they'll use that keen intelligence of theirs to manipulate you. And if they can't control you, they'll try to squash you."

"Consider me warned." He nodded. "Coming here was obviously a power play. They think they have the upper hand because they've chosen the time and location of the showdown. They're trying to establish themselves as the decision makers in the relationship. What about your mother? She seems harmless enough."

"Um, no." Wendy thought about it. Of all the family members, her relationship with her mother was the most complicated. There were times when she actually liked her mother. Of course, she loved all of them, but her mother she actually liked. But she'd never understood her. And her mother had her moments of being just as vicious as Uncle Hank. "In all those scuba-diving trips you take, you ever been in the water with a jellyfish?"

"Several times. They sting like hell."

"Exactly. They look delicate and frail, but they have more than enough defenses. That's my mother in a nutshell. She can play the victim, but she's as smart as—" That's when it hit her. "Oh, crap."

"What?"

"The bedroom!" She leaped to her feet and dashed for the stairs.

Jonathon snagged her arm on the way past. "What?"

She whispered, just in case anyone was close enough to hear, "The guest bedroom. Where I slept last night."

He continued to stare blankly at her. Seriously? Mr. Genius couldn't figure this out?

She lowered her voice to a hiss. "Last night. On our wedding night. I slept in the guest bedroom." She resisted the urge to bop him on the forehead. "And now my mother is upstairs with Peyton. And if she sees the guest bedroom, she'll realize we didn't sleep together last night."

This time, she didn't wait around to see if his sluggish brain had started working at normal speed. Instead, she pulled her arm from his hand and made a break for the stairs. He was hot on her heels as she took the stairs two at a time.

She stopped at the top, breathing rapidly through her mouth and she looked around for her parents. A long gallery hall ran from the top of the stairs to the guest room at the end. They'd have to pass the nursery to get there.

Crap, crap and double crap.

This was going to be tricky. She crept down the hall, praying that Jonathon would walk as softly. Or head back downstairs if he couldn't.

She tiptoed right up to the doorway and pressed herself

against the wall, listening. She heard the faint, steady creak, creak of a rocking chair.

If her mom was sitting in the chair rocking Peyton, there was a good chance Wendy could sneak past to the guest bedroom, make the bed and sneak out with anyone being the wiser. Or more importantly, becoming suspicious.

Slinking past the door, she heard two things that would have stopped her in her tracks if she hadn't been in such a desperate hurry. The first was Jonathon's heavy footfall behind her. The next was her father's voice from within the nursery.

She glanced through the open door, but saw no one. Maybe they'd make it. But when she heard the rocking chair still, she grabbed Jonathon's hand and made a dash for it.

If her parents heard them and followed, she and Jonathon would never have time to actually make the bed. Certainly not neatly enough to put her father off the scent.

And this wasn't the day to leave up to fate.

Pulling Jonathon into the room after her, turning him so his back was to the door, she flashed him a wry smile. "Sorry about this."

"About what?"

She only had an instant to appreciate how charming he looked with that bemused expression on his face before she launched herself at him. They both tumbled backward onto the bed in a tangle of arms and legs. He might have gasped with surprise. She didn't have a chance to notice, as she pressed her mouth to his and kissed him.

The second Jonathon felt Wendy's mouth on his, he gave up trying to figure out what she was doing. She'd been babbling about the bedroom one minute and kissing him like a woman overwhelmed by desire the next. A smart man knew when to hold his questions for later.

Instead, he wrapped his hand around the back of her head and deepened the kiss. Her lips moved over his in sensual abandon, her tongue stroking against his in the kind of soul-deep kiss that made a man forget everything except the burning need to possess.

Desire pounded through him, heating his blood and tightening his groin. He fought against the desperate need to strip her naked and plow into her. A need that had been building within him for what seemed like years. Hell, probably had been years. As desperately as he wanted her, he didn't want this. This frantic, rapid rush of sex without fulfillment.

He wanted more. He wanted all of her.

Rolling her over onto her back, he took control of the kiss. Her hand had started pulling his shirt out from his waistband. If her hot little hand so much as touched his bare chest, he'd lose the last shreds of his control. So he grabbed both her hands in his and pulled them over her head, pinning them there. She let out a low groan, arching her back off the bed.

Yes. This was what he wanted: her, on the brink. As desperate and needy as he felt.

He slowed the kiss down, exploring every sweet corner of her mouth. Loving her sleepy flavor, the faint hint of coffee. The smooth heat of her tongue against his. Her hips bucked against his as she ground the vee between her legs against the length of his erection. Even through the multiple layers of her clothes, he could feel the heat of her.

But it wasn't enough. Merely kissing her would never be enough. Not when there was so much of her body left to explore. That silken shoulder that had been tempting him for so long. That tender swath of skin along her collarbone. The hollow at the base of her throat. The glimpse of her belly he sometimes saw when she rose up on her toes to get a fresh ream of printer paper.

His hand sought the hem of her shirt. He slipped his hand up to her rib cage, relishing how incredibly soft her skin was. He felt the edge of her bra and hesitated. He'd waited years to touch her naked skin. His hand damn near trembled at the prospect.

But was this really what he wanted? A quick grope in the guest bedroom when her family was just down the hall?

No, he wanted her naked. Laid out before him like a feast. He wanted hours. Days.

He wanted—

Jonathon's head jerked up as he pulled back from Wendy and sent her a piercing look.

Her family was just down the hall. What the hell had she been—

A sound came from the doorway. A man clearing his voice.

Jonathon whipped his head around and saw Wendy's parents standing in the doorway. Her mom, a perfect, older version of Wendy, stood with her hands propped on her hips, but the teasing smile on her lips softened any reproach in her gaze. Wendy's father, on the other hand, looked ready to throttle him.

With good reason.

The man had just caught him groping his daughter like a desperate teenager.

Wendy's dad growled—actually growled—with displeasure and took a step toward him. Wendy's mother grabbed her husband by the arm. Though the petite woman couldn't possibly have had the strength to stop the man in his tracks, her touch still gave him pause.

"Wendy, your father and I will be waiting for you in the hall. Why don't you come out in a minute when you've had a chance to get yourselves…under control."

A moment later the guest bedroom door closed.

Jonathon rolled off Wendy, planted his feet firmly on the ground and dropped his head into his waiting hands.

What a mess.

Wendy's parents—waiting in the hall with her dad looking as if he wanted to chew his ass out—were the least of his worries. Whatever criticism they'd deliver he'd take.

None of it would come even close to the talking to he was going to give himself. He'd completely lost control. For several moments there, he'd forgotten where they were. Forgotten that she wasn't really his to take whenever he wanted. Forgotten that this was merely a sham.

Worse still, she hadn't. Clearly, she'd manipulated the situation—manipulated him—all so that her family wouldn't notice the fact that she'd obviously slept in the guest room. And it hadn't even occurred to him that that's what she had been doing.

He drew in several deep breaths, but barely felt calmer. The scent of her was heavy in the air, and with every breath she only seemed to fill more of the room, rather than less. That faint pepperminty smell that was uniquely her. His very hands seemed steeped in her.

He sat fully up, looking over his shoulder. She'd scrambled back into the corner of the bed, pressed against the headboard. She looked almost afraid of him. He didn't blame her. His control felt too shaky just now to offer her any reassurances.

She bit down on her lip as she tucked a strand of hair behind her ear. It was a ridiculous effort, fixing that one strand of hair when the rest were still so mussed.

"I—" she started to say, then cleared her throat. "Boy, that was close."

Not trusting himself to say anything just yet, he merely raised one eyebrow. Apparently she had no idea just how close that had been. Just how lucky she was that her parents had walked in, since he'd been about three minutes away from taking her right there.

"I—I'm sorry," she stammered. "I couldn't think of any other way to distract them from the bed."

He pushed himself to his feet. "I doubt your parents noticed the bed."

She scrambled up onto her knees. "No. I mean, that was the idea, right?"

He gave a tight little nod, hating her a little bit in that

moment. Or at least hating that she was still thinking coherently when he'd lost the ability. "Yeah," he said as blandly as he could manage. "Apparently it was."

"I—" She climbed off the bed, coming to stand right beside him. "I'm sorry."

He was struck suddenly by how petite she was. Standing flat-footed beside him, the top of her head barely reached his chin. And yet, she never seemed small. She had more than enough personality to fill a woman half a foot taller. And more than enough strength of will to stand up to him.

He hadn't been able to face her father without embarrassing himself a few minutes ago, but her endless stream of excuses certainly killed the mood. She hadn't been as affected by the kiss as he had. Fine. But she could damn well stop harping on it.

"Stop apologizing," he ordered. "We all make mistakes. I'm just not used to making such stupid ones."

She opened her mouth as if to say something, but snapped it shut again when he brusquely smoothed down her hair. Then, since he couldn't seem to keep his hands off her, he pressed one quick kiss to her forehead. "Let's go face your parents."

Eight

Some things are embarrassing no matter what your age. Having your father stare down your boyfriend is one of them.

At seventeen, she and her boyfriend had been caught necking in the back of his truck. The make-out session had been bad enough. Worse still was the fact that her date had been high. Her father wasn't very forgiving of that sort of thing. Never mind that she hadn't known it at the time. She'd gotten reamed. He'd had the poor boy arrested. And had her hauled in and tested for drug use just to make a point. Was it any wonder the next year when she went to college she'd picked one thousands of miles away?

She'd always assumed that would be the low point of her boyfriend/father debacles. But this—oddly enough—felt worse.

Maybe it was because Devin—or had it been Drake?—had been carefully chosen for his many red-flag qualities. He'd been guy number twenty-six in her ongoing teenage quest to piss off her parents.

As she followed Jonathon into the hall, she held her breath, half afraid of the argument to come and half relieved to be escaping Jonathon's one-on-one scrutiny.

Her parents were waiting for them in the hall. Her mother sent a wan smile, a hint of apology in her eyes. Her father, on the other hand, looked as if he could happily strangle Jonathon with his bare hands. Which was saying something, because Wendy had always figured it her father was going to murder someone, as a lifelong hunter and a member of the NRA, he would opt for a gun rather than sheer brute force.

Even with Devin—or was it Derek?—her father hadn't seemed this mad. Normally, she knew how to handle her parents. Twenty-three solid years of pushing their buttons made her an expert at undoing the damage. But just now, she was drawing a blank. Every brain cell she had was still stuttering with the memory of that soul-searing kiss.

He could have taken her right there, with her parents on the other side of the door, and she would have been okay with that. More than okay. She would have been begging for more.

Not a good thought, that one.

Since she could barely put a single coherent thought together, she was infinitely thankful that Jonathon seemed to be recovering more quickly than she was.

He draped an arm over her shoulder in a possessive, but nonsexual way. Giving her parents a distant nod, he said, "Mr. and Mrs. Morgan, I'm sorry you saw that."

"Oh, no need to apologize—" her mother began.

"You're sorry we *saw* that." Her father talked over her mother. "Or you're sorry you *did* it?" His tone was as ice-cold as his reproof. "Because to my way of thinking, a man who loves his wife doesn't fool around with her in the middle of the morning when her family is in the house and the child they hope to rear is in the next room."

"Dad!"

"Now, Tim—"

Jonathon held up a hand, stopping both her protest and

her mother's. He drew out the moment just long enough for everyone to know he wasn't about to just kowtow to her father's bullying. "And to my way of thinking, a family that respects their daughter doesn't show up on her doorstep unannounced."

Her mother opened her mouth, looked ready to say something, then pressed her lips into a tight line and stomped off down the stairs.

Wendy's father continued to glare at Jonathon. Jonathon did a damn fine job of glaring back.

"If you think making my wife cry will endear you to me," her father said through gritted teeth, "then you're sorely mistaken."

Wendy wanted to protest. Those hadn't been tears in her mother's eyes. Just anger. But Jonathon didn't give her a chance to point it out.

"The same goes for you. Sir," Jonathon bit out. But apparently he couldn't leave well enough alone. Because a second later he stepped closer to her father and said, "And I'll have you know, that before she agreed to marry me, I never once so much as touched your daughter at work. I have the greatest respect for her intelligence. And her decisions. I'm not sure you can say the same."

Both men seemed to expand to fill their anger. Any second now, they would either start bumping their chests together like roosters or one of them would throw the first punch.

She figured they were equally matched. Her father was a solid six-five, and a barrel-chested two hundred and fifty pounds. Plus, he'd worked on rigs alongside roughnecks in his youth. Jonathon, on the other hand, had grown up poor, spent a few weeks in juvie, and had two older brothers, both of whom had criminal records. She figured he could probably handle himself.

She looked from one man to the other. Neither of them seemed to be willing to budge. Finally, she just shook her head. "I'm going to go talk to Mom. You two, sort this out."

She gave Jonathon's arm a little squeeze, willing him to see her apology in her eyes. Then, as she walked passed her dad, she laid a hand on his arm. "Dad, I'm not seventeen anymore. And if Jonathon was planning on besmirching my honor or whatever it is you're worried about, then he probably wouldn't have married me. Give him a chance. You have no idea how good a guy he is."

She went down the stairs, half expecting her father and Jonathon to come tumbling down after her in a jumble of brawling arms and legs. And she tried to tell herself that if they did, it wasn't any of her business.

Peyton was apparently asleep again, because a stream of lullabies could be heard through the baby monitor sitting on the kitchen counter. Her mother was doing what most Texas women do when they're upset. Cooking.

Wendy gave a bark of disbelieving laughter.

Her mother's head jerked up, her eyes still sharp with annoyance. She had a hand towel slung over her shoulder, paring knife in her hand and a chicken defrosting in the prep sink.

She gave a sniff of disapproval before returning to the task at hand, dicing celery.

Wendy bumped her hip against the edge of the island that stretched the length of the kitchen. That honed black granite was like the river of difference that always divided them. Her mother on one side: cooking to suppress the emotions she couldn't voice. Wendy on the other: baffled at her mother's ability to soldier on in silence for so many years.

"You might as well just say it," her mother snapped without looking up from the celery.

"I didn't say anything," Wendy protested.

"But you were thinking it. You always did think louder than most people shout."

Wendy blew out a breath. "Fine. It's just…" Anything she said, her mother would take as a criticism. There was probably no way around that. "You're alone in the kitchen for less than five minutes and you start cooking?"

Her mother arched a disdainful brow. "Someone has to feed everyone. You know Mema isn't going to want to go out to eat. God only knows what the food is like up here."

Wendy laughed in disbelief. "Trust me. There are plenty of restaurants in Palo Alto that are just fine. Even by your standards. And we're a thirty-minute drive to San Francisco, where they have some of the best restaurants in the world. I think on the food front, we're okay. And if Mema doesn't want to go out, there are probably two dozen restaurants that would deliver."

Naturally, having food delivered wasn't something that would have occurred to her mother. Back in Texas, all of the Morgans lived within a few miles of each other, in various houses spread over the old Morgan homestead, deep in the big piney woods of East Texas. Sure you could have food catered out there, but not delivered. As a kid, Wendy used to bribe the pizza delivery guys with hundred-dollar tips, but that only worked on slow nights.

Her mom sighed. "I've already—"

"Right. You've already started defrosting the chicken." Here her mother was, making chicken and dumplings. Wendy could barely identify the fridge, given that it was paneled to match the cabinetry. She walked down the island, so she stood just opposite her mother. "Give me a knife and I'll get started on the carrots."

Her mother crossed to a drawer, pulled out a vegetable peeler and knife, then pulled a cutting board from a lower cabinet. A few seconds of silence later and Wendy was at work across from her mom.

Her mother had always been a curious mix of homespun Texas farmwife and old oil money. Wendy's maternal grandparents had been hardscrabble farmers before striking oil on their land in the sixties. Having lived through the dustbowl of the fifties, and despite marrying into a family of old money and big oil, her mother had never quite shaken off the farm dirt. It was one of the things Wendy loved best about her mom.

"You used to love to help me in the kitchen," her mother said suddenly.

Wendy couldn't tell if there was more than nostalgia in her voice. "You used to let me," she reminded her mother. She paused for a second, considering the carrot under her knife. "But you never really needed me there. I stopped wanting to help when I realized that whatever I did wasn't going to be good enough."

Her mother's hand stilled and she looked up. "Is that what you think?"

Wendy continued slicing the carrots for a few minutes in silence, enjoying the way the knife slid through the fibrous vegetable. As she chopped, she felt some of her anger dissipating. Maybe there was something to this cooking-when-you're-upset thing.

"Momma, nothing I've ever done has been good enough for this family." She gave a satisfying slice to a carrot. "Not my lack of interest in social climbing. Not my unfocused college education." She chopped another carrot to bits. "And certainly not my job at FMJ."

"Well," her mother said, wiping her hands on the towel. "Now that you've landed Jonathon—"

"No, Momma." Wendy slammed the knife down. "My job at FMJ had nothing to do with landing a husband. If all I wanted was a rich husband, you could have arranged that for me as soon as I was of age." Picking the knife back up, she sliced through a carrot with a smooth, even motion. Keep it smooth. Keep it calm. "I work at FMJ because it's a company I believe in. And because I enjoy my work. That's enough for me. And for once in my life, I'd like for it to be enough for you and Daddy."

"Honey, if it seems like I've been trying to fix you your entire life, it's because I know how hard it is to not quite fit in with this family. I know how hard this world of wealth and privilege can be to people who are different. I didn't want that for you."

"Momma, I'm never going to fit into this world. I'm just not. Your constant browbeating has never done anything except make me feel worse about it."

Her mother blanched and turned away to dab delicately at her eyes, all the while making unmistakable sniffling noises. "I had no idea."

Wendy had seen her mother bury emotions often enough to recognize this for the show it so obviously was.

"Oh, Momma." Wendy rolled her eyes. "Of course you did. You just figured you were stronger than I was and that eventually you'd win. You never counted on me being just as strong willed as you are."

After a few minutes of silence, she said softly, "I'm sorry, Mom."

Her mother didn't pretend to misunderstand. "Apology accepted."

"I really do wish you'd been here for the wedding. I guess I should have made sure you knew that."

Her mom slapped the knife down onto the counter. "You *guess?*"

"Yes," she said slowly, putting a little more force into the chopping. "I *guess* I should have."

"I am your mother. Is it so wrong for me to wish you'd wanted me here enough to—"

"Oh, this is so typical," she said. "Why should I have to beg you to come to my wedding? I've lived in California for over five years. When I first moved here, I invited y'all out to visit all the time. You never came. No one in the family has shown any interest in my life or my work until now. But now that baby Peyton is here, you've descended like a plague of locusts and—"

"My land," her mother said, cutting her off, her hands

going to her hips. "And you wonder why we didn't want to come before now, when you talk about us like that."

Wendy just shook her head. Once again, she'd managed to offend and horrify her mother. Somehow, her mother always ended up as the bridge between Wendy and the rest of the Morgans. The mediator pulled in both directions, satisfying no one.

"Look, I didn't mean it like that. Obviously I don't think you're a locust. Or a plague."

"Well, then, how did you mean it?"

"It's just—" Bracing her hands on either side of the cutting board, she let her head drop while she collected her thoughts. She stared at the neat little carrot circles. They were nearly all uniform. Only a few slices stood out. The bits too bumpy or misshapen. The pieces that didn't fit.

All her life, she'd felt like that. The imperfect bit that no one wanted and no one knew what to do with. Until she'd gone to work for FMJ. And there, finally, she'd fit in.

Her mother just shook her head, sweeping up the pile of diced celery and dumping it in the pot. "You're always so eager to believe the worst of us."

"That's not true."

"It most certainly is. All your life, you've been rebellious just for the sake of rebellion. Every choice you've made since the day you turned fifteen has been designed to irritate your father and grandmother. And now this."

"What's that supposed to mean?"

"Remember when you were fifteen and you and Bitsy bought those home-perm kits and gave yourselves home perms four days before picture day at the school?"

She did remember. Of course she did. Bitsy had ended up with nice, bouncy curls. But she'd been bald for months while her hair grew back out. Her father had been so mad his face had turned beet-red and her mother had run off to the bathroom for a dose of his blood-pressure medicine.

That had not been her finest moment.

"Or the time you wanted to go to Mexico with that boyfriend of yours. When we told you no, you went anyway."

"You didn't have to have the guy arrested," she said weakly. She couldn't muster any real indignation.

"And you should have told him you were only sixteen."

Also, not her proudest moment.

"And don't try to say we were being overprotective. No sane parent lets their sixteen-year-old daughter leave the country with a boy they barely know."

"Look, Mom, I'm sorry. I'm sorry I was such a difficult teenager. I'm sorry I never lived up to your expectations. But that has nothing to do with who I am now."

"Doesn't it?" Her mom swept up the carrots Wendy had been chopping and dumped them into the pot, lumpy, misshapen bits and all. She added a drizzle of oil in the pan and cranked up the heat. "You've rushed into this marriage with this man we've never even met—"

There was a note of censure in her voice that Wendy just couldn't let pass. "This man that I've worked with for years. If you've never met him, it's because you never came out to visit."

Her mother planted both her hands on the counter between them and leaned forward. "Jonathon seems like a very nice man. But if you married him solely to annoy us then—"

"Oh, Marian, don't be so suspicious."

Wendy spun around toward the kitchen door to see her father and Jonathon standing just inside. She and her mother had been so intent on their own conversation that neither of them had heard them enter.

The two men had obviously come to an understanding about the argument upstairs. Her father had his arm slung over Jonathon's shoulders as if they were old buddies. The smile on his face was downright smug.

Jonathon looked less comfortable. In fact, he rather looked

like he'd swallowed something nasty. Slowly his gaze shifted from her mother to her. Obviously, he heard everything her mother said to her. And he didn't like it.

Nine

"I'm sure," Wendy's father was saying, "that our little Gwen here has grown out of her rebellions."

Jonathon swallowed the tight knot of dread in his throat. "Mrs. Morgan, I assure you—"

But Wendy's mother sent both of them withering glares and he was smart enough to shut up when a woman wielding a butcher knife sent him a look like that.

Wendy pointed the tip of her own knife in her father's direction. "You stay out of this." For the first time in years she felt as though she and her mother were actually talking. She wasn't about to let her father muck it up.

Turning her gaze back to her mother, she continued as if the men hadn't entered at all. "I'm not a rebellious teenager anymore. I'm a grown woman. With a job I love. I may not have married the next political golden boy and I may not be VP of Twiddling My Thumbs at Morgan Oil, but I'm successful in my own right. And a lot of people would be proud to have me as their daughter."

"It's not that we're not proud," her mother began. "But—"

"Of course there's a but. There's always a but."

Her mother ignored her interruption, slicing to the point of the matter as easily as she sliced through the joints in the chicken. "But you've always delighted in rebelling against your father at every turn. If I thought for a minute that marrying Jonathon and raising Peyton was truly what you wanted—"

"It is."

"—and not just another one of your rebellions then I would support you wholeheartedly."

Wendy threw up her hands. "Then support me!"

"But I know how you are. If Mema or Big Hank, let alone your daddy, announced that the sky is blue, the very next morning you'd run out and join a research committee to scientifically prove that it's not."

"You make me sound completely illogical." Wendy shook her head as if she didn't even know how to defend herself against her mother's accusations. "It's like you haven't heard anything I just said."

"Well, you tell me whether or not this is just rebellion." Her mom propped her fists on her hips. "Everyone in this family thinks Hank Jr. and Helen should raise Peyton, except you. Do you have any logical reason why you're so darned determined to raise this baby?"

Jonathon had had enough. He stepped away from her father. Pulling Wendy back against his chest, he said calmly, "I believe that's the point, isn't it? Everyone in the family except for Wendy. And Bitsy. Since Bitsy didn't want her brother raising her daughter, shouldn't that be enough for everyone?"

Marian snapped her mouth closed, narrowing her gaze and setting her jaw at a determined angle. He'd seen that look often enough on Wendy.

"You didn't know Bitsy," she said to him, obviously making an effort to moderate her tone. "Bitsy was never happy if she wasn't stirring up trouble. I don't like to speak ill of the dead, but has it occurred to either of you that naming

Wendy guardian might just have been her way of creating conflict from beyond the grave?"

He felt Wendy pulling away from him, tensing to speak. He tugged her back soundly against him and said, "I may not have known Bitsy. But I know Wendy. I know she's going to make a wonderful mother."

Her mom studied him for a second, apparently searching for signs of his conviction. Finally, she nodded. "Hank Jr.'s wife, Helen, sees that baby as little more than a crawling, crying dollar sign. Peyton is a fast ticket to a bigger chunk of Mema's estate. Helen will fight you for that baby."

"Helen has three boys of her own that she's done a crappy job raising," Wendy pointed out. "If she hadn't shipped those boys off to boarding school the second they were old enough to go, maybe I'd see things differently."

"Just be prepared. Helen's like a bulldog with a bone when money's involved."

"That may be true," Jonathon said. "But Helen isn't here now. And we have all weekend to convince Mema that we'll be the best parents for Peyton."

Her mother harrumphed. "Don't think Helen hasn't figured that out as well. Mark my words, girly, you might be glad we came to visit you here instead of waiting for you to come to us. This might be your only chance alone with Mema to convince her that you and Jonathon are the happy, loving couple you want us all to believe."

There were few things that terrified Jonathon. He thought of himself as a reasonable and logical man. Irrational fears were for small children. Not adults.

At nineteen, he'd spent a solid hour in the dorm room of a buddy, holding the guy's pet tarantula in his hand to get himself over his fear of spiders. At twenty-three, about the time he'd made his first million, he'd spent three weeks in Australia learning how to scuba dive. That trip had served the joint purpose of getting him over his irrational fear of sharks and his equally irrational fear that FMJ would go under if he wasn't available 24/7.

He now took annual diving vacations. After the first, he'd stayed closer to home.

He was a man who faced his fears and conquered them.

Which didn't entirely explain why at nearly midnight on Saturday, he was still sitting in the kitchen sipping twenty-year-old scotch with Wendy's father and uncle. He'd been there for hours, listening to them tell stories about Texas politics and—as her father colorfully called it—"life in the oil patch."

Her family was entertaining, to say the least. And that was the sole reason he hadn't headed to bed much earlier. This had nothing to do with the fact that Wendy was now sleeping in his bed.

He'd been dreading sleeping in the same bed, but that was unavoidable now. As if that wasn't bad enough, now he couldn't get her mother's words out of his head.

After reminding Wendy over and over again that his own motives were selfish, why did it bother him to think that hers might not be so pure? He didn't know. All he knew was that he hated the idea that their marriage was just one more rebellion in a long line of self-destructive behaviors. Worse still was the idea that she'd quickly lose interest in him once the tactic failed to shock her parents.

If she offered herself to him, he wouldn't be able to resist. Even knowing what he did now, the temptation would be too sweet.

To his chagrin, he actually felt a spike of panic when her uncle stood, tossed back the last of his drink and said, "Jonathon, I appreciate the hospitality—and the scotch—but I know I'll regret it tomorrow if I drink any more."

Wendy's dad stood as well. "Marian is gonna have my hide tomorrow as it is."

Jonathon held up the decanter toward Wendy's father. "Are you sure I can't offer you another?"

"Well…"

But Hank slapped his brother on the arm in a jovial way. "We're keeping him from his bride."

"Don't remind me," her father grumbled.

"No man should have to entertain a couple of old blowhards when he has a lovely new wife to warm his bed."

Jonathon nearly smiled at that, despite himself. He liked Wendy's family far more than he wanted to admit. He knew she found them overbearing and pretentious, but there was something about their combination of good-ol'-boy charm and keen intelligence that appealed to him.

Besides, the longer he kept them here, shooting bull until all hours of the night, the greater the chance that Wendy would be fast asleep by the time he got up to the bedroom.

However, before he could even offer them yet another drink, Wendy's father and uncle were stumbling arm in arm up the stairs to the guest bedrooms where they were staying. He winced as they banged into the antique sideboard his decorator had foolishly put outside his office. And then cringed as her father cursed loudly at the thing. Maybe he should consider himself lucky that all of their fumbling didn't wake Mema.

He waited until they vanished down the upstairs hall before he followed, turning off lights as he went. That afternoon, he and Wendy's father had moved Peyton's crib from the nursery to the master bedroom. Ironic, since it had only just arrived in the past week. They'd moved the spare mattress up from the garage and now the guest-bedroom-turned-nursery was once again a guest bedroom. Throughout the process, Wendy kept insisting that her family should just book rooms at one of the many hotels in town. Mema had looked scandalized. Marian had looked offended. And Wendy had eventually caved.

And so, after thirteen years of living completely by himself, he now had six additional people under the roof. Maybe he should buy a bigger house. One with more bedrooms. Though a dozen bedrooms wouldn't have saved him from this. When the family of your new wife was visiting, they all expected you to share a room with her. There was just no way around that.

After putting it off as long as he could, he finally bit the bullet and let himself into the master bedroom. The room he'd be sharing with Wendy. His wife.

Despite his numerous prayers, she wasn't asleep.

She sat up in the bed, her back propped against the enormous square pillows his decorator had purchased—personally he'd never been able to stand the damn things and wasn't entirely sure why he continued to pile them on the bed every morning.

Peyton was asleep on Wendy's chest, her tiny fist curled near her face so that she sucked on one knuckle. Wendy was on his side of the bed. The bedside lamp was on and in her other hand, she held a Kindle.

He glanced at the bedside table. Scratch that, she held his Kindle.

She looked up as he closed the door behind him. Try as he might, he couldn't force himself to walk into the room more than a step or two.

Wendy smiled sheepishly. "Sorry to steal your Kindle," she whispered. "She fell asleep here and I didn't want to risk waking her by digging around for my own book."

She was dressed in a white tank top and Teenage Mutant Ninja Turtle boxer shorts. Her legs were stretched out in front of her. How a woman as short as she was had ended up with legs that long was a mystery, but damn, they seemed to stretch for miles.

Her skin was creamy white, her legs lightly muscled, ending in perfect, petite feet. And her toenails were painted a sassy iridescent purple. He had to force his attention away from her bare legs, but couldn't make his gaze move all the way up to her face. He got caught on her arms, which were just as bare as her legs and somehow nearly as erotic.

In all those years that they'd worked together, he hadn't

ever seen her in something sleeveless. Her upper arms were just like the rest of her. Small and lean, but lightly muscled. Unexpectedly strong.

There was something so intimate about the sight of her holding Peyton on her chest, dressed for bed. In *his* bed.

His muscles practically twitched with the need to cross the room and pull her into his arms. To do all kinds of wicked things to her body. Or maybe to just sit on the bed next to her and watch her sleep.

That thought—the idea that he'd be content without even touching her—that was the thought that scared the crap out of him. Physically wanting her, he could handle that. He'd been fighting his desire for her for years. He always won that battle. But this new urge to just be with her. He didn't even want to know what the hell that was about.

Suddenly his master bedroom seemed way too small.

That new house he was going to buy—the one with a dozen guest bedrooms—apparently the master would need to be four times bigger. He was going to have to move out to Portola Valley to find a house big enough.

"You're mad, aren't you?" Wendy asked.

He dragged his gaze up to her face. She was frowning in that cute way she did, biting down on her lower lip in a half frown, half sheepish grin. He walked closer so that he didn't have to speak louder than a whisper. "Why?" he asked.

"You're mad that I borrowed your Kindle." She flicked the button on the side to turn it off. "I didn't even think. That was a horrible invasion of your privacy."

He wanted to stand here watching her sleep and she was worried that reading from his Kindle was an invasion of his privacy. She had no idea.

"It's okay. No big deal."

"Are you sure?" Despite the whisper, her voice sounded high and nervous. "Because you look really annoyed."

If anything, he probably looked as though he was trying

not to kiss her. Good to know she interpreted that as annoyed. "It's just a Kindle. Not a big deal."

Then he crossed automatically to his side of the bed. The side she was sitting on. He took off his watch and set it on the valet tray on the bedside table. The familiarity of the action calmed his nerves. Of course, normally there wasn't an empty baby bottle beside the lamp, but still…

"Did you have trouble getting her to fall sleep?" he asked as he pulled off his college ring and dropped it beside the watch. Then he hesitated at the simple gold band on his left hand. Since he'd slept in Peyton's nursery last night, he'd had both rings and the watch on all night. This was the first time he'd taken off the wedding ring.

"No." Wendy rubbed at her eyes a little before arching her back into a stretch. "I think she's finally getting used to the new feeding schedule. I woke her at eleven for that bottle and she went right back to sleep.…"

Jonathon looked up when he heard her voice trail off. Like him, she was staring at the ring on his hand. Her gaze darted to his and held it for a second. He watched, entranced, as she nervously licked her lips. Something hot and unspoken passed between them, once again stirring that need to kiss her. To mark her as his own. To bend her back over the bed and plow into her.

Thank God, Peyton was asleep on her chest, keeping him from doing anything too stupid.

He yanked the ring off his finger and dropped it onto the tray beside his watch and his class ring.

Her gaze dropped to where his watch and rings lay on the nightstand. Then it snapped up to his face again. She gave another one of those wobbly, anxious smiles. "I'm on your side of the bed, aren't I?"

"It's fine."

"No, I'll move. Just give me a second." Bracing an arm at Peyton's back, she half sat up, then hesitated. Peyton squirmed and Wendy's frown deepened.

"Just lie her down in the center. She can sleep there."

"You sure?"

"Absolutely." Was it wrong that he was scheming to get Peyton in the bed between them? A little devious maybe, but not wrong. He wouldn't make a move on Wendy as long as Peyton was in the same room. But having her in the bed was a stroke of genius. Better than an icy shower, he was sure. And less conspicuous. Besides, he even had sound scientific reasoning in his corner. "I've been reading this book on—"

"Attachment parenting?" she asked as she waggled the Kindle. "I've been stalking your Kindle, remember?"

That playful, suggestive tone of hers was like a kick in the gut. Maybe he'd still need that cold shower. "I should just sleep on the floor."

"Don't be ridiculous."

She leaned over and rolled Peyton from her chest to the center of the bed. Then came up onto her hands and knees to climb over the still sleeping baby. The thin cotton of her boxer shorts clung enticingly to her bottom and his groin tightened in response to the sight.

She had no idea just how far from ridiculous he was being. This was him at his most practical.

Hell, forget the floor. He'd just sleep in the shower. With the cold water on.

"I don't mind."

"Well, I do," she said, tossing the pillows on that side of the bed onto the floor—the side that from this moment on would always be *her* side of the bed. "When I think of all the things you've done for me in the past few weeks…"

"Don't make me into some kind of hero. You know why I married you." The problem was he was no longer sure *he* knew why he'd done it. "My motives weren't altruistic."

At least that was true.

She flashed him a smile that was a little bit sad. "I know. But neither are mine. And I'm not about to kick you out of bed."

Ten

"Not about to kick you out of your *own* bed," she corrected, a blush tinting her cheeks.

As if she wasn't irresistible already.

He wanted to argue about the sleeping arrangements. Dear God, he did. But he couldn't logically make an argument for sleeping in the tub. Besides, he'd doubt he'd fit.

"Oh, I get it," she said with teasing concern. "You're embarrassed about your body."

Clearly she was trying to hide her own embarrassment. "Wendy—"

"You're probably all pasty white under those dress shirts, huh?" She clucked her tongue in sympathy. "Maybe you put on a few extra pounds over the holidays? Is that it? Is that why you're standing there like a statue, refusing to get undressed?"

He wasn't about to tell why he really wasn't getting undressed. If she hadn't figured out how thin her tank top was and how much that turned him on, then he wasn't going to be the one to tell her.

"Hey, I won't even look," she teased, making a great show of rolling over to face the wall. "Now I can't see you. You can even turn out the light if you want."

Rolling his eyes at her silliness, he reached over and turned off the lamp before starting on his buttons.

"I guess you made peace with my dad," she said after a minute.

"I guess so," he admitted, slipping off his shirt and tossing it vaguely in the direction of a nearby chair. He toed off his shoes and socks. "He's not such a bad guy."

"No." Her voice was small in the darkness. "He's not. Everyone comes around eventually."

He hesitated before unbuttoning his jeans. He hadn't slept in anything other than his underwear since college. He didn't even own a pair of pajama bottoms. First thing in the morning, he was buying a pair. No, twenty pair. Maybe thirty just to be safe.

A moment later he lay down so close to the edge of the bed that his left shoulder hung off the side. His awkward position was still not uncomfortable enough to block out the scent of her on his pillow. It smelled warm and feminine and faintly of peppermint.

He lay there stiffly, eyes resolutely closed, keenly aware that she too was still awake. He searched for something to say. "I never knew you liked the Teenage Mutant Ninja Turtles."

Damn, was he smooth or what?

He heard her roll over in the dark and prop herself up on her elbow. "Doesn't everyone?"

He turned just his head to look at her, but found himself eye to eye with Peyton. Her tiny face was seven inches from his. Her lips pursed as she dreamed about eating. He remembered his niece doing that, from all those long years ago when he used to help feed his sister's kids. Lacey would be in college now. He felt a powerful punch of longing. The kind he normally kept buried deep inside. To push it back down, he rolled up onto his elbow to look at Wendy.

At least he understood the longing he felt when he looked at her. Pure sexual desire. He got that. He could control it—at least, he thought he could. God knew, he'd controlled it so far. But this unfamiliar longing to reconnect with his family? That was new and terrifying territory.

He doubled his pillow under his head, allowing him to look over Peyton to where Wendy lay. She'd moved the night-light in from the nursery, a glowing hippo that cast the room in pink light and made Wendy's skin look nearly iridescent. When he looked back up at her eyes, her gaze darted away from his, as if she was all too aware of the desire pulsing through his veins.

He could see she was about to lie back down, so he said, "No, not everyone loves Teenage Mutant Ninja Turtles. Most people don't even know they were a witty and subversive comic book before becoming a fairly cheesy movie marketed to kids."

She gave a playful shrug, smiling, either because the topic amused her or because she was relieved he'd stopped looking at her like something he wanted to lick clean, he couldn't tell which.

"That's me, I guess." She imitated his hushed tone, obviously no more willing to wake Peyton than he was. "A fan of things witty and subversive."

"Yeah, I get that. What I don't get is how I never knew it until now."

"Oh." She gave another shrug, this one self-effacing.

"For five years, you've dressed like the consummate, bland executive assistant." Whispering in the dark as if this made the conversation far more intimate than the topic was. "Bland clothing in a neutral palate. Demure hair. Now I find out you've been hiding a love of violet nail polish and eighties indie punk rock." He nodded toward her boxers. "Not to mention the Turtles."

She frowned. "Punk rock?"

"The Replacements T-shirt you had on the other day."

"You recognized them?" She gave him a pointed once-over. "And yet you don't seem like a fan of eighties alternative."

"I'm a fan of Google. And you couldn't possibly have been old enough to attend the concert where that T-shirt was sold."

"I'm a fan of eBay. And of defying expectations."

"Which brings me back to my original question. Why didn't I know this about you?"

She paused, seeming to consider the question for a long time. Then she sank back and stared at the ceiling. He watched her, lying there with her eyes open as she gazed into the dark, long enough that he thought she wasn't going to answer at all.

Finally she said softly, "Working at FMJ…" Her shoulders gave a twitch, as if she was shrugging off her pensive mood. "I guess it's been the ultimate rebellion for me. When you're from an old oil family, what's worse than working for a company that's made their money in green energy."

"We do a lot of other things too," he pointed out.

"Well, sure." She rolled back to face him. "But even then, it's all about innovation and change. My family is all about tradition. Maybe when I was working for FMJ, I never felt like I needed to rebel."

He felt his heart stutter as he heard her slip. *When I was working for FMJ,* she'd said. Not *now that I am working for FMJ,* but *when I was.* But she didn't seem to notice, so he let it pass without comment.

"Working at FMJ," she continued, her voice almost dreamy, "I felt like I had direction. Purpose. I didn't need to define myself by dying my hair blue or getting my navel pierced or getting a tattoo."

The image of her naked belly flashed through his mind. The thought of a tiny diamond belly-button ring took his mind into dangerous territory.

"A tattoo?" He was immediately sorry he asked. Please let it be somewhere completely innocuous, like her…nope.

He couldn't think of a single body part on Wendy that didn't seem sexy.

She gave a little chuckle. "One of my more painful rebellions." Then—please God, strike him dead now—she lifted the hem of her white tank top to reveal her hip and the delicate flower that bloomed there.

He clenched his fist to keep from reaching out to touch it. For a second, every synapse in his brain stopped firing. Thought was impossible. Then they all fired at once. A thousand comments went through his brain. Finally, he cleared his throat and forced out the most innocent of them. "That doesn't look like it was done in a parlor."

As lovely as it was, the lines were not crisp. The colors weren't bright.

Wendy chuckled. "Mine was done by a boyfriend." She held up her hands as if to ward off his criticism. "Don't worry, his tools were all scrupulously sterilized and I've been tested since then for all the nasty things you can get if they hadn't been." She gave the tattoo a little pat and then tugged her hem back down. "I was eighteen, had just finished my freshman year at Dartmouth and I wanted to study abroad. My parents refused and made me come home and intern at Morgan Oil. So I dated a former gang member who'd served time in county."

Jonathon had to swallow back the shot of fear that jumped through his veins. She'd obviously survived. She was here now, healthy and safe, but the thought of her dating that guy made his blood boil.

He unclenched his jaw long enough to say, "And you wonder why your parents worry about you."

She gave a nervous chuckle. "Joe was actually a really nice guy. Besides, after spending the weekend with my family—"

"Let me guess, now he works for Morgan Oil? Interns for your uncle in Washington?"

"No. Even better. He went on to write a book about how to leave the gang life behind. He teaches gang intervention throughout Houston and travels all over the U.S. working with police departments."

"You sound almost proud," he commented.

She cocked her head and seemed to think about it. "I guess I am proud of Joe. He turned his life around." Then she gave a little laugh. "Maybe my family should start a self-help program."

"Tell me something. What's with all the cautionary tales?"

"What do you mean?"

"This is the second boyfriend you've told me about whose life was changed by meeting your parents."

"I'm just warning you." Her tone was suddenly serious. "This is what they do. They'll find your weakness—or your strength or whatever—and they use it to drive you away from me."

"No," he said. "That's what they've done in the past. That's not what they're going to do to me."

"Don't be so sure of that." She looked at him, her expression resigned. "Can you honestly tell me you haven't considered how helpful my uncle could be in securing that government contract?"

"That contract has nothing to do with this."

"Not yet. But they're doing it already."

"I don't—"

"You were up late drinking scotch with my dad and uncle, weren't you?"

"How—"

"I can smell it on your breath. And you don't drink scotch."

"How do you know that I don't drink scotch?"

"You never drink hard liquor." Her tone had grown distant. "Never. You keep very expensive brands on hand at the office—and I assume here—for associates who do drink. You read *Wine Spectator* magazine, and can always order a fabulous bottle of wine. You don't mind reds and will drink white, if that's what your companion is having, but you don't really like either. You prefer ice-cold beer. Even then, you never have more than two a night."

He leaned back slightly, unnerved that she knew so much about his taste. "What else do you know about me?"

"I know that anyone who has such strict rules for themselves about alcohol, probably has a parent who drinks. I'd guess your father—"

"It was my mother."

"—but that would just be a guess."

"You have any other theories?"

Between them Peyton stirred. He reached out a hand to place on Peyton's belly to calm her. Wendy reached out at the same time and their fingers brushed. Wendy hesitated, then linked her fingers through his.

"I didn't say it to make a point. I'm just…" She brushed her thumb back and forth over his. "There's something about my family that makes people want to impress them. It's made you want to impress them, or you wouldn't have bent your no-hard-liquor rule."

"My mom did drink," he said slowly. "'Functioning alcoholic' is the term people use now. You have any other old wounds you want to poke?"

The second the words left his mouth, he squeezed his eyes shut.

Christ, he sounded like a jerk.

He opened his eyes, shoving up on his elbow to look at her. He fully expected to see a stung expression on her face. Instead, she just gave his hand a squeeze and sent him a sad smile.

"I'm sorry," he admitted.

"Don't apologize. I got a little carried away with the armchair psychology." She was silent for a minute and he could hear the gears in her brain turning. "But since you mentioned it…"

"Okay, hit me with it. What horribly invasive question are

you going to ask next? You want to know my deepest fear? Clowns. How much I'm actually worth? About—"

"Actually I wanted to know about Kristi."

He fell silent.

"She was your—"

"I know who you mean."

He didn't say anything for a long time, all but praying she'd let it drop. She shifted in the bed beside him. Fidgeting, but saying nothing. She wasn't going to let it drop, and if he didn't respond soon, she'd think Kristi was a bigger deal than she had been.

"She was just someone I knew in high school. Who told you about her?"

He wanted to know who to kill. He hoped it wasn't Matt or Ford, because murdering one of his business partners would probably be the end of FMJ.

"Claire," Wendy answered.

Well, crap. He couldn't very well kill a woman. Especially when she'd just married his best friend.

"Don't be mad at her," Wendy continued. "I practically begged for information."

"Why on earth would you beg for information about my old high school girlfriend?"

"I dunno." She rolled over, but with his eyes squeezed shut, he couldn't tell if she was rolling toward him or away from him. "As dead set as you are against love…well, no one feels that way unless they've been hurt."

"What did Claire tell you about Kristi?"

She didn't answer right away. "Just that you were crazy about her. And she left."

She'd paused long enough for him to know she'd been fabricating her answer. Condensing it down to the barest details.

But in his mind, he could all too easily imagine the longer version. The real version. The one where he made a complete ass of himself over Kristi. Where he handed her his whole heart...and did nothing but scare her away.

"And?" he prodded.

"I figured...she must have been the one."

"And that's what you surmised from Claire's story? That Kristi was the one to break my heart?"

"Am I wrong?"

What exactly was he supposed to say to that? Kristi *had* broken his heart. But he'd only been eighteen. "That was a lifetime ago."

"What happened with her? What really happened?"

He forced his eyes open and tried to sound casual. "You're the armchair psychologist. What do you think happened?"

She tilted her head to the side, considering. "I think that you, Jonathon Bagdon, are a pretty intense guy."

He looked up at her. In the dark of the room, her skin was luminous. Her eyes were so dark they looked almost purple. She was so beautiful, it made his heart ache. As well as plenty of other parts of him.

Damn, but he wanted her. Not just her body. But all of her.

Thinking of her comment, all he could was mutter, "You have no idea."

"The way I see it, I'm a grown woman. Someone who's used to dealing with strong personalities. And there are times when even I'm a little overwhelmed by you. So this girl—Kristi?—she probably didn't have a chance. I'm guessing you falling in love with her must have scared the hell out of her."

"Yeah. That's about it." He let his eyes drift closed again. "This thing between us," he began, but then corrected himself, "this physical thing between us, it's pretty intense."

"Yes, it is," she agreed softly. He opened his eyes to see her still sitting up, looking down at him. The look in her eyes made heat churn through his body, but it was her words that made his heart pound. "I'm not scared of you, Jonathon."

"Maybe you should be."

She tilted her head, studying him in the pink glow of the

hippo. Indeed, she looked more aroused than frightened. "Maybe."

"Scratch that. You should definitely be afraid. If you knew half the things I want to do to you…"

She arched a brow, her expression a little curious, a little challenging. "You think you're the only one with pent-up desire and an active imagination?"

Was she purposefully trying to destroy any chance he had of getting some sleep? Ever again?

"I think," he answered her, "there's a damn good chance you underestimate how sexy you look in a tank top." It was hard to tell in the pink light, but he could have sworn she blushed. He couldn't stop himself from going on. "And I also think you underestimate just how hard it is for me to keep my hands off you."

Her chest rose as she sucked in a deep breath, highlighting all the wonderful things that tank top of hers did.

"You think you're the only person this is hard for?" she asked.

"I think I'm the only one who's a big enough jerk to wait until there was an innocent baby here in the bed between us, just to guarantee I'd keep my hands off you."

She gnawed on her lip for a second then, looking secretly pleased with herself. He squeezed his eyes shut, blocking out the image of her and that sexy bow mouth of hers.

He felt the bed shift as she lay back down. Then, so softly he thought he might have imagined it, she said, "Don't be so sure about that."

Eleven

She'd fallen asleep with her body fairly throbbing with un-fulfilled sexual tension and she woke up alone. The feeling of jittery anticipation stayed with her as she headed for the bathroom and dug through the suitcases she'd left in Jonathon's closet the day before. She quickly pulled on an oversize gossamer shirt and a pair of black leggings and headed downstairs to search out food and her family.

She walked into the kitchen just in time for her mother to pile her plate high with the last batch of buttermilk pancakes. Peyton was gurgling happily in the high chair beside the table, being cooed to by Mema. The kitchen was as warm and as welcoming as a Hallmark special. The tangy scent of pancakes mingled with the bitter zing of the coffee to stir long-forgotten memories of her childhood. She swallowed back a pang of loneliness and regret. She'd chosen to leave Texas and to distance herself from her family. That didn't mean she didn't miss them.

But with all that was going on in the kitchen, there was one thing that was missing. Jonathon.

Or to be more precise, three things: Jonathon, her father and Big Hank.

She didn't notice at first, so caught up in as she was in the pancake-scented time machine. But she paused, that first bite halfway to her mouth, and listened with her head cocked toward the kitchen door, mentally reviewing the walk down the stairs.

She set down the fork, heavenly bite uneaten. "Okay, where'd you send them?"

Mema's back stiffened. "Why would you assume I'd sent them anywhere?"

Wendy shoved the bite of pancakes into her mouth and chewed out her frustration. "Well, they're not here, are they? That means you've sent them off somewhere. Either so you can ply him for information. Or me, I suppose."

Her mother and grandmother exchanged a look that made her very nervous. She forked off another bite and crammed it in. Weren't carbs supposed to be calming? So why didn't she feel any more relaxed?

She felt a niggling of fear creep up her spine. If she was honest with herself, she knew why she didn't feel any calmer. When a pride of lions went hunting, they'd separate the weaker members of the pack from the rest to make it easier to pick them off.

Jonathon had just been separated from the herd.

"Where did they go?" she asked, feigning a calmness the pancakes hadn't provided.

"Seriously, it's nothing nefarious. Jonathon offered to show them FMJ's headquarters. It's not like they've taken him out back to beat him or anything."

No. Maybe it wasn't like that. But she feared how buddy-buddy they'd be when they got back.

She and Jonathon had only been married for two days and already her family was driving a wedge between them.

* * *

It was no easy task slipping out of the house when her mother and grandmother were there hovering. In the end, she lied. She wasn't proud of it, but she did it.

I just want to run out to the grocery store for a few things, she'd said. *Diapers. New formula. Oh, right. There are several cans in the pantry. But Peyton's been so fussy I want to try a different brand.*

Who knew motherhood would provide such ample opportunity for lying?

"I think between the two of us, Mema and I have raised enough children to muddle through," her mother had said as Wendy headed for the door.

Wendy took the grocery store at a mad dash, storming the unfamiliar baby aisle as if it were the target of a shock-and-awe military campaign. She raked into her cart five different varieties of formula and enough diapers to keep Peyton dry until college. Then, back in the car, she retraced her path, bypassing Jonathon's street and heading for FMJ's headquarters.

Stopped at a light—mentally urging it to change more quickly—she took one brief minute to question her motives. Why was she so worried? What was the worst that would happen?

A few hours alone with her family wouldn't convince Jonathon to revamp his entire life, write a tell-all and travel the country on the lecture circuit. After a single night of tossing back scotch with her uncle, he wasn't going to quit FMJ and accept a position at Morgan Oil. Or worse, run for office.

But none of that logic slowed the pounding of her heart. Nor did it dry out her damp palms.

She so desperately wanted to believe that Jonathon was different than every other guy she'd ever dated. But what if he wasn't?

He had to know how influential her uncle was within the

government. One word from Big Hank and that contract they'd been working on could be a done deal. All Jonathon had to do was sell her uncle on the idea.

And when it came to FMJ's proprietary technology, no one was a better salesman than Jonathon. If he had the chance to schmooze her uncle, he'd be a fool not to take it. She'd just hoped he wouldn't have a chance.

By the time she swiped her security card at the campus gate, she was twitchy with anxiety. Part of her wanted to just drive. Not back to his house, not even back to hers, but just drive. She'd had a friend once who hopped in her car and drove to Cabo San Lucas every time life got messy. It was a twenty-eight-hour drive from Palo Alto. By tomorrow afternoon, Wendy could be sipping tequila on the beach. But none of her problems would go away. And then she'd be drunk or hungover and two thousand miles from them. That hardly seemed like the perfect solution. Twenty-seven years of rational decision-making wouldn't let her go the Shawshank route.

She scurried into the front office, dropped her purse on the desk and sank into her chair. The simple familiarity of the actions settled her nerves. How crazy was it that the faint scent of ozone coming off all the computer equipment in the other room could be so calming?

Maybe her family was right and she was a nut for loving this job so much, but she couldn't help it. Everything felt right in the world when she sat behind this desk.

She knew it was an illusion. If she went down to the R&D lab, she'd find Jonathon there with her father and uncle. And she just wasn't ready to see that yet. Apparently, she'd run across town for nothing.

Letting out a sigh, she crossed her arms on the desktop and dropped her head into the cradle of her elbows. Then she heard a faint sound coming from the back office that Ford, Matt and Jonathon shared. She stilled instantly, listening. Slowly she stood and crossed to the door, giving it a nudge so it swung inward.

Jonathon stood behind his desk along the west wall. She was unused to seeing him in casual clothes, and couldn't help admiring how good he looked in a simple cotton T-shirt and jeans. Though his laptop was out on his desk, it wasn't open. There was a manila file in his hand.

"Oh," she murmured as he looked up. "It's you."

His lips twitched. "Who'd you expect?"

"I…" She paused, momentarily stumped. Finally, she admitted, "I thought you were downstairs in the R&D lab. With my father and Big Hank."

"Nope." He frowned, obviously puzzling through why she would have thought that. "We ran into Matt. He offered to show them around."

"Oh." Relief flooded her. He wasn't off schmoozing her family. He hadn't fallen under their spell.

"Why'd you come in?" he asked.

"Oh, well I…" Not wanting to admit she suspected him of underhanded business tactics, she made a vague gesture toward her office. "Same as you. Wanted to catch up on some work."

Suddenly, now that her fears about Jonathon had been dispelled, another emotion came rushing into the void left by them: desire. Or maybe it had been there all along, right under the surface, waiting for an excuse to rise to the top, as it always did.

"Right." He nodded. "Since I figure we won't be in tomorrow we might as well—"

"Why won't you be in tomorrow?" she asked, without really listening for the answer, because her mind was back in the bedroom, the night before, hearing him confess how much he wanted her. And she was remembering how he'd looked in the light of that ridiculous pink hippo, the bedsheet pulled only to his waist, the muscles of his chest so clearly defined despite the dim lighting.

"Your family. They'll still be here then."

"So? What does that have to do with your work?"

"While they're here, our first priority is convincing them we're a happy couple. We can't do that if we're not together."

"But work—" she protested.

"Can wait for a few days."

Work? Wait? Who was this guy?

Whoever he was, she didn't like it. Not one bit. She was going to have a hard enough time sleeping in the same bed with him for the next week. She'd been counting on their time at the office to return to normalcy. Now more than ever, she needed him to be the hard, analytical boss she was used to.

Her mind was still reeling from that little bomb when Jonathon said, "Since we're both here, why don't you go grab your computer and we'll try to get some work done?"

"The thing is, Jonathon, I—"

Then she broke off abruptly. Because what could she really say? He was waiting, expectantly. Looking so handsome it made her heart ache. "The thing is, I don't know if I can do this."

"Do what?"

"Slip so easily between the work me and the me that has to pretend to be your wife. I don't know why it seems so easy for you, but—"

"You think this is easy for me?"

"Well. Yes. You barely seem aware that at this time yesterday you were kissing me. Or that last night we slept in the same bed." She paused, waiting for him to say something. Though his gaze darkened, he didn't comment and suddenly she felt ridiculous for saying these things aloud. "Which is fine, I mean, this is my problem. I'll figure it out. But I think I just need to get out of here for a couple of hours. Get my head on straight."

Maybe that trip to Cabo wasn't such a bad idea after all.

She turned and had made it most of the way to the door when he grabbed her arm and turned her around. She barely caught her balance when he pulled her roughly against him and kissed her.

Twelve

His mouth was hot and firm on hers. It only took a second for her to lose herself in the sensation of being kissed by him. No, not just kissed, devoured. She felt completely swept away by it. By him. By the sensation of his hand gently cupping her jaw. By his arm at her back, pressing her body to his. The feel of his lips as they moved over hers in a hundred delicate kisses.

"This is not easy," he pulled back just long enough to say. And then he kissed her again. "It's never been easy." Another kiss. "Not once in five years." And another kiss. "Not once has it been easy." And another. "To stay away from you."

And then his tongue was in her mouth, seducing her with long, slow strokes, stirring heat in her body. Making her all but tremble with need. She felt as though her skin was overheated. Tingly and antsy. As if she was on fire. Her nipples prickled, demanding to be touched and she arched against him, pressing her breasts to his chest, desperate for some kind of contact. And still it wasn't enough.

Wrapping her arms around him, she twined her fingers into his hair and pulled him back just enough to ask, "Then why did you stay away?"

He gazed down at her, his eyes foggy with lust. "I don't know."

And for the life of her, she didn't know either. Honest to God, she couldn't think of one damn reason why they shouldn't be together. It had nothing to do with Peyton or the marriage. Nothing to do with her family or the rebellious tendencies she'd thought were long dead. This was about them. It had always been about them. And now that she was kissing him—now that his hands were all over her, making her tremble—she couldn't think of any reason why they should stay apart. When it was so obvious that they were meant to be together.

His lips moved from her mouth down to her neck, leaving a delicate trail of red-hot nibbles. She arched into his lips, all but praying he'd move lower and take her breast into his mouth.

"Oh, Jonathon," she murmured. "Please..."

She wasn't sure what exactly she was pleading for. Not when there were so many things she wanted him to do to her. So many places on her body she wanted him to touch and explore. All she knew was she wanted more. All of him.

Then abruptly, he let go of her and stepped away. Her body sagged with mounting desire, her legs limp and barely able to hold her up.

Thank goodness, she didn't need to support her own weight for long. His hand grasped her bottom, lifted her firmly against him and she automatically wrapped her legs around his waist. The position was perfect. Exquisite. As if her body had been precisely designed to wrap around his.

Her leggings were thin enough that she could feel the denim of his jeans through the delicate fabric. She felt every seam, every ridge. The hard line of his erection beneath his zipper pressed against the very center of her. She rocked her hips, increasing the pressure against her core, sending fissures of pleasure rocketing through her body.

He groaned low in his throat, still kissing her. Then he pulled his mouth away from hers. "You're killing me here."

She grinned, brimming with pure feminine pride. "Am I?" she asked, shifting her hips again, delighting in tormenting him. But the sensation was too divine and she shuddered as well.

He muttered a curse that was half exasperation, half pride. "I shouldn't do this," he muttered. "I should be stronger than this, but I can't..." He nipped at her neck in a primal, animalistic sort of way that sent a shower of pleasure radiating across her skin. "I can't stay away any longer."

A second later, she felt him bump against the edge of his desk. He lowered her slowly down the length of his body. She didn't have even a moment to miss his warmth or the pressure against her sensitive skin, because he reached under the hem of her shirt and hooked his thumbs under the waistband of her tights and pulled them down her legs in one smooth movement, stripping away her panties as he did so.

She kicked off her shoes as she stepped out of her leggings, naked from the waist down. Her shirt hit her mid-thigh, but the fabric was gossamer thin and left her feeling scandalously exposed. Standing in her boss's office, half-naked, trembling with desire.

He stepped back to look at her. The heat in his gaze made her skin prickle. Suddenly she was very aware of her hardened nipples pressing against the thin cotton of her bra. Of the moisture between her legs and the cool air on her thighs.

A feeling of vulnerability started to creep in under the heat of desire. Then she looked up and saw the expression on Jonathon's face. It was part dumbstruck awe and part reverent glee. Like a little boy standing in front of a Christmas tree, staring at the presents, wondering which one was his.

She brought her hands to the buttons running down the front of her shirt. Then flicked them free, one by one. His gaze stayed glued to the progression of her hands. He didn't move an inch. Except for his hands, which slowly curled into fists. As if it was all he could do not to reach for her and rip the shirt off her body himself. As if she was his deepest fantasy come to life.

For all she knew, maybe she was.

She wanted to think so. Needed to believe it. Because he was certainly hers.

It wasn't a fantasy she'd consciously entertained. Never something she dwelled on. Nevertheless, the idea of being with Jonathon, of seeing exactly this expression in his gaze... it had always been there. Right beneath the surface of her thoughts. Niggling at the edge of her awareness. She'd pushed it aside countless times. But now she pulled it from the depths of her mind and let it out into the light of day.

She wanted this. For years she'd wanted this. And now he was about to be hers.

Her hands reached the last button. She slipped it free of the buttonhole, letting the shirt fall open.

With a sweep of his arm, Jonathon knocked everything off his desk except for the blotter. Then he set her down carefully on the desk.

"You can't imagine the times I thought about doing this." He pressed a hot kiss to her neck as he nudged her shirt off one shoulder. "Every day." He nipped at her collarbone, sending hot spikes of desire radiating down through her chest. "I pictured you sitting here." His fingers popped open the front closure of her bra and peeled back the cups to reveal her bare breasts. "Right on my desk." Her bra dropped off and she arched her back as he trailed the tip of one finger from her collarbone down to her nipple. "Completely naked."

With a groan he dropped to his knees in front of her. As if he could no longer resist the temptation she presented. He parted her thighs, moved her bottom right to the edge of the desk and placed his mouth at the very core of her.

He devoured her in tantalizing licks. She dropped back

onto her elbows, her eyes almost closed as wave after wave of pleasure washed over her. He was patient and thorough.

The pleasure was so intense that her eyes nearly rolled back in her head, but she couldn't make herself look away from the sight of his head between her legs, his close-cropped dark hair in such sharp contrast to her pale, quivering thighs.

Just when she thought she couldn't take it anymore, he focused his relentless attention on the tiny bundle of nerves so central to her pleasure, stroke after stroke, until she could hardly catch her breath. Then she felt his hand at her entrance. One finger, then two, plunged into her. She dropped onto her back, arching off the desk. As her climax crashed over her, she cried his name.

It felt like more than five years. Maybe his whole life he'd been waiting to see her like this. Spread out before him on the very desk that had so often been between them. She was the most delectable treat he'd ever sampled. Hot and moist with desire. Trembling from the aftereffects of a climax. His name still a whisper on her lips.

Now, here she was. Just like he'd always wanted. And he couldn't find a damn condom.

He had them here. Somewhere in the desk. Because he'd known for years how much he wanted her. And that some day he might act on it. Hell, there had been no "might" about it. With only the slightest hint of interest from her, he'd have acted on it. She needn't have stripped naked for him here in his office, though that certainly had been a dream come true.

And now he couldn't find the damn things.

He pulled one drawer out completely, dumping the contents on the floor. And then he did the same with the next drawer. And the next. Finally he found them, just when he thought the sight of her might make him come in his pants, just when his erection was twitching with the need to be inside of her.

When she saw what he'd been looking for, she was as eager as he was. He ripped open the package with trembling fingers, even as she unbuttoned his jeans and shoved them down around his hips. Then a second later, he was inside of her, her legs spread wide, her arms outstretched as she leveraged herself against the desk. Her hips bucked off the surface as he plowed into her over and over again. The feel of her body clenching around him was exquisite. The taste of her, still on his lips, was divine. But it was the sound of her cries of pleasure that sent his own climax rocketing through his body.

He knew in that moment, that he wanted her—just like this—forever. And that scared the hell out of him.

As soon as Wendy was able to move again, she sat up, pressing her face against his chest and wrapping her arms around him. She breathed in the musky scent of him. Relished the feeling of his taut muscles beneath her fingers and of his warm skin beneath her cheek. She wanted to sit like this forever, wrapped around him. Clinging to him. Her body still thrumming with pleasure. The feeling of complete and utter contentment cocooning her from the rest of the world.

But the world was out there and it wouldn't stay away forever. So when he stepped out of her embrace, she let him go, when what she really wanted to do was hold on fast.

She moved slowly, pulling her bra back on and then her shirt. Her fingers were still fumbling with the buttons when he spoke.

"This can't happen again."

Her head whipped up and she stared at him. He'd turned away from her, but she could read the tension in his back as he zipped up his jeans. "Why not?"

"It's not a good idea." His voice was terse.

She felt that tension like a solid wall between them. She could feel him building it up. One brick at a time. One brick with each word. Part of her screamed that this wasn't the time for an argument. That the more they talked about it, the higher the wall would become, but she just couldn't let it go. It wasn't in her nature to back down from a fight.

"Not good for whom?" she asked.

"For anyone." He paused, then turned back to face her. His gaze drifted to her shirt, which hung open, her fingers having stilled midway up on their progress. "I'm afraid it'll be bad for you."

"Um, then you weren't paying attention," she said snarkily as she hopped off the desk. "Because that was extremely good for me."

She was naked from the waist down. True, her shirt was long enough that it hit her mid-thigh, but she still felt extremely exposed. Twenty minutes ago, before he'd rocked her world off its axis, that had been a good feeling. Now, not so much.

She swiped her tights off the ground, uncomfortably aware of how his gaze followed her every movement.

"Exactly. And good sex is addictive. You'll have a problem with that."

That cool, clinical tone of his made her blood pressure creep up. How the hell did he sound so calm? So rational?

"What kind of problem am I supposed to have with this… this extremely addictive sex?" And damn it, her tights were inside out. She rammed her hand down one of the legs, trying to snag the ankle hem so she could right them, but anger made her clumsy.

"I just don't think it's a good idea. It's not good for Peyton."

Watching Wendy's frustration grow as she wrestled with her tights, Jonathon wondered if perhaps he should have taken a different route.

"We're her parents now," she snapped, clearly exasperated. "I can't see how it would possibly hurt her for us to sleep together."

"You can't?" Why did she have to be so strongheaded?

Why couldn't she just make it easier on both of them and agree with him for once?

"No. I can't. In fact, since we agreed that this marriage could last up to two years, I actually think it's a good idea."

"Then you haven't thought it through."

Of course, nothing was ever that easy. Not with Wendy.

One of the things that made her such a great assistant was that she never hesitated to give her opinion. No mindless agreeing for her. If she had a better idea, she said so. If she spotted a problem he'd overlooked, she pointed it out. Unfortunately, right now, it made her a pain in the ass.

Because what he really wanted—no, damn it, what he needed—was for her to stop talking about sex.

"Okay, maybe I didn't think it through." Finally—thank God—she got her tights right side out and stepped into them. "But now that I am, I don't know that I see a downside. Two years is a long time. And—" She broke off, appearing to grit her teeth before spitting out her next words. "And I'm not going to tell you that you can't see other people while we're married."

"Wendy—"

"No. Just let me say this, okay?" She swallowed visibly, not quite meeting his gaze, though he could tell she was mustering the gumption to do so. "I'm not going to forbid you from…doing what you need to do. But goodness knows, I'm not going to be registering on eHarmony anytime soon. So, maybe it's not a bad idea to—"

"What?" he asked. "To hook up anytime either one of us has an itch?"

She rolled her eyes. "What is wrong with you? Are you purposefully being the biggest jerk in history for a reason?"

"What is wrong with *me*? What's wrong with *you*?" He swept a hand toward his desk, as if displaying the destruction they'd done. "Five minutes ago we were having sex on that desk and now you're talking about me being with another woman? How is that normal?"

This had to be the most awkward conversation in his entire

life. And considering that he sometimes talked to complete strangers about their finances, that was saying something.

She looked stricken by his words. Not for the first time either. She gave a little rapid blink, her eyes not quite reaching his gaze, and then swallowed. "I'm trying to be logical here. Two years is a long time and—"

"And you don't think I can keep my zipper up?"

Her gaze snapped to his face. "Let's just say, given that I've had a front-row seat to your dating practices for the past five years, I'm skeptical."

"Trust me. I can keep my zipper up."

She gave him a searing once-over. "All evidence to the contrary."

He gave her an icy, wolfish smile. "Is that really a stone you want to throw?"

"What do you want me to say? That I'm so impressed by your monkish fortitude?"

What *did* he want her to say?

He wanted her to say that she didn't want anyone else. That she wanted only him. And that she wanted him for some reason other than he was going to be convenient for the next two years.

"Okay, you want the truth? I don't think we should sleep together again, even if it means two years of celibacy. For both of us. I don't want you to get hurt, and you're too emotionally involved already."

"I'm too emotionally involved?" she scoffed, her voice dripping with sarcasm, but he could see the flash of pain in her gaze and knew he'd nailed it on the head. "*I* am? That's funny, because I wasn't the one just now who couldn't stop talking about how much I wanted this for the past five years. About how desperately I needed this."

Of course it would come back to that. He'd sounded like a lovesick fool. But neither of them would benefit from imagining he was some romanticized hero.

"Right," he said, bitterness seeping into his voice. "I talked about how I wanted your body. How much I wanted you physically. Not how much I loved you." As he spoke, the tear that had been clinging to her lashes, finally gave up its battle and dropped down onto her velvety cheek. He gently brushed it off with his thumb, then held it up as evidence. "And I'm not the one crying now."

"You bastard. I can't believe you said that." She stepped back, putting some distance between them. "And you're wrong about one thing. I won't be begging to sleep with you again anytime soon. Not now."

She stormed off, but made it only as far as the office door before turning around. Propping her fists on her hips, she said, "I need to know now. Are you in or out?"

"What?"

"Are you in or are you out? Do you still want to do this, or are you wigging out on me?"

"I'm in," he said slowly. Undoubtedly deeper in than he should be.

"Are you sure? Because two years is a long time. And I'd rather know now if you're having second thoughts."

"I said I'm in."

"Good. My family wants to meet yours. They're planning a reception for us. We leave for Palo Verde on Friday."

She didn't wait for his reply. It probably wouldn't have occurred to her that two years without sex wasn't nearly as off-putting as the idea of going to visit his family. A second later he heard the door to her office slam as she stormed out.

All alone in the office, he sank into his desk chair. Everything that had once been on his desk now lay scattered on the floor as well as the contents of three drawers. Years of keeping his life meticulously under control, of keeping his emotions neatly compartmentalized, and he'd blown it all in one reckless act.

He propped his elbows on his desk and dropped his head into his hands, ignoring the fact that his own cheeks felt suspiciously damp.

Thirteen

She wanted to stab him on her way out. There were several things in the office sharp enough to leave a nice puncture wound without being fatal. She took it as sign of great personal development that she didn't use any of them.

Then she sat in her car for several long minutes trying to hash out her feelings. Retrace her steps. Figure out where she'd gone wrong. In the end the only conclusion she could reach left her deeply unsatisfied.

Jonathon was right. She *was* too emotionally involved. She was up-to-her-tonsils-and-sinking-fast emotionally involved. Damn it.

Worse still, she couldn't follow her first instinct, which was to run like a rabbit and hole up somewhere until she sorted through her emotions. No, with her family here, watching her like a hawk… Or maybe a pride of ravenous lions was a better analogy? Whatever hungry predator they were, she couldn't bolt. They'd attack at the first sign of weakness. She had to remember what was important. Keeping Peyton.

Then she thought of what she'd seen just yesterday morning. Jonathon sitting in the rocking chair with Peyton cradled in his arms. He may not know it yet, but she wasn't the only one who was emotionally involved.

He may not care about her—beyond her body, which he was obviously rather fond of—but he did care about Peyton.

Whether or not he wanted to admit it, he was a good father. He was a better father than he was a husband. Well, she could live with that. For the time being, she had to.

The days before the trip to Palo Verde passed quickly. Jonathon insisted she take the time off to visit with her family. Which seemed counterintuitive to her since the whole point of the marriage was to keep her at work. But every time she brought it up, he just stared at her stiffly and reminded her that taking off work to bond with Peyton would go a long way toward convincing them that she would be a good mother. He assured her that they still had plenty of time to work on the contract proposal. He, however, went stalwartly into work alone. He never again mentioned taking time off himself to play the part of the loving husband. Apparently—after they'd had sex at the office—that would have strained even his resolve. She assumed that when he said she should spend time with her family, what he really meant was that she should spend time with anyone other than him.

Truth be told, she let him put her off over and over, because she wanted to avoid the office too. She wasn't ready to be in the office where he'd made love to her with such abandon. Scratch that. Made love to *her body* with such abandon. And she damn sure wasn't ready to see him sitting behind the desk, working as if nothing had ever happened.

So she spent the days playing tour guide to her family. Mema was determined to hate everything about California and Big Hank flew back to Texas for the week, but her parents seemed to actually enjoy the time she spent with them. Even more shocking, she enjoyed it too.

She assumed that would change by the end of the week, when Big Hank, Hank Jr. and Helen would arrive. Helen had insisted on planning the wedding reception Mema had suggested the Morgans host. Without even leaving Texas, Helen had arranged a venue, invited guests and booked lodgings for the Morgans, which was no small feat to accomplish in just a few days' time. Whenever Wendy offered help, she was firmly rebuffed. Helen had even located and invited Jonathon's family. Though, apparently, only his older sister, Marie, had returned Helen's phone calls.

Wendy could hardly blame Jonathon's family. By the end of the week, she was sick of talking to Helen. The only thing worse than dealing with her was dealing with Jonathon.

At the end of each day, he'd arrive home and she'd have to—once again—pretend to be a loving wife. With the tension between them as strong as it was, she doubted she fooled anyone. Jonathon, however, did a bang-up job. She could barely turn around without having him there to touch her. To wrap his arm around her shoulder and drop a careless kiss on her forehead.

The nights were the worst. She could make it all the way through the day, she could even pretend in front of her parents, but her stomach knotted every time they closed and locked the bedroom door. She didn't know if her family found it odd for them to be locking the door, but she didn't dare risk having them walk in unannounced and seeing his pallet at the foot of the bed, where he'd been sleeping. The closest they came to communicating was the moment each night when she threw the pillow at him. Unfortunately, he always caught it. Damn him.

And before she knew it, it was Thursday. The week had slipped by and they'd be driving out to Palo Verde in the morning.

She lay there in the dark, unable to sleep and staring at the ceiling, irritated by the rhythm of his slow, even breathing from the foot of the bed. Thirty minutes passed. Then another twenty. Then she heard him roll over and sigh.

"Are you still awake?" she whispered in the dark.

"Of course. I'm on the floor and you're tossing and turning so much it sounds like a bounce house over there."

She bolted upright and snapped on the bedside lamp. "Would you just get into bed."

He blinked up at her, wedging his elbows under him. "Turn off the light. Try to get some sleep."

"I'd be able to sleep better if I didn't know you were uncomfortable sleeping on the floor."

He lay back down and stared up at the ceiling. "It's not that bad."

"It's two blankets and a pillow. It can't be good. You'll be safe sleeping in the bed. I'm not going to attack you or anything."

"It's just better if we limit our contact as much as possible. I'm trying to be noble here."

"Yeah." She snorted, falling back onto the bed. "I think that ship sailed the day we had sex on your desk."

"You're going to wake up Peyton."

Even though Big Hank had left, they'd decided to keep Peyton's crib in their room. She'd slept so much better when she was only a few inches away from them.

And though she knew Jonathon had a point—winning the argument wasn't worth waking Peyton, who would want to be fed in a few hours anyway—it only irritated her more. She yanked her pillow out from under her head and threw it at him. There was a satisfying whump as it landed on his torso.

"I already have a pillow."

"I know. I just wanted to throw something at you."

"Very mature."

"I know." Smiling, she snapped off the light.

He brought the pillow back to her, standing next to her side of the bed in the dark and holding it out to her. "I don't need it."

"Keep it. Maybe it'll make the floor a little less uncomfortable."

"Wendy—" he growled.

"I'm trying to be *noble*."

"Fine," he snapped and went back to lie down.

It was wrong how pleased she was by the irritation in his voice. He may act as if he was completely indifferent to her, but she was still able to get under his skin. That shouldn't make her happy. But it did.

A few minutes later, she fell asleep smiling. And woke up in the morning with the pillow under her head.

At eighteen, Jonathon had left Palo Verde with $5,168.36 in his checking account—all earmarked for living expenses. His only other possessions were a partial scholarship to Stanford, two suitcases, a desk lamp, a used laptop, a backpack and a veritable mountain of student loans. He'd hitched a ride from their hometown to the coast in Matt's BMW. Jonathon hadn't been back since.

Palo Verde was a small but historic town on the highway between Sacramento and Lake Tahoe. When he'd left in the mid-nineties, it was only just beginning to climb out of the economic slump that had cursed it since the gold rush ended more than a hundred years before. Now Sacramento had grown enough—and was expensive enough—for people to commute from Palo Verde. On a purely intellectual level, Jonathon supposed Palo Verde wasn't such a bad place to live. The town had a certain charm to it. Not the sort that any teenage boy would appreciate, but surely plenty of people liked musty old buildings and the gently rolling foothills of the Sierra Nevada mountains.

Nevertheless, during the drive Jonathon practically itched to turn the car around and get the hell out of there. If someone had asked him a month ago, he'd have sworn that nothing short of the coming apocalypse would have enticed him back to Palo Verde. Maybe not even that. If the world was coming to an end, why would he go there?

As they entered Palo Verde, with Peyton safely nestled in her car seat in the backseat, and Wendy beside him in the front, Jonathon clenched his hands so tightly around the steering wheel that he feared he might snap it in half. Sure, it was unlikely, but if anything was going to imbue him with Incredible Hulk-like powers, it would be this.

Wendy's family was in the rented minivan behind them on the highway. She sat with her iPhone, carefully dictating directions from the GPS map, as if he hadn't spent the first eighteen years of his life trapped in this God-forsaken hellhole.

"Okay," she said in a half whisper since Peyton was asleep. "It looks like this road will merge with Main Street just ahead."

"I know."

She ignored him. "And then, a couple of miles into town, Cutie Pies will be on your left."

"I know."

"It looks like there's parking on the street, but according to Claire's email, it fills up pretty quickly, so if we don't get a spot, we should circle around to the back of—"

"I. Know."

Wendy dropped the phone in her lap and held up her hands. "Hey, I'm just doing my part as navigator."

"I grew up here." He blew out a slow breath, prying the fingers of his left hand off the steering wheel and giving them a flex. "I don't need a navigator."

"Things can change a lot in fifteen years."

He didn't need her to tell him that. He was a completely different man than the boy who'd left town straight out of high school. He'd always thought it odd that spending his whole life wanting to escape from Palo Verde, he'd end up living in a city with such a similar name. Of course, Palo Alto was a completely different kind of town. The bustling intellectual hotbed of technological development. A city with many brilliant, very rich men. And he was one of them. So there was no reason at all that just breathing Palo Verde air should stir all his rebellious instincts. Yet it did.

It made him twitchy with energy and shortened his already strained temper. As if she sensed his mood—not that he was doing a great job of hiding it or anything—Wendy reached out a hand and gave his leg a stroke that she probably meant to be soothing. "It's just been a while since you've been back. I was trying to help."

He could feel the heat of her hand through the fabric of his jeans and it made his thigh muscles twitch. Instantly, he knew what he really wanted. The one thing that would expel all the anger and tension roiling inside of him. Sex. Good, clean, emotionless sex would do the trick. He could skip the drive through town to Cutie Pies and head up to the hairpin turns of Rock Creek Road, pull off into the trees, tug Wendy onto his lap and screw her right here in the front seat.

It was a good plan if he ignored the baby sleeping in the back of the car. It'd be even better if he didn't know emotionless sex was impossible with Wendy.

And then there was the minivan full of in-laws behind them. And the wedding reception Wendy's helpful cousins had planned for them.

He took little pleasure in knowing that once the wedding reception was over, he could leave Palo Verde and never look back. It didn't even help knowing that tomorrow Matt, Claire, Ford, Kitty and Ilsa would arrive for the reception. Having his best friends and their families there would make things better, but only a little bit. Before he could get through that reception tomorrow night, he still had lunch at Cuties Pies— that part wouldn't be bad. But he'd begun to wish he'd refused to come into town the day before the reception. Two whole days in his hometown was way too long.

It meant a lot of time dreading meeting with his family. Oh, he knew it was unavoidable. That was—after all—the sole purpose in having a wedding reception in Palo Verde. But he certainly didn't relish the idea.

In short. It sucked. The whole situation sucked.

He'd been acting like an ass ever since they'd had sex in his office. Of course, he didn't need Wendy's faux armchair psychology degree to figure out why. He was pushing her away every chance he got. Now if he could just get her to actually *go* away. So far, she wasn't budging.

He knew there were infinite explanations for the tenacity with which she clung to their relationship. The very fact that she was desperate enough to marry him in the first place was testament to that. With her family hovering nearby for the past week, she couldn't very well boot him out the door. And then there were those defiant urges of hers. She'd said it herself. For a woman from an old oil family, a man who made his money from green technology was the ultimate rebellion.

He'd been trying all week to distance himself emotionally from her, and he'd only made things more awkward. Since actively driving her away didn't seem to be working, it was time to own up to his mistakes. "I'm sorry. I just—"

"You're sorry?" She laughed. "Why on earth are you sorry? It's not your family who's bullied us into this stupid reception. I'm the one who should be apologizing."

"No, I've been acting like a jerk."

"No argument there," she muttered.

"And it's been worse for the past couple of days. I just—" Why was this so hard to say aloud? "I just don't look forward to having you meet them."

"Them?" she asked, her brow furrowing in confusion.

"My family."

"Why? Because my family's so great? With the manipulation and the backstabbing?"

"But they're..." he let the sentence trail off, realizing how it would sound.

"They're what?" When he didn't answer, she arched a

brow. "They're rich. That's what you were going to say, isn't it? You think wealth excuses bad behavior? Well, it doesn't."

"That's not what I meant."

"Then what are you afraid of? Do you think I'm going to think less of you once I meet your family? Once I see firsthand that you grew up in poverty?"

There was enough indignation in her voice that he knew better than to say yes. That's exactly what he was afraid of.

As he pulled the car to a stop at a light, she shifted in the seat so she half faced him. "Be forewarned, I don't care about your past or where you came from, but the rest of my family might. And Helen is a real piece of work. If she thinks she can make you look bad by yanking the skeletons out of your closet, she'll do it. Just remember, no matter what she says, the fact that you come from a poor family doesn't make you less worthy in my eyes. It makes you more worthy. Yes, my family is wealthy, but so what? I didn't have to work for any of that money. You've worked for every penny you have. In my book, that says a lot."

Listening to her words loosened some of the anxiety in his chest. He could almost believe that she was right. And that where he came from made him a better man.

Almost. But not quite.

Fourteen

She'd heard a lot about Cutie Pies, but most of it had been from Matt. Considering that his wife owned the place, she'd expected all the praise to be exaggerated, but was pleased to find that it wasn't. It was a classic small-town diner on main street. It could have been found in any town in the United States. But rather than the standard greasy-spoon fare, the food was fresh, tasty and unique. However, at lunch, none of that made up for the tension hovering over the table like a dense, poisonous gas.

The atmosphere—compliments of Helen—was largely due to the fact that she'd invited Jonathon's sisters and brothers to the lunch without mentioning it to him or to her.

What had promised to be a stressful meal anyway was made even worse by Helen's interference. They arrived at the restaurant to find Helen and Hank Jr. out in front. Helen—as always a picture of moneyed, blond sophistication—looked horribly out of place in the homey diner. She gave air kisses to everyone, then linked arms with Mema and sashayed through the front door, the chime over her head tinkling, ringing the death knell of any hope Wendy had that this visit would go smoothly.

"I tried to call from the jet to reserve a table," Helen was saying, "but apparently, this little place doesn't even take reservations."

Wendy surveyed the restaurant with its simple red upholstered booths and gleaming bar stools. "It's a diner," she said dryly. "Of course it doesn't take reservations."

The interior of Cutie Pies was clean but worn, the staff friendly but unsophisticated. Wendy instantly loved it. Helen—who would turn up her nose at anything just to show she could—offered strained smiles, as though it was a horrible burden to be forced to eat in such a place. She didn't bother to hide it when she pulled an antiseptic wipe from her Gucci bag and gave the table a quick scrubbing before letting anyone sit down.

Then before anyone even had a chance to look over a menu, she hopped back up, standing behind Hank Jr. and talking as though she were hosting an elaborate dinner party.

"H.J. and I just want to thank y'all for coming for this reception we're throwing for our little Gwen."

Jonathon leaned close and whispered, "*Their* little Gwen?"

Wendy shot him a surprised look at the obvious amusement in his voice. Apparently poking fun at Helen's extravagant efforts to stay in the spotlight was enough to dissolve the tension between them.

Secretly pleased, she whispered back, "Fair warning—if you ever call me 'your little Gwen,' I'm stabbing you in the leg with a pickle fork."

Peyton sat in a high chair between them, happily gurgling away on a ring of rubber keys. Jonathon smiled and their eyes met over Peyton's head. For that moment—with Helen spewing utter nonsense at the end of the table, surrounded by her family with all their ridiculous eccentricities—she felt a bone-deep connection to Jonathon. Somehow, being with him made all of this—this weird family stuff she was having to deal with—seem more manageable. Yes, her family was overbearing, controlling, borderline obsessive. But for the first time, she felt strong enough to handle it. Because he was here with her.

That's when it hit her. She loved him.

This newfound feeling of being at peace with her family— hell, with the whole world—was due to him. Having him in her corner made her believe that she was capable of anything.

Wendy shook her head, rattled by the sudden—and damn scary—insight. At the head of the table, Helen said something that she must have intended to be funny, because she gave a tittering laugh. Peyton let out a loud squawk of protest. To calm her down, Wendy reached a hand over to pat her on the back. From the other side, Jonathon did the same and their hands touched. For an instant, they both stilled. Then Jonathon brushed his thumb across the back of her hand. Such a simple gesture, but the first time he'd voluntarily touched her since they'd had sex at the office.

A feeling of calm swept over her. They were going to be all right. Sure, they'd have some tough times ahead, but they could work through them. She was pretty sure. She tried to keep her smile to herself, but didn't quite manage it.

But then she glanced at Jonathon and realized he'd gone stone still. His gaze was pinned to a woman by the door. She was dressed simply in worn jeans and a T-shirt. Her hair was long and dark, with an inch-thick gray streak arcing over her forehead. She looked both earthy and beautiful. And her eyes were the exact same shade as Jonathon's.

"Oh, good!" Helen clapped her hands. "You must be Jonathon's sister, Mary. It's nice to meet after all the emails exchanged."

"Marie," the woman said, her gaze sweeping over the cluster of tables that now dominated Cutie Pies.

"I was afraid no one from Jonathon's family would make it." Helen made a grand show of bustling over to Marie.

She hesitated, as if trying to figure out how to give Marie a welcoming hug without actually touching the other woman. She settled on giving an air kiss in the vicinity of Marie's cheek. "Welcome to the family."

Marie arched a brow, practically sneering her derision.

Wendy liked her instantly.

Unfortunately, it was obvious that Jonathon did not feel the same way.

Marie had never liked rich people. Of course, under these circumstances, Jonathon couldn't blame her. Helen was pretentious and obnoxious. She clearly thought she was better than Marie—probably better than everyone in the whole town—and she didn't bother to hide it.

Jonathon wasn't surprised that after all these years, Marie could still get her nose bent out of shape so easily. He also wasn't surprised that she was the only one in his family who would bother to show up. Family was everything to Marie. Even for family that had long ago deserted her.

Still it was obvious she didn't want to be there, in everything from the way she ordered nothing but tea, to the generous space she managed to wedge between her seat and the others near her.

Helen seemed doggedly determined to ignore the tension that hung over the table.

"So, Marie," Helen said brightly. "Tell us what you do."

Marie shot an annoyed look at Jonathon, as if he was somehow to blame for the inquisition. "I stay at home with my kids."

"Oh," was all Helen could say.

"What, you don't think that's real work?"

"No. I—" Helen fumbled for an answer. Jonathon couldn't help but enjoy her discomfort. After all, she had it coming. "I stay at home with my children myself. I know what a big job it is."

Beside him, Wendy snorted into her iced tea, trying to hide

her laughter and keep from spewing her drink. Hadn't Wendy said Helen's kids went to boarding school?

Wendy stepped in to rescue Helen before she made an even bigger ass of herself. "Marie, will more of Jonathon's family be able to make it to the reception tomorrow? We'd love to meet his parents."

Marie shot him a confused frown. "Our dad died when Jonathon was in high school."

He felt, rather than saw, the stillness sweep over Wendy. "Oh. I'm sorry to hear that."

He should have told her. Of course he should have. But it wasn't the kind of thing that came up in normal conversation and he'd never particularly wanted to talk about it with anyone.

"Cancer," Marie said. "Probably from all those chemical pesticides."

"Oh," Helen said, trying to smooth over the awkward pause. "Is your family in agriculture?"

"Our dad worked in the apple orchards, if that's what you mean, but I wouldn't fancy it up by saying he was *in agriculture.*"

"I see." Helen managed to sound almost sympathetic, but the faint glimmer of satisfaction in her eyes ruined the effect. "And your mother?"

"She lives in Tucson now, with her sister."

"And are there other siblings?" Helen asked.

Beside him, Wendy stared sightlessly down at her plate. He could practically read her mind. All the things he hadn't told her about his family were coming back to bite him on the ass. And there wasn't a damn thing he could do about it. He couldn't very well call a time-out, pull her back into the kitchen and pour out his whole miserable life's story. Even if he was the kind of the guy who would do that.

Before Marie could answer, Jonathon cut in. "Enough, Marie." Marie sharpened her gaze into a glare and looked as if she wanted to respond, but he didn't let her. "Enough acting defensive. If you're mad at me for not visiting more often or whatever, fine. We'll talk about it later." He turned his gaze on Helen next. "And enough from you too."

Helen looked as if she'd been slapped. He suspected that it was rare for anyone to put her in her place. "I never—"

"If you want to know about my family, ask me. Chances are, none of us are going to meet with your approval. My father worked in the orchards. My mother checked groceries. There are a lot of babies born out of wedlock. A sprinkling of jail time, but no felons. On the bright side, all of my nieces and nephews who are old enough have graduated from high school and most of them have gone to college. On scholarship. Not many families can say that. All in all, we're mostly just hardworking people you'd look down your nose at." He swept his gaze from Helen to the rest of the table. "Any other questions?"

No one spoke. After several seconds of silence, he pushed his chair back and said, "Wendy, why don't you grab Peyton and we'll go check into the hotel."

He dropped some cash by the register on the way out and waited for her on the sidewalk.

The second he left Cutie Pies, he knew it was a mistake. People like Helen were emotional vultures. Once she saw his vulnerabilities, she'd be circling overhead until something else brought him down. Then she'd pick over his carcass.

There was a bench out on the sidewalk, just a few steps away from the door to the diner, but still out of view of the interior. He sank to the bench and propped his head in his hands.

"That was brilliant, by the way."

He looked up to see Wendy standing there, Peyton on her hip, purse slung over her shoulder.

"That was stupid," he replied.

"No. Brilliant. Helen needs to have someone stand up to her occasionally. She puts on airs too often. If she knew how much Mema hated it, she wouldn't do it." Wendy gave a sly grin. "Which, I suppose is why I've never told her that Mema hates it."

"It was still stupid." He stood, rolling his shoulders to release some of the tension there.

"No, I agree with Wendy," came a voice near the door.

Jonathon looked around Wendy to see Marie standing just behind Wendy. "You know how I feel about putting people in their place."

"Yes, I do. I'm just not sure the patented Bagdon method of dealing with things is the way to go."

"What?" Marie asked. "The old beat-the-crap-out-of-someone-until-they-agree-with-you wouldn't work on her?"

He chuckled, despite himself.

"Look," Marie said, taking a step closer and giving him a little pat on the cheek. "It was good to see you. Even if it meant putting up with Ms. Snooty-pants in there."

Marie turned and headed down the block.

"Wait!" Wendy called out. "Won't we see you tomorrow at the reception?"

Marie sent her an amused look. "No offense, but no Bagdon is going to set foot in the country club. It's just not going to happen."

"But—"

"Sorry. It was nice to meet you."

Wendy watched Marie walk away for a second before thrusting Peyton into Jonathon's arms and rushing after her. "Then where should we have it?"

"Excuse me?" Marie stopped and looked at Wendy as if she'd grown another head.

"Forget Helen and her stupid ideas about a wedding reception. The only point in actually having a reception— and having it in Palo Verde—is so that I can meet Jonathon's family. If none of them will come to the country club, then I would like to know where we should have the party so that his family will come."

Marie looked warily at Jonathon, undoubtedly trying to figure out if Wendy was serious. All he could do was shrug. After all, he couldn't very well tell either woman that the last thing he wanted was to see his family again, let alone introduce them to his new wife.

"Isn't the party tomorrow night?" Marie asked. "You won't be able to plan a new party in twenty-four hours."

Wendy just grinned. She nodded toward him. "I keep FMJ organized and running. This will be a breeze."

Marie looked from Wendy to him and then back again, but she still looked doubtful. "Okay. If you want…" Marie got a shifty look in her eyes, one he remembered all too well from his childhood. She'd always had a knack for pushing boundaries and his gut told him that just now she was going to see how far she could push Wendy. "You should have it at my house."

"Marie—" he warned.

"I can't ask you to do that," Wendy said, cutting him off. "It's too much of an imposition."

"Or…" Marie said archly, "you think my house won't be nice enough."

He watched Wendy carefully, curious whether she'd pick up on Marie's subtle manipulation.

"No, no!" Wendy began. "That's not what I meant."

But Marie ruined whatever advantage she might have had by letting just a hint of smug satisfaction creep into her smile.

Wendy caught it. For the briefest second, she looked puzzled, but she recovered quickly. "I'm sure your house is lovely. What time would you like us to be there?" She didn't give Marie a chance to answer, but linked arms with the other woman and began walking toward the back parking lot, where Marie had been headed before Wendy had stopped her.

Jonathon had little choice but, with Peyton in his arms, to fall into step behind the two women and observe the battle of wills from what he hoped was a safe distance.

"Do you want me to try to find a caterer?" Wendy asked.

"A caterer?" Marie said the word as if it was a curse.

Jonathon would bet she'd never had a catered meal in her life.

"No, you're right," Wendy responded. "If Jonathon's family would be offended by the ostentation of the country club, then a caterer wouldn't be good either. We'll just show up with food, if you don't mind us using your kitchen. My mother is an excellent cook. And my father and Big Hank make some of the best barbecue in the state. Texas, that is." She flashed a bright smile. "Of course, we'll have to arrive early for that. Say, seven?"

"In the morning?" Marie squeaked. "You might as well stay with us overnight."

Wendy pretended not to hear the sarcasm in Marie's voice. "Jonathon and I would love that! We'll come over as soon as we get the rest of my family settled at the hotel. I assume Jonathon knows where the house is?"

Marie looked as though she'd been sideswiped by a fast-moving vehicle. "It's the house he grew up in."

Marie stopped in front of an old Ford. The car was worn, with a dented bumper and enough scratches that it looked as if it had been mauled by a lion. There were booster seats in the back and toys littering the floorboard.

"Great! We'll get my family settled at the hotel and see you in a few hours." Wendy launched herself at Marie and gave her a hug. "I've always wanted a sister."

Wendy stood beside him, her arm around his waist and her head resting on his shoulder while they watched the flabbergasted Marie back out of the parking lot and drive away.

As soon as the car was out of sight, Wendy straightened and sent him an exasperated look as she took Peyton back from him. "You should have warned me how things were between you and your siblings."

He shrugged. "You were the one who's been so sure you know me."

She considered his words and then nodded. "Okay. Fair enough." She studied him, her head cocked to the side, her expression pensive. "Do you ever see them at all?"

Instead of answering, he asked a question of his own. "You realize, don't you, that Marie didn't really invite us to stay with her?"

Wendy scoffed. "Of course I do. I'm not an idiot. But I'm not going to let her believe that we think she's not good enough."

"The last time I saw it, the house I grew up in was a total dump. It *isn't* good enough. Certainly not for your family."

"Let me worry about what's good enough for my family. Helen may be a fool, but…" She exhaled a long, slow breath. "Well, they're certainly difficult, but they know when to keep their mouths shut. And don't forget, Big Hank has been in politics for twenty years now. You don't get as far as he has without appreciating the hardworking middle class."

"But—"

Wendy cut him off. "Come on, we don't have time to debate it. We've got an impromptu wedding reception to plan."

She turned and headed back to the restaurant, but he snagged her arm as she passed. "What exactly is it you think you're doing here?"

She arched an eyebrow. "Isn't it obvious?"

"Unfortunately, it is. You think you're going to repair my relationship with my family."

She shrugged. "Well, somebody has to."

"No." He dropped her arm and shoved his hands deep into his pockets. "No one has to do it at all. My relationship with my sisters and brothers is nobody's business but mine. Stay out of it."

"I'm not going to." She said stated it so simply, only a hint of condescension in her voice. "This is your family. I'm not going to stay out. You obviously regret how strained your relationship with them is. Someone has to bridge the gap."

"And what exactly is it you think you're going to gain by doing this for me? You want me to be thankful? You want me to drop down onto my knees in gratitude? What do you expect?"

A tiny frown creased her brow, as if she didn't understand the question. "I expect you to be happy."

"Mending the rift between me and my family isn't going to make me happy."

"Are you sure?" She cupped his jaw with her hand, her blue-violet eyes gazing up into his with such compassion it nearly took his breath away. "Because you want to know what I think? I think you've never forgiven yourself for walking away from them. I think, when you left to form FMJ, you never looked back and that you've always regretted it."

"If I did walk away from them and never looked back, maybe it's because I don't want them in my life. Did that ever occur to you? Maybe I'm just a selfish enough bastard that I want to enjoy my wealth and success without any reminders around of where I came from."

"I don't believe that."

"You don't have to believe it for it to be true."

"You know what I *do* believe? I believe you don't have any idea how to bridge the gap between you, so you just let it stand."

He didn't know what to say, didn't know how to convince her that she was spinning fantasies about him that just weren't true. And whatever words he might have used to convince her got choked in his throat anyway. So he said nothing and let her continue talking.

"I've seen you with Peyton. I know how good you are with her. How caring. And I know you must have felt that same way about your family. Your real family. I think you haven't married and had kids of your own because it's your way of punishing yourself for abandoning them. That's the real reason you wanted to marry me. By marrying me, you could lie to yourself about your motives, but you'd still have the family you've always wanted."

"That's bull." He said it with more conviction than he felt. "I married you because FMJ fell apart without you. But don't think that the freedom you have in running FMJ's office extends to meddling in my personal life."

"What personal life?" she scoffed. "That's the point, isn't it? That's why none of your romantic relationships last longer than a financial quarter and why Matt and Ford are your only friends."

He wasn't even going to dignify that with a response. Instead, he stalked toward her until she backed up a step and then another. "I'm going to make this real simple for you. Back off."

"No."

"No?" He stopped, flabbergasted by her gall. "What do you mean, no?"

"I mean, no, I'm not going to back off."

"Why the hell do you even care about this?"

"Because we're married now. And I care about you." She crossed her arms over her chest, bumping up her chin as if she was challenging him to argue with her. "There. I said it. I care about you and I want you to be happy. I don't think this—this thing where you cut yourself off from everyone is going to make you happy. So I'm going to do everything in my power to fix it." She took a step closer to him and gave his chest a firm poke. "And unless you want to fire me, admit to everyone that our marriage was a ruse and give me an annulment right now, there's not a damn thing you can do about it."

With that, she turned on her heel and marched away, back around the corner to Main Street and back to her family waiting for them in Cutie Pies. Where presumably she'd announce her plan to move the wedding reception to Marie's house. All in the interest of repairing familial bonds.

Ah, crap.

This marriage thing was ending up to be much more work than he'd anticipated.

Fifteen

Jonathon did not want to spend the afternoon becoming reacquainted with his big, sprawling mess of a family.

He did not want to spend the night in the tiny, three-bedroom, two-bathroom tract house where he'd grown up.

Hell, he didn't even want to leave the comfort of Palo Verde's one luxury hotel. Luxury being a somewhat fluid term. In this case, meaning historic, not decrepit and possessing a well-stocked bar.

After lunch, he'd drawn out the afternoon as much as possible, his annoyance with Helen surpassed only by his aversion to spending more time with his own family. So he showed Wendy's family around town, lingering over checking them into the hotel. Anything to avoid bringing Wendy to his sister's house.

Which was why he was now hiding out in the bar, waiting for Wendy to walk her grandmother back to her room.

He sat there, the ice-cold Anchor Steam almost untouched

in front of him, considering his options for getting out of sleeping on his sister's living-room floor on a blow-up bed.

While the place may or may not be quite the dump it had been when he was growing up, it was still smaller than his sister's five kids needed. And for some reason he'd never understood, his sister doggedly clung to the damn thing. While he didn't keep in touch with any of his siblings, he kept tabs on them and their finances. He didn't want to be involved in their lives, but he didn't want any of them out on the street either. And he'd made sure his sister could afford better if she wanted it. Apparently she didn't.

Now he wished he'd given up on being subtle and respecting her pride and had just bought her a damn mansion. Hell, maybe it wasn't too late. What were the chances he could find a twenty-four-hour Realtor?

He took one last swig of beer and then pushed away from the mostly full bottle. Before he could even stand up, Big Hank sauntered in.

"Thank God, you're here." Big Hank pulled back a chair for himself without waiting for an invitation.

"Is something wrong?" Jonathon asked, poising to head for the door if there was.

"No, no," Hank muttered. The big man pulled off his cowboy hat and settled it onto one of his knees. "I just hate to drink alone." Then he laughed as if he'd told the funniest joke.

Jonathon smiled, humoring the older man until the waitress could come over to take his drink order. For the first few minutes, while they were waiting, Hank spun his particular brand of good-ol'-boy charm.

Jonathon was too wise to underestimate him. Instead he said little and mostly listened to one over-the-top story after another. He knew better than to take the stories seriously. But also knew that every word out his mouth could be the truth. With a guy like Big Hank, just about anything was possible.

Just as Jonathon was finishing his beer and about to make his excuses, Hank settled back, stretched an arm along the back of his side of the booth and said, "But enough about me." If the past thirty minutes were any indication, he wasn't a man who could ever say enough about himself. "I want to talk to you about Gwen."

Something in his tone gave Jonathon pause. "What about her?"

Hank gave the ice in his scotch glass a little swirl. "When you left the restaurant today, Mema sent me to find you. I overheard your conversation in the parking lot."

Which could mean almost anything, depending on how much of the conversation Hank had heard. "And?"

"And I know your marriage is a sham."

"And?" Jonathon asked again.

"You know what I think? I think Gwen put you up to this. I think she's trying to worm her way into Mema's good graces, so she can avoid a custody battle." Hank chuckled, raising his glass as if in toast to Wendy's ingenuity. "What I couldn't figure out at first was how she roped you into going along with her." Hank gestured with the glass he held in his hand. "You're a smart man. I doubt you'd get involved with this scheme of hers unless it benefited you."

"I love Wendy," Jonathon said, the rehearsed words sounding flat on his tongue.

"No," Hank muttered. "I don't think you do."

Jonathon leaned forward, propping his elbows on the table. "You can't prove I don't love her."

Hank took a gulp of his drink and gave his head a sharp shake of his head. "I think she convinced you that a marriage to her would benefit FMJ. I think that's how she got you to marry her."

"She didn't *get* me to marry her. I proposed."

Hank studied him for a moment, then his lips twisted in a sly smile. "FMJ does some extraordinary work."

The sudden change of topic gave Jonathon only a moment's pause. "What's your point?"

"I know you're putting together a big proposal for the

Department of Energy. Those smart-grid meters of yours are mighty interesting. Matt said if y'all win this government contract, every government building in the country will be retrofitted with one of those meters. Could save the nation millions in electric bills."

"Matt wasn't supposed to show you the smart-grid meters."

"He got a little overenthusiastic. And I found them mighty interesting."

"And let me guess, if I do something you want, you'll make sure FMJ gets that contract?"

"No. Certainly not. That would be nepotism." He scoffed as though the idea were repugnant. Then added, "But what I could do is make sure that the FMJ doesn't get the contract."

"And what do I need to do in return?"

"Get an annulment. Send Wendy home with her family."

"No," Jonathon said without even considering an answer.

"Just think about all those smart-grid meters of yours," Hank said, his voice taking on a slick and oily quality. "All those fantastic widgets of yours. Sitting in a warehouse, doing nothing."

"You're threatening me."

Hank smiled. "More to the point, I'm threatening FMJ. Make no mistake about it. If you walk away from this marriage, I can make fabulous things happen for you and for FMJ."

"But only if I walk away. From Wendy and from Peyton."

"Exactly."

"Just tell me this. Why? Why go to all the trouble to blacklist me over one tiny baby. Wendy thinks it's all about the money. But I don't believe that. Did Mema put you up to this?"

"No. All she really wants is for Wendy to visit more often. She'd be happy with a promise to bring Peyton to Texas every once in a while."

"So why not just let Wendy raise her?"

Big Hank pinned him with a steely stare. "Now don't get me wrong, boy. I have a lot of respect for your Gwen. It takes some *cojones* to stand up for yourself in this family. And your Gwen certainly has a pair. Probably bigger than Hank Jr.— though Helen could give her a run for her money. The thing about Helen, at least I know how to control her. She always follows the money. But Gwen…Gwen's a loose cannon. She doesn't give a damn about the money."

Jonathon thought about Wendy and knew that her uncle was right, about the money at least. She didn't care about it. She cared about the baby. After a minute, Jonathon looked up to find Big Hank studying him. "What about me?" he asked.

Hank studied him shrewdly. "You're a businessman first and foremost. You haven't spent the last thirteen years of your life building a company from the ground up just to throw it away over a baby. Or even over a woman. You'll do what's right by FMJ."

Jonathon pretended to think about it. Mostly because Big Hank would never take seriously someone who would turn down his deal without considering it. Then he shook his head, chuckling a little under his breath. "You know, she said you'd do this."

Big Hank smirked. "Do what?"

"She said that her family always found a way to twist what someone wants. Turn it against them. Or rather turn them against her."

For a second, Big Hank looked as though he might deny the accusation. Then he just shrugged his shoulders and owned up to it. "Most of the time, she's made it easy. Wendy always dated men who were weaker than she was." Big Hank gave Jonathon a slow and assessing look. "But not you, son."

"No. Not me." He scraped a line of condensation off his beer bottle. "So tell me something. From what I understand, you tried to control your daughter, Bitsy, and in the end you only drove her away. So why are you trying to do the same thing to Peyton?"

"Why did the scorpion sting the turtle? It's in my nature.

And people don't really change, no matter how they wish they could."

Jonathon pushed back his chair. "Well, sir, with all due respect, I've lived my whole life in Northern California. And I don't understand homespun analogies about scorpions. Never seen a scorpion in my life."

"Is that your way of telling me you're not going to take me up on my offer?"

"I suppose it is."

Big Hank arched a skeptical brow. "You fancy yourself in love with Gwen? You think you're going to impress her by turning me down?"

For one overly long instant, time seemed to stop. As if everything in his body came to a complete and utter standstill, but the rest of the world kept turning and slammed against him with full force.

Love? Was he in love with Wendy?

The idea was preposterous. Ludicrous.

And yet...

He shook his head, partly in answer to Big Hank's question and partly to dispel the very idea before it could take root in his mind. "No. I don't think this will impress her. I don't plan on her ever finding out about your offer."

"You know my offer goes both ways. I could guarantee you get the contract. I could make sure every government building in the country uses one of your smart-grid meters. Hell, I could get one in every house built in the next decade. Or I can guarantee that FMJ never sees another drop of government money. Not on this project. Not on any project. Ever."

"You make it sound so tempting. Would you like a swivel chair to sit in and fluffy white cat to stroke while you repeat it?"

For a second, shock registered on Big Hank's pudgy features. Then he burst out laughing. "You know, Jonathon, I like you. It's a shame you're not going to be my nephew-in-law."

"I'm not going to accept your offer."

"Not yet. But you will eventually. You'll sit down and think about it. Do the math—which won't take you very long, if what Gwen says about you is true. Once you realize how much money I'm talking about, you'll come around. No woman is worth that much money."

The truth was, he'd already been doing the math. Calculations had started running through his mind the second Big Hank had spoken. "Maybe you're right. Maybe no woman is worth that. But where you're wrong is in thinking that Wendy is the reason I'm saying no." Big Hank's gaze narrowed, but he didn't interrupt. "This thing you do, this good-ol'-boy manipulation, this under-the-table way of doing business—" Jonathon gave his head a shake. "It isn't FMJ's style. We do things out in the open. We win contracts because our products are the best on the market, not because we have connections. FMJ's an honorable company. We don't make the kind of deals you're talking about."

Big Hank leveled a shrewd look at him. "That may be FMJ's policy. But I've done my research on you. The kind of background you have makes a man hungry for success. If there's one thing my twenty-five years in politics has taught me, it's that there's not much an ambitious man won't do if you offer him the right incentives."

"I suspect you're right. About me. But I'm only one-third of FMJ. And you're wasting your time."

And with that, Jonathon turned and left.

He only wished he knew what drove him away: the fear that Big Hank was right and he really had made that decision for Wendy's sake, or the fear that if Big Hank kept talking, eventually Jonathon would cave. Either way, he figured he was pretty much screwed.

Sixteen

Knowing what she knew about Jonathon's childhood, Wendy half expected the house Jonathon grew up in to be a decrepit shack. But Marie's house was just an average tract house, in a neighborhood that may have been on the low end of middle class. Though small, the house was obviously well cared for, with a neat, flower-edged lawn in front. Bicycles and toys littered the yard, a testament to the number of kids who lived there.

Jonathon parked his Lexus out in front. He studied the house, his expression grim, his hands tight on the steering wheel.

To lighten the mood, she said, "Oh, you're right. This place is horrible. A real dump. Maybe we should go get our hepatitis C shots before going in."

He glared at her. "It was worse when I was a kid."

"Everything always is." She could all too easily imagine how hard an impoverished childhood would have been on Jonathon, with his stubborn pride and his desperate need to control everything. She gave his thigh a pat. "Come on, let's go in."

She hopped out of the car, knowing he'd follow along if she forged ahead. By the time she'd removed the bucket car seat from the back, he was there to take it from her, but the tight line of his lips hadn't softened at all.

"Think about it like this…whatever happens, they can't be any worse than my family is." She meant to make a joke of it, but the oddest expression crossed his face. She frowned. "What?"

"Nothing." He shook his head, gripped the car seat a little tighter and headed across the street. "Let's get this over with."

"Great attitude, by the way," she muttered under her breath. But he ignored her, trudging up toward the house with such determination that she had to jog a few steps to catch up with him.

A moment later, the door was being opened by a lovely young woman. Wendy guessed she was in her early twenties. She had Marie's dark glossy hair and the Bagdon green eyes. There was only a moment's hesitancy in her expression before she threw her arms around Jonathon. "Uncle Jonny! It's so good to see you!"

Shock registered on Jonathon's face, then slowly, he wrapped his free arm around her back. "Hey, Lacey."

Lacey pulled herself out of his arms and gave him a once-over. Nodding in apparent approval, she said, "You haven't changed a bit." Jonathon looked as if he wanted to disagree, but she didn't give him a chance. Instead she moved on to Wendy, giving her a hug that was just as enthusiastic. "You must be Wendy. Welcome to the family."

Then she darted off into the house, calling out, "They're here! Momma, why didn't you tell us she was so cute?"

Jonathon—looking shell-shocked—just stood there for a moment. So Wendy pushed past him to enter the house. "You coming, Jonny?"

His gaze narrowed. "Shut up," he muttered, but his tone

was playful, which she figured was the best she could hope for under the circumstances.

Wendy met so many people in the next hour, she quickly lost track of them. There was Lacey, the oldest of Marie's three kids. Or was it four? Then there were two additional step-kids as well. Neither of Jonathon's brothers had come—though Marie insisted she was still working on them and hoped they would be there for the big reception the next afternoon. His other sister came by and brought three of her four kids. Even Lacey's boyfriend was there.

Everyone greeted her warmly and oohed and aahed over Peyton. But Jonathon spent most of the evening standing stiffly in the corner, giving monosyllabic responses any time someone talked to him and looking deeply uncomfortable.

Photo albums were brought out and pizza was ordered. Someone brought soda and beer. Someone else brought cupcakes. Wendy could see why none of them would have wanted to go to a party at the country club and she was glad Marie had spoken up and told them so.

She was talking to Marie's husband, Mark, when Lacey came up and coaxed Peyton out of her arms. "I have to cuddle with babies whenever I can," she explained. "Mom's forbidden me to get pregnant until I'm at least three years out of college."

"Useful rule."

Lacey, however, was already ignoring Wendy in favor of rubbing her nose against Peyton's.

Wendy glanced around the busy living room and noticed that Jonathon was nowhere to be seen. She asked around and finally, one of the many children huddled around the video games being played on the TV yelled over his shoulder that Jonathon had gone out into the backyard.

She grabbed a sweater that was draped over one of the kitchen chairs by the back door on her way out into the darkened backyard. Slipping her arms into the sweater, she shivered as she waited for her eyes to adjust. The night air was cool against her skin. The unfamiliar landscaping cast deep shadows over the lawn. She skirted the furniture scattered around the tiny patio and stepped out onto the grass. In the light from the half-moon overhead she could barely see Jonathon.

Picking her away across the lawn around horseshoe sets and toy dump trucks, she crossed to where he stood beside a sapling tree.

He turned as she approached, studying her in the moonlight.

"Are they really so bad you had to come out here to escape?" she teased.

"I wanted to see if it was still here." He nodded toward the tree. "I planted an acorn here on the day we buried my dad. I picked it up from the lawn at the cemetery."

Though the tree was taller than he was, it still looked gangly and young. "That tree couldn't be more than ten years old."

"Almost twenty years now," he said softly. "Trees grow more slowly than people do."

She nodded, but looking at him, wondered if that was true. Sometimes, it felt as if people didn't grow at all. "I don't know about that," she admitted. "Here I am at twenty-seven, making the same mistakes I made at seventeen." She let out a dry bark of laughter. "And at seven."

"You sure about that?" he asked. "You seem to be getting along with your family pretty well these days."

"Maybe." She shrugged. "My mom said something the other day that surprised me. She said the reason Mema is so against single mothers is—"

"Because she was a single mother herself," Jonathon finished the sentence for her.

She shot him a surprised look. "How did you…?"

"Your Uncle Hank's father died in Korea. He was just six months old. She didn't marry your grandfather for another two years."

"And you know this…how, exactly?"

He raised his hand. "Fan of Google. Remember?"

"You researched my uncle?"

"Well, your family. There's a Wikipedia article on the Morgans. You're sort of a footnote."

"We live in a weird world." She just shook her head, wrapping her arms more tightly around her body. "I never thought to Google myself. If I had, I guess I would have known that about Mema and Uncle Hank's father."

"You didn't know?"

"It was only vaguely familiar. I must have heard it years ago and forgotten. I've never even heard Mema mention her first husband. And when Papa was alive he treated Uncle Hank and Dad like they were both his children. He set up trusts for all of us grandkids. Just like Hank Jr. and Bitsy were his own." She felt tears prickling her eyes, and blinked them back.

It had been so long since she'd thought about her Papa. He filtered through her thoughts nearly every day, but she didn't often take out the memories and dust them off.

"He used to love having the whole family together," she said, suddenly wanting to share those memories with Jonathon. "He loved the holidays most. When all the grandkids were running around. He'd have adored Peyton."

For the first time, it occurred to her that maybe the tenets of her trust hadn't been designed to control and manipulate her. Maybe he'd just wanted all the family to stay together forever. How disappointed he'd be.

Of course, he'd never met Helen. He probably wouldn't want to be around her either.

Still, the thought of Papa's disappointment snatched her breath away and she found herself shivering again.

Jonathon must have noticed. He unzipped his windbreaker and pulled her close so her back brushed against his chest. Then he wrapped the edges of the jacket around her, enveloping her in his warmth.

She leaned her head back against his shoulder, looking at the tree he'd planted so long ago, marveling that he'd planted a single acorn and it had actually grown into something. Not something big yet, but with the potential to someday be massive and strong.

"Tell me something, Wendy," he murmured, his voice close to her ear. "If there was a way for you to keep Peyton without being married to me, without moving back to Texas, would you do it?"

Everything inside of her went dead still at his question.

She squeezed her eyes shut again. This time, not to shut in tears but to block out her dread. She knew every modulation of his voice. The question wasn't pure speculation. She knew if she could see his face, he'd be wearing his I-solved-the-problem expression. Was he wondering—as she was—if this greater understanding of Mema could be used to convince her that Wendy was a suitable mother, with or without a husband?

"No," she admitted softly. Barely a whisper. She was not even sure she wanted him to hear it.

But he did hear it. She felt it in the faint stiffening of his muscles.

And a moment later, he stepped back from her and held out his hand. Nodding toward the house, he said, "It's almost Peyton's bedtime."

She let him lead her back across the lawn and into the boisterously cheerful company of his family. Although she smiled brightly as everyone said goodbye and started heading home, she couldn't dislodge the lump of dread in her throat.

She'd admitted to him that she'd stay married no matter what, but he had—rather obviously—not done the same. And she couldn't help wondering, did he fully realize what she'd admitted? Did he know that she was already in love with him?

By the time Jonathon followed Wendy back into the house, Marie had noticed how sleepy Peyton looked and was beginning to shuttle people out the door. Wendy stood stiffly to the side, seeing people off. The bright smile on her face didn't quite reach her eyes. He wasn't sure what he'd done to upset her, but it was obvious that he'd made a mess of things.

Finally Marie showed Jonathon and Wendy to one of the bedrooms. There were bunk beds along one wall and—just as Jonathon had predicted—a blow-up bed on the floor. Marie had pulled a Pack 'n Play out of the attic and wedged it between the head of the bed and the room's only dresser. Toys had been piled up on the lower bunk bed to clear space on the floor for the blowup bed, which barely fit as it was. Unless one of them wanted to sleep on the top bunk, they'd be in the same bed tonight.

As soon as they were alone, Jonathon asked, "You sure you don't want to head back to the hotel?"

"I've stayed in worse," she said, her tone determinedly cheerful as she lay Peyton down on the bed and started to change her clothes.

He arched a brow. "Really?"

"Yes, really. I took a year off college to backpack around Europe." She dug through the suitcase and pulled out the pink footie pajamas Peyton liked. "I've even stayed worse places on FMJ's dime."

"I doubt that."

"Then you've obviously forgotten that hotel in Tokyo." With Peyton sitting on her lap, she began the complicated wiggle-and-giggle of dressing a squirming child. "The rooms were the size of shower stalls and the beds were too short even for me."

"I must have blocked it out."

"Yeah. I bet." She chuckled as she rolled Peyton onto her back to work on the snaps, leaning down to give the baby a raspberry on the belly. Peyton let out a sleepy squeal, kicking her arms and legs. Wendy zipped the pj's up and patted Peyton on the belly.

It was an action so intrinsically mothering it made his

breath catch in his throat. He knew in that instant that she was going to be okay. She and Peyton may have gotten off to a rough start, but they were going to be just fine. With or without him. He knew something else as well. He should tell her the truth about her uncle. Tell her what Mema really wanted.

It was such a simple solution. And if he told her, she wouldn't need him anymore.

She looked up to find him studying them and she frowned. "What?"

He gave his head a little shake. "Nothing. You're just getting good at that."

"Yep, that's me. Nearly a month of mothering under my belt and I've mastered the art of zerbert delivery."

"No. I mean it. You're going to be a good mother."

Despite the compliment, her frown deepened. She sat cross-legged on the center of the bed, her expression pensive as she picked up Peyton and set her on her knee.

The air between them was thick with all the things that had gone unsaid, but before he could say anything, she hobbled up, setting Peyton on her hip.

"Peyton and I are good here." She snagged the bottle she'd prepared earlier and gave it waggle. "We're all set. Maybe you should go hang out with your family for a while. While I get her to sleep, I mean."

"No. I—"

"I insist." She gave his shoulder a gentle shove. Then for effect, she rubbed her finger along her brow as if she was warding off a headache. "This weekend has been really hard on me. I just want a few minutes alone with Peyton."

He saw right through the ruse, but he didn't call her on it. Maybe she needed time alone. Maybe she just needed time away from him.

He left the room, all too aware that he hadn't told her about her uncle. Nor had he mentioned that she probably didn't need to stay married to him in order to keep Peyton. He hadn't told her yet. And he wasn't going to.

Seventeen

Wendy had no more answers when she woke up than when she'd fallen asleep. And to make matters worse—after more than a week of waking at the crack of dawn and hightailing it out of the room, this was the morning Jonathon decided to sleep in. So she woke to find herself draped across his body, her head resting on his chest, her left knee nestled against the hard length of his erection.

There was a moment when she didn't quite remember where she was. When all her sleep brain could process was the unbelievable feeling of total contentment.

That moment passed in a flash the instant she felt him move. She shot off the bed.

Or rather rolled to the edge, only to feel the bed give way beneath her weight. She sank to the floor and tried to stand, but the bunk beds were in the way. She clung to the upper bed's railing, the lower bed bumping her legs as she inched her way to a spot of open floor space.

"Morning," Jonathon muttered.

She stilled, then looked over her shoulder. He was awake, watching her awkward progress. "Um, hey." His gaze dropped to her bottom. Suddenly aware of the cool air on the cheeks of her buttocks, she gave the hem of her boxers a tug. "Good morning."

He just smiled, looking awfully smug. The jerk.

She finally reached the foot of the bed where there was about a four-inch gap between it and the wall. She shuffled around until she reached the dresser.

"I'm just going to—"

She didn't even finish the sentence. She just grabbed her clothes and ran for it.

Ten minutes later, out of her skimpy pajamas, clothed in as many layers as she could scrounge and determined to buy a pair of long johns to sleep in from now on, she made her way to the kitchen and the divine scent of freshly brewing coffee.

She found Lacey there, a cup of steaming coffee at her own elbow as she greased up a waffle iron. The younger woman smiled brightly. "Hope you're ready for the patented Bagdon Banana Chocolate Chip Waffles. You're a fan, right?"

Some wise person had left an empty coffee cup beside the coffee maker and Wendy poured herself a cup. "Of waffles? Sure."

"Not just waffles. These are the Banana Chocolate Chip Waffles. His signature dish."

Feeling unable to follow the discussion without caffeine, Wendy took a generous gulp. Whatever criticisms Jonathon might have had about his family, they brewed damn good coffee. Which in her book, about put them on the level with the gods.

A moment later, her brain caught up with the conversation. "Whose signature dish?"

Lacey, who was in the process of pouring a ladleful of batter onto the hot iron, looked up. "Jonathon's." She sprinkled chocolate chips across the top. "He has made them for you, right?" Lacey closed the lid, then pegged Wendy with her gaze.

"Um…no."

"Oh." The waffle iron released a fizzle of steam. A frown creased Lacey's forehead. "He used to make them all the time for me. He taught me how."

Caught off guard by the girl's wistful tone, Wendy was torn. The girl looked as though a cherished childhood memory had just been stolen. But Wendy couldn't exactly tell Lacey the truth. And for all she knew, Jonathon actually made waffles for all of his real girlfriends. He'd just never made them for his fake wife.

"Maybe," Wendy supplied, "he doesn't make them now because they remind him too much of you."

She couldn't imagine the Jonathon she knew behaving in such a sentimental manner, but the girl might fall for it.

Sure enough, Lacey's lips curved into a smile and she nodded slowly. "Yeah. That sounds like him."

"It does?" Wendy tried to hide her surprise behind a sip of coffee. "I mean, it does. Definitely."

The waffle iron beeped and Lacey bent down as she lifted the lid. Wielding a spatula with surgical precision, she pried the waffle free and flipped it onto a plate. She put on the finishing touches with a flick of a butter knife and drizzle of syrup, then held the plate out to Wendy. "Ta da!"

Wendy took the plate. Lacey stood there, her gaze darting from the waffle to Wendy and back like an overeager puppy.

"Now?" Wendy asked. "Shouldn't I wait until everyone else is here?"

"Nope. First come, first served, and you eat them while they're hot." As she poured the next waffle, Lacey flashed a wicked grin that reminded Wendy of Jonathon. "House rules."

Imagine that. House rules about waffle eating. Or, for that matter, house rules about anything food related that weren't restrictive and oppressive.

"Are you going to try it?" Lacey asked, her forehead starting to furrow again.

"Just taking a moment to enjoy house rules about food that aren't designed to inspire guilt or shame. I think I'm in heaven."

"And you haven't even eaten the waffle yet."

Since Lacey was still watching her expectantly, Wendy forked off a bite and popped it into her mouth. The sweet buttery banana contrasted nicely with the dark bittersweet chocolate. The waffle itself was light enough to melt on her tongue. Her eyes drifted closed in bliss.

Even though Wendy hadn't said anything, beside her, Lacey said, "I know. Right?"

"Divine," Wendy enthused before taking another bite. If Jonathon *did* make these for his real girlfriends, that went a long way toward explaining why they put up with his emotional distance for as long as they usually did. These waffles plus fantastic sex, and what girl would care if her boyfriend was a jerk?

Somehow depressed by the thought, Wendy took her waffle and wandered over to the table. She scooted the chair back with her foot and sat, stuffing another bite into her mouth with a fervor that had more to do with therapeutic stress release than with hunger.

A moment later, Lacey joined her, a waffle of her own on her plate, the waffle iron temporarily off since no one else was waiting for one.

They ate for a few minutes in silence.

Lacey gave a sigh of deep contentment. "Uncle Jonny used to make these for me when I was little. Mom worked at the Giddey-up Gas on weekend mornings."

"You must have been…what? Six or seven?"

"I was eight when he went off to college."

Went off to college and walked away from his family completely. As far as she knew, he hadn't seen a single family member since then. Okay, she could get walking away from the no-good mother who had been more interested in raising a bottle than raising a family. But walking away from his siblings? She'd wanted a brother or sister her whole life. So that was a grayer area. But walking away from an eight-year-old niece? A little girl he'd made waffles for every morning for years? Who did that?

Had it been hard? Had he ever looked back? Ever wondered about the family he'd left behind?

"And you haven't seen him since?" Wendy had to ask, even though in her heart she knew the answer to the question.

"Not really." Lacey shrugged, though her expression was more thoughtful than sad.

"What do you mean, *not really?*" Most of the time, she knew Jonathon's schedule better than her own. If he'd been within fifty miles of Palo Verde in the last five years, she would have known about it.

"I mean, sure, he never visits." Lacey spoke around a mouthful of waffle. "But it's not like we don't all know he's out there. Keeping an eye on us."

"Keeping an *eye* on you?" Wendy asked.

"Sure. Just watching out for us, you know?"

No. Wendy didn't know. She didn't have the faintest clue what Lacey was talking about. Luckily Lacey was a babbler and kept talking.

"Just little stuff mostly." She rolled her shoulder in a shrug. "Though sometimes it was big stuff. It used to make Mom so mad."

"What kind of stuff?"

"Like, oh, I don't know. I guess it started with the lab at school."

"Uh-huh," Wendy said encouragingly.

"That was about ten years ago. I won the regional science fair, but we didn't have the cash for me to go to the state competition. The newspaper ran this article about a fundraiser we were doing at school to raise money for it. Then—bam—anonymous donor steps in to cover the costs. The next year, the school district science labs were completely remodeled—middle school, all the way up to high school."

Lacey forked off another bite of her waffle, while Wendy poked listlessly at hers.

"I used to think that we were just incredibly, unbelievably lucky."

"What do you mean?"

"Well, like the science lab. I needed money and it magically appears. Or the time when Mom was out of work—this was before she got married—and this frozen-food delivery truck broke down right outside our house. The driver begged us to take the food inside to our own freezer before it went bad. Stuff like that happened all the time."

"And you think Jonathon was responsible?"

"Well, sure. Who else could it be? It's always made Mom so mad, but I kind of like it. It's nice knowing he's out there, keeping an eye out for us."

"Why does it make your Mom mad?"

"Because she always says it'd be nicer to have her brother back."

It was so like him. He wanted to help. Always wanted to be the hero, but never wanted the credit for it. He never wanted to be beholden to anyone. Never wanted to risk having someone know he was a decent guy beneath the mantle of corporate greed he wore. And he never let anyone close enough to see the man he really was underneath.

No wonder it pissed off Marie. Hell, it pissed her off.

"He finally wore Mom down," Lacey was saying. "I think it was the scholarship that did it."

"There's a scholarship?" Wendy asked, then instantly realized how stupid that sounded. With Jonathon's fervor for education, *of course* there would be scholarship.

Lacey nodded. "Ten top science students in the high school get a full ride to the university of their choice as long as they major in a science or engineering program."

"Naturally."

How had she not known about any of this?

She had thought she had her thumb in every pie on his plate, but here was this one element of his life that she'd never glimpsed until now.

He'd told her he'd cut himself off from his family entirely. Claimed that he had nothing to do with them anymore. And yet now she found out he'd been meddling in their lives for years. Not bad meddling, just…from a distance.

Which was the way he did everything. God forbid he let anyone get truly close.

"Hey. Yoowoo?"

Wendy looked up to see Lacey waving her fork back and forth in front of Wendy's face. Apparently she'd been caught drifting off into what-the-hell-have-I-got-myself-into land. "Oh. Sorry. I was just lost in thought."

Lacey smirked. "Obviously. No one lets waffles this good go uneaten without good reason."

Well, at least confidence ran in the family.

"I was just…wondering what to think about all this."

"All what?"

"The generosity. The altruism."

"Really?" Lacey's expression turned shrewd and assessing. "Because if I was with a guy like that, it would be one of the things I loved most about him."

"Well, sure. It would have been. If I'd known about it." She gave her waffle a particularly savage poke.

"Oh, no." Lacey had gone pale. "I've made you doubt him."

"Lacey—"

"This is my fault." She shoved back her chair, stood up and waggled her hands frantically. "He's finally met someone he can be happy with, and I have to go and screw it up."

"This isn't your fault." Wendy jumped to her feet and grabbed Lacey's hands before she could knock herself out with one of them. "If this is anyone's fault, it's his. He's the one who's emotionally unavailable."

"No!" Lacey interrupted. "He's totally available! I promise! He's just…shy!"

Wendy paused, staring at Lacey with raised eyebrows. "Shy? You think Jonathon is *shy?*"

"Okay," Lacey admitted. "Not shy. He just doesn't talk about his feelings much."

"Or at all."

"But I know he has them. I know he does. He just doesn't talk about them. I mean, not to you. But he does to Peyton," Lacey blurted out, trying to be helpful.

And here she'd thought her eyebrows couldn't go any higher. "He talks to Peyton? About his feelings?"

Sure, he was good with Peyton. Great with her as a matter of fact, but Wendy couldn't actually imagine him pouring his heart out to her.

"Yes, he does!" Lacey's words flew out in a garbled rush. "Last night, I woke up around one and I went to the kitchen for a glass of water, but before I got there, I heard him talking to Peyton. He was holding her on his lap and giving her a bottle and he told her that she was worth more to him than a hundred peppermint Pop Rocks."

Lacey stopped, her eyes wide and hopeful. As if what she'd said was supposed to convince Wendy. Or make sense.

"Um…it is possible you were dreaming?"

"No. This definitely happened."

"Jonathon told Peyton she was worth more to him than *peppermint Pop Rocks?*"

Lacey frowned. "I guess that's strange, huh?"

"A little." She didn't think they even made peppermint Pop Rocks.

"Okay, maybe I heard wrong. I didn't want to interrupt, so I snuck back to bed."

Wendy dropped Lacey's hands, her mind suddenly whirling. "Peppermint Pop Rocks" made no sense. But "government contracts" did. That sounded more like it.

Wendy fished her phone out of her back pocket and pulled

up her mother's number. After a few seconds of ringing, her mother answered. "Hey, Mom, are you at breakfast yet?" She rolled her eyes as her mother answered. "Yes, I know it's early. I need to talk to Uncle Hank. Put him on. Right now."

Eighteen

She ended the call after only a few minutes. It didn't take long for her to verify what she already suspected. Then she made a beeline for the guest bedroom where they'd slept last night, dodging two kids jumping gleefully on a blow-up bed in the living room. Neither Jonathon nor Peyton were in the guest bedroom. But the door to the master bedroom was open, and when she glanced inside, she saw Peyton gurgling happily on the bed as Natalie, one of Jonathon's teenage nieces, dangled a toy over her.

"Honey," she asked, struggling to keep the simmering anger out of her voice. "Do you know where Jonathon is?" It was a struggle to keep her voice light.

The teenager looked up. "He asked me to watch Peyton while he took a shower."

"Thanks."

Wendy spun on her heel and stalked out into the hall to the bathroom. She gave the door a tap, and waited only until she heard him say, "Just a minute." She slipped through the door without waiting for an invitation.

"What the—"

"We need to talk."

She shut the door behind her, looking up just in time to see him grabbing a towel to cover himself. Behind him the shower was already on, pumping steam out into the room. Despite her anger, she felt her gaze clinging to the sight of his naked chest. Logically, after a week of sleeping in the same room with him, she should have started developing a Jonathon immunity. But instead, the sight of him affected her even more strongly. All that bare skin. Lightly tanned. The muscles that were defined, but not pronounced. The towel slung low across his waist as he tucked it in. It was all very, very…she drew in a slow breath…just very masculine. And distracting.

She forced her gaze up to his eyes, only to find him grinning at her. As if he could read every salacious thought in her head.

"Do you need something?" he asked in a low voice.

His arrogance brought her anger back to her in full force.

Yeah. She needed something. She needed to take his ego down a couple of notches. And then she needed some answers.

"Did my uncle try to blackmail you?"

Every muscle in Jonathon's body tensed. At least, every muscle she could see. Which was a lot of them.

Despite that, he kept his expression carefully schooled. If he hadn't been nearly naked, she might not have realized how strong his reaction was.

"Who have you been talking to?" he asked.

"Just answer my question."

He opened his mouth, clearly debating what to say.

Then there was a knock on the door.

"Give me a minute," he snapped, and she wasn't sure if he was speaking to her or to the person knocking.

"I have to go pee-pee and someone's in the other bathroom," came a small voice from the other side of the door.

Jonathon glared at her as if this was her fault.

She shrugged and mouthed the name "Sara."

Jonathon nodded her to the door in a get-out gesture.

Wendy shook her head.

"I need to go really, really bad!"

Little wonder since just a few minutes ago she'd seen the girl jumping on the bed.

"I don't think I can hold it!"

They could hear the thump-thump-thump of the girl bouncing up and down.

Wendy toed off her shoes and socks and kicked them near the wastepaper basket. Jonathon arched an eyebrow in question, but she ignored him as she pulled back the shower curtain and stepped into the steaming shower. The last thing she saw before she pulled the curtain closed was the expression of pure exasperation on his face. As if this was all terribly beneath him.

"Come on in," she heard him say. "But be fast."

"Ugh. Uncle Jonny, you're naked!" she heard the girl say.

"I was about to get in the shower," he said, his tone far dryer than Wendy now was. Even pressing herself toward the back wall, the spray kicked up onto the legs of her jeans.

"Aren't you going to go?" she heard Jonathon ask.

"Not while you're watching!" the girl whined.

"I'll turn around." Wendy heard the impatience in Jonathon's voice.

"Just get in the shower. And don't listen!" There was a moment of silence, during which Wendy imagined Jonathon mustering his patience. "Go!"

She saw Jonathon's fingers wrap around the edge of the shower curtain. She stepped under the showerhead to make room for him. An instant later, he pulled back the curtain and stepped in, towel still slung low across his hips.

The water slashed down, wetting her hair and clothes.

She was drenched within moments. Jonathon raked his gaze over her, his expression dark. She felt his stare like a touch, searingly hot and disconcerting. A shiver ran down her spine and she tried to tell herself that her damp clothes had made her cold, but she knew that was a lie. She wasn't cold at all. How could she be when Jonathon was so close? And nearly naked? He looked her up and down, making her painfully aware of her clothes clinging to her skin and of her nipples hardened against the silk of her bra. Desire mingled with her anger in a potent mix that made her head spin.

From the other side of the curtain, she could hear Sara moving in the bathroom. Then the girl started singing "The Ants Go Marching." Jonathon arched an eyebrow at Wendy and suddenly the mood shifted, and she barely suppressed a giggle. The toilet flushed. The water ran colder for a few seconds, making Wendy shiver for real. Then the sink ran. A moment later the bathroom door opened and closed.

Suddenly, they were alone. In the shower. She was drenched and he was nearly naked.

This seemed like a very bad idea.

"Now," he said, his tone tight and controlled, "will you please get out of the bathroom? Let me finish my shower. In peace."

"No." The word left her mouth before she could even fully process his request. But the instant she said it, she knew it was the right response. "I'm not leaving. Not until you answer me. Did my uncle blackmail you into getting an annulment?"

"No. Now get out."

"But—"

"Get out. Now. Or I can't be responsible for my actions."

"I'm not leaving until you explain—"

He didn't even give her a chance to finish her sentence, but pulled her to him and crushed her mouth with a kiss.

Her hands shoved uselessly at his shoulders even as her hips bumped eagerly against his. Her mouth opened under his assault, her tongue stroking his, savoring the taste of his hunger. Of his impatience. Every instinct she had screamed at her, but she could hardly distinguish her warring desires. She wanted him. She didn't want to want him. Her body desired him, but every shred of common sense she had warned her to stay away. He could bring her body enormous pleasure, but he'd surely crush her heart.

But when he touched her like this, she simply didn't care.

His kiss was deep and needy, as if he were trying to consume her. His hands seemed to be everywhere at once, meddling with the water coursing over her body in a chorus of stimulation. He touched her hair, her neck, her breasts. Teased the sensitive skin of her waist and massaged her nipples through her bra. Then under her bra. He peeled off her shirt and bra and they fell to the floor of the shower in a sodden lump. Then he was caressing her again. It was as if he was trying to absorb her very essence through his hands. As if he was binding her to him.

Or maybe that was just her, projecting her own emotions onto him. Because she couldn't stop touching him. Couldn't keep her hands from exploring all that glorious naked skin. Her fingers trembled with need as she reached for the towel. But stopped herself just in time. Instead, she flattened her palm against his chest and pushed.

"Stop," she said.

He stilled instantly, pulling back from her. She sank against the wall of the shower, her breath coming in ragged breaths.

This was the problem with their relationship. Physically, they were a perfect match. And if that was enough for her, then…this would be enough for her.

If all she wanted was fantastic sex, then it wouldn't matter to her that Jonathon had prevaricated about her uncle. If all she wanted was a husband to satisfy her family, then Jonathon would still be the perfect man. But she wanted more than that now. She wanted all of him.

Shaken to her very core, she reached over and turned off the water. She yanked back the curtain and grabbed a towel off the rack. Giving her hair a quick rub, she climbed out of the shower.

She looked over her shoulder and saw that he'd turned his back to her. He stood with his arm braced against the wall, resting his head on his forearm. As if he was struggled for control. Yeah, well, she felt the same.

"Why'd you lie?" she asked.

He looked up, turning around. "What?"

It was an effort for her to keep from looking down, but she managed it. "About my uncle. Why'd you lie about him black-mailing you?"

"I didn't." He grabbed a towel as well and scrubbed it down his face.

"I talked to my uncle. I know the truth."

For an instant, surprise flickered across his face, but he hid it well. "Then you know that he didn't blackmail me. He made the offer. I refused. That's not blackmail. That's attempted blackmail."

She stared at him blankly and after a moment all she could do was let out a bark of laughter. "That is just like you to try to get off on a technicality."

"You're mad at me about this?" The confusion in his voice was real. "What good would it do you to know that your uncle is a jackass?"

"I already knew that." She fished her shirt off the floor of the tub and gave it a vicious twist to wring out the water. "What good does it do you to try to hide it from me?"

"I was just—"

"Trying to protect me?" she finished for him as she pulled the shirt over her head. "Yeah. I get that. But you've got to stop doing me favors. Because it's not helping things at all."

"I don't know what you mean."

"Of course you don't." She gave a sharp, bitter laugh. She shook her head. He may be brilliant when it came to money, but when it came to emotions, he was an idiot. "I now know why you've been so determined to make this work. I just don't think you understand it yet."

"What are you even talking about?"

"You walked away from your family when you were so young and you still haven't found a way back to them. And you haven't made peace with that either."

"What does my family have to do with any of this?"

"You love kids. You'd be a great dad, but you don't feel worthy of having a family of your own. Not when you walked away from your family. So Peyton and I, we're consolation prizes. You get to have a family, but you get to lie to yourself and pretend you're doing it for FMJ or to protect me."

"You're wrong."

"I don't think I am. You're just so out of touch with what you really want, that you don't even recognize what's going on. Think about it, why did you marry me in the first place?"

"So you could keep custody of Peyton."

"No, that's why I married you. Not why you married me. You asked me to marry you, because it was supposed to be best for FMJ. I was going to leave and you were trying to protect the company. But somewhere along the way, you lost track of that. The company is supposed to come first for you."

His jaw tightened and his gaze drew dark. "It's not supposed to come before my wife."

"No. I'm your assistant. Before I was your wife, I was just the incredibly efficient, supremely organized, very best assistant you've ever had. That's why you married me. Because it was best for FMJ." She cupped his jaw in her hand and gently tilted his face down so he met her gaze. "I'm going to make this easy for you. Your loyalties lie with FMJ. With Ford and Matt. That's where they've always been. That's okay."

"Stop it!" He barked the order, jerking away from her hand. "It's not your decision to make."

She felt her lips curving in a bittersweet smile. "You really think it matters to my uncle which of us capitulates? Hell, he'll probably be glad it was me who broke."

"Is that what you're doing? You're giving in to your uncle?" There was a sneer of scorn in his voice, but she knew the pain it hid.

"If I accept my uncle's bargain for you, you get that government contract. FMJ wins."

She kept her voice calm and reasonable, even though her emotions were tearing her apart.

"I am not—" he growled "—going to sacrifice our marriage just so FMJ can win some stupid government contract."

"No. But I'm going to. You're not the only one who loves this company. I believe in it. And I believe you're going to continue to do great things with it, even if I'm not there. So don't disappointment me, okay?"

"That's it?" Jonathon asked, outrage pouring through him. "You're just going to walk away?"

"It's what I should have done to begin with."

"No. I don't believe that. I don't believe *you* believe that." She didn't even look at him as she straightened her sopping-wet shirt. Didn't even meet his gaze. And for the first time since this ridiculous conversation started, he considered the possibility that she was actually going to do it. That she was really going to walk out the door and leave him.

He grabbed her by the arm and turned her to face him. "If you really want to leave me, then fine. I can live with that. But don't lie to me and tell me you're doing it because it's what's best for FMJ. Don't lie to yourself either."

"Okay, you want the truth? Here it is—I know how important this deal is to you and I can't let you throw it away. Not for me. If I did, you'd only end up resenting me someday. And I couldn't stand that."

Then he said the one thing he thought might make a difference. "Don't forget, we've slept together. That annulment won't be so easy to get now. And I'm not going to make it easy for you to walk away from me."

She looked at him, meeting his gaze directly. There was something so sad in her eyes that his heart actually contracted a bit as she looked at him. Her lips curved into a smile that held no humor, but brimmed with warmth and sorrow. "It was never going to be easy to walk away from you. I knew that all along."

And with that, she left the room, her clothes dripping water in her wake. For what must have been a full minute, he stared after her, shocked that she'd actually done it, even though she'd said she would.

Then he slung a dry towel around his waist and ran after her, following the drops of water like a little trail of breadcrumbs. He dashed through the family room, barely aware of the curious gazes that followed his half-naked progress through the house. Then he stopped and ran back to the guest room where he and Wendy had slept the previous night. Natalie sat alone on the bed, looking confused.

"Did she take Peyton?" he demanded.

"Yeah." Natalie gave a confused shrug. "She ran in here, grabbed the baby and the suitcase and ran out. Where is she—"

He didn't wait to hear the rest of her question, but dashed back through the house. He heard adult laughter and one of his nieces ask, "Mommy, why is he naked?"

He made it out onto the front lawn in time to see Wendy close the backseat door and then climb into the driver's seat. The towel slipped as he ran for the car. Holding the drooping ends of the towel in one hand, he banged on the window with the other. But she didn't stop or even slow down. And a second later, he was left standing on the street. In a towel.

And since she'd taken his car, he had no way to get home.

Scratch that. Since she'd left and was taking Peyton with her, he no longer had a home.

Nineteen

Jonathon stood there in the road for a long time, watching the corner around which his Lexus had just disappeared.

He might have stood there all day, shock pinning him to the ground, if his sister hadn't walked out in the street to stand beside him. Arms crossed over her chest, she looked him up and down. "Wow, you really effed that up, didn't you?"

He shot her a look of annoyance. "After all these years, how is it that you're still this irritating?"

She grinned. "I'm a big sister. It's our moral obligation to point it out when you make a colossal mistake."

"Thanks," he muttered dryly. "Very helpful."

Glancing back at the house, he realized that Marie's brood—all five kids, plus the husband—had poured out onto the lawn after them. In fact, they'd even attracted the attention of a few neighbors. Little wonder. How often did you see a guy in nothing but a towel running after a car?

He turned around and headed back to the house. Marie fell into step beside him. "What are you going to do?"

"What do you think I'm going to do?"

Marie smiled. "The brother I remember would chase her down and win her back."

He nodded, hoping he looked more confident than he felt. "I'm going to need to borrow your car."

"Borrow?" Lacey laughed. "No way. You think we're going to let you do this all on your own?"

"I did hope," he admitted in exasperation. But when had his family ever done what he wanted them to do?

"Too bad," Mark said. "This is the most entertaining thing that's happened since that toy company's truck crashed on our corner and all the kids on the block got free toys the week before Christmas."

Wendy briefly considered skipping the hotel and driving straight back to her apartment in Palo Alto. After confronting Jonathon, the last thing she wanted was to see her own family. However she still needed to convince Mema she was the best mother for Peyton and abandoning them without a word in Palo Verde would do little to help her cause. And since she wasn't going to have that rich husband in her favor anymore, she figured she needed all the help she could get.

Besides, she had unfinished business with her uncle.

The historic Ellington House hotel sat in the middle of town, on Main Street, a block or two from Cutie Pies. She nabbed one of the parking spots on the street. She dug around in the suitcase and pulled out a dry shirt and jeans. It was tricky changing in the car without drawing attention to herself, but she managed it. Plus it gave her time to muster her courage, before she extracted Peyton from the car seat and headed into the hotel.

When she'd called her mom earlier, her entire family had just met for breakfast on the terrace of the hotel's dining room. If she was lucky, they'd be just finishing up and she could get this all over at once.

Striding with purpose, she carried Peyton through the

lobby and up the stairs to the second-story dining room. On another day, the hotel's elegance and meticulous restoration might have impressed her. As it was, she barely noticed the velvet-trimmed antiques and heavy oak furnishings.

Instead, she made a beeline for the double doors leading onto the patio. That was where she found them, sitting at a long table overlooking Main Street. Mema was at one end, Uncle Hank at the other. Her parents, Hank Jr. and Helen scattered in between. They all looked at ease among the fine china and sterling teapots, the poached eggs and hollandaise sauces. The meal was so perfectly her family.

No homemade banana chocolate-chip waffles here. Just elegant dining and a steely determination to ignore the tension simmering beneath the surface. This would be her life from now on.

She dreaded this with every fiber of her being. Yet it was still preferable to the life she was walking away from. She knew how important FMJ was to Jonathon. Its success had always been his first priority. She couldn't knowingly ruin all he'd planned for the company.

If she did, she'd be stuck on the sidelines in her own family, Jonathon's heart forever just out of her reach.

She stopped at Mema's end of the table. Peyton still propped on her hip, Wendy said, to the table in general, "Okay. You win."

Uncle Hank's face split in a wide grin. Helen's eyes lit up as if someone had just offered to sprinkle full-carat diamonds on her plate as a garnish. Hank Jr. just looked bored, as he had ever since setting foot in California.

Her mother and father exchanged worried looks. Looks that seemed—for once—to reveal actual concern for her. Maybe there would be an upside to this debacle after all. Her heart would be broken into a thousand pieces, but maybe the pieces her parents had broken years ago would start to heal. It gave her hope that maybe the parts Jonathon had broken would someday heal as well.

Mema dabbed at her mouth with her napkin, then nodded to a spare chair at another table. "Well, Gwen, since you've interrupted our meal yet again, you might as well pull up a chair and explain yourself." Then she shot an annoyed look at Helen. "Helen, dear, please try to contain your glee."

Somehow despite the situation, Wendy felt herself smiling. Funny how her overbearing family wasn't quite so unbearable now that she was an adult in her own right. Now that she was coming to them on her own terms.

Her father jumped up to pull a chair over for her and Wendy seated herself between her mother and her grandmother. Surveying the table, she felt oddly at peace about her decision. Yes, this would be her life from now on. Sometimes.

She would inevitably have to deal with them and so would Peyton. But this wouldn't have to be their only life. The two of them, together, could find their own way as a family. They could endure hollandaise sauce every once in a while, as long as they had banana chocolate-chip waffles most of the time.

Pinning her uncle with her gaze, she started with, "I fully expect you to honor the deal you offered Jonathon."

His grin widened only slightly. "Why, certainly."

Then she turned to her parents. "Mama, Daddy," she began. "I'd like to finally accept—"

But before she could tell them she'd like to take the job at Morgan Oil, the door to the terrace swung open behind her. Mentally cursing the wait staff for interrupting her big moment of capitulation, she turned in her seat to send them away.

Only it wasn't some overeager busboy. It was Jonathon. Along with what—at first glance—appeared to be every Bagdon in the county.

She jolted to her feet. "What the—"

"I'm not letting you go," he said unceremoniously.

For the first time since she'd known him, Jonathon looked decidedly disheveled, if that was possible for a man who kept his hair trimmed into such neat submission. He was dressed in jeans and a rumpled denim work shirt open over—bizarrely enough—a T-shirt, for some rap group, which was obviously too tight.

Clutching Peyton tighter to her chest, she tried her damnedest to glare him down. "I'm not having this discussion here."

"Then you shouldn't have rushed off." He quirked his eyebrow. "If you want, we can drive back over to my sister's and finish the conversation in the shower."

Helen gave an indignant huff, but beside her Hank Jr. sniggered. Then there was the unmistakable whack of someone getting kicked under the table followed by his grunt of pain. Wendy glanced over her shoulder to see Mema smiling faintly.

"My dear, since there is now no hope of us finishing our breakfast in peace, you should at least hear him out."

"Okay." She eyed him suspiciously. "Start talking."

But before he could say a word, Lacey darted between them and held out her hands. "Let me take Peyton. I have the feeling you're going to want your arms free before this is over."

"She's fine here," Wendy said stubbornly.

"Oh, for goodness' sake, Wendy," muttered her mother, standing. "If anyone is going to take Peyton, it should be me." Her mother practically wrestled the baby out of Wendy's arms.

With nothing to hold, Wendy wrapped her arms around her chest. "Go ahead," she said to Jonathon.

He opened his mouth, then snapped it shut again, casting a wary glance at the crowd around them, her family on one side, his family blocking the only door back into the hotel. He grabbed her arm and navigated her around the few empty tables to the far corner of the terrace.

"I want another chance to make this work. You and I are good together."

"Good together in bed?" she asked softly. "I'm not going

to argue that. Good together at work? Absolutely. But I want more than that." She swallowed. "I need more than that."

Jonathon scrapped a hand over his short hair, his mouth pressed into a straight line as he seemed to be mustering his words. He studied her face, looking for what, she wasn't sure.

Refusing to meet his gaze, her eyes dropped again to the absurd T-shirt. Frustrated that he claimed to want to talk, but still wasn't talking, she asked, "And why on earth are you wearing that T-shirt?"

"That's mine!" called a voice from near the door, shattering the illusion of privacy.

She looked around Jonathon's shoulder to see Lacey's younger brother Thomas holding up a hand.

Jonathon rolled his eyes in obvious exasperation. "You took our suitcase. I didn't have any clothes other than the jeans."

"Oh." She cringed. "Sorry. I didn't mean to leave you with nothing—"

"Then don't leave me with nothing," he interjected. "Don't you get it? If you leave at all, you leave me with nothing."

The tightness in her chest loosened a little. "Go on," she prodded.

"I don't know, maybe your wacky theory about me leaving my family is right. Maybe I have never forgiven myself for walking away from my family. And maybe that's why I haven't married before now. But that's not why I married you."

She finally let herself meet his gaze. The naked emotion she saw there stripped her breath away. But just seeing it wasn't enough. She needed to hear it. She needed him to say it aloud. "Okay, then. Why did you marry me?"

"Why do you think I married you?" he countered.

"If it was enough for me to just intuit how you feel about me, then we wouldn't have a problem. But it's not enough. I need to hear the words. From you. I need you to say it aloud." Frustrated, she reached up and cupped his jaw in her hands, forcing him to look her in the eyes. "Whatever you feel, it isn't going to scare me off."

"I love you, Wendy. I think I've always loved you." His lips curved into a smile. "That may not scare you, but it scares the crap out of me. Because I don't know what I'd do if you left me."

She bit down on her lip, trying to hold back the tears of joy threatening to spill over. "Better," she said finally. "Go on," she coaxed.

"Okay." He blew out a rough breath. "The way I see it, you can't leave me without voiding the terms of the prenup."

Her eyebrows shot up. "Huh?"

"You were the one who said that when the marriage ends, we each walk away with everything we had when we started. But if you left now, you'd walk away with my heart."

Someone behind them groaned. Then Thomas called out, "Dude, I hope that sounded cooler in your head. 'Cause that was lame."

Jonathon's eyes drifted closed for an instant and he gave a nod of chagrin. "It actually did sound cooler in my head."

"I thought it sounded great!" Lacey called out.

Wendy threaded her fingers through Jonathon's hair and pulled his mouth down to hers. Just before his lips touched hers, she admitted, "I thought it sounded pretty good too."

His mouth was warm and moist over hers. The kiss sweet and gentle. Full of love. Full of potential.

When he lifted his head, she said, "I love you, Jonathon Bagdon. If this scares you, then you're not alone. Because it terrifies me too. Everything about it. But I figured, at least we're not alone in it."

He flashed her one of those rare smiles that squeezed her heart and didn't let go. "I love you, Gwendolyn Leland Morgan Bagdon. Will you marry me?" Then he grinned and added, "Again."

She flung her arms around him and whispered a yes into his ear. Then added, "You know I prefer just the simple Wendy Bagdon."

She glanced around Jonathon's shoulder to see Lacey

giving her a big thumbs-up. Thomas was still shaking his head, as though the uncle he barely knew had been a huge disappointment. Marie had leaned her back against her husband's chest and he'd wrapped an arm around her. They were both grinning widely.

Wendy's own family looked less exuberant. Uncle Hank was scowling. Hank Jr. had pulled out his BlackBerry and was checking his messages. Helen had her arms crossed over her chest, looking about ten seconds away from a meltdown. But her mother was smiling and as Wendy watched, her father gave her mother's hand a squeeze. Even Mema seemed—almost—to be smiling.

Wendy nodded in her uncle's direction and whispered to Jonathon. "What about the government contract?"

He scoffed. "Who cares? One decision isn't going to change the course of FMJ's future. One government contract won or lost isn't going to make or break the company."

"It's a lot of money."

"And we're a diverse company. We'll be fine."

"You're sure?" she asked, because she hated to think he might regret the decision down the road.

By way of answering, he grabbed her hand and pulled her back over to the table where her family still sat.

He draped an arm over her shoulder and pulled her against his chest. "Henry," he began formally. "If you'd like, we can negotiate visitation rights for you, but only if you back off." He shifted his gaze to Helen. "If anyone in this family wants to fight for Peyton, then bring it on. Just know that we're going to fight for her. We have every intention of winning. No matter how much it costs. And if you do bring this fight to our doorstep, when you lose, you won't ever see Peyton or Wendy again."

Before Uncle Hank could say anything, Mema pushed back her chair and stood slowly. "I don't think we need to worry about that. Though I do expect to see both my granddaughter and my great-granddaughter more often now that she's settled down."

"We can do that." Jonathon nodded formally. Then he gave Wendy's shoulder a squeeze. "Now, if you'll excuse us, I'm going to take my bride and my daughter and we're going to go have breakfast." He glanced down at her. "How does a doughnut from Cutie Pies sound?"

"Perfect."

She didn't mention the banana chocolate-chip waffles. That seemed like a lifetime ago anyway.

They walked the few blocks to Cutie Pies with Jonathon's family trailing behind. They'd almost reached the restaurant, when Wendy asked, "When did you realize you loved me?"

He stopped walking and looked down at her. "I think I've always loved you." Then he laughed. "You didn't really think I asked you to marry me just to keep you from quitting, did you?"

"Yeah," she admitted. "I did."

"Come on, nobody's that good of an assistant."

She socked him in the arm. "Excuse me, but yes I am!"

"You are an amazing assistant." He dropped a kiss onto her forehead. "But you're an even better wife."

* * * * *

THE TEXAS
BILLIONAIRE'S BABY

BY
KAREN ROSE SMITH

Award-winning and bestselling author **Karen Rose Smith** has seen over sixty-five novels published since 1991. Living in Pennsylvania with her husband—who was her college sweetheart—and their two cats, she has been writing full-time since the start of her career. She enjoys researching and visiting America's west and southwest where this series of books is set. Readers can receive updates on Karen's latest releases and write to her through her website at www.karenrosesmith.com or at PO Box 1545, Hanover, PA 17331, USA .

For survivors

Acknowledgment:

Thanks to Stephanie Fowler for helping
with research sources.

Chapter One

Gina Rigoletti's heart pounded as she followed the sounds of deep male laughter and happy baby squeals to a child's playroom in the Barnes mansion. She'd been here before…years ago. Back then, this room had been a sitting area attached to Logan Barnes's bedroom. Fate had brought her here again.

On the threshold of the playroom, she shut down the memories before they paralyzed her altogether to focus on Logan Barnes. He was sitting on the floor in front of an easy chair. With ease, he lifted his fourteen-month-old son high in the air. Little Daniel giggled and his dad laughed again.

The love between father and son was palpable as Gina took a step toward them, swallowing her anxiety. She called softly, "Logan?"

The tall, muscled, tawny-haired Texan stilled. Then

he got to his feet and slowly turned—his son in his arms—and faced her.

"I should have called you after your pediatrician set up this appointment with me for Daniel. But I knew the conversation would be awkward. And Tessa gave you my name so if you'd wanted to cancel—"

"I did my homework on you after Dr. Rossi made the appointment," he cut in, stopping her.

Though he had been relaxed before she'd entered, now his shoulders were straight, his stance taut and determined as he went on, "You're the only expert near Sagebrush with your credentials—an M.A. in pediatric physical therapy and a Ph.D. in infant and toddler development. When did you move back here and open the Baby Grows practice?"

Yes, he *had* done his homework. She should have expected that.

She moved into the playroom, settling her bag of evaluation materials on the round coffee table, then nervously pushed her tangle of curly black hair behind one ear. "I returned to Sagebrush about six months ago."

When she'd learned the Family Tree Health Center in Lubbock—fifteen minutes from Sagebrush—was looking for a baby development practitioner, she'd impulsively submitted her résumé. It was the first impulsive decision she'd made in a very long time.

In the palpating silence, her heart beat hard and fast, and words seemed to jam in her throat. She had to act perfectly normal. She had to act as if years and distance and memories didn't make any difference.

"I'm living in the Victorian where Tessa used to live," she added, "sharing it with another doctor from Family Tree."

Logan's son, Daniel, was staring at her, just like his dad. Now the little boy tilted his head, laid it on Logan's shoulder and gave her a smile.

She'd take whatever she could get. "And *you* must be Daniel."

The toddler straightened again and babbled a combination of "Da da" and "Dan Dan" with a few other syllables thrown in. His hair was sandy-brown like his dad's, his eyes the same shade of green. He was adorable in his cargo pants and red T-shirt, much more casual than his father who was still wearing a white shirt and dress slacks.

"Do you do all your clients' evals?" Logan asked, patting his son's back. "You couldn't have sent someone else?"

"I do the evaluations. I have therapists who work with the children, but they follow my plan."

Although Logan had been confident and assured from the day she'd met him in the estate's barn when she was eighteen, now he seemed to be debating with himself.

Suddenly Daniel leaned forward as if to take a better look at her. She raised her hands automatically as she would with any child, and he practically jumped into her arms.

"Hello, there!" she said with a laugh, comfortably clasping him securely. After all, she was used to being around babies.

"You have him?" Logan looked worried, hovering close, his arms practically around her and his son.

Oh, how she remembered the strength of those arms. Oh, how she remembered Logan's six-foot-two height, his protective consideration that had made her feel like a princess. So near to him again, she could feel his body heat, could feel her own rise.

It had always been that way between them.

Daniel put his tiny hands on her cheeks, one on each side of her face, and looked into her eyes.

She was fascinated by this little boy who, if his records were correct, hadn't learned to walk yet at fourteen months. He'd been a preemie and she didn't know the whole story behind that.

Logan seemed to decide she was capable of holding Daniel and stepped away. He pointed to the flannel bag on the coffee table. "A bag of tricks instead of a briefcase?" he asked.

At one time, Logan's green eyes would have twinkled and there would have been a smile at the corners of his mouth. But now he was making conversation, trying to figure out what was going to come next.

"It's more interesting than a briefcase, don't you think?"

The blue flannel bag almost looked like something Santa Claus would carry, only it was the wrong color.

The housekeeper, who had introduced herself as Mrs. Mahoney, peeked in the door. In her late forties, she wore her brown hair in a gamine cut. After a smile at Gina, she asked Logan, "Is there anything you need?"

"No, Hannah." He glanced at Gina. "You two have met?"

"We introduced ourselves when I came in," Gina assured him.

Mrs. Mahoney made her way into the room and ruffled Daniel's hair. "I forgot to tell you Daniel had his supper early so he should be in a good mood until he starts getting sleepy. Logan, you have leftovers in the oven. I'll be watching TV if you need me."

Mrs. Mahoney bent and gave Daniel a kiss on the forehead. "I'll see you at bedtime, big boy." Then with a wave to them all, she headed out the door toward her quarters.

The silence of the big house surrounded the three of them.

The three of them.

Gina tightened her hold around the warm cuddly weight in her arms. This toddler could have been her life. This child could have been *hers*. If only she'd turned around and come home. If only she hadn't gone to that frat party and had her life changed forever.

Too late. Too late. Too late.

The window of opportunity with Logan had passed. Even if it hadn't, she wasn't the same woman now that she'd been then. Nothing had ever been the same after her freshman year at college. She'd had to rebuild her world…alone.

Gina shifted Daniel to get a better idea of his weight and balance. When she tickled his tummy, he giggled.

"Maybe we'd better get started." Logan's voice was low and husky.

Her gaze met his and what she saw there shocked her as much as what she didn't see. His eyes used to be expressive—caring, amused, warm, simmering to share what had begun with one chaste kiss. Now they were turbulent, and she couldn't hold eye contact. That one look had made her feel such guilt. How could he do that without saying a word?

Fortunately Daniel was getting restless, rocking back and forth in her arms, and she could focus on him. "Where does Daniel spend most of his playtime?"

"Here."

"Good. I want to evaluate him with his own things around him."

Daniel wriggled more vigorously and Logan reached for him. "Do you want me to take him?"

Her pulse sped up with Logan so close. She noticed the way his cheeks had gotten leaner over the years, though his shoulders had grown more muscled. His waist was still tapered, and she recalled exactly how taut those stomach muscles had been.

Apparently Daniel thought his dad was going to pull him away from her. The baby slid his fingers into her curls and held on tight.

For years Gina had straightened her curls into more manageable waves. But over the past few months, she'd decided to let it curl naturally again. Now her concern was more for Daniel and his desire to hold on to her than her hair. "It's okay, little one. I'm not going anywhere. We're going to play for a bit."

Instead of scolding his son, Logan settled his hands over Daniel's and loosened the boy's fingers. When his tall, hard body leaned into her, Gina was overwhelmed with emotion—and memories. Logan's fingers in her hair reminded her of the time he'd stroked her curls as they lay on the sofa in the poolhouse.

"God gave you too many curls to count so they'd drive me crazy."

"Crazy?"

"Silky and soft and I want to touch every one of them."

Now, however, Logan just tickled his son, letting his laughter spill around them. Then he lifted Daniel from Gina, high into the air, causing the little boy to give a cry of joy.

Watching them together, Gina's heart hurt and her

arms felt so empty. She wrapped them around herself, knowing her evaluation had to be objective.

She could do this…she really could.

Logan sat straight on the cranberry leather sofa watching his son. Daniel crawled to Gina gleefully as if he'd been doing it ever since he could.

Maybe he just wanted to reach those bright-colored pegs on the board she held on her lap.

Unclenching his fist, Logan attempted to relax his posture so he didn't look like a man on guard. Why should he be on guard? Gina was just evaluating his son.

His son. His and Amy's son…the son his wife had died to save.

He might as well admit it. He was angry Gina was in his house, reminding him of a time he'd shoved behind him, reminding him of her desertion, reminding him of his father's stroke and the fact she'd left and hadn't looked back.

As Daniel plopped beside her on the floor stretching his hand toward the pegs on her board, Logan had to ask, "Why did you come back to Sagebrush?"

She didn't answer right away, rather set the board aside, picked up the remote-controlled car she'd removed from her bag and set it on the floor in front of her.

"My mom heard about the opening at the Family Tree Health Center and called to tell me about it. She and my dad have always wanted me to move back here, or at least closer than New England."

She pressed the button on the remote and the car skittered across a patch of hardwood floor. Daniel crawled after it as fast as his little legs would go.

"You know he can crawl," Logan grumbled. "Why keep encouraging him to do it?"

"I'm not encouraging him to crawl," she answered quietly. "I'm watching how he problem-solves, what he reaches for first, what muscles he uses when he does. He's not even thinking about using the coffee table or any other piece of furniture to stand up, and I'm wondering why."

Logan wondered the same thing.

Tessa had given Logan exercises to do with Daniel since he was a few months old. But recently, with his son still not walking, Logan had worried. Was Daniel simply a premature baby, slow in development? Or was there another problem, perhaps more serious? Gina was here to assess that possibility.

She directed the car back to where she sat and Daniel followed it. Levering herself to her knees, she clasped the little boy at the waist and encouraged him to stand. He did…while she supported him. Slowly she let her arms take less and less of his weight until he was standing on his own.

"You're such a big boy! Can you take my hands and come over to me?" She offered them to him, but he ignored her and plopped back down onto the floor as if that was where he was safe.

Suddenly she asked Logan, "Do you and Mrs. Mahoney carry him wherever he wants to go?"

Logan tried to restrain his impatience. "The house is huge. Usually I just scoop him up and bring him along. I guess Hannah might do the same."

If Gina noticed his impatience, she didn't respond to it. Instead she asked, "What about when you're relaxing in here, watching cartoons, something like that? Do you go to Daniel if you want him? Or do you encourage him to come to you?"

Logan thought about it. "Now that you mention it, I probably go to him and take him what he needs."

"Like a puzzle, or crayons, or blocks." She saw all those on the colorful shelves to the side of the room.

"Are you saying this is my fault?" He knew he sounded defensive and, dammit, he was. After all he'd been through with Amy, as well as Daniel, he'd done the best he could.

Gina handed Daniel a plastic bowling pin and watched him turn it upside down. "I think you can call Mrs. Mahoney now. I'd like to talk to you about Daniel and I think it would be better if he's not in the room."

"He's not going to understand—"

Gina's concerned brown eyes locked to his and her voice held conviction. "Daniel will understand our tone of voice. He'll understand our expressions. He'll understand if we're happy, sad, angry or frustrated."

Gina Rigoletti *was* the baby expert and with reluctance Logan recognized that fact. He pressed a button on the console where the cordless phone sat on the end table.

Long minutes later, Hannah entered the room. "Is Daniel ready for bed?"

"If you could get him ready, that would be great," Logan said. "I'll be in as soon as Dr. Rigoletti leaves."

As soon as Hannah left with Daniel, Gina began gathering assessment sheets and toys she'd stacked on the coffee table and the floor around her. She slipped the papers onto her clipboard. The rest went back into that flannel bag.

She stood, seemed to debate with herself, and then joined Logan on the sofa. "I'll e-mail your copy of my formal evaluation tomorrow. For now, I'll give you the highlights." She looked down at the notes she'd taken. "First of all, Daniel was a preemie. He's within the normal range of walking, which is fifteen months. I think with encouragement—the right kind of encouragement—that can happen."

"What do you mean the *right* kind of encouragement? I'm always asking him to come to me."

"We'll get into that." She checked her notes again. Because she didn't want to look at him?

"I know you're doing exercises with Daniel now. We're going to expand those a little if you decide to put him under my care. I'd like you to do them with him daily in between sessions. In addition, you have to stop carrying him when he can get somewhere on his own. You need to be patient enough to wait for him, encourage him to stand and walk with you. I think he'll do it if you simply let him lag behind. He won't like that. He needs motivation to get up and walk. You have to help him develop that."

Logan let out a sigh and ran a hand through his hair. "I thought kids learned to roll over, sit up, crawl and walk instinctively. I never expected Daniel to have problems with those things."

"He might be slower talking, too—sometimes preemies are. But you can encourage him in that area, also. The more verbal he becomes, the sooner he'll talk. He already understands more than you think he does. If you bring him what he wants or needs without him asking, there won't be any reason for him to ask."

"So his *not* walking yet isn't a permanent problem?"

"In my opinion, I don't think it is. In a few weeks, we'll know better."

"In a few weeks, he'll be walking?"

"I didn't say that. Children have their own timetable. But I'll set up a program where we'll strengthen his muscles, encourage him and motivate him."

Logan made a sudden decision before he thought better of it. "You'll be able to come here to do it?"

Her eyes widened in surprise. "I thought just the evaluation would be here."

"I'll pay double. It will save me time running back and forth to your practice in Lubbock."

She thought about it. "I suppose one of my therapists—"

He cut in, "Aren't *you* the most qualified?"

"Yes, but…"

"Then I want *you* to handle his care." Logan couldn't believe he was inviting Gina back into his home. Judging by her silence, she was just as surprised. But he had to do what was best for Daniel. On the other hand, if he was honest with himself, he also had to admit he wanted to see the woman she'd become…if she felt regrets for leaving the way she had and turning her back on him.

Why did he even care?

He cared because when he looked at her…his body responded as it had when he was in his twenties. He resented that fact. He'd been happily married. He still missed the woman who had given her life for their son. Any reaction to Gina came from the past and he had to douse it. Daniel was his only focus now.

When Gina's gaze met his, he saw emotion flicker there. He thought he saw the corner of her lip quiver. That used to happen when she was upset or nervous. He was sure she was going to refuse his offer.

Instead, she straightened her back and didn't look away. "I can handle some of Daniel's treatment here, but I'll need him at Baby Grows for sessions, too. I can't start a program without you agreeing to that."

There was a bit of steel in her tone and an assertiveness she'd lacked as a teenager. She'd obviously grown into a strong woman.

Just as Amy was strong, an inner voice reminded him. Just as Amy had been unbending in her determination to keep Daniel safe.

"How often?"

"That depends on my schedule. I can commit to one evening a week."

"That's fine." He thought about his busy May schedule...watching Gina with Daniel even on a limited basis...and added, "When I can't be here, Hannah will be."

"Logan, you need to participate in the program I set up. That's important to Daniel."

Something about his name on her lips shook him a little. It cracked the vault of memories he'd carefully sealed and buried. "All right, I'll make sure I'm available. Is there anything else you need from me right now?"

She looked as if she was debating with herself but finally answered, "No."

"Daniel and I have a routine at bedtime. I don't want to disrupt that. Hannah will see you out."

The room had become stifling with them both in it. Memories seemed to dance between them, muddling the past with the present. He needed to hold his son and forget about what had happened so long ago.

He headed for the doorway.

"Logan?"

When he turned to face Gina again, she looked vulnerable. He almost crossed the room, almost gave in to the instinct to reassure her that everything would be all right, as he might have once done.

Now he kept silent.

Appearing flustered for a moment, she finally said, "Call me tomorrow to set up an appointment." She took a card from her pocket, covered the distance between them, and handed it to him. "All my numbers are on there. If you can't reach me at Baby Grows, you can reach me on my cell phone or at home."

His fingers grazed hers as he took the card, and he willed his body not to record the brief contact. His voice became rough as he responded, "Thanks."

Then he left Gina in Daniel's playroom and breathed a deep sigh of relief.

On Saturday morning, Gina sat in the small parlor off the living room in the old Victorian house in Sagebrush, tapping her foot, too edgy to admire the chintz material on the love seat, the dragonfly Tiffany lamp sitting on the corner of the library table she and her housemate, Raina, used as a desk. Her heart practically tripped over itself as she waited for Logan to answer his cell phone. She had to change the appointment the two of them had set up for Daniel a few days ago. It just couldn't be helped.

"Barnes," he answered in a clipped voice and she heard machinery in the background.

"Logan, it's Gina."

"Hold on a minute," he said to her. "I need to move into an area where I can hear you."

She guessed he was at the denim factory the Barnes family had owned and operated for decades.

Finally he said, "Okay, I'm in my office. What's up?"

Anyone listening in would think they knew each other…would think maybe they were friends again. Friends. Could they even come close to that?

"Logan, I need to change Daniel's appointment. Can we switch it from Monday night to Wednesday night?"

He was quiet for a few moments, then responded, "Gina, if you don't have time to do this, maybe I *should* find someone else."

They were going to have to clear the air at some point and bring everything out into the open…what had happened since she'd left. Not even her parents knew she'd been raped during her first year at college. But now just wasn't the right time to go into it with Logan.

"I'd like to help Daniel if I can, but Family Tree set up a meeting for all its practitioners on Monday evening. There are budget and billing concerns and the decision to have the meeting was made just last night. It's not something I can opt out of."

The only sound she heard was her pulse in her temples, then Logan's deep baritone, a little lower and huskier now. It affected her the way it always had, making her nerve endings come alive.

"I see. I shouldn't have jumped to the conclusion you didn't want to treat Daniel. But in our situation—"

"I don't run from clients who need me."

"No, but you might run from *me*."

Because she had run once before. She couldn't get into that over the phone. "So will Wednesday at six work for you?" she asked, ignoring his comment.

After a pause, he agreed, "It will work. We'll see how Daniel responds at that time of evening. If you think the appointments need to be during the day, I'll take off work if I have to."

"You're there now?"

"Yes. A malfunction with one of the machines."

"Is it unusual for you to be there on a Saturday?"

"Not really. If we have orders, we cut the material. That's the only way to stay ahead these days. Fortunately, denim is as popular as it ever was, all different grades, old ways of making it and new."

They could talk about his business or…she could say what was in her heart.

"Logan, the other night…I wanted to tell you how sorry I am about your wife."

"Thank you." His voice was strained.

"Sometime maybe you can tell me about it. That might help me with Daniel."

"You have his medical records. You know he was premature. That's all you need."

She shouldn't have said anything because he wasn't going to give an inch with her…even after all these years. He wasn't going to tell her what his life was about, except for Daniel. Maybe she'd feel the same way if she'd lost her spouse.

"I didn't mean to pry. Really. But children are little sponges. Emotions play into their physical development."

She could hear Logan blow out a breath. "If there's anything that I think will help Daniel, I'll tell you. I'll see you at six on Wednesday."

"Six on Wednesday," she repeated. She thought she heard him murmur, "Goodbye, Gina," but she couldn't be sure.

When she said goodbye, he was no longer there.

Chapter Two

The following Tuesday evening, Gina stirred the pot of soup then tasted it. She wrinkled her nose. Why didn't her minestrone ever taste like her mother's?

She was replacing the lid when she heard the front door slam. Raina called, "I'm home. What smells so good?"

"Soup. And I stopped for a loaf of bread to go with it. Are you hungry?"

"For *your* soup? Yes."

Raina Greystone Gibson entered the kitchen. She was a beautiful woman with a Cheyenne heritage. Her hair was long, flowing past her shoulders. Usually she wore a headband or clipped it back in a low ponytail the way it was tonight. It appeared black until she stood in the sun and chestnut highlights gleamed. Gina had liked Raina, a pediatric ear, nose and throat doctor, immediately when she'd met her at Family Tree. She'd learned that Raina had returned to Sagebrush from New York City, where her husband, a firefighter, had been killed on September 11.

"Is Lily still joining us?" Gina asked, hoping the fertility specialist also practicing at Family Tree hadn't been held up.

"Yes, I told her she could drive over with me, but she had errands to run first. She'll be here in a little while. She was glad we invited her for dinner since Troy had a meeting. I'm not sure how she'll handle it when he's deployed to the Middle East."

This summer Lily's husband, Troy, a member of the Texas Army National Guard, would be deployed for pre-mission training. Lily couldn't even think about later in the summer when he'd be gone.

"The support group for military families will help her and so will we."

Raina went to the cupboard and began removing dishes she could use to set the table. "Speaking of support, I really enjoyed dinner with your family on Sunday."

Gina removed the lid from the soup once more and stirred. "My mom said you're invited again this week. Everyone liked you. Especially my nephew Evan. I think he has a crush on you."

Raina laughed. "Since he's twelve, give him a week and he'll have a crush on someone else."

Shortly after Raina had moved in with Gina, she'd admitted she didn't date. She'd also confided she intended never to marry again. She understood loving and losing better than most.

Maybe that was what prompted Gina to ask, "Do you know Logan Barnes?"

After closing the cupboard, Raina glanced at Gina. "*The* Logan Barnes? The CEO of Barnes Denim? The mover and shaker who dines with the governor and owns real estate from San Diego to Sydney…the man who set up a charitable foundation to fund cancer research?" She'd listed some of his accomplishments as if to say that *everyone,* especially in the state of Texas, had heard of him.

"That would be the one," Gina confirmed.

"We don't exactly move in the same circles," Raina said, flashing Gina a grin. "Why?"

"I met Logan the month I graduated from high school. His father hired me to work in the stables on the estate. Logan and I…well, we connected that summer."

Raina took the dishes to the table. "How seriously?"

Gina remembered Logan's mother's antique locket that he'd given her after they'd made love for the first time. She'd returned it when she'd said goodbye. "He wanted me to stay and marry him, but I left and went to college," Gina explained as simply as she could. "I ran into him this week and…it's obvious he's still angry with me."

Now Raina studied Gina. "Does it matter to you? That he's angry?"

If *that* wasn't a perceptive question. "Yes, I guess it does. After all these years, I thought maybe he'd think of me less harshly."

"Was college the only reason you broke up with him?"

One of the qualities Gina admired most about Raina was her ability to see deeply into any situation.

"Lots of reasons." She thought about Logan's father, his warning that he'd disinherit Logan if she got too serious about him. She recalled her parents' advice and her older sister Josie's practical admonition not to marry too young—because *she'd* had to. "I had a full scholarship," Gina explained to Raina. "No one in our family had graduated from college. But mainly Logan's father had his own ideas about who Logan should marry. I was too insecure to stay and fight for our love. I didn't think I had a chance. I thought about coming back and marrying him after I got to college, but then something happened that changed my life and I was on a different track."

"Changed your life?"

Even though Gina and Raina had only known each other a few months, Raina was fast becoming a trusted friend. Gina considered telling her about the date rape that had occurred two months into her first college semester.

The doorbell rang.

"That must be Lily," Raina said, halting their conversation with a concerned look.

"It's okay," Gina assured her. "We can talk about it another time."

Raina nodded. "Any time you want to."

When the doorbell rang again, Raina crossed the kitchen to the living room, unaware of what Gina had been about to disclose.

Moments later, Gina heard Lily's voice. As she entered the kitchen, Gina smiled broadly at the bubbly blonde who seemed to bring sunshine with her whenever she stepped into the room.

Lily held a bag in her arms and set it on the island counter.

"I told you you didn't have to bring anything," Gina protested.

"I didn't bring much. Just a couple of deli salads

and…" She produced half of a chocolate cake with peanut-butter icing. "I thought we needed a little decadence."

Gina didn't know when she'd last felt decadent.

"Thank you," she said, meaning it, glad she'd taken the time to get to know Lily at a practitioners' cocktail party at the Family Tree. Lily's specialty practice enabled women to conceive. She was upbeat, always ready with a smile and a hug.

Lily glanced around the kitchen to the patio beyond. "You two are lucky to have found this place. It's a great house."

"It's big, but it's cozy, too," Raina assured her. "It kind of wraps itself around you. When I first walked into the foyer to consider living here with Gina, it felt like home. It's hard to explain."

"You *have* heard the rumor about it, haven't you?" Lily asked.

"What rumor?" both women returned.

"Well, since Tessa Rossi, Emily Madison and Francesca Fitzgerald all lived here and have now gotten married, the rumor is that any woman who lives here will find true love."

"I like the rumor," Gina said. "But I think it's wishful thinking."

"Maybe for me," Raina decided. "But what about *you?*"

Lily looked from one woman to the other. "What don't I know…besides the obvious million things?"

Gina felt heat creep into her cheeks. "I…ran into someone I used to date before I left Sagebrush for college."

"There's a story there." Lily's blue eyes twinkled.

"There certainly is," Gina agreed. "But it will keep.

Bring over those soup dishes and we'll start our meal with minestrone."

"An old family recipe?" Lily asked hopefully, apparently aware Gina wanted to change the topic. "One that you can share?"

"Well, I can share it. Just don't ever tell my mother that I put canned tomatoes in the pot. She'd be horrified."

Gina focused on the soup recipe and the meal she was about to share with her two friends, sure she could prevent herself from thinking about Logan and Daniel.

Couldn't she?

Logan never expected to be in this position…in his house with Gina playing with his son in the family room. His and Amy's son.

On Wednesday evening, Gina encouraged Daniel to fall onto the ball that was just his size. She'd brought a mat along, too, so if he tumbled off, he wouldn't hurt himself.

"Come on, Daniel. Let's rock back and forth." She was holding his hands as he lay over the ball and pushed with his feet.

Logan knew they weren't actually playing. They were working. But Daniel would never suspect that, not from the way Gina interacted with him.

"We never use this room," Logan said to himself, but it must have been loud enough for Gina to hear.

"Why not? It's a beautiful room."

She was right. It was. The carpet was plush and an ocean-blue. The draperies were thick. The furniture was a mixture of tan and gray and blue-green, cushiony and comfortable. If he ever wanted to watch a game on the huge flat-screen TV, he'd feel as if he were in the middle of it.

Something Logan couldn't define urged him to be honest with Gina. "My wife redecorated this room. I thought we'd be playing on the floor with Daniel, watching kid videos with him on the TV."

After their gazes held for a long moment, Gina broke eye contact and let Daniel roll off the ball. She tussled with him a couple of minutes, making him laugh, then she let him sit with a few toys just to see what he would do.

"Would you rather I move Daniel into his playroom? I'd like him out of his comfort zone so he'll have to go a distance to get to wherever he wants."

"The room's here," Logan responded offhandedly. "We might as well use it."

Their gazes locked again, and he saw something on Gina's face that stabbed at his heart. Was it regret? Was it guilt?

He almost moved closer to her, anything to relieve the tension that had pulled between them from the moment she'd walked back into his life.

The tension was abruptly broken when Hannah came rushing into the room. "That reporter's here again, Logan. He wants to do a story on you for the Style section of the Sunday paper. What should I tell him?"

"I'll take care of it," Logan assured her and strode out of the room, glad for the interruption, glad to escape the web of emotion that seemed to surround him whenever Gina was within arm's reach.

After Logan left the family room, Hannah declared, "He doesn't like publicity, so that makes reporters want to come after him even more."

Before Gina could think better of it, she said, "If I

remember correctly, Logan's father didn't like publicity, either."

Hannah shot her a quizzical look. "You knew Elliot Barnes?"

"I can't say I *knew* him. He was my employer one summer."

Watching Daniel play with the toys Gina had given him, Hannah sat on the sofa. "Oh, I see. The two men are as different as night and day, though. Mr. Barnes, senior, didn't want publicity because he just didn't want to be bothered. After his stroke, he became quite a recluse. Little by little, he turned everything over to Logan. Now Logan, on the other hand, doesn't want publicity because he thinks it's foolish and should be saved for something important—like the charities he backs—not a dinner he's giving or an event he's attending. But reporters always want to know all about his life. That's when Logan clams up."

Gina hadn't known Elliot Barnes had suffered a stroke. Had it been severe? She was about to ask Hannah when Daniel crawled to the housekeeper and pleaded, "Up?"

She looked down at him with a fond smile. "Oh, no. I'm not picking you up. Those are the new rules."

Gina laughed. "I'll bet they are. That smile of his and those green eyes could melt any heart."

Daniel tugged on Hannah's slacks.

"I gave him quite a workout," Gina relented. "I think we're finished for today."

"We've gotten an official okay," Hannah said to Daniel as she stooped over and lifted him. "Time for your supper." She glanced at the balls, blocks and the push toy Gina had brought along. "Do you need help gathering all that?"

"Oh, no. You take care of Daniel. I'll be fine."

After Hannah left the room with the toddler, Gina began collecting what she'd brought. She'd been strung tight ever since she'd entered the house. Usually when she was working with a child, that baby was her main focus. Daniel *had* been her focus, but she'd also been aware of Logan watching her…aware of Logan. There was a vibrating energy connecting them, like a live wire. She didn't know how to break it, deflect it or let it burn out.

When Logan reentered the room, he'd rolled up his white shirtsleeves and opened the first few buttons of his shirt. He looked strong. Totally male. Absolutely sexy.

She swallowed hard, realizing how much she was still attracted to him. "Trouble?" she asked, just to say something.

"No. Just an eager journalism student wanting to make a name for himself."

Gina moved toward the corner of the mat she'd opened on the plush carpeting to give extra padding. As she folded it, Logan came to help her. They practically brushed shoulders. Both jerked away.

She knew she had to do something about the awkwardness between them. "Logan, I don't have to be the one who helps Daniel."

Logan rubbed his hand up and down the back of his neck. "No, I suppose you don't. But he obviously relates well to you. I don't want to mess with that. Hannah's been the only woman in his life since he was born."

"What happened?" Gina asked softly.

Logan's green gaze was penetrating as he studied her, trying to decipher why she wanted to know.

Finally he answered, "One day Amy and I were on

top of the world, the next an earthquake destroyed everything we thought we were building."

As if he knew he was being cryptic, he sat on the sofa, studied the carpet for a few moments, then met Gina's gaze. Something in his eyes drew her to him and she lowered herself beside him, though not too close.

When he started talking, Gina knew he didn't discuss this often because his voice was strained.

"Amy was ecstatic when she discovered she was pregnant," he began. "We'd been married a few years, and we both wanted kids. She'd been working hard at her career—she was a real estate agent and intended to keep selling properties after our baby was born. But soon after she learned she was pregnant, she had symptoms that sent us to a neurologist and then a neurosurgeon. She had a brain tumor."

Gina desperately wanted to reach out to Logan, to touch his arm. Yet she couldn't. She had no right. "I'm so sorry." She was. She'd never wanted anything but happiness for him. That was why she'd left.

Logan didn't seem to hear her. He stared across the room and explained, "Her doctor wanted to treat the cancer aggressively, but Amy wouldn't let him do surgery or put anything in her body that could damage Daniel. She decided if she survived the pregnancy, she'd have treatment after our baby was born. But that day never came. She had a stroke at thirty-two weeks. The doctors performed a C-section and she died shortly after."

One look at Logan's face and Gina knew he was reliving that time in his life. Did he want comfort? Did he want sympathy? Or did he just need to look forward?

Gina didn't want to trample over sacred ground so she asked, "How long was Daniel in the hospital?"

"Eight weeks…a terrifically *long* eight weeks."

"Who was his doctor?"

"Francesca Talbott. I think it's Fitzgerald now."

"Yes, it is. She shared the house with me until she got married," Gina said softly.

"It really *is* a small world, isn't it?" he asked, finally looking at her.

"It can be."

After a silence-filled pause, Logan asked, "Did you marry?"

His question surprised her. "No."

What would he say if she told him what had happened? It really made no difference to their relationship. She'd left him, no matter what had happened afterward. "I've been focused on my work all these years, trying to make a name in my field."

"So why come back to Sagebrush *now?*" He looked genuinely perplexed.

"I'm not exactly sure. I began missing my family more. I knew I needed something different—closer friends, bonds, actual fun."

The lines on Logan's face told her he hadn't had fun in a long time, not since before his wife died. Daniel might bring him joy, but Gina had the feeling it was fleeting.

"We really don't have to work in here, Logan. I understand how memories can suck the air out of the room."

Logan shrugged. "If I get used to seeing Daniel playing in here, crawling in here, maybe eventually walking in here, it will be fine."

She could only imagine what Logan had been through—his wife's diagnosis, losing her and at the same time dealing with Daniel's hospital stay. "It takes a while to recover from any trauma." She knew that all too well. Counseling sessions and talking and crying and just putting one foot in front of the other, even when you thought you couldn't, took energy, motivation and sometimes steel will. Logan had all of those. Still…

Logan stared at a picture of Daniel on a side table.

Gina assured him, "He's a wonderful little boy. Quick and learning more each day. When I arrived, I suggested to Hannah if you fill two of the bottom cupboards in the kitchen with pots and pans, colorful containers, anything Daniel might feel he'd like to get into, that might give him more motivation to explore his world."

Logan was quiet a moment, then he turned his focus to her. "I guess parents are always supposed to teach their kids to explore the world."

"That gets scarier for both the parents and kids as they get older. Learning to walk across the room suddenly becomes all-day kindergarten and then piano lessons, and then driving and dating!"

Logan remarked, "Your parents encouraged *you* to explore your world. Your education was as important to them as it was to you."

"It wasn't just my education," Gina said quietly, hoping she could break through the icy wall Logan had constructed between them.

"I know. There was your younger sister. Did she eventually go to school?"

"Yes, she did. Angie is a nurse and I'm proud of her." If only they could keep talking—

Suddenly Logan stood. "It's good you don't have any regrets."

She hadn't said she didn't have regrets.

Logan went on, "This is bath night and it's one of the things I enjoy doing most with my son, at least until he gets old enough to ride a horse. I'll help you gather this up and walk you out."

As he stuffed a toy elephant and lion into one of her drawstring bags, she asked him, "Are you still angry that I left?"

His answer was slow in coming as his gaze finally met hers. "I'll probably always be angry that you left. But…if you hadn't left, I wouldn't have Daniel. I love him more than anything in this world."

There was nothing she could say to that.

A few days later, when Gina stopped in at the Target that had recently opened in Sagebrush, she ran through the baby department. It was a habit, keeping her eye on the latest trends in toys and car seats, in strollers and play furniture. Tonight, she pushed her cart around the corner into the toy department. There, she stopped cold.

Logan stood in front of a shelf, holding a remote-control car in one arm, studying the RC truck directly in front of him.

For a nanosecond, Gina thought about turning around and going the other way. Logan didn't have to know she'd seen him. He didn't have to know she was here. But that was the coward's way out. She was no longer a coward. At least she hoped she wasn't.

Rolling her cart up beside him, she asked, "Looking for a new hobby?"

He went still, then he turned to face her. "No," he drawled in that Texas deep baritone that had always curled her toes. "I thought Hannah and I might take bets on who could run their car across the yard the fastest."

Gina laughed at his wry tone. "I bet Daniel would enjoy that. He might even chase one."

"That's the idea," Logan assured her.

At that moment, they both understood the motivation Daniel needed to learn to walk. It was the first tension-free moment she and Logan had shared.

He nodded to her cart filled with three pairs of shorts and a few knit tops. "New wardrobe for summer?" he joked.

Actually it was. She didn't owe him any explanations but she explained anyway. "I lost a few pounds so I needed something that fitted a little better than what was in my closet."

"Intentionally?"

"What?" she asked, lost in his eyes for the moment.

"Did you lose weight intentionally?"

He was looking at her in a way that made her nerve endings dance. She hadn't felt that way when a man looked at her for a very long time. "No, not intentionally. With the move, a new job, a new life really, it just happened."

"Are you glad you moved back here?"

Standing here face-to-face with Logan, she wasn't quite sure how to answer. Finally she responded, "I like the life I'm building. I like the new friends I've made. My practice is rewarding and it's good to be near family again."

"You stayed away a long time."

"Yes, I did, in part because I didn't want to face you."

For a moment, Logan's guard slipped and he looked astonished. Was he surprised she'd been so honest? Maybe that was what they needed between them, some old-fashioned honesty. Just how far was she willing to go with it?

"You didn't have to face me," he said evenly.

"We live in a small town, Logan. I knew eventually I'd run into you."

"Why didn't you send someone else from Baby Grows to evaluate Daniel?"

She expected this question had been bothering him since the night she'd appeared at his house. "As I told you, I do all the evaluations. I wasn't going to shirk my responsibility."

He seemed to mull that over. "You're an expert in your field."

"Some people would say that."

"And now that we *have* come face-to-face?" he asked, his voice challenging.

"I'd like you to forgive me," she blurted out, without considering the consequences.

There seemed to be a sudden hush all around them. Then Logan shifted, adjusting the toy under his arm. "I don't know what to say to that. When you left, the bottom dropped out of my world in more ways than one. I've never forgotten how that felt. I've never forgotten how you didn't even have time to have a conversation when I called you in Connecticut."

She couldn't deal with this here. What had she expected when she'd started this? That it would be easy? That he'd forgive her and they'd go on being friends?

"Logan, things had happened…"

He gave a short laugh. "Yes, I'm sure they had. You probably met someone at school and—"

"No, nothing like that."

He looked startled at her vehemence. "You're not the same Gina you were fourteen years ago."

"I certainly hope not." She tried to keep her tone

light. They hadn't spent enough time together to *know* how each other had changed.

Logan cocked his head, studying her with those penetrating eyes that had so often seen right through her. But not tonight. She held secrets he'd never know about unless they could find more common ground than this.

If she brought the conversation back to Daniel, maybe the tension between them would ease. "I was thinking…" she said slowly.

He waited for her to go on.

"Can you bring Daniel to Baby Grows on Saturday? I'd like to ask Tessa to stop in with her two children and I want to watch Daniel react with them, play with them. We have more equipment there, too."

"Tessa won't mind giving up her Saturday morning?"

"After rounds, she usually takes the kids to the library. She said she'd just bring them to Baby Grows instead."

"All right, I can do that. Do you have appointments before Daniel, or do you want me to pick you up?"

Logan had always been a gentleman, and thoroughly polite. He was being courteous now and she shouldn't read any more into his offer than that. "I do have other appointments, but thanks for offering." Before she saw more recriminations in his eyes, she pointed to the shelf. "So, which one are you going to buy?"

"You have a car when you work with him. I think I'll go with the truck."

"What about Hannah?"

He rewarded her with a small smile. "Maybe she'd like the motorcycle."

Gina laughed. "She probably would."

After he stacked the motorcycle on top of the truck, he asked her, "Are you finished shopping?"

"Yes."

"I'll walk you out."

More courtesy? Her heart was already in overdrive and now it sped up a little more.

Walking beside Logan, she was reminded just how tall he was, just how broad his shoulders were, just how slim his hips were in his black jeans. He kept enough distance between them that their arms wouldn't brush. She didn't glance at him, but she felt *him* looking at *her.* She pretended not to be affected either by his presence beside her or his gaze on her, but she was.

At the checkout line, they didn't speak as she used her credit card, then picked up her packages. He went through and paid in cash.

Then he took her bag from her. "I'll carry this to your car for you."

Being with Logan was a combination of bittersweet and exciting. She knew he'd be relieved if he went his way and she went hers, yet she didn't want to leave his company. Just like so many years ago.

At her car, she used the remote to unlock the doors and pop the trunk. They went around to the back and he dropped her purchases inside. There was a duffel bag there.

"Do you belong to a gym?" he asked as if he *was* curious about her life now.

"No, but I walk whenever I can. In Lubbock at lunchtime, sometimes I do a couple of laps around the center. In Sagebrush, I like to take the trail around the lake."

"You always did like the outdoors." He slammed the lid of her trunk.

"I still do. I hiked a lot in New England. Here, I'd like to take up riding again. Francesca and I have gone on a couple of trail rides at her ranch. I've ridden at Tessa's, too. I'd forgotten how wonderful it feels to be on horseback."

Logan walked to her car door and stood very close, so close she could reach up and touch his jawline, so close she could see that the lines around his eyes and his mouth weren't superficial. They'd been carved from pain. All she wanted to do was ease them away.

"You asked me about forgiving you…" His voice was low and husky.

She held her breath and waited.

"I can't give you an answer, Gina, and I don't know if time will help or not. That night after we split up, my father had a stroke."

That night. A rush of dread made her cold all over. "What happened?"

He looked away from her as if warring with himself over the answer. "We argued about you."

Her chest felt tight. "Why?"

"I went riding after you left, trying to figure out what to do. When I got back to the barn, Dad confronted me. He said I was better off without you. But I didn't believe that. I was going to talk to your parents…convince them they were interfering and they shouldn't be…convince you that we could make something work long-distance. Dad grabbed my arm. I tore away. And then—suddenly he couldn't speak and he collapsed."

Gina was stunned. A tiny shard of guilt pierced her heart at the realization that she hadn't been there for Logan.

"I called the paramedics and he was rushed to the hospital. We managed to keep all of it quiet. Dad

abhorred publicity and the hospital and medical personnel were cooperative. His recovery took about three
months. He was fortunate he regained his speech and
most of his mobility. But the whole process was—"
Logan halted as if he didn't want to admit how much
his father's collapse and recovery had affected him.

"I'm so sorry," she managed to say, feeling so
much sympathy for him that tears welled in her eyes.
"Three months," she murmured. "That's around when
you called—"

"I was hoping we could just talk. I was hoping—"
He shook his head. "But you didn't have time to talk.
You had to run off to take a test."

"You never called again," she said softly, remembering how numb she'd been for such a long time after the
rape. She *had* had a test that day. But more important,
she'd been too raw to talk to anyone. Should she tell
Logan that? Could he possibly understand?

No. This wasn't about her. The distance between them
was all about her letting down Logan in so many ways.
If she had fought for the love she'd felt for him, then
maybe more than one tragedy could have been avoided.

"Logan, I don't know what to say."

"You don't have to say anything."

She heard a car door slam…children laughing near
the store's exit.

So much had happened to both of them. She'd lost her
sense of safety, her trust in her judgment, her trust in men.
Logan had gone on to marry and lost a wife he'd obviously loved. He now had a son his wife had died to save.
How much more he must love her for that. How much
he must cherish Daniel as the gift his wife had given him.

The twelve-foot-high parking-lot light lit up the area

where Gina's car was parked. In the blink of an eye, she thought she saw a flash of tenderness in Logan's eyes. But then whatever emotion he'd felt disappeared.

They'd been standing as close as two people having an intimate conversation would be, but now he took a step back. "I'll see you Saturday morning at Baby Grows."

Her throat tightened and she wanted to reach out and hug him, hold on to him, cry with him. Instead, she simply nodded.

A few feet away, Logan waited until she slid into her car, closed the door and started the engine. Then he strode to his car as she drove away, swiping at the lone tear that rolled down her cheek.

Chapter Three

Logan could hardly hold on to Daniel Saturday morning. His son peered around at the colorful equipment in the therapeutic workroom at the Baby Grows practice, pointing to a big red ball. "Baw!"

As soon as Gina came toward them, Daniel reached for her and practically jumped into her arms.

"It's so good to see you again," she told the little boy, her face lighting up as it always did when she was around him.

In spite of common sense telling him to let it go, Logan couldn't help but wonder how she felt about seeing *him*, especially after their goodbye in the parking lot. Why couldn't he just tell her he forgave her?

Because it wouldn't be honest. It might smooth the waters, but it wasn't the truth. He didn't know what *was* the truth. Ever since Amy had died, his life had taken on a manage-each-day quality.

"I wasn't sure you'd come," she said to Logan.

He saw vulnerability in her brown eyes but didn't know what to do about it. "I've learned over the years avoidance only buys time. It doesn't solve the problem. So we're here to get Daniel walking."

"Logan, I just want to say again I'm sorry about everything that happened."

He could see she didn't want to let their conversation in the parking lot go, but he did. "Let's put the past behind us for now, okay?"

She seemed to tear her gaze reluctantly from his to focus on his son. "So what do you think we should try first?" Gina asked Daniel as if she had this kind of conversation with a fourteen-month-old every day.

"He's never tried a sliding board." Logan didn't know if that piece of information would be useful or not.

"The sliding board is a great idea. If he likes to ride down, he might try to climb up."

She took Daniel over to the three-foot-high sliding board and sat him on top. "No more carrying. Anywhere you want to go today, you have to get there on your own steam."

His green eyes sparkling, Daniel tilted his head and studied her face. Then he raised his legs up and down on the slide portion of the equipment and said, "Go...go...go."

"Great exercise," she encouraged him, watching his leg movement. "That will help strengthen those muscles." She crouched down at the bottom of the board. "Come on. Let's see if you can push yourself off."

After a few moments of squiggling and squirming,

gravity helped Daniel slide sideways down the short board. He careened onto the soft mat beneath it and grinned up at Gina.

Logan felt as if his heart was cracking into a few more pieces. Daniel should be looking up like that at his mother.

If Amy had lived—

Logan might not have Daniel.

If Gina had stayed—

Logan might not have Daniel.

How could he regret any part of his life when his son was the result of it?

Suddenly, from the reception area, Logan heard a woman's voice call, "Is anyone here?" He also heard the chatter of children.

Tessa Rossi entered the room in obvious mother mode. On her left side, she held the hand of nineteen-month-old Sean and on her right, that of little Natalie, who looked to be over two. Logan remembered hearing about the little boy and girl from Hannah, who knew Tessa's nanny and housekeeper. The children had been through a lot in their short lives, and now Tessa and her husband, Vince, were in the process of adopting them both.

Tessa headed straight for Logan. "Hi! Gina said Daniel could use some playmates."

"I never really thought about it," Logan admitted. "I was an only child and learned to occupy myself. I guess I thought Daniel would do the same."

"Oh, but they learn so much from each other—good *and* bad," she confided with a wise smile.

He laughed. "I suppose that's true."

Sean and Natalie both looked up at Tessa. When she gave a nod, they ran over to Gina and Daniel.

Logan watched as the kids both gave Gina hugs. "They seem to like her."

"Oh, they love her. She knows just what to say to them, just how to handle them, and it's all genuine."

"How long have you known Gina?"

"Since January. A mutual friend introduced us."

"Francesca Fitzgerald."

"That's right." Tessa's gaze asked how he knew.

"Gina mentioned Francesca and I told her she was Daniel's neonatologist."

"They're both women who are dedicated to helping babies."

Maybe so. But he was still curious about something. "I'm surprised Gina came back here."

"Why are you surprised?"

"According to everything I discovered when I searched her name on the Internet, she was headed up the career ladder. After undergraduate work, she earned her Ph.D. at a larger university. Then she moved on to become the dean of a teaching program in early development at a college in Massachusetts. All along she's published in well-respected journals. A couple of years ago she moved back to Connecticut to head up a new baby study at her alma mater. Lubbock just seems small potatoes compared to what she could be doing and where she could be going."

"Have you really *watched* her with the children, Logan?"

They stood about twenty feet away from Gina. He had to admit, up until now, he got distracted just looking at her. He always wanted to run his hands through the tumbled curls, to tap his finger on the little bump on her nose.

Now he really looked at her—the expert, the teacher,

the therapist. She was a combination of all three. As Natalie and Sean tumbled and pushed on a beanbag chair, Logan noticed Gina using more than the tools in her repertoire. Yes, she was competent, decisive and knowledgeable. But on top of all that, there was a pure love in her eyes for the children she was with.

"Gina just wants to work with babies who need help. When I met her, I wondered immediately why she hadn't married and didn't have a brood of her own," Tessa mused.

"Did she ever tell you why she hadn't married?"

"Not really. I think she was just too busy earning her degrees."

Too busy? Or some other reason? Gina herself had told him that something had happened after she left Sagebrush. Had she moved around so much for professional reasons? Or something else?

"Sean and Daniel seem to be getting along well," Tessa commented.

To Logan's surprise, Daniel crawled after Sean. Tessa's little boy found a stack of chunky blocks. While Logan held his breath, Daniel pushed himself to his knees and, using a small table for leverage, pulled himself up. But then his son sat again and stacked one block on top of another with Sean's help.

"He's teetering on the edge," Tessa said. "He could walk anytime."

"I think he might forget himself and just do it if he's playing with Sean."

"Kids help each other develop skills. It's wonderful to watch."

For the past couple of years, Logan's employees had been voicing their opinions about opening a day-care center at the factory. First he'd dismissed the idea because of the expense. But after doing feasibility research, he'd been much more open to it. Now he could see even more benefits, not just for the parents, but for the children themselves. He was glad the center was in the planning stages and he'd be meeting with the architect soon.

As he watched the children, Gina joined the boys, helping them decide what to build. Logan suddenly wondered if Gina would help with the project. He knew there were companies who sent representatives in essentially to take over and even staff the center. But he wanted to use a local contractor as well as someone from Lubbock to staff the facility. Maybe Gina could help with the preliminary stage.

Was he looking for an excuse to spend time with her?

Of course not. He didn't need one with her treating Daniel.

A half hour later, Tessa and her children waved goodbye. Daniel had obviously enjoyed their company, but he looked as if he'd had enough of these activities and was ready for something else.

Logan lifted his son into the air and wiggled him. "How about the Yellow Rose Diner and cheese fries?"

Daniel babbled, "Da da da. Fwies," and Logan laughed.

"I think that's a resounding 'yes.' Are you going back to Sagebrush?" he asked Gina.

"Yes, I am. Raina and I made a pact to clean the house this afternoon, then we're going to a movie as a reward later."

"Girls' night out?"

"You could say that."

"If you're going back to Sagebrush, how about stopping at the diner with us and having some lunch? There's something I'd like to discuss with you."

When Daniel fussed to be let down, Logan lowered him to a mat. "We could talk about it here, but I think Daniel needs a change of scene and something in his tummy. What do you say?"

He could tell Gina was giving his invitation major consideration. She asked, "Is this about Daniel?"

"No, it's not."

She seemed to think about the pros and cons but he knew what her answer would be. She wouldn't deny him this simple request because she still felt guilty about what had happened. He didn't want to push that button. She'd have to let go of the guilt and he'd have to let go of the bitterness. Maybe they could do that if they worked on the day-care center together.

Finally, she nodded. "Okay. I have to pick up some folders and lock up. I'll meet you at the diner."

Logan found himself looking forward to sitting across the booth from her and didn't examine his reasons why too closely.

Logan was settling Daniel into a high chair as Gina walked into the Yellow Rose and spotted them. She ruffled the little boy's hair as she settled into the booth and smiled at the dish of cheese fries on the table. "You must have called ahead."

Logan broke a cheese fry into pieces and set them on his son's tray. "I did. Experience is a great teacher."

Their gazes collided and the noise of the diner faded away. Damn, he was *still* attracted to her! Why couldn't he shut it down? Why couldn't he control the rush of adrenaline that wired him when she entered a room? At first he'd relegated that rush to tension, to regrets, to emotion packed away for a long time. But today, he knew better.

An auburn-haired waitress came over to take their orders and raised an eyebrow at Logan as if to say, "So when did this start?" Mindy kept her fingertip on the pulse point of anyone who came to the Yellow Rose Diner.

He ignored her curiosity. After a brief examination of the menu, he and Gina ordered and their waitress hurried away.

Fingering her knife, Gina moved it to the side of the placemat. "You surprised me when you said you were coming here. It wasn't a place I imagined you having lunch."

"No sterling silver or crystal goblets?"

"Hannah could make you anything you want at the estate and there are other restaurants that are a little more private."

"I'm not a hermit, Gina. I don't need electric gates around the house or a high wall to keep reporters out. There are much more interesting characters around than me. I know I can't live a normal life because I have more than most, but I don't have to live such a different life, either."

"Your father wanted—" She stopped abruptly. Picking up a cheese fry, she wiggled it into a scoop of ketchup.

"My father wanted what?" Logan asked.

"I think he wanted you to live the same life he did."

Logan hadn't realized that Gina and his father had had many conversations. His father had hired her to work in the stables and that was about it. But she *was* right. His father had wanted him to travel, to be invited to the governor's mansion, to have friends in even higher places. But his perspective on raising a son was much different from his father's, and that wasn't a subject he wanted to discuss.

"I read the articles you published online," he said, changing the subject as he poured water into Daniel's sippy cup.

That seemed to surprise her. "I see."

He doubted that she did. "I wanted to know what you had done with your life and the type of work you accomplished."

She took a sip of her water, then set down the glass. "Why?"

"I was curious whether the reasons you told me you left were honest."

Her cheeks took on some color. "They were honest, Logan. That full scholarship put me on the first rung of the ladder. I had a job when I was earning my master's and sent money home to help put Angie through school. I became the first college graduate in my family. When I earned my doctorate, even my dad had tears in his eyes."

She seemed to brace herself as if he might ask her something else. Like what? Was it all worth it? He couldn't go there. Not now. Not here.

"One of your articles concerned day-care centers. I'll be starting construction for one in June for my employees' kids, and I wondered if you'd give me some input, maybe give the architect I've chosen some input. You know what kids need. I would need it to be appropriate for ages two to five. What do you think? Would you be interested? I'll pay you a consultation fee."

She looked totally taken aback. "You've surprised me, Logan. Do you mind if I think about it?"

"No, I don't mind. I have a meeting with James Wolfe—he's the architect who designed the new elementary school in Sagebrush—on Wednesday. If you're interested, I'd like you to be there, too."

Their gazes locked. When she didn't look away and neither did he, he felt his chest tighten and other parts of his body come awake.

Had he just made a huge mistake?

On Wednesday evening, Gina sat in Logan's den at a long library table next to his architect, James Wolfe. She was studying the plans—and felt Logan studying *her*. He was sitting across the narrow table from them in a leather desk chair.

"So what do you think?" the architect asked her. His brown eyes sparkled with interest she didn't return. He was good-looking enough…but he wasn't Logan.

She concentrated on the plans. "The square footage looks about right for the number of children you're anticipating providing for. But—"

"But?"

Directly across from her, Logan's leg brushed hers as he leaned forward to take a closer look at the architect's drawing.

She swallowed and smiled. "I think you need to utilize the space better, maybe two rooms instead of one. That way the younger children can be taking a nap while the older ones are playing or working. You also need a common area where they can share snacks. But that's just my opinion."

James shrugged. "She makes sense."

In professional mode now, Gina tapped another line of the blueprint. "You might also want to consider a wall with an observation window. That way if a parent doesn't want to come in and get involved, they can just make sure their child is okay."

James grinned and patted her shoulder. "That's an excellent idea."

Reflexively, Gina leaned back and his hand fell away. Even after all these years, she didn't appreciate a man touching her without her giving the signal it was okay. But James didn't seem to notice that she was uncomfortable with his gesture.

Logan stood, signaling the meeting was over. "Work on those changes, Wolfe, and then bring the plans back to me."

Realizing the meeting had come to an end, James Wolfe stood, rolled up the plans and inserted them into the protective tube. "I'll take a few days with these then give you a call. When's the ground-breaking ceremony?"

"Mid-June," Logan responded. "As soon as I finalize the changes, we'll move forward."

James extended his hand to Gina.

She clasped it and shook it. "It was nice to meet you," she said politely.

"It was good meeting you, too. Take care now. Logan, I can see myself out."

Moments later, she and Logan were standing alone in his study. "I didn't mean to throw a wrench into what Mr. Wolfe had already designed."

"I invited you to this meeting for your input. I'm pleased you gave it. Your ideas are sound." Logan reached for the knot on his tie and pulled it loose.

"I know kids," she said softly. "And what they need."

After unfastening the shirt button at his neck, Logan came around the table and stood close to her. She didn't feel crowded by *him*. Oddly, she welcomed his nearness in the same way she'd shied away from James Wolfe's proximity, as well as his touch.

Logan's voice was low when he asked, "And what do *you* need, Gina?"

His green gaze was piercing and unsettled her. "I don't know what you mean."

"My architect is interested in you."

"He was just being friendly."

"But you weren't being friendly back."

"I…" She stopped, took a deep breath, then gave a nonchalant shrug. "I wasn't interested."

Logan came another step closer. Her temperature went up a few notches, especially when he said, "You're not stepping away from *me.*"

What was he doing? Testing her? Trying to identify any attraction between them? Did he still feel attracted? Was that possible?

"I know you," she murmured, standing her ground.

"Not anymore, you don't. I'm not that kid who didn't know up from down or right from left, or much about what made women tick."

"You know what makes women tick now?" she teased, trying to lessen the intensity in the room.

He gave a short laugh. "Not by a long shot. But I *do* have a hint. After all, being married gives a man much-needed insight. If he doesn't learn fast, he'll go under without a lifeline."

Trying to take a step back from the sexual tension that had developed between them, she responded, "Basically, I guess men need to know women want to be respected, and listened to and that most care deeply about love and family."

Logan still held her gaze. "I learned family is important and children are the most important. Amy died so Daniel could live. I had trouble wrapping my mind around *that* one for a while. She gave up her life and *our* life for our little boy."

Immediately, Gina felt sympathy for Logan because he still seemed perplexed by the idea. Yet she knew a father's love could be as fierce as a mother's. "Logan, if you were in the middle of the ocean and Daniel fell overboard, you'd jump in after him without a second thought to try to save him." She'd seen him with Daniel. It was obvious that Logan cared about his son and wouldn't let anything hurt him if he could help it. Just as his wife had done, in her own way.

Shaking his head, Logan said almost to himself, "You're still that young, compassionate girl who could talk to a horse and understand the expression in its eyes, aren't you?"

"Why does that unsettle you?" she asked, feeling as if this conversation was quickly going down a dangerous road.

"Because I wanted you to have changed. To have become hard and ambitious and uncaring, because then I still wouldn't…be attracted to you."

She practically stopped breathing. His words made her feel as if she was eighteen again, and they were standing close, about to kiss.

She shook her head, anxious to get rid of the rush of emotion. "We're not who we were back then." She knew that more than anyone.

"Maybe not. But I feel something when we're in the

same room, just like I did back then. In fact, this close, I know exactly what I feel."

What should she do? She hadn't been involved seriously with a man since Logan. After the date rape, she couldn't think about "serious," though she'd tried over the years…tried without success. Counselors had told her she'd find a satisfying relationship when she found a man she could trust. But she never had.

Was Logan saying he wanted to kiss her? Should she let him?

He laid his hands on her shoulders, maybe just to see how that would feel. It was a contact that was almost chaste, a contact that could be comforting. Yet it wasn't chaste *or* comforting.

"Why did you ask me to work with you on the day-care center?" she asked, not sure if she wanted to hear the truth.

"I told you, you're an expert. I wanted your input."

"The *real* reason."

He cocked his head as if to say at one time she never would have questioned him. "I really did want your ideas. But I guess I also wanted to see what would happen if the two of us were together in the same room, without Daniel."

"Did you get your answer?"

"Oh, yeah."

His hands tightened slightly, but she felt no sense of panic.

"Why did you agree to work on the project?" he asked.

"I guess I wanted to see what type of man you'd become."

"You couldn't tell from our sessions with Daniel?"

"Daniel was a buffer. You could hide behind father-hood."

His eyebrows quirked up as if he definitely didn't like her conclusion.

She added, "You could concentrate on Daniel and not give me a second thought."

"Did you want a second thought?" he returned quickly.

"As impossible as it is, I already told you what I want." She had returned to Sagebrush hoping for his forgiveness. Now...since she knew about his father's stroke, it really seemed impossible. How could she tell him why she'd really left when it would change forever how he viewed his dad and their relationship?

Logan's gaze searched hers. He must have seen the corner of her mouth quiver because he focused there. "Dammit, Gina." He bent his head and before she had time to think, to protest or to back away, Logan Barnes was kissing her with more passion, more heat than he had when she was eighteen.

At first she stiffened, ready to run. Then she told herself to relax. This was Logan. To her surprise, she *wasn't* panicking. She wasn't imagining she was some-where else. In fact, she was enjoying his kiss. It swept her back into the dream of romance that she'd given up.

Yet this wasn't a dream and she doubted if romance was on Logan's mind. When he put his arms around her to hold her tighter and his tongue slid into her mouth, she balked, put her hands on his chest and pushed away.

He released her. "I'm sorry. I know I shouldn't have done that but I wanted to see—" He swore.

She felt almost dizzy...breathless...and completely unnerved, too. "A kiss has to mean something, Logan. That one didn't. It was some kind of test. If we want to heal what happened between us, we have to do it with talking, not acting on a remnant of attraction that will only embarrass us both."

"Heal what happened between us?" Logan asked incredulously. "How would we *ever* do that? It was as if our breakup had a domino effect. How do I heal the fact that my father had a stroke and I was powerless to help him—and *you* weren't here for me when I needed you?"

"Are you saying you don't want to try to tear down this wall between us?"

Instead of answering her, he asked, "What do you know about walls?"

She realized he was merely taking a stab in the dark. "I know they protect us. Things happen, Logan. Things hurt us when we least expect. We want to keep ourselves safe. That's why we build walls."

He didn't respond, just ran his hand over his face then stuffed his hands into his front pockets. "I'll understand if you don't want to continue to work with Daniel."

Because he'd kissed her? Because there might be more left than that spark of attraction? She'd returned to Sagebrush to finish something with Logan. She had to see it through.

"I want to work with Daniel. He's making progress, and one of these days, he's going to grab on to a piece of furniture and take steps away from it without even realizing he did. I'd like to see that. And I'd also like to see your day-care center come together for the sake of the children."

Logan gazed out the window over the expertly manicured grounds and pool area. Then he swung around to face her. "Are you doing this to make up for leaving?"

There were so many reasons to help him and Daniel…and not all of them had to do with guilt. "I do feel I owe you something. But for now, I just want to help Daniel walk."

Maybe by the time she did that, she'd figure out if Logan could ever forgive her. Maybe she could tell him at least one of the secrets she'd kept hidden for way too long.

Chapter Four

The Rigoletti household was unusually quiet when Gina let herself in. Gina knew her mom was happiest when her kids were all under one roof, talking, laughing and eating.

"Anyone home?"

"In here," her mother called from the kitchen, as expected.

"In here," her dad called from the living room where he sat in his favorite easy chair watching golf. The ranch-style house wasn't big, but it had always held a lot of love.

Gina went to the living room first and kissed her dad on the cheek. "Who's winning?"

"Nobody you'd know," he returned with a smile that said it was okay if she didn't follow golf. "Go help your mom. She and Angie had some to-do and she's a little…frazzled."

Ever since Gina had returned, there had seemed to be more than the usual tension between her and her younger sister. They had been close once, but now that she was back in Sagebrush, Angie was keeping her distance. Gina knew that when her sister was ready to talk, she'd talk. But for now it made for uncomfortable Sunday dinners. Had her mother mentioned their rift to Angie?

Gina patted her dad on the shoulder. His face was weathered from all the hours he'd spent as a mail carrier walking his beat, so to speak. He always said his route kept him in shape and he didn't want to give it up. But last year, the heat and his new blood pressure medication hadn't mixed, and he'd decided to retire.

"I *do* want to know who wins," she told him with a wink, then she went to the kitchen.

Her mother's favorite room resembled a homey café with its bright yellow cupboards and blue-and-yellow gingham curtains. She took pride in everything about it, from the copper-bottom pan on the stove, to the hand-worked placemats on the table. The house didn't have a dining room, but the kitchen table was long enough for the whole family, grandkids included.

Gina hugged and kissed her mother and received a warm hug in return. "What can I help you with?"

The spaghetti sauce was already simmering on the stove, the smell of fresh garlic, tomatoes and onion wafted in the air. She also caught the scent of fresh-baked bread.

"I'm almost finished with everything for today. Are you bringing Raina to dinner tomorrow?"

"She said she'd love to come again." Gina hesitated a moment, then commented, "Dad said you and Angie had a disagreement?"

Gina's mother's black hair was straighter than her own and she wore it tucked behind her ears. As a little girl, Gina had thought her mom was the prettiest woman in the world and she still did. Mary Rigoletti was usually talkative, but now she kept silent.

"Mom?"

"You and Angie haven't talked much since you came back to Sagebrush."

"No, we haven't," Gina admitted. "She doesn't seem to want to talk…or to be around me. When I ask her what's wrong, she says nothing. But she seems uncomfortable and I wish she'd tell me why."

Mary sighed. "She feels beholden to you."

"Why?"

"You know why. You helped her through nursing school. Without your help, she would have been saddled with more loans than she has."

"We always planned that I would help her. That's why I accepted the scholarship." *And left Logan.* She didn't say it aloud, but she knew her mother could hear the words anyway.

"I think she wants to start paying you back."

"That's ridiculous!"

"Not where pride's concerned. If she comes to you with the idea, don't refuse her outright. Think about it."

After studying Gina, her mother asked, "How about a slice of fresh-baked bread?"

"That sounds great."

A few minutes later, the two women sat with glasses of iced tea, munching slices of buttered bread. "Why did you stop in today?" her mother asked.

"Can't I come over to visit?"

"Sure. But I think you have something on your mind."

Of course, she did. She might as well tell her mother what was happening before she found out from someone else. Gossip traveled the streets of Sagebrush with frustrating regularity.

"I saw Logan Barnes."

Her mother set her bread on her dish. "You *saw* him? What does that mean?"

Fourteen years ago, her parents had opposed her association with Logan on the grounds that she was too young, that she had a future ahead of her, and engagement and marriage were out of the question. After all, her older sister had opted for a young marriage and it had been hard going for her. Now Gina didn't know what her mother would think about her life colliding into Logan's again.

They'd never discussed him after she'd left Sagebrush for college. They hadn't discussed him throughout the years. But now she supposed they had to. However, as a professional, she could reveal nothing she knew from Daniel's records or her sessions with him.

"What do you know about him?" Gina asked, hoping to jump off from that.

"Only what's in the newspapers, and the rumors at the butcher shop. After his daddy died about five years ago, he took over the denim factory and everything else. He'd already expanded into other businesses in Dallas and Houston and even in foreign places. Rumor has it, the Barnes empire is three times the size it was when his father was living."

"I meant about his personal life," Gina murmured.

Her mother studied her daughter, then folded her hands in front of her on the table. "Actually the Barnes family wasn't in the news much for a couple of years after you left. Then, about five or six years ago, Logan married Amy Dunlap, who moved here from Dallas and made her mark in real estate. There was a splash about that in the paper. She was at the epitome of her career when she got pregnant. I'm not exactly sure what happened after that. I just know the baby was delivered early and she died and Logan now has a son. I think Angie knows the whole story but she's not talking. She just says that little boy fought for his life and won."

"Daniel is a cutie."

"You've met him?"

"Yes, I have. I can't say more about it than that."

Her mother didn't need Gina to spell it out. "And I can't ask any questions because you can't answer them. Just tell me this, are you and Logan interested in each other again?"

Gina was shaking her head before any words came out of her mouth. "That won't happen. He's still angry I left. In fact…his father had a stroke that same night. I know Logan believes it happened because they argued about me."

"Oh, Gina. The same night? I heard he was ailing but never heard the cause."

"I think Logan blames me for his father's stroke."

Gina and her mother had always been close. She'd confided in her about every teenage aspiration and dream, though they'd disagreed about her situation with Logan. Her mother had known exactly how she'd felt about everything. But that had changed after the rape. Gina hadn't told anyone about it except the counselor she'd seen. Even now, all these years later, she couldn't bear to see hurt in her parents' eyes. If she told them—

She didn't want to revisit the shame. She didn't want

to *feel* again as if some of it were her fault. On some level, she knew it wasn't. Her counselor's voice still echoed in her head every time she thought about it. *You did nothing wrong. His actions weren't your fault. You said no. He didn't listen.*

Still, Gina had gone to the party knowing full well there would be liquor there. She'd gone with the boy up to his friend's room. She'd been stupid and naive and had paid dearly for it. To admit all that to anyone close to her wouldn't have helped back then. There was no point in divulging it to her mother now.

"What's troubling you?" her mom asked.

Gina sighed. "At some point, Logan and I are going to have to talk about all of it."

"To make peace?"

"I don't know if we'll ever make peace. When someone hurts you as badly as I hurt him, peace is hard to come by."

"Not if the two of you want it."

She knew *she* did, but she wasn't sure about Logan. If he could forgive her—

That seemed to be an unreachable dream.

"I don't know how often you're seeing Logan…" Her mother hesitated then went on. "But we're planning a picnic and softball game at the pavilion at the lake next weekend. Why don't you ask him and his little boy to come?"

"Mom, you can't be serious."

"Didn't you say you want to make peace?"

"Yes, but I don't think he'd ever accept."

"You won't know until you ask, will you?"

"Why are you willing to get involved? Logan knows you disapproved of us being together."

"Time has passed. He's a grown man. You're a grown woman. I don't regret the choice we helped you make. Not only do you have your Ph.D. and the satisfaction of knowing you helped your sister through school, but your older brother and sister look up to you."

Yes, she had accomplished what her parents wanted. She was happy—wasn't she?

Then why did you return to Sagebrush? a little voice in her head asked.

To make peace with Logan? Is that why fate had brought him to her?

"I'll think about your suggestion, Mom, but don't get your hopes up."

"My hopes are always up," her mom reminded her with a grin.

Gina couldn't help but laugh as she stood, rounded the corner of the table, and hugged her mother. She was glad she'd come home.

Logan entered the kitchen on Monday evening from the garage, eager to see his son. Gathering Daniel into his arms was always the best part of his day. Yet tonight, he knew Gina was with Daniel. Her car was already in the driveway.

Suddenly he heard his little boy's cry. The sound of it made Logan shift his briefcase to the counter. He took off for the family room.

As he rushed into it, he found Gina holding Daniel, murmuring to him. But Daniel was crying and shaking his head and Logan couldn't tell if he was hurt or not.

Still, he tried to keep his voice calm as he took Daniel from Gina's arms. "Did he fall?"

"No," she answered without a reasonable explanation.

He leaned away from his crying toddler. "Are you okay? Did you get a bump or—"

"He didn't hurt himself," she said quietly.

Daniel was hiccupping, his cries softer now that he was in his dad's arms.

"Where's Hannah?"

"She said she had a batch of laundry to take out of the dryer."

Worried, Logan carried his son to the sofa and sat with him on his knee. "So why is he crying?"

In watching Gina with Daniel, he knew she was careful. He knew she didn't put his son in danger. Yet he hadn't been here to protect Daniel so *anything* could have happened. So much for returning that last call. Daniel was always his main priority. Just because his son was with Gina was no reason to let down his guard.

Snatching one of the small plastic animals from the floor, he handed it to Daniel. His son's cries subsided as he became interested in the toy.

Gina was studying them both as she explained, "He stood up by the chair. I wouldn't just hand over his toy, so he got stubborn, sat down and started crying. Mrs. Mahoney said he didn't have his nap today. He could just be tired, or…he could finally be realizing we're not going to give him everything he wants just because he hollers for it."

When Logan looked into Gina's eyes, his heart practically turned over in his chest. Damn, but she had the most beautiful brown eyes he'd ever seen. They were the color of brandy and had always melted him.

"Have you been here long?"

"About half an hour."

"I'm sorry I'm late."

"That's no problem, Logan. Sometimes it's better if you aren't watching."

"Excuse me?"

Her cheeks reddened a little. "I just mean Daniel responds differently when you're here than when you're not."

"How's he different?"

"He expects you to protect him, to make sure his world is right-side-up."

"That's a dad's job."

"Most of the time it is. But he's getting to the age where he's striking out, learning to do for himself. It's a long process. He needs the confidence to know he can."

"You're saying I'm still treating him like that preemie in the incubator who needed my every prayer to live."

With an understanding smile, Gina came over to the sofa and sank down beside him. "Your concern and worry for Daniel are normal. You almost lost him. But he's healthy and happy, and just trying to catch up to where he belongs." She held her hands out to the baby to see if he'd come to her.

Daniel looked up at his dad, then back at Gina. With a grin, he plopped down on his dad's legs and squiggled over to her.

She lifted him into her arms, held him up and laughed. "You're a charmer, but don't think that smile is going to get you everything you want."

Daniel smiled and babbled at her, and she laughed again.

Logan had noticed that Gina was different when she was with his son. She was the teenager he'd fallen in love with—lovely and sparkling and laughing. Since she'd reentered his life, he'd decided the tension between them had taken the sparkle from her eyes. Now he wasn't so sure. Maybe something else had. Something that had changed the girl he used to know. His years with Amy had changed him. What had changed Gina?

He told himself he didn't care, but a gnawing in his gut urged him to find out what had happened to her since they'd parted ways. Maybe she was struggling to let go of something in her past other than what had happened between the two of them.

He'd struggled to let go of Amy, but she was still there in Daniel's smile, the laughter in his eyes and the color of his hair. But he'd had no choice—he'd had to let go of her to concentrate on Daniel, to enable him to live and thrive.

Maybe he could let go of Gina, too, and be free— free to focus on his son and the life they'd built—if they were more honest with each other.

When Gina settled Daniel on her lap, he yawned a big, wide, baby yawn that told them both he'd had enough for today.

Logan had, too. He gathered his son up once more and stood. "I'm going to put him down for the night."

Gina looked uncomfortable, rubbed her hands on her jeans-clad knees and said, "I'll collect my paraphernalia and be going."

After he started for the doorway, he debated with himself. Turning back to her, he asked, "Would you like to go for a ride after I put him to bed? I don't think Hannah would mind sitting with him for a while."

Gina looked torn. "You need to clear the cobwebs from a long day?"

"I do. Silence isn't always the best way to do that, and the horses won't always make conversation with me."

She smiled, and this time the sparkle was there, even though they weren't talking about Daniel.

She pointed to her shoes. "I only have my sneakers."

"You know there are always spare boots in the barn. I'm sure there will be a pair there that will fit."

Her expression told him she did indeed remember the spare boots...and she remembered other things, too.

So did he.

He had the sudden urge to ask her to put Daniel to bed with him, but that was a bonding time with his son. He didn't want Gina that involved with his life. He nodded to the flat-screen TV and the magazines on the coffee table.

"Make yourself at home."

Although she nodded, she looked a bit lost. That was the way he felt now that he'd invited her for a ride. What did he really expect to come of it?

A half hour later, Gina walked beside Logan to the barn, well aware they'd taken this walk together before— almost fourteen years to the day. His silence told her he must have been conscious of it, too. Their romance had begun on a night like this—when the air was fragrant with damp grass, a three-quarter moon glowing in the twilight sky, begging their gazes to linger on it. His father had been away so often that summer they'd pretty much had the run of the place—swum in the pool, gone riding and made love in a vacant stall. She could still remember the scent of clean hay, the roughness of a wool blanket on her skin, Logan's passionate kisses and tender touches.

The scent of roses wafted to her on the breeze and she noticed the yellow roses alongside the barn were in full bloom.

Years ago the stable at the Barnes estate had been stone and wood. Now it had been modernized and weatherized and was relatively maintenance-free. The decades-old stone facing had been cleaned and preserved and the door Logan opened for her didn't squeak as the old one had.

As they passed the tack room, Logan stayed a few strides ahead of her, out of touching distance. No chance of elbows grazing as their steps slowed in unison, no conversation. Turning to look around, she saw that only four of the stalls were occupied now.

Logan suddenly stopped and faced Gina. "I'm going to give you Aquarius to ride. She's sure-footed and in-tuitive. Do you still remember how to saddle up?"

"That's something a rider never forgets. I saddle my own horse at Francesca and Grady's, and at Vince and Tessa's."

"Good. Then I don't have to worry about the saddle sliding around to the side after you're in the paddock."

His suddenly lighter tone gave her hope. "When I love to do something, I become an expert at it."

"That always was one of your qualities I admired."

Immediately a conversation vividly played in her mind. It had taken place in this barn…in a vacant stall. They'd made love for the second time, a week after the first. Logan's father had been home at the estate during that week. Gina's parents had disapproved of her dating Logan and had kept her at home with chores and baby-sitting most days. But on Friday night, Logan's dad had gone out of town and her parents hadn't found another excuse to keep her at home. After all, she *was* eighteen.

Eighteen, in love and confused about what her future could be. Eighteen and uncertain about everything from her looks to her intelligence to her capabilities. Logan had lain beside her on the blanket in that stall, stroking the curls around her face. She'd been bolder with him that night, touching him more, reacting to every one of his caresses.

Holding her chin in his hand, he leaned forward and took another deep, wet kiss. She surprised him by wrapping her arms around his neck, pulling him down to her, returning each stroke of his tongue.

When he broke away, he laughed. "You catch on fast."

They were still naked and she took advantage of that, running her hands down his chest, over his stomach...and lower. "You're a wonderful teacher. When I'm really interested in a subject, I can become an expert in no time."

"An expert, huh? In the art of loving me?"

She panicked when he'd asked her that. After all, her love for Logan was new and frightening—because it had the power to change her life. She'd already committed herself to a future her parents approved of, to helping her younger sister through college, then working in a field where she could make a difference.

Still, she couldn't ignore her heart. "I'd like to become an expert in the art of loving you."

She'd been living in the moment, wanting to feel Logan's arms around her again, needing his approval, too. And she had loved him. She just hadn't realized how much until it was too late.

Now she saw him looking at her and knew he was remembering that night, too. What could she say? "I meant it, but I was so young and naive"? "I didn't know what love meant until your father warned me away from you"? "Until my heart broke when I left"? "Because I felt unworthy of you and unable to tell you what had happened"?

Logan stepped toward her, his hand raised as if to reach for her. But then he abruptly turned and unlocked Aquarius's stall door.

Gina felt shaken, wanting to get close to Logan again at least in friendship—but not knowing how. She placed her hand on his arm. "Logan."

He acted as if she wasn't touching him. "She'll read your slightest signal," he said. "The easiest touch on the reins is all she needs."

"Logan," she repeated. "Maybe we should talk about—"

"I don't want to talk, Gina. Not now. Let's just saddle up and get out on the trail. That's the only place I seem to find peace these days."

She dropped her hand from his arm, not wanting to stir the cauldron of emotions that wouldn't help either of them.

A few minutes later, they'd left the safety of the paddock and were headed along the marked trail by the white fence line. Thought and planning had gone into the trails that wound through the trees as if they were a natural route rather than a groomed one. The canopy of live oaks made their ride quiet and intimate, the last lingering light spilling through the leaves, dappling their path.

"Do you have time to ride as far as the lake?" he asked.

The Barnes property held a natural lake of its own. It was surrounded by cottonwoods and willows and was one of Gina's favorite places, day or night.

She answered softly, "I have time."

They rode side by side and Gina felt a companion-ship in that, as if they were gaining some footing, finding that common ground from so many years ago. But Logan must have been thinking of *other* things.

As they drew up to the cottonwoods on the shore of the lake, he said, "Amy and I didn't come here much."

Gina went still, then she asked conversationally, "Did your wife like to ride?"

"No, she didn't. I mean, she would ride because *I* liked to. It was a pleasant way to spend a Sunday afternoon when she wasn't showing properties. But she didn't have a real yearning for it. It was a pastime, like golf." He looked over his shoulder at Gina. "And I think she pre-ferred golf."

Their legs almost brushed as Gina drew up beside him. "Did *you* learn to prefer golf?" She'd seen her friends' lives change with marriage and maybe Logan's had, too.

"Actually, I hate golf. I'm not bad at it. I learned the game for business reasons as well as social ones after I met Amy. The idea of chasing a ball from hole to hole doesn't hold much interest for me. I'd rather be on a horse, learning his nature, learning his habits, learning how we can communicate. Do you know what I mean?"

"You're talking to a believer. I know exactly what you mean. I enjoyed skiing in New England. It's chal-lenging in its own way. But it's not part of me like riding is, like horses are. Are you going to buy Daniel a pony?"

"Maybe. Do you think it's a good idea?"

"Sure. Under the right supervision, horseback riding can teach children balance in a way not much else can. In fact, I've often thought about organizing a horseback

riding camp for developmentally challenged children."
She shrugged, a bit embarrassed by sharing that with
him. "It's just one of my dreams."

"Do you have a lot of them?"

She laughed. "An assortment. I've considered volun-
teering in Appalachia, too. The children and families
there need so much help. I've also considered writing a
book for parents, and I would love to tour Alaska
someday."

"You have a lot of dreams left."

"Don't you?" She hated to think his dreams had died
with his wife.

"My dreams now are for Daniel. Will he want to
become a world leader, an economist, a soccer player?
Should I let him take piano lessons as well as try out
for a football team? How soon should he learn Spanish,
climb a tree, have a pet other than a horse? Small
dreams and big ones."

"You still need your own dreams, too."

"No," he said quickly. "Not anymore. Raising a child
and running a business can keep a man busy for a lifetime."

She could hear what he wasn't saying. That his
dreams had gotten crushed and he wasn't going to invest
in them again.

"Do you believe in fate?" she asked.

"Fate or coincidence?" he asked with a sideways
glance.

"I think fate brought Daniel's chart to my desk."

"Or coincidence."

"Maybe I was meant to work with Daniel so that I
could make up for the hurt I caused you."

He brought his horse closer to hers so the animals'
noses were almost touching. He leaned forward and

looked into her eyes. His were shaded by the brim of his Stetson and she couldn't see them clearly.

But she definitely heard the vehemence in his voice. "The past can't be fixed. You can just try to move it aside and go on. After you left, I got over it. Amy died, and I'm trying to get over that. Fate has *nothing* to do with Daniel's chart landing on your desk. This really *is* a small world, Gina," he returned. "You know Tessa. She's Daniel's pediatrician. We all link together, one way or another."

He made the coincidence sound so reasonable. But she felt she'd come back here, not only to be with her family, but to mend fences with Logan. Fate had made that a little easier.

That was what she believed but she also knew she was the one who had to choose the next step. She wasn't sure what that step was going to be.

"Enough of the lake?" Logan asked.

She could never get enough of the lake—or enough of him. But his the-past-can't-be-fixed attitude proved that he didn't forget or forgive easily.

And she didn't know how she was going to change that.

Chapter Five

Gina glanced at the sky with its thousand tiny twinkles of light, the moon softly brilliant and illuminating their return path. This could be a romantic ride if only—

If only what? As far as she could tell, Logan didn't even want to be friends. Why would he? Telling him what had happened to her wouldn't change the fact that he'd felt deserted by her.

When they reached the paddock, Logan dismounted to unhitch the gate. In jeans, boots, snap-button shirt and a Stetson, he was every inch a Texan, every inch a strong, compelling, virile man. He had more confidence now than he'd had at twenty-two. He was quieter and more introspective, but then so was she.

He walked and she rode until they reached the exterior doors to the barn. There she stopped Aquarius, intending to dismount.

But distracted by memories of the past and the tension of the present, she caught her foot in the stirrup and almost landed on the ground.

Logan was quick and caught her around the waist, holding her snugly until she pulled her boot free. She felt tossed back into a time when being in his arms like this had been right. Now she felt awkward and embarrassed, afraid to face him and see nothing in his expression. But she had to do it.

The brim of his Stetson might have hidden his eyes but as he set her back on her feet, the barn light lit the angles of his face. They were standing close, much closer than they should. She held her breath, not knowing what he might say, not knowing what to expect. The night air drifted across them, but she wasn't chilled, not when she was standing this near to Logan, feeling the heat of his body. He reached out and slid his hand under the hair at the back of her neck. She couldn't breathe, couldn't speak. She just stared into his eyes, hoping to see a glimmer of the gentleness she once knew.

"Gina?" His voice was rough.

The desire she saw in his gaze made her tremble. He wanted her. That was obvious in the tension in his fingers, the tightening of his jaw, the tautness of his stance.

The anticipation of another kiss brewed and ripened between them. Yet she knew what she had to do…until they could find an emotional bond once more.

She stepped away from him before anything could happen, before the desire in his eyes became another kiss they couldn't undo.

His expression changed, becoming remote, guarded.

"Logan—"

"I'm sorry. I don't know what I was thinking, or I guess I wasn't. For a minute old memories made things seem different than they are."

"So many things have changed," she murmured.

"For both of us," he agreed.

She could tell him now. She could just open her mouth and let it all come pouring out. But the timing seemed off. They didn't even have a friendship to lead them to share.

Yet if she wasn't honest with him, they'd never be able to share anything substantial. "Logan, I didn't back away because I didn't want you to kiss me again. I backed away because I thought it was the right thing to do."

At her words, he studied her with deepening determination, looking behind them and underneath them. "Right for you, or right for me?"

"For both of us. We have enough regrets between us. I didn't want to add to them."

"You have regrets? You did what you had to do."

"It isn't that simple."

"Nothing in life is simple, not even what seems right. I found that out when you left. I found that out when Amy died."

He stiffly handed her the reins and led his horse into the barn, saying, "We'd better groom them."

Grooming horses together felt familiar, too, yet she knew familiar wouldn't be comfortable. Nothing was comfortable between her and Logan now. She'd been right to back away from another kiss.

Yet she knew she'd dream about it tonight.

After keeping his distance for a couple of days, Logan called Gina and asked her to his office on Thursday to examine the revised day-care plans.

This wasn't complicated, he told himself as he ushered her in to his office. But the perfume she wore, some kind of fruity floral scent, had already distracted him.

Gina had never dressed provocatively—she'd dressed practically. In summer she'd worn mostly jeans and T-shirts, or a pair of shorts when they weren't going riding. She'd never needed clothes to enhance her beauty. Now, however, it was as if she chose clothes that would hide her womanly curves.

This evening, she wore a shapeless navy pantsuit— a boxy jacket, slacks with wide legs—and navy ballet flats. As always, though, his attention went directly to her face, to her huge dark eyes, to the full mouth that he'd almost made the mistake of kissing again. He was still attracted to her, damn it, whether they were on a night ride, or in his office. So he'd better be careful.

"Hi," she said brightly, as if the other night hadn't happened at all.

Just wipe it off the slate? he wondered. The same way she'd wiped him out of her life for the past fourteen years?

How could he be angry with her when he'd done the same? No point asking, really—he still was. Even though he'd met, fallen in love with and married Amy, he'd never forgotten Gina's betrayal because she'd been the first woman he'd really cared about.

He pulled one of the burgundy leather captain's chairs from in front of his desk around the corner, next to his own. "I think you're going to like these. James took all of your suggestions seriously."

Setting her purse on his desk, she came around the corner. Instead of sitting, she studied him. "You didn't need me to look at these plans. If this is about the other night—"

"This is about the day-care center, Gina. I asked for your ideas because I thought they'd be valuable. If you don't want to see what the architect has done, just say so."

After another long look at him, she turned the chair slightly toward his and slid into it. "Okay, show me."

Those words—*show me*—thrust him into the past, into the pool house after an evening swim. *"Show me how you want me to touch you,"* she'd requested. *"Show me how to make* you *satisfied, too. Show me what passion is all about."*

He could hear her voice in his head now, as he sometimes did in his dreams.

"Logan?"

He had to get a grip. After all, this was a business meeting of sorts. Blueprints carried a serious message—Job in Progress. They were going to focus on that job.

They had to sit close together or they couldn't see the plans. His arm brushed against hers as he leaned forward. The tension between them was already ratcheting up and he knew talking about it would only make it worse. So he acted as if sitting with her like this was the most common occurrence in his world.

He pointed to the blueprint of the day-care center. "That's a small kitchenette. Great idea so the personnel can deal with snacks. We'll be feeding the kids from the cafeteria. Those meals can be wheeled in on individual trays or we can keep the food hot with warmers. We have either option. And James divided the larger space into two with observation windows in both."

Gina pointed to the outside space. "I like the shape of the area with the jungle gym and the swing sets."

"The equipment and ground covers are made of the latest materials. Safety is a major issue."

"This really looks perfect, Logan," she said enthusiastically. "If your personnel are as great as the facilities, I wouldn't hesitate to send my child there."

"Are you as good at furnishing day-care centers as you are at planning them? I also need a list of equipment that might be useful."

She glanced down at the plans and then back at him, and he knew what was coming.

"Are you sure you want me to help you with this? Wouldn't you be more comfortable with a professional?"

"You *are* a professional."

"Logan, you know what I mean. Whether we want to admit it or not, everything is still awkward between us. Do you want that interfering with planning the day-care center?"

She was so damn honest. She always had been. It was one of the qualities he'd liked about her. Amy had always softened her opinion when she knew he might disagree, but Gina had never done that. But he shouldn't be comparing his wife with Gina.

"We're adults. Working together doesn't have to be awkward."

"The other night was awkward."

Moving his hand through his hair, he thought about what his reply should be, then decided to be as honest as she was. "I don't know what got into me. Probably memories. We spent a lot of time in that barn and outside it. I almost felt as if I were twenty-two again."

She ducked her head for a minute, then returned her gaze to his. "I know what you mean. Wouldn't it be nice if we could escape that easily?"

What did Gina have to escape from? Was she running from something in New England? Or was she trying to escape into the past instead of looking for a future? He knew all about that.

They were still sitting very close, almost leaning into each other. He knew he should move his chair, get up and walk around the room, anything to be away from her perfume, her softness, the understanding in her eyes. That understanding twisted a knife in his gut.

"More than anything else, Logan, I want to be friends again."

Friends. Could he do that? Could he relegate Gina to that category? Even in friendship, there had to be loyalty. His rational mind told him she'd been young. She'd had a future ahead of her. She'd been afraid to risk believing in them. Yet another part of him wondered about that loyalty and if she'd break it again.

However, risking friendship was a hell of a lot easier than risking more.

He had no intention of risking more ever again.

"I don't know, Gina. It can't be forced."

Sadness clouded her eyes as if she knew the trust she'd broken with him was going to affect them for the rest of their lives. Still, she forced the clouds away and smiled. "I won't force anything. That would make us both uncomfortable, but—"

She looked pensive and uncertain for a few moments. Finally she said, "My family is having a picnic by the lake on Sunday. We'll probably play softball, eat hamburgers. Would you and Daniel like to come? There will be children for him to play with." She stopped. "You probably already have plans."

He imagined extending this invitation hadn't been

easy for her. They still weren't from the same side of the tracks. Their lifestyles were very different. That didn't matter to him—but did she feel the same way?

"What about your parents? They weren't fans of mine."

"My dad respects what you've done with your father's company. And my mother knows we're not young and naive anymore."

He couldn't keep from touching Gina. He just couldn't. He held her chin gently and asked, "When did you stop being naive?"

Something flickered in Gina's eyes that almost made his breath hitch. For that moment, he thought he glimpsed excruciating pain. But from what? Another breakup? Was that her MO? Love 'em and leave 'em?

She recovered quickly, all expression dropping from her face.

She responded, "College was a learning experience for me. I lost my naïveté there."

Partial truth? Complete truth? Just when in college had she lost that naïveté? He had the feeling it had to do with a boy and it had to do with sex. That was an old story. But he didn't press her for more.

Suddenly emotion flickered in her eyes and he could see she was worried that asking him to the picnic had crossed a line. Maybe it had. Long ago he'd told himself that if she ever came back to Sagebrush, he'd avoid her. So why had he asked her to become involved in the day-care center? Why continue Daniel's care with her?

Why continue thinking about her night and day?

Because Gina was a puzzle to him now, one he wanted to unlock, to understand. Maybe he never would but he had to try. Maybe if he tried and succeeded, some of his own shadows would finally vanish.

"All right," he decided. "I'll come to your picnic. I'm sure Daniel will find it a lot more fun than crawling around his playroom with me. Hannah will be gone for the weekend and it will be just the two of us."

"Gone?"

"She does have a life," he said with a smile. "She's made us her family, but she has a son in college as well as a sister and nieces and nephews in the area."

"You trust her, don't you?"

"Implicitly. She was our housekeeper before everything turned…serious. She was wonderful with Amy and when Daniel came home, she mothered him when he needed it most."

Gina's eyes grew shiny.

"What are you thinking?" he asked, leaning closer, reaching out and twirling one of her curls around his finger. "Everything's in your eyes, no matter how you try to hide it."

"You've had a tough road," she murmured, her voice catching.

She was obviously feeling compassion for what he'd gone through and that touched him in a way a woman hadn't in a long time. Maybe that was why he revealed, "When Amy died, I wanted to—" He halted, then went on. "There's that old saying, *Fake it until you make it.* So I did, for my sake and Daniel's. About six months ago, I stepped outside one morning, took a deep breath of fresh Texas air, stared up at that blue, blue sky, and realized I was glad I was still here."

"And how do you feel about Daniel?"

He withdrew his hand, wondering why she could possibly be questioning his feelings for his son. "I love Daniel."

"I don't doubt that, Logan, but after Daniel was born, how did you feel then?"

"I told you, I faked it. I put one foot in front of the other and got through each day. I spent most of my hours at the hospital, watching over him."

"But how did you *feel?*"

His jaw tightened. He could feel the muscle in his cheek jump. Finally he gave in to her question. "I felt nothing. Amy died so he could survive. I couldn't absorb it. All I knew was that she was gone and I had a son who might not live, either. How do you *think* I felt?"

She studied him with huge, dark, sympathetic eyes. "Have you ever talked about this with anyone?"

Now he shrugged and ran his hand through his hair. "Talk about it? Gina, get real. Why would I want to talk about it? Talking only brings up everything I want to forget." He sighed then blew out a breath. "I'm not clueless. I know what you're getting at. You think I didn't bond with Daniel."

"I didn't say that."

"You didn't have to. And the truth is, I didn't the first month. He was so frail... I could touch him, but couldn't hold him. He was hooked up to machines in a plastic bubble. But eventually...he grabbed my heart. Luckily I have a good team at the factory because I took a lot of time off. And when he came home, I was there, along with Hannah."

"I can see you and Daniel have a wonderful relationship."

"But..." he said warily.

She laughed. "Nothing. Except maybe..." She smiled. "You indulge him a little too much. But that's a parent's prerogative, right?"

"Except when it gets in the way of Daniel functioning as well as he should."

"You're doing all the right things, Logan. Just give him some time. If you come to the picnic, he'll have kids to play with and sights to see and new foods to try."

"So you're inviting me to this picnic for *his* sake?"

"No, I'm inviting you both so you can relax. My family can be fun."

He knew what she was thinking. He'd never had a chance to know them because they hadn't approved of him. Maybe now that would all change. Did he really care if it did?

Logan couldn't stop the collision.

Rounding the bases during the Rigolettis' softball game, he and Gina reached home plate at the same time. Her shoulder slammed into his. Somehow their feet tangled and they both went down.

The end-of-May sun shone brightly on them as his arms went to protect *her* rather than the ball in his glove. He didn't know why, but holding on to her at that moment was more important than winning the game.

They landed with a jolt, his worse than hers because he was on the bottom. That was good and that was bad. He could feel the hard ground under him—his shoulders pressed into it. But *Gina* was soft. Her T-shirt had ridden up and his hands were on soft skin. Her body was everything a woman's body should be as he registered the imprint of her breasts and her pelvis, her thighs stretched along his. Memories flooded back of another time in this position and he knew that she knew he was aroused.

"Damn it, this was supposed to be a safe game of

softball." He didn't realize he'd said it aloud until she'd scrambled off him as fast as she could.

He reached for her and snagged her arm. "Gina, I just meant—"

She was kneeling beside him, her face red. "It just meant you came today for a beer and playtime for Daniel. Don't worry, Logan, I understand that."

He didn't let go of her arm. "Are you okay? I mean, did you get hurt in the fall?"

"No. Did you?"

Other players were gathering around now and they were close enough to hear what he and Gina were saying. He levered himself to his feet and held a hand out to her. "I'm fine. I think we both just had the air knocked out of us."

Gina's brother, John, who'd pitched the ball to Logan, shook his head at his sister. "Sorry, kiddo. He caught it about a second before you slid in. You're out."

"Only for this inning," she said with a smile Logan knew was forced. Then she walked away without a backward glance and headed for the cooler of water.

Logan was still staring after her when he felt a presence close beside him and turned to see Angie, Gina's younger sister, rolling Daniel toward him in his stroller. The little boy was grinning from ear to ear, kicking his feet and babbling his enjoyment of the day and the company. Gina's mother and sister had convinced Logan to go play the game while they took care of Daniel. He'd seemed perfectly comfortable with them, so Logan had agreed.

Now he took his little boy from the stroller. "Are you having fun?"

Daniel babbled and leaned forward to put his little arms around Logan's neck.

Angie laughed. "He likes us, but he likes *you* better."

Logan knew Angie was twenty-seven now. She was a beauty with dark brown wavy hair and golden-brown eyes. She was a little shorter than Gina, but slender like her sister. Now she tilted her head at Logan and asked, "So I guess you and Gina are…friends again?"

He shifted Daniel to a comfortable position in his arms, much more comfortable than answering that question. "We're not friends, exactly. She's working with Daniel so we're getting to know each other…again."

"You mean you can't go back to what you once had." Angie was frowning and looking troubled.

"You can't relive the past, Angie, no matter how hard you try." They were both watching Gina, and Logan found himself saying, "She's different now."

"Different how?" Angie asked warily.

"She's quieter, more introspective, even around all of you. She sort of sits back and watches, rather than entering the fray. Do you know what I mean?"

"Yeah, I do. She changed after her first year of college, but we all just thought—"

"What did you think?"

"We thought it was because she really missed you."

Had the decision to leave him been much more difficult than he'd imagined? She'd never looked back. She'd been too busy to take his call when he tried to reach her at school. In fact, he could remember the conversation even today. Three months into his father's rehabilitation, he'd been worn-out and overwhelmed. Gina had been the one person who could understand that. He'd thought—hoped—that she might have changed her mind…that they could work out some way to stay connected…to eventually be together.

"*Logan, I can't talk right now,*" she told him. "*I have a class and a test.*"

"*Can we talk later? Just because you're in Connecticut doesn't mean we can't keep in touch.*"

She paused for a long few moments. "*You and I both know a long-distance relationship won't work. And, Logan, I can't see me ever coming back to Sagebrush. Not for more than a visit. So I don't think there's any point…to talking.*"

Had her voice caught? Did she wish she hadn't chosen the path she was on?

It had taken him three months to set aside his anger and his pride and call her. But during that painful conversation, his pride had reared its head again. Her life had been going on, his would, too. Next semester if his dad continued to make progress in his recovery, he'd be working on his MBA. There had been more than one woman who'd shown an interest in him. Gina had chosen her path and her rejection had only made him more sure of his.

Or so he'd thought—

"You *could* become friends again," Angie said, intervening in the past, as if she was hopeful about the future.

The sensation of Gina's body on top of his, his fingertips on her skin, the fresh scent of her hair, taunted him. "We could. But I don't know if we will," he commented and slipped Daniel back into his stroller.

After a nod to Angie, he pushed his little boy over to the bench where he would wait until his turn at bat.

Chapter Six

"So tell me, Logan," Gina's mother said. "What does it feel like to be CEO of your father's company?"

Gina looked at her parents, who were sitting next to each other across the picnic table from her. Daniel was happily kicking his legs in a high chair at the end of the table. He grinned at them as he poked little round cereal Os into his mouth.

Gina wished *she* felt like grinning. What was her mother up to?

Suddenly conscious of Logan beside her, his elbow lodged next to hers now and then, she wasn't sure inviting him here today had been a good idea. He and Daniel seemed to be having fun but her stomach was tied up in knots and she wasn't even sure why.

Logan didn't seem to be bothered by her mother's

question. "It's an honor to run an enterprise he built from scratch."

"I heard you're running it better than he ever did," Angie said, looking Logan in the eye.

Logan just shrugged. "New styles for denim as well as advancing technologies have made it easier for me to expand markets. I see change as opportunity."

"That's a good way to look at it," Gina's mother decided. "I hope Gina sees her return to Sagebrush as a new opportunity. I don't want to believe she did it just for us."

Feeling Logan's gaze on her, Gina shrugged. "Everyone's life needs a change at some point. Now seemed to be a good time." She stood and picked up the empty dessert plates. They'd all eaten every bit of her mother's homemade pies.

At the next table, her brother, John, called, "Hey, Gina. If you want to clean up our table, too, I'll leave you a tip."

She wrinkled her nose at her brother. "Be careful. The next time you want me to babysit, I might not wash off their sticky fingers before they point to their favorite characters on your new fifty-two-inch TV."

Everyone laughed, but Gina still felt the heat of Logan's gaze. That made her excited and nervous all at the same time. She dumped the plates into the trash can and heard her mother say, "Gina waited tables when she was in college for extra money. I think she was even a short-order cook at one point, weren't you, honey?"

"I was," she answered, turning from the trash can with a bright smile. "Eggs overeasy, burgers medium well. They were my specialty."

"She suddenly decided she didn't like waitressing, that

she'd rather be back in the kitchen. I didn't get that because as a cook, she didn't get tips," her brother explained.

"I worked more hours that way because nobody else wanted to do the short order."

Logan suddenly stood and climbed out from the picnic bench. Approaching his son, he unfastened the tray from his high chair.

Angie asked, "You're not leaving, are you?"

Gina wondered what that was all about. She told her sister, "Daniel has a regular routine at bedtime. Logan probably doesn't want to disrupt that."

Logan's eyes settled on her once more and she felt hot from head to toe, even though the day had simply been pleasantly warm.

"Gina's right. In a little while, he'll be good and cranky. I find I can get him to sleep easier if I do it on his timetable."

"The world revolves around our children," Gina's mom said, nodding. "Most men don't get that."

"I had to get it," Logan said seriously.

Gina's mother stood now, too, and went to Logan and Daniel. "I just want to tell you how glad we are you could come today."

"Yes, we are," Angie said quickly. "You'll have to come to one of our family dinners. Mom makes the best ravioli."

Gina didn't understand what her sister was doing. Why was she pushing Logan's continued connection to her family? Gina had to have a talk with her and soon. There were times when Gina had wanted to start a serious conversation with her sister, but Angie always found an excuse not to. They *were* both busy women. Angie didn't always work the same shift. She was also signed up for the hospital's disaster relief team and flew out unexpectedly when they were needed. Besides Angie's commitments, Gina often stayed late at Baby Grows. That didn't make getting together easy.

"Maybe sometime," Logan answered diplomatically, already gathering Daniel from his chair.

"Would you like me to take him while you pack up?" Gina asked.

Already leaning toward her, Daniel wanted her to hold him. But she didn't want to overstep any boundaries.

"That would be a help," Logan said. "Before I round up his diaper bag, toys, food and chair, not to mention his stroller, he could be asleep."

Gina laughed.

Suddenly Logan leaned close to her and murmured near her ear, "If you want to stay with your family, I'm sure one of them will take you home. You don't have to leave now."

Logan had insisted on picking her up this afternoon and she didn't know now if he was offering simply because he thought she might want to stay, or because he didn't want to be in close quarters with her again. He hadn't indicated at all how he felt about being around her.

What about that kiss?

That kiss had been on her mind way too much. But she couldn't help wondering if Logan thought about it, too.

"I'm ready if you are. I have an early appointment in the morning," she assured him.

Her mother heard that. "Do you? I was hoping you'd come back to the house for a while."

"Not tonight, Mom. I promise, I'll come visit soon."

While Logan loaded up his vehicle, she and Daniel made the rounds of her family, giving hugs and saying goodbye. Angie, her sister-in-law, Kristi, and her older sister, Josie, were standing together so she really couldn't ask her younger sister why she'd almost invited Logan to dinner. But she'd find out. After she gave Angie a squeeze, her sister hugged her back.

Angie readjusted one of the shoulder straps on Daniel's overalls. "You are one of the cutest little boys I've ever seen."

Daniel laid his head on Gina's shoulder, cuddling in close to her neck.

"He's getting attached to you," Angie said.

"No, he's just a friendly little guy. He'd cuddle with anyone like this."

Angie adamantly shook her head. "I doubt that. You know—" she lowered her voice "—he could probably use a mom."

Gina didn't have a chance to respond as Logan returned from his trek to the Range Rover and held out his hands to his son. Daniel didn't fuss but went to his dad, poking his thumb into his mouth, closing his eyes as he laid his head on his dad's shoulder.

"Aha," Logan said. "I thought so. Fresh air and sun will do it every time."

After a final round of goodbyes, he and Gina started down the path to the parking lot.

Gina was still thinking about Angie's last remark, and what might have caused her to voice it.

"Are you tired?" Logan asked her.

"Not really." Then she added, "It was fun just to be outside and get some real exercise."

"As opposed to…"

"As opposed to the treadmill Francesca left behind. I'm beginning to hate that thing, even though it's great to have when I'm up too early to walk outside or I return home late at night. I thought about joining that new gym in town, but I don't know when I'd find time to go."

They walked in silence in the growing dusk until they reached the Range Rover. Gina helped buckle in Daniel and took her place in the passenger seat.

After Logan climbed inside, he started the ignition. "Your family made me feel welcome today. I wasn't exactly sure what would happen."

"My mother wouldn't have invited you if she didn't want you there. I think today was meant to make up in part for their attitude toward you."

"I suppose."

Logan put his hand on the gearshift and Gina thought they'd back out of the parking place and be on their way. But he didn't put the vehicle into Reverse; rather he glanced to the backseat and saw that Daniel's eyes were closed already.

He shifted as well as he could with his seat belt on and faced her. "You're different than you were when you were eighteen."

"Aren't we all?" she joked, hoping to deflect his perceptive observation.

"Something's different, Gina, that I can't put my finger on. I knew you well, very well. You were irrepressible, joy-filled, ready for any new adventure. Now—"

"Now I'm mature, and I like my world a little more organized."

He shook his head. "No. The old Gina comes out with kids. You played tag, you told jokes, you even swung Daniel on the swing like that girl of eighteen. But the rest of the time, you're quieter, more…withdrawn.

So I guess I'm asking, what had the greatest impact on who you are today?"

"It must have been that short-order cooking," she teased.

"Gina."

The gentle expression in his voice was hard to miss. But did she really want to tell him what had happened, here with his son sleeping in the backseat? She really believed what she'd told him early on when working with Daniel—children were little sponges, no matter what the age. She didn't want to go into something as serious as date rape with Daniel around.

She took a deep breath. "When I was in college, something happened to change the way I looked at the world."

"Some*thing*, or some*one?*"

"A mixture of the two, but I don't talk about it. There's no point. I'm sure there are things that happened that gave you your view of life today. You said you see change as opportunity. Your father didn't. I remember how he fought against bringing in the newest types of machinery. He liked the old ways of doing things."

"I swore I'd never be like him."

"I'm sure his stroke and passing affected you."

"They did. I was pressed into responsibility in a way I'd never experienced after his stroke. We became closer than I ever thought we could. But we weren't talking about *me,* and I'm not so self-absorbed that I didn't notice you changed the subject."

"You have to get home and put Daniel to bed."

He looked frustrated but then gave her a wry smile. "You know how to escape a sticky conversation."

"I do my best."

He put his hand on the gearshift again and shifted into Reverse. "We'll have to finish this soon."

He wasn't going to let it drop, and she supposed she didn't want him to. The time would be right soon.

And then what?

That was the problem. The traumatic event in her life had nothing to do with them and with what Logan felt about her. She had to regain his trust if she wanted even friendship between them. But even then, could she tell him about the threat his father had made? How could she ruin Logan's image of his dad? Somehow she had to rebuild her relationship with Logan without hurting him. But she knew regaining trust would be as difficult as rewriting history.

Gina's emotions had held a tug-of-war with her logic since the picnic. Maybe she should have told Logan about the rape. On the other hand, was he ready to hear? After she told him, she couldn't take it back. After she told him, he'd look at her differently.

On Monday evening Gina decided to tell Logan the truth—about everything. She had an excuse for stopping by. She'd brought lists of requirements for staff for the day-care center and catalogs for furnishings. But as she pulled into the circular driveway in front of the house, she noticed the black stretch limousine.

Logan had company…apparently important company. She pulled up behind the limo, thought about her timing then switched on the ignition again ready to pull away.

However, before she could, Logan came to the door. Seeing her, he beckoned her inside.

She would simply hand him the information. The rest would have to wait.

Parking quickly, she ran up the walk and handed him the manila envelope. "Just some catalogs with things I thought you might need for the day-care center. You'll have an idea of cost estimates when you go through them. Staffing requirements, too."

Logan was dressed in a Western-cut suit, white shirt and bolo tie and looked as if he'd stepped out of the pages of *Country Gentlemen* magazine. In her jeans and sandals she felt as she had fourteen years ago on the evening his father had told her he would never let his son marry a nobody.

"I didn't mean to interrupt your evening. I wasn't thinking. I should have called."

He took the envelope from her. "You're not interrupting, believe me. I'm just having dinner with an oil man and his wife who are interested in donating to the foundation."

"Foundation?"

"After Amy died, I set up a foundation for donations to help with research for women who are pregnant and have cancer. That seemed to be one of the most positive things I could do to try to get over feeling powerless."

Logan admitting to that feeling surprised her. Maybe she really *didn't* know him. Maybe she hadn't known him all those years ago, but had just been caught up in romantic dreams, without the maturity to realize what was real and what wasn't.

"That's a wonderful cause. I wish you luck tonight. What will it take for your guests to write a huge check?"

"Lots of conversation, martinis and a look at my horses. Chad's thinking about purchasing a couple of new ones and would like some tips."

"You should do okay then."

After a long moment, when they couldn't seem to look away from each other, Logan broke into a smile. "Why don't you stay and have dinner with us? I'm sure Chad's wife would like to talk about something other than baseball scores and the price of crude."

But Gina was already shaking her head. She knew where she belonged and where she didn't, and if she wanted to help Logan make an impression, she certainly couldn't do it dressed like this. "I think I'll pass, but thank you for asking."

"You didn't even give it a minute of thought." He sounded more puzzled than annoyed and she saw now that he had meant that invitation seriously.

"I didn't have to, Logan. I might have professional credentials, but I'm not prepared for an evening of suits, upswept hair and jewels."

His mouth turned down in a frown and now he *did* look annoyed. "So you're a reverse snob?"

The word *snob* made her stumble for an answer. She wasn't one and never would be. But maybe she needed to give Logan some understanding of why she'd left. To heal past hurts they needed honesty between them. "Your father hired me to work in the barn. Whenever I enter this estate in any capacity, I think of myself as a hired hand. Your dad never thought I was good enough for you and he told me so. So no, Logan, but on a night like this, dressed as I am, I wouldn't feel comfortable joining you. Think about it—how would you feel coming to one of *my* department meetings?"

"My father told you you weren't good enough for me?" He'd heard what she'd said and understood what it had meant.

Should she say more? They couldn't get beyond the past if she didn't, could they? "You and I were…becoming more involved. Your dad came home early from a trip and found us together in a chaise by the pool. When you went inside the pool house to change, he told me I shouldn't even consider a relationship with you because I was a nobody, and he had plans for you to marry someone in your same social stratum."

"Gina! Why didn't you ever tell me?" His voice showed his shock and he looked troubled.

"At the time, I thought it was best not to, and then…it didn't matter." She heard laughter float from an interior room. "I shouldn't have told you now. I just wanted you to understand why I didn't feel comfortable staying tonight. But I do appreciate the invitation."

When she turned to leave, he caught her arm. "You can't just go like this."

"Yes, I can. Have a good night, Logan. I'll see you Wednesday for Daniel's session."

"You always run away before we're finished," she heard him mutter. But she didn't linger and listen to anything else he had to say. His reaction to her revelations had indicated to her that he might have stood up for her. The fact that he'd wanted her to stay tonight said he didn't care about appearances.

All those years ago, Gina had thought she'd left Logan for all the right reasons. But now she realized she'd simply been too insecure to stay and fight.

Logan rang the doorbell of the Victorian, not sure what he was doing there. He just knew he and Gina had to talk. For almost twenty-four hours, he'd mulled over what

Gina had said about his father. Long dusky shadows were beginning to fill corners as he pressed the bell again.

Suddenly the door opened and Gina was there, looking breathless and beautiful in jeans and a lime-colored blouse. "I was out back," she explained. "The evening was just too nice to stay indoors."

"Are you home alone?" Logan asked, thinking they could go for a drive if she wasn't.

"Yes, Raina is at her brother's. Come in," she said, motioning him inside.

She switched on the Tiffany light in the foyer and its jewel tones dispelled the shadows. When she led him into the living room, he noticed the kitchen beyond, then the hall that led to other rooms. It was an intriguing house, definitely large enough for two or three women to share.

"Would you like something to drink?" she asked. "I have…a local wine, soda, juice, beer."

Did she think he'd turn down anything but the finest champagne? Did she have the beer for men friends she might invite over?

"I'm fine."

She nodded as if she didn't know what to do next.

"I thought we should talk," he said bluntly, motioning to the sofa to indicate this wouldn't be a quick conversation.

They rounded opposite sides of the coffee table and met in the middle.

He waited for her to be seated, and then he lowered himself a good six inches away. "I want to know more about the conversation you had with my father."

She took one of the fringed throw pillows into her lap and held it as if she needed something to hold on to. "I'm not sure there's any point."

"I believe there is."

Staring across the room rather than at him, she pulled the pillow into her chest. "The truth is—I wasn't mature enough or assertive enough to stand up for myself, but I think that's because I believed he was right."

"That you were a nobody?" She'd been intelligent and bright and sweet.

"*You* made me feel like somebody, but I knew that wasn't enough. I felt I had to be your equal. Your father didn't think I was, didn't see that I was, so I was sure I wasn't."

"You really believed that?"

She nodded and swung her gaze toward him. "I didn't have the latest clothes. I wore Josie's hand-me-downs. I wasn't a cheerleader or even a debater because I always had to get home to take care of Angie. I never resented that because I found satisfaction in taking care of her and fulfilling my role in my family. It was important to me, and it helped my mom bring home a paycheck, too. But that role also kept me isolated from my classmates. When I met you, you didn't know that I wasn't the most popular girl in school. You didn't care that I wasn't a cheerleader. You were somehow beyond all that. At least, that's what I thought."

"But my dad made you feel differently."

She hesitated, then seemed to choose her words carefully. "Your dad made me see who I truly was. That wasn't going to change unless *I* changed it. I could do that by going to college. I could not only change who *I* was, but who Angie could become. Oh, Logan, I wanted to stay. But there were so many pressures that pushed me to leave. Once I was in college, I still had regrets, but I—"

The look on her face forewarned him that he

wouldn't like what was coming. For a moment, just a moment, he glimpsed that something soul-shaking had happened to her.

"So when I called, why didn't you talk to me? Did you really have a test?"

She looked down at her hands folded across the pillow. Her dark lashes were so feminine on her cheeks, but he sensed her calm exterior was hiding a wealth of turmoil underneath.

"I had a test that day, but…I couldn't call you back."

More than anything, he wanted to reach out and take her hand. He wanted to reach out and touch her face. When they touched, all heaven broke loose and he could use a little of that now. But this wasn't about him and his feelings. It was about *her.* He'd never put himself into her shoes because he hadn't wanted to, because her reasons for leaving weren't as important as the reasons she should have stayed.

"Tell me what happened."

It was a request more than a command, but the intensity behind it made her hold the pillow tighter.

"You'll never look at me the same again if I tell you," she said, so reasonably he almost believed her. But then he saw she wasn't being reasonable at all. She was afraid…afraid of his reaction.

"What happened?" he asked again, gently so she'd know she had nothing to fear.

He saw the pulse at her neck was beating fast.

She took a deep breath, held it, then let it out. "I was date-raped."

She uttered the words very softly, but they slammed into him like a body blow. Their impact took his breath away. If they did that to *him,* he could only imagine what they did to her. Should he gather her into his arms? Let her explain? Tell her she didn't have to say anything else?

He was at a total loss. He felt frozen.

She must have seen how absolutely he'd been affected by what she'd told him because she said, "You don't have to say anything. I just wanted you to know why I didn't come back, why I didn't call, why I felt even more insecure about the differences between us."

"My God, Gina, insecure? You were raped! Insecurity has to be the least of it. Who in the hell did this? Did you press charges?"

Agitated now, she tossed down the pillow and walked over to the bay window looking out into the front yard. "I didn't bring this up to rehash it. I got counseling. It's over."

He couldn't stay away from her now. Crossing to her, he gently laid his hands on her shoulders. "If you don't want to talk about it, that's okay, but please turn around and look at me."

She did then, and he could tell it took an effort for her to keep her chin lifted. He could feel the tension in her body, see the lines on her brow, and abruptly he realized what facing him like this cost her. Without a second thought, he wrapped his arms around her and brought her into his chest. They stood that way for what seemed to be a very long time.

Seconds passed. Minutes passed. He didn't know how many.

When Logan finally leaned back to look at her, he thought he might see tears in her eyes, but he didn't. That surprised him.

"You say you're over it, but can you really be over something like that?"

A long sigh escaped her lips. "For the most part. I still have some trust issues with men, trust issues in general, really. I didn't tell anyone what happened. It would have been a 'he said, she said' situation. He didn't even go to the college I attended. He was a friend of one of the frat guys and just happened to be at the party that night. I was lonely and had drunk punch that was spiked. I don't know how much liquor was in it. But that was no excuse. I never should have gone with him to that room. I thought we were going to talk." She let out a humorless laugh.

That laugh was like a lance to Logan's heart. Gina had been trusting and innocent, shy and vulnerable. How much of that had been taken away from her? He was filled with righteous anger.

She pushed away from Logan. "I can see what you're wondering. I said *no,* Logan. After a few kisses, I said *no.* But he wouldn't listen, and he was stronger and bigger than I was."

"Don't, Gina. I'm not doubting you."

"Aren't you? The counselor warned me about any responses a man in my life might have. That's why I never told my parents. Can you imagine what my father's response would be?"

"And your mother doesn't know, either?"

"No, no one does. It happened in Connecticut. I dealt with it there. I didn't want it intruding on my family or on any time we spent together."

"Don't you think they had a right to know so they could help you?"

"They *couldn't* help me, Logan. I had to handle it on my own. I had to take my power back. I had to work through the anger, and then I had to go on."

"But did you go on? Or is this the reason you never married and had a family?"

"I don't know. I do know I got caught up in my studies and my work and that's what became all-important to me."

As he studied Gina, he saw there were no external remnants of what she'd been through. But he suspected on the inside, she'd been changed in an elemental way. As he thought about everything she'd told him, he found his fists clenched by his sides.

She glanced at him warily. "You're going to be different now, aren't you? Please, Logan, don't be. I just told you all this so you'd understand why I couldn't...stay in touch."

"Essentially, you didn't trust me to understand. You thought I'd blame you."

"Trust? I don't think that even entered into it. It took me a long while to recover—months, a year, probably even longer than that. I just put one foot in front of the other and took a step each day. My counselor and group therapy were a large part of my college years. I made excuses not to come home until I had put myself back together."

He instinctively wanted to touch her again, but didn't know if he should. "Does it bother you to be...close to a man?"

"Strangers. Sometimes if they get close, I pull away. But with you, I'm...fine."

Was that longing he saw in her eyes? Longing for what? What they might have had? For his kiss? For his forgiveness? He'd come here to settle something between them. Instead, everything had gotten more complicated. He was at a loss as to what to say or do, and he wondered just how he would have reacted if she'd told him right after the rape had happened.

"So the guy who did this—"

"I didn't even know where he was visiting from, or who his friend was. I only knew he was charming and complimentary and seemed like a genuinely nice guy until after we went into that room. Could I have found out who he was? Maybe. But I wasn't in any position to play detective. Shouldn't I have discovered who he was and outed him? Yes. As soon as it happened, I should have gone into the hall and screamed bloody murder. But I didn't. What I did do was rebuild my life. I made my parents proud. And I helped put Angie through school."

She walked away from him, over to the sofa, agitated, as if telling him had brought everything out of the dark of the basement, and she didn't want to see it in the light. He couldn't blame her. He shouldn't have asked her questions. He should have just listened.

Logan went to her, caught her hand, and tugged her around to face him. "Do you have plans this evening?"

She looked flustered. "No."

"Then come home with me. We can spend some time with Daniel and take him to that carnival that's in town. He's never seen Ferris wheels or merry-go-rounds. I'd like to take some pictures when he sees all of it for the first time."

"Why are you inviting me?" she asked, her huge brown eyes direct. "I don't want you to feel sorry for me. I put the past behind me and I have a life I'm proud of."

No matter how courageous, forward-looking or optimistic anyone was, trauma colored their future. He remembered the weeks by Amy's side as she was dying, Daniel's birth, not knowing whether his son would live or die. He'd pushed all of that to the back of his mind and to the back of his heart, but it never really went away.

"I'm asking you along because Daniel and I want to enjoy his first carnival with someone, and you're the someone I'm choosing. There's nothing complicated about it, Gina. Just cotton candy, a merry-go-round and an escape from everyday reality for a little while."

When she didn't respond immediately, he prodded her. "So what do you say? Will you ride on the merry-go-round with us?"

Chapter Seven

*W*hat are you doing here? Gina asked herself later.

Beside her, Logan pushed Daniel's stroller over the ruts and bumps of the unpaved walkway in the field where the carnival had been set up, heading toward the cotton-candy vendor.

She knew Logan had only asked her along because he felt sorry for her. That had been the problem with telling him about what had happened. She didn't want his pity and knowing he felt sorry for her might put even more walls between them.

Or maybe he thought she was a coward for not trying to prosecute her attacker. He might also believe she'd invited what had happened. She'd analyzed her behavior over and over again until her counselor *had* told her she had to let it go. But that was difficult to do.

Every time Logan glanced at her now, she thought

he looked at her a little more kindly. But she didn't want that, either.

What *did* she want?

Wasn't that the most mind-boggling question she'd ever encountered? She'd said she wanted Logan's forgiveness, but maybe what she really wanted was to find the missing piece of herself she'd left behind in Sagebrush fourteen years ago.

Logan had wheeled Daniel up to the cotton-candy cart that sat next to a corn-dog stand and a funnel-cake maker. "Can you watch him while I get the cotton candy?" he asked her.

He trusted her more and more with Daniel and that made her feel better than she should.

She gave Logan a smile and crouched down with Daniel to talk to him in his language for a few minutes, to play with the small toys on the tray on his stroller. It was a state-of-the-art stroller with all the bells and whistles, sturdy and solid with a canopy that would protect a child against almost any element. She could only imagine what it had cost. In the future, how would Logan keep from spoiling his son and buying him the best and the finest? How would he teach Daniel he had to earn what he wanted most? Would Logan even make him do that? She remembered how Josie had married right out of high school—secondhand supplies were all her older sister had ever known for her kids. It had broken Gina's mother's heart and she'd helped provide what she could, but the rest of the family had been on a thin budget, too.

When Logan returned, his smile was bittersweet.

Gina had been at a carnival with Logan that summer she was eighteen in another small town an hour away.

They'd wanted just to be themselves, go someplace they weren't known and where people wouldn't talk. They'd shared a stick of cotton candy and gotten it all over their mouths, their fingers, their hands. They'd kissed it from each other. When Logan turned her way, she could see that he was remembering that night, too. Those sparks of desire in his eyes were easy to decipher.

Now, however, he merely offered her a pink wisp of the candy. She took it, feeling her fingers get sticky. When she touched it to her lips, she remembered Logan feeding it to her that summer night when they hadn't had a care in the world. At least that was how it had seemed until Logan's father had warned her away from his son…until her parents had talked to her about the future and her dreams…until her older sister described being saddled with a baby when she was practically still a child herself. If she had followed her own heart back then and fought for the love she and Logan shared, there might not be this distance between her and Logan now. There would have been no trauma to explain.

Daniel reached out to her swath of pink fluff, filling one little hand with it and squeezing it into his fist. It turned into pink goo. Daniel chortled and touched her cheek with his messy hand, leaving sugary fingerprints. Gina heard Logan's camera beep.

Laughing, she took Daniel's hand and kissed it, then wiped it and her face as best she could with her napkin.

Logan's voice was husky when he said, "I have a jar of baby food in the backpack of the stroller. There's a canopied dining area over there. If you want to head that way, I'll grab some food and drinks. Root beer, right?"

He'd remembered. Tears formed in her eyes. She didn't know why that little thing unlocked the door where feelings waited to rush out, but it did. Still…it took until she found them a table in the cordoned-off area, until she took Daniel from his seat and held him on her lap, for the tears to stop. She'd had an unexpectedly emotional evening. That was all.

A few minutes later, Logan came toward them managing to balance two boxes—one with food, another with drinks. She helped him unload the corn dogs, burgers and chili, then the sodas.

While Logan held Daniel, Gina fed him the baby food.

"It must be awful to be down there sitting in that stroller all the time, unable to see what's going on up here."

"Do you think he minds?" Logan asked, as if he hadn't considered the idea before.

"I just think he'll like it better up here."

Daniel seemed content to stare at all the sights while they ate. Lights were beginning to come on now, transforming the carnival into a magical place.

"I forgot to ask if you got donations for your charity from the oil man," Gina said, finished with her cup of chili, needing to make normal conversation so emotion wouldn't get the best of her again.

Logan's eyebrows lifted. "I wish you had come in for dinner."

She kept silent.

"You're going to have to deal with your insecurities, Gina," he said, a little sternly. "You have a Ph.D. and a successful practice. You have nothing to be insecure about."

She glanced around, seeing that nobody sat at the tables close to theirs, and anyway, everyone else was involved in their own conversations.

They were being so honest with each other. Should

she tell him what his father had threatened to do? She'd always wondered what Logan would have chosen. Would he have chosen a life with her, without riches? Or would he have turned his back on her for the life his father had planned for him?

"What are you thinking about?"

She shook her head. "Nothing."

He frowned. "Nothing you want to talk about, you mean."

"You think you can still read my mind?" she joked.

"Obviously I can't."

Daniel squirmed to be let down, ready to explore something else. "Why don't we take Daniel on a pony ride?" Logan suggested. "After that, maybe we can listen to the bluegrass concert. I have a blanket in the car we can spread out. He might fall asleep on it if we're lucky."

"And if we're not?"

He shrugged. "We can take him home."

Logan seemed more relaxed with Daniel's schedule tonight than he'd been the evening of the picnic with her family. Maybe he'd been uncomfortable with them, but tonight he was at ease with her. Or maybe he sensed what was best for Daniel and just followed his instincts.

Gazing into his eyes now, she knew that was the case. "You really understand putting kids first, don't you?" she asked softly.

"I do," he said.

A bond of understanding tied them together. A hot tingle skipped up her back as she gazed into his green eyes and remembered all the things she'd felt as a teenager. Now she was feeling more…excited? More wishful? More intoxicated by his mere presence?

Why *was* she here?

Maybe by the end of the night, she'd find out.

Logan's gaze fell on Gina for the umpteenth time as they sat on a blanket listening to guitars strumming along with a banjo and fiddle. He couldn't get her revelations out of his mind. The rage he felt for her was similar to the fury he'd felt against Amy's cancer. His wife had been a beautiful, vibrant woman, cut down by an evil disease. There had been no good answers for her, not where she and Daniel had been concerned. So she'd lived with the decisions she'd made, and she'd died because of them…without regrets.

Admitting he had regrets was difficult. He regretted that they hadn't laughed more and traveled more and tried to have a baby sooner. He wished he'd been more attentive. Then he might have caught her symptoms sooner, maybe even before *she* had. Those feelings still weighed him down in the middle of the night. He was always digging through it all, coming to terms with the pain, learning to live with it.

And Gina…she sat here tonight, years removed from what had happened to *her*. But he knew trauma like hers couldn't be left behind so easily. He'd already noticed the ways it had affected her personality, making her quieter and more self-conscious where men were concerned. He'd seen that with James Wolfe.

Yet she'd kissed *him* without hesitation. Because he'd surprised her? He'd surprised himself. That kiss hadn't been the kind of intimacy they'd once known. How would she handle *that* kind of involvement?

Why was he even asking?

There were many sleepless nights when still he tossed and turned because of the decisions he'd let Amy make…because of the way he hadn't bonded with his son the first month, because he'd been afraid Daniel would die. After Amy's memorial service, he'd vowed loving a woman hurt too much. When he was ready, he'd have no-strings sex. It would be about having a physical need fulfilled, no more. But he hadn't even contemplated it. He hadn't gone out on dates, or asked a woman to any of the dinners he attended, the cocktail parties, the charity functions. He went alone. Because?

Because it was safer. Because he only had the energy for Daniel and work. Because getting involved in any fashion just hadn't been in the cards he'd been dealt.

He did *not* want to get involved with Gina now. Yet sitting on this blanket across from her made his insides jump, made him feel heat under the collar of his shirt, made him resurrect the past when that was the last thing he should do.

"You're frowning," she noticed, her voice soft in the growing darkness as the band took a break. "Is it getting too late for Daniel? We can leave anytime."

Daniel was sitting on the blanket between Logan's legs, chewing on a plastic giraffe he liked to carry with him. Suddenly the giraffe held no more interest and he tossed it at Gina. As she grabbed for it, her T-shirt sneaked up her midriff and Logan caught sight of skin. She was as slim as she'd ever been, her breasts still as pert.

Unnerved by desire that had no place here tonight, he picked Daniel up from a sitting position and balanced him on his feet. His little sneakers rocked on the blanket but he kept hold of Logan's hands.

Gina turned to face Logan squarely, and touched her

feet to his, making a channel between them. She lifted Daniel's giraffe and waved it at him. "Look here, Daniel, see what I've got. Do you want him?"

Logan turned Daniel around so he was facing Gina. He knew what she was trying to do and he held his breath to see if it would work. But at that moment, Daniel decided to plop down onto the blanket and knee-walk toward her.

She gave him a bright smile. "Well, *that's* new."

He took the giraffe from her and began to gnaw on it. A drum roll startled all of them and, for a moment, Logan thought Daniel was going to cry. He was ready to go to him and comfort him, but Gina already had her arms around his son. She stood him up, supported his hips and pointed to where the band started to play again. She looked like any mother would, her face close to Daniel's, her lips at his cheek, telling him about something new.

But *Amy* was Daniel's mother. Logan could never forget that. He could never let Daniel forget it, either.

So why *had* he invited Gina tonight? Because he felt sorrow for what she'd gone through? Because he wanted to know more? Because the old attraction was tickling his libido in a way he couldn't scratch?

He crossed one ankle over the other, kept his gaze on his son and concentrated on the music.

"He's still asleep," Gina murmured as Logan pulled into the driveway at the Victorian, feeling as if the ground beneath her feet had shifted again.

Ever since she'd told Logan about the rape, he'd been different. During the concert, he'd distanced himself from her. Yet that shouldn't be a surprise. He'd been doing it ever since fate had brought them together again.

"If I'm lucky, I can get him into bed before he wakes up too much. I think he had a good time tonight."

"Did *you?*" She probably couldn't eliminate the distance between them if Logan was determined to keep it there, but she could chop at it.

"Yes, I did," he responded, but Gina knew it was a reflexive, polite response.

"I shouldn't have told you."

Logan put the Range Rover into Park, but let the engine idle. "What do you want me to say, Gina?"

"I want to know what you're feeling. You're thinking I deserved it for leaving? Do you—"

"No, Gina. For God's sake, don't you know me better than that?"

"I don't know. Everything between us is so complicated. One minute I think we're becoming friends again, then I feel this wall between us. Tonight, we were having a good time and then suddenly, you were a thousand miles from me. I felt as if I'd done something wrong."

Logan cut her a sideways glance. "You and Daniel have bonded."

"Isn't that a good thing? If he and I have a connection, when I work with him, we'll make better progress."

Logan kept his gaze straight ahead at the detached garage twenty yards away. "You don't understand what's happening, do you?"

She wished she did. Maybe he'd explain the turmoil she felt in him when they were together. "Tell me."

The engine of the Range Rover hummed in the background. The only other sound was the pounding of her heart as she waited, giving Logan time to put his thoughts together.

Finally he wrapped his hands around the steering wheel, still not looking at her. "Hannah and I have cared for Daniel since he came home from the hospital. I trust her to care for him the same way I do. I'm used to seeing them together."

In a jolt of insight suddenly Gina knew where this was going, and her heart hurt for this man she'd left.

"You together with Daniel," he went on, "that's different. When he looks up at you and laughs, when he puts his little hands on your face, whenever you hold him, I think about Amy and the way this should have been."

"Logan, I can bow out of your life. I can have one of my therapists work with Daniel and you won't ever have to see me."

Already Logan was shaking his head. "That's the thing, Gina. If we do that, nothing's resolved. Do you understand?"

Oh, she understood. She'd returned to Sagebrush to resolve something in her life, something that had to do with Logan. "Maybe what happened between us and what happened afterward will never be resolved."

She touched his arm, her fingertips aware of the strong sinew of his muscles, strength in Logan that he also used as a defense mechanism. "You miss Daniel's mother. I do understand that. You not only miss her, but you miss the life you would have had together…you *should* have had together. Nothing I can say will change that."

In the silence, Gina could hear Daniel's little sighing noises as he slept. He was becoming dear to her, maybe too dear. Maybe in trying to reconcile the past with Logan, she was setting herself up for another world of hurt.

Releasing Logan's arm, she wasn't sure what to do. She sensed he'd said everything he was going to say.

Maybe they'd had enough of talking and they were both better off if they kept a lid on the emotions they considered private and too painful to share.

She unfastened her seat belt. "I'd better go in. You have to get home and put Daniel to bed."

He didn't protest or argue, and she knew she was right. Daniel's next appointment was scheduled for tomorrow evening. "If you want me to find another therapist for him, just let me know."

"I'd walk you to the door, but I don't want to leave Daniel alone in the car."

"I know. I don't have far to go," she said lightly, hoping Logan would at least look at her.

"I'll wait until you're inside." He did glance at her then. It was only a glance. She understood why he didn't make eye contact. If he looked at her, they'd both feel more than they already did—more regret, more sadness, more uncertainty about the future.

She opened the car door and climbed out. When she closed it, she felt as if she were shutting the door on a chapter in her life. She looked over her shoulder, wishing she could give Daniel a kiss, wishing she and Logan could wipe the slate clean.

With her heart hurting, she hurried up the walk to the Victorian, unlocked the door and stepped inside. As the door clicked shut, she heard Logan backing out of the driveway.

Raina called, "How was the carnival?"

Gina had left a note on the refrigerator so her housemate would know where she was. When she walked into the living room, Raina took one look at her and from the easy chair used the remote to turn off the TV. "What's wrong?"

Gina shook her head and dropped down onto the sofa. "It can't be so obvious."

"You sat in the driveway for a long time, so either you were making out or having an intense discussion."

"We could have just been talking about the weather," Gina tried to joke.

"When I was married, Gina, my husband and I had a few of those in-the-driveway talks and make-out sessions. Young love was wonderful—all highs and lows and not much room for anything in between."

"I remember," Gina said solemnly. "I made the biggest mistake of my life when I left and turned my back on Logan."

"Why didn't you return to Sagebrush sooner?" Raina asked, reaching for a hair band on the end table, sliding it into her hair.

Gina knew it was time that she started letting go of the past, too. A part of her letting-go process had to be talking about it.

"When I left Logan, I told myself I was doing the best thing for both of us. I tried to forget about him and throw myself into my studies and into college life in general. About two months into the semester—"

She revealed to Raina what had happened to her at that frat party.

As soon as she was finished talking, Raina came over to her and gave her a hug. Sitting beside her on the sofa, she said, "I'm so sorry that happened to you."

"I told Logan about it today. I wanted him to know why when he called, I couldn't talk to him, why I couldn't make contact afterward. I've never talked to anyone about it but my counselor. Now you and Logan in the same night."

"I'm glad you confided in me."

"We haven't known each other long, but I feel I can trust you."

"I feel the same way," Raina agreed. "I couldn't have moved in with just anyone." She patted Gina's hand. "How did you and Logan leave it tonight? What was the discussion about?"

"It was about everything, although a lot went unsaid. Do you know what I mean?"

"Oh, yeah. I know exactly what you mean."

"I think Logan believed he was ready to move on with his life. But when he sees me with Daniel, he misses his wife."

"I don't doubt that. But there's got to be a reason he also wants to spend some time with you. If everything he felt for you was in the past, he wouldn't feel the need to be with you now."

Gina could only hope that was true, because she was falling for Logan all over again. This time, the fall could be even more devastating than the last time.

The knock on Logan's home-office door was a welcome intrusion. He'd been distracted for the past week and not very productive in whatever he'd tried to accomplish.

"Come in."

Hannah did and asked, "Got a few minutes?"

Logan checked his watch and the video monitor on his desk where he could see Daniel sleeping. "Shouldn't you be hand-deep into a bowl of popcorn, watching your favorite detective show?"

Hannah smiled broadly. "I will be in about ten minutes. I just wondered if you're going to make an appointment with Gina this week."

Logan's back stiffened and he told himself not to be defensive. Yet he was. He'd canceled this week's appointment, knowing it *wasn't* the best thing to do. But he'd needed some time to think. "I'm not sure yet, why?"

"Because he misses her and because I think he's right on the verge of walking. She might be the motivation he needs."

"*We* aren't enough?"

"Apparently not, or he'd be walking by now, don't you think? Logan, I don't know what happened between you and Gina, but don't let Daniel suffer for it."

"It's one session," he muttered.

"One session right now could make a difference. Besides that, he needs another woman in his life, one who cares about him as much as Gina does."

"And just how do you know she does?"

"Don't play games with me. I can see it whenever she's with him, and she cares about *you,* too."

"Hannah—"

"I know. I should stay out of your personal life." She glared at him. "Not that you really have one. Don't you think Amy would be glad if you found someone to look after you and Daniel?"

"*You* do that."

Hannah just rolled her eyes and shook her head. "You need more than work and you need more than Daniel, whether you'll admit it or not."

Logan leaned back in his chair and studied his housekeeper/nanny. "So your reason for interrupting me tonight is…"

"Make an appointment for Daniel and keep it. Or better yet, make a date with Gina and keep it."

"You're overstepping," he grumbled.

"No, I'm not. I've been with you long enough to express my opinion."

When he didn't respond, she came toward his desk, put her hands on it and leaned forward toward him. "You need to start living your life again, Logan. There's no point being here if you're just going through the motions." Then she straightened, smiled, said, "You know where I'll be if you need me," and left his office.

Logan stood and paced across the room. He went to the back window and stared at the outside floodlights illuminating the pool area. So much…and so little.

After a few moments, he shifted his gaze again to the monitor on his desk where he could see Daniel. His son appeared to be so peaceful, so caught up in baby dreams.

Dreams. Logan had told Gina he didn't have them anymore. Should he dream, or should he just take what came, day by day?

Gina had dropped into his life on one of those days and she'd shaken up his universe. Denying his attraction to her was absolutely useless, especially when it seemed to be mutual.

What could come of it?

Didn't they both deserve the chance to find out?

He checked his watch again. Ten-thirty. Too late or not too late?

Again he studied his sleeping son, then he picked up the phone on his desk. It rang three times and he was almost ready to hang up when Gina answered. "Hello?"

"It's Logan."

"I know. Caller ID."

"Right." There was an awkward pause and he knew

he had to be the one to fill it. "I shouldn't have canceled Daniel's appointment."

"I see," she said slowly. "You want to schedule another one now?"

He had to smile. "Yes…and no."

"I have my appointment book downstairs." Her voice was still filled with puzzlement.

"Gina, I called because I'd like you to spend some time with me on Saturday. I thought Hannah could pack a picnic lunch and we could take it to the lake. I still have a rowboat and…" He felt at a total loss for words. "And there's a family of baby ducklings you might want to watch."

She laughed. "Baby ducklings."

He swore. "I'm not doing this very well. I'd like to spend some time with you, just you and me. What do you think?"

Her answer seemed forever in coming, but finally she answered him. "I'd like that. What time should I come over?"

"Around noon."

"I'll see you then."

When Logan hung up the phone, he wasn't sure if he'd done the right thing. He'd find out on Saturday.

Chapter Eight

Logan balanced on his feet in the rowboat beside the cooler, holding his hand out to Gina, who was standing on the dock.

Gina thought he looked too tall for the rowboat. Too muscled, too broad-shouldered, too ruggedly ready for rowing. This was a different boat from the one they'd taken out on the lake fourteen years ago. Thank goodness. As it was, a memory of the night they'd kissed under a full moon while floating in the middle of the water slid before her eyes as if it had happened yesterday. Was Logan remembering, too?

Since she'd arrived, his expression had been unreadable. She wasn't sure exactly how to act or what to think. Was this a *date?*

When she stepped down into the boat, Logan held her hand a little longer than he had to. The warmth around her fingers made her feel safe, though the boat teetered a little.

"Do you want to have lunch on the lake, or should we just row for a while?"

"Let's just row. We have the cooler. If we get hungry, we can eat." She didn't know whether to sit beside Logan or across from him. Across from him, she could see his eyes and look at his face. Maybe at that vantage point, she could interpret glimmers of what he felt.

Logan settled himself with the oars and began rowing.

"Do you want me to help?"

"I'm good. I've been coming out and rowing around the lake for exercise. It helps work off frustration." As soon as the words came out, he looked sorry he'd said them.

"Frustration from work? Or frustration from having me back in your life?"

He grinned ruefully. "You always did see too much."

"I don't think I saw enough. I'm only four years younger than you, but back then, those four years meant a lot. I hadn't broken my ties with my parents yet, definitely not with my family."

"I didn't know about the kind of ties you had with your parents," he said. "After my mother died, my father really started earning his fortune. He was never home. We lost a lot of years until he was interested in me because I was growing up and could be groomed to take over the business."

She heard his father's voice echo again. *If he marries you, I'll disinherit him.*

"Did you *want* to take over the business?"

"I don't think I ever thought about it. To me it was expected. On the other hand, it did interest me. I knew the business here could lead to a wider range of opportunities. I've invested in condos in Sydney, a winery in the Loire Valley, and I even have an interest in a high-rise in Hong Kong. Not that I'm trying to impress you," he said with a grimace. "I'm just saying my father didn't have the curiosity I do for the world at large."

Would Logan have developed those interests if she hadn't left? Did she want to tackle that subject, too? Maybe in a roundabout way. "How do you feel about the rest now that you have Daniel?"

He continued rowing slowly, his Stetson shading his face so she really couldn't see his eyes.

"Now my world revolves around Daniel," Logan responded. "That means when I'm working, I think about leaving him a legacy like my father left me. It means I make time away from work to be with him. It means nothing is more important than *his* welfare."

"You can't give him a perfect world," she warned.

"No, but I can do my best to make sure it is in every way possible."

Suddenly Logan stopped rowing. He was looking over her shoulder and he patted the seat next to him. "Come here."

She wasn't sure what he wanted her to see, but she gingerly managed to step over the cooler to sit beside him on his seat.

He pointed to the edge of the lake under the willows and she had to smile.

"Ducklings!" There were five of them all swimming after their mama. "You weren't kidding," she said, laughing again.

"No, I wasn't." The gravel in his voice turned her head toward him and their gazes locked.

In that moment, everything he'd been through and

everything she'd been through fell into the background of their lives. She was close enough to him that she could feel the restrained desire in his body, the kiss that was brewing in his thoughts. If he kissed her again, what would it mean? More than the fact that he was still attracted to her?

"The last time I kissed you, afterward you said a kiss has to mean something. I understand that better now. So I have to ask how you feel…about being close to a man. Being intimate."

She took a deep breath, stared at the diamond sparkles on the water and considered his question carefully.

"Gina?"

When she looked at him, she wanted to tell him desire was a good thing. It was healthy. She'd felt it once more when he'd kissed her. But it was a complicated issue. "I can't give you a simple answer to that. I had counseling, Logan. Yet, faced with a man's desire, that's a different thing than talking about it, analyzing it or even wishing for it. I've dated since the rape. I've been kissed and I didn't panick. But I don't know how much I was there for it, either. I didn't respond very well and I guess that's why the relationships didn't go any further. Maybe I just wouldn't let them."

He was studying her, trying to figure out what was behind the quiver in her voice, the emotions she still kept in check. "What do you mean, you weren't *there?*"

"Do you know what dissociation is?"

"I've heard the term, but tell me what it means for you."

"When he started violating me, I went away in my mind. He was strong and big and I couldn't escape, at least not physically. But I disappeared mentally and emotionally. I closed down because I didn't want to feel anything that was happening."

"Gina," Logan murmured, his voice filled with tenderness as he took her hands.

"It took a couple of years to let myself feel in the moment because afterward I filtered everything, everybody. I just wanted to be alone and study and focus on the print in a textbook because there wasn't any danger there. I kept my apartment door dead-bolted and chainlocked. I had a can of mace in my purse and kept it under my pillow. When the counseling began to have some effect, I became more proactive. I took several self-defense courses and then finally I started getting 'me' back. I found my people-radar was darn good and I had absolutely nothing to fear from children. They were honest and innocent and responded to love. I could totally be there for them. They didn't question motives or agenda. I just wanted to help them develop into healthy adults."

She felt unsettled by everything that had poured out. "That's more information than you wanted to know, I guess."

He squeezed her hands and his thumbs moved over her palms in soothing circles. "It's hard to hear. But I want to know, Gina."

"I think that's enough for now," she said with a small laugh, wanting to cut the tension that had coiled around them.

"You were *here* during our kiss, unless I'm totally off the mark."

"Yes, I was. I don't know if it was because the kiss was a surprise or because of what we once had, or because I'm not afraid of you."

"I hope that's the reason," he said with heartfelt sincerity.

"I haven't talked about this with anyone because I don't want them to walk on eggshells around me. I don't want *you* to walk on eggshells."

"I suppose all we can do is be honest with each other." He brushed a tendril of hair from her cheek and she wanted to curl into him, lie against his chest, feel his strong arms around her. But that might never happen for lots of reasons. Today, the most she could hope for, was that they would finally begin to reestablish a real friendship again.

Beside Logan now, she helped him row to the other side of the lake. There was no dock there so they paddled as fast as they could into the shore and pushed with the oars to find a secure mooring. As they climbed out, mud squished around their feet. Gina's foot slipped and Logan caught her. His arm held her securely around the waist, and she reached to his shoulder for support. The willow branches seemed to stop swaying, the birdcalls faded, the sun's heat mingled with theirs.

"I don't know how to treat you," Logan said huskily.

"How do you want to treat me?"

He shook his head. "I'm not sure."

"Then we shouldn't do anything we'll regret," she decided reasonably, not feeling reasonable at all.

His gaze lingered on her lips, then his hands released her as he mumbled, "Right."

After he fetched the cooler, he carried it through some brush and over grass laced with tiny blue and white wildflowers. The quilt Logan had brought for the occasion looked brand-new.

"We'll get it dirty," Gina protested as he spread it over the grass near a cottonwood.

"Hannah says it will wash. I use it on the ground for Daniel when I take him outside."

"Do you do that much?"

"Not enough. I've had too many conference calls lately. This week I've been discussing foundation work with the governor."

"You're trying to find more funding?"

"That and we're planning activities that go state-wide—coordinated walk-a-thons, bike races, that kind of thing."

As they lowered themselves to the quilt, she and Logan settled their backs against the same tree trunk.

"I've been thinking about the day-care center," Gina said.

Logan seemed to be relieved at that subject. "What about it?"

When she didn't respond quickly, he opened the cooler and took out two wrapped sandwiches.

"Do you have a name yet?"

He shrugged. "I hadn't thought beyond getting it built. What's your suggestion?"

"How about the Amy Barnes Day-Care Center?"

His hand with the sandwiches stopped in midair.

"It's just a suggestion, Logan. I wasn't sure if it would be a good one or a bad one. How do you feel about it?" She knew "how do you feel" was a very different question than "what do you think?" Would she get either answer?

"I didn't consider that. Naming the center after her would be a tribute to her, wouldn't it…a tribute for what she did for Daniel."

"And you."

"Right. And me."

He laid one of the thick roast-turkey sandwiches in front of her on the quilt. "As Daniel grows older, he'd understand better what his mother did for him." Logan seemed to be warming to the thought. "Thank you, Gina, it really is a wonderful idea. I don't know why I didn't think of it."

Gina knew suggesting his wife's name had been the right thing to do. She also knew that the day-care center would be a huge reminder of the life Logan had shared with Amy.

She picked up her sandwich, unwrapped it and began to eat. But she had no appetite.

Later, as Logan drove back to the house, Gina sat quietly, staring out into the cotton fields.

"Are you up to a game of tennis?" he asked.

Her attention veered from the rows of green leaves to his profile as he drove.

"You don't have to entertain me, Logan. If you'd like to look in on Daniel, we can do that."

She'd always had the damnable habit of reading him too well. Amy had never even attempted to read his thoughts. She expected him just to tell her if he had something important to say.

Don't compare, he told himself sternly.

"I'd like to look in on Daniel," he said. "But tennis might be good afterward. I haven't had anyone challenge me in a while. Have you kept your game?"

He'd taught her how to play and she'd been good.

"I still play now and then, but I doubt if I'm as good as you are."

A recognizable tune played somewhere in Gina's

vicinity. She said, "Sorry," and dug in her purse. She brought out her cell phone and checked the caller ID. "It's my mom. I'd better take this."

Logan knew Gina's family came first. She'd proven that. When he glanced at her, their gazes held, and he suspected she knew what he was thinking once again.

Her cheeks became a little brighter as she answered. "Hi, Mom. What's up?" There was a pause. "Sure I'll be there tomorrow. I wouldn't miss Josie's birthday… I can pick up the balloons. Okay, I'll see you tomorrow."

Gina closed her phone.

"A birthday party?" he asked.

"My older sister's. My mom wanted to make sure I'd be there."

"You're not as close to your family as you once were."

"It was hard to stay connected when I was so far away."

"But now you're back." After a pause, he added, "Maybe you should tell them what happened."

"I can't do that!" The idea really seemed to horrify her.

"Why?"

She sighed. "I think my parents are still fairly naive. They were sending me to a good college where I'd study hard and find a brilliant future. They would never even imagine something like that could happen there."

"But it did. Don't you think your mom and dad have worried about the changes they see in you?"

"I always acted perfectly normal when I called, and it was almost a year afterward until I came home for a visit. They didn't suspect anything."

"Oh, I'm sure they *did*. They just couldn't put their finger on what it was. Even my father, as remote as he was sometimes, could read me better than I liked."

"Tell me what happened after he recovered."

He knew what Gina was doing—switching the focus from her to him. "I'd taken a semester off to help with his rehabilitation. At the start of the new year, he insisted I go back and get my MBA. He had a valet who was with him twenty-four hours a day. He also had a physical therapist and a nurse when necessary. I knew he was well taken care of so I got my MBA at Texas Tech instead of going back to Texas A&M. I was around as much as he wanted me to be around. Since I'd taken over most of his business dealings during those first few months, I kept my hand in. After I earned my degree, I started some ventures of my own. He didn't approve of condos in Sydney or even of the golf courses in Arizona. But I wanted to build, and I felt I had the foundation to do it. After a while, he stopped protesting. He had some memory problems after the stroke. Because of the weakness on his left side, he'd stopped riding and hated that. He hated having someone help him do anything."

"He died five years ago?"

"Yes. A year after I married Amy."

"Did he like your wife?"

"He adored Amy. He'd known her father and—" As soon as Logan said it, he knew he shouldn't have. "Gina, I didn't mean—"

"It's okay, Logan. Your father knew the kind of woman he wanted you to marry."

"I didn't ask Amy to marry me because of my father."

"I wasn't insinuating you did."

"You were insinuating I chose from the right crowd."

"Logan, I was not. You chose the woman you loved. Your father happened to approve. That was good."

Logan knew he shouldn't have sounded so touchy

about it, and why was he? He had married the woman he wanted. But deep down, he'd known his dad had disapproved of his involvement with Gina. Had he suspected that was one of the reasons she'd broken off her relationship with him?

The stifling silence was only broken by the sound of the tires on the gravel lane as Logan wended his way toward the house.

Ten minutes later, Logan found Hannah and his son playing in the sunroom.

"I thought he could use some fresh air," his nanny explained, motioning to the sliding doors that pushed open to reveal long screens. The windows were all open, too, giving the feeling of being outdoors.

As soon as Daniel saw Logan, he waved, and said, "Da da da da," then jumped up and down in his play saucer. Logan felt deep abiding happiness make his chest swell. He picked up Daniel, kissed him on the cheek, and tucked him into the crook of his arm.

"Did you miss me, buddy?"

Daniel babbled something Logan took as a definite yes. "I missed you, too. Gina wanted to come say hello. We came to play with you for a while. What would you like to do?"

Daniel pointed to the big exercise ball that Gina often used with him. "Baw," he said.

"Good choice." Gina captured the ball and sat on the floor with it as Logan brought Daniel to her.

Instead of going for the ball, Daniel crawled straight to her, saying, "Gee, gee, gee," and climbed into her lap.

When Gina hugged him close, Logan's heart ached. How could he feel so many things at once—Amy's absence, regrets about Gina, worry that Daniel had bonded with Gina, the intensity of his attraction to her?

He took off his Stetson and tossed it onto a side table. Then he lowered himself to the floor to enjoy playtime with his son.

Gina knew Daniel's attention span and switched from one activity to the next before he got cranky. They were playing with blocks on top of a step stool when Hannah brought in a snack for Daniel, bites of banana on a dish. "Look what I have for you," Hannah said, setting the dish on the wicker table.

Daniel didn't seem interested. He was too busy watching Gina build a tower.

Logan was engaged in building a bridge, hoping his son would help him. His hip was lodged against Gina's. Once in a while, their arms brushed. Leaning this close to her felt unsettling as well as exciting. Sitting like this, playing with Daniel, felt simply…nice.

Gina added a blue block to Logan's all-orange structure. "You need some variety," she teased.

He stared at her tower. "This from a woman whose building wobbles with every new floor."

They both laughed.

Daniel, suddenly interested in the dish of fruit, crawled over to it on his knees. Unable to quite reach the top of the table, he pulled himself up to stand and snacked on a bite of banana.

"The blocks will stay together now," Logan warned her. "They'll have sticky fruit between them."

"Oh, look." Gina pointed to a prairie dog who had just run between the bushes near the side of the room.

"Daniel, look there," Logan directed.

The little boy turned, saw the animal, planted his legs

wide apart and took three toddling steps away from the table toward it.

Logan's gaze went to Gina's, both of them realizing what had just happened.

Gina quickly held out her hands to Daniel.

"Come here, honey. Let's go over to the window and see if we can find him."

His toes pointed out, Daniel shakily walked the three steps it took to put his hand in Gina's. When he did, she squeezed him tight. "Oh, you wonderful little boy! Do you know what you just did?"

Logan clapped, then hugged his son.

"You walked six whole steps, six whole steps. That was terrific! Can you do it again?"

Propping himself at the chair next to Gina, Daniel looked uncertain for a long while. Logan just waited with his hands held out. "Come on, buddy. I know you can do this. I'll catch you. Come on."

After a look at Gina, a glance at where the prairie dog had vanished, then a look at his father, Daniel grinned and took three lurching steps toward his dad, who caught him and swung him up, laughing, so grateful his son was walking.

"What's all the commotion?" Hannah asked, coming in.

"Daniel *walked*. About nine whole steps."

Hannah clapped and made a fuss for a while. Finally she said, "You know what? Those first steps deserve a scoop of ice cream. Want to come with me to get it?"

Apparently Daniel knew those words because he bobbed his head and held his arms out to Hannah. She scooped him up and said, "We won't be long."

When Hannah left, Logan grinned at Gina and pulled her into his arms for a hug. "Thank you."

She leaned away from him. "I didn't do much. I just encouraged his natural tendencies."

Logan felt more elated than he had since Daniel had come home from the hospital, and *his* natural tendencies were telling him exactly what he wanted to do. He lowered his head to Gina's and began what was supposed to be a quick, simple, thank-you kiss. But as his lips settled on hers and the warmth of their compression burst into heat, the kiss became more than a simple thank-you. He didn't want to go too fast. He knew he couldn't push too hard. Would she even react or respond?

That question was a moot point as her arms wrapped around his neck. When she pressed closer to him, she proved to him she definitely *wanted* to respond. He remembered what she'd said, and he wanted her to be *here* for him, *here* for them. He gave her time to think about what they were doing by nibbling at the corner of her mouth, tantalizingly licking her lower lip, pressing both of his lips to hers again. She laced her fingers in his hair and her fingertips started moving. He knew what that meant. She was becoming as excited as he was.

He knew that at any time he'd have to stop. He knew that at any time he might have to put the brakes on, forget about his need and acknowledge whatever she was feeling. Yet she didn't seem to want to stop. She opened her mouth to him and he accepted the invitation. When his tongue slid over hers, he heard her moan. When hers dashed around his, he groaned. They were in sync as they'd always been, giving and taking, reacting and responding, participating in a dance that had so many places to go.

Yet, when he reluctantly broke away, her lips clung to his. She gazed at him with undisguised passion—and more than a hint of confusion. After she took a deep breath, she caressed his face. "Well…where do we go from here? What did that mean, Logan?"

His stomach sank as his elation met reality. Because despite the desire he could no longer deny, he didn't have the faintest idea where they were headed.

Chapter Nine

Gina held her breath, hoping for the answer she wanted. Had the kiss meant forgiveness? Or something more?

Logan frowned. "What did it mean? Don't analyze everything to death, Gina. We were both happy about Daniel walking. It was an expression of gratitude. You helped him."

She couldn't let this go, not that easily. "So you would kiss anyone who helped him?"

"Don't be ridiculous." He was scowling and his stance was defensive.

"Then I don't think my question was so out of line. Why does it bother you? Because you don't want to think about what you're feeling?"

"You might have had lots of counseling, but I don't need it," he snapped. "Don't analyze me."

She took a step back from him, her fears confirmed. *That's what happens when you share your worst experience with someone. They could use it against you.*

Immediately he saw that he had hurt her and he reached out.

But she moved away. "Logan, I'm confused enough. I don't want you holding me and patting my head, or holding me and denying you feel anything."

"I'm not denying what I'm feeling. I'm attracted to you…and you're attracted to me."

"But does the attraction come from the past…or now? Is that confusing you as much as it's confusing me?"

"That kiss didn't seem confused, did it?" he asked in an I-don't-want-to-admit-this voice.

"No, it didn't. But it had little to do with Daniel walking."

Now he closed the distance between them and looked down at her with tenderness and maybe more. "I had a really good day today. How about you?"

It had had highs and lows, but at the end of it, they *were* still connected. "Yes, it was a good day and I especially liked the ducklings."

He chuckled. "I thought you might." He took her hand, drew it to his mouth and softly kissed her knuckles. His lips were warm and firm and seductively erotic.

Tingles streaked down her spine and she wanted to be in his arms again, longed to kiss him again. But neither of them knew what would happen if they went further. Logan didn't want to feel more. She was afraid she'd feel too much. They'd both be thinking about her last experience. How could they ever get over that hurdle?

They could if they loved each other.

Gina suddenly realized her love for Logan had never truly faded. When she'd left, she'd had to deny the depth of her pain. That pain had to be less important than what her parents wanted for her, what her sister needed and what she herself wanted to accomplish. It couldn't compare to the pain Logan would have felt had he known his father could disinherit him.

Nevertheless, her love for him had always been there. What would have happened if she'd run back to him after the rape? Would he have supported her, stood up against his dad or backed away? It simply didn't matter. But she knew now, she still loved him. She'd returned to Sagebrush to find out if she had to bury that love for good. What she was finding was that it was more alive than it had ever been.

He still held her hands as he said, "I want to issue a special invitation to you for the groundbreaking of the day-care center. Can you take an hour off on Monday when we dig the first shovelful? The ceremony is at four o'clock."

"I'll see if I can rearrange appointments and let you know."

He gently tugged her toward him and placed a kiss on top of her head. They stood that way a few seconds and then she pulled away.

"I really did have a good day," she assured him.

"Me, too. It was the first really good day in a long time. Thank you."

He looked as if he wanted to kiss her again. "I'd better go."

"You *could* spend the evening. We could play tennis and later watch a DVD with Daniel."

"Enough is enough for today," she said, not wanting

to go but deciding leaving was best for now. "I don't want to spoil the day by expecting too much."

He studied her face…brushed his thumb over her lips. "You're right. We should take this slowly whether it's friendship or attraction or whatever, not only for our sakes but for Daniel's."

His finger on her lips brought back the sensations from their kiss. Yet the mention of Daniel's name brought all of her focus to his little boy. She already loved Daniel. But if she told Logan that, she'd be moving way too fast.

He dropped his arm around her shoulders. "I'll walk you to the door."

He didn't stop at the door but went outside with her. The evening air was cool and Logan kept his arm around her the whole way to her car.

At her door, he tipped her chin up and kissed her again. It was a light kiss and carried feeling as well as that indefinable taste that Logan wanted more. That taste wouldn't go away until she saw him again. It wouldn't go away until it became hotter, bolder—until it became desire they were both ready for.

White, puffy clouds skittered across the blue sky as Gina stood in the group of onlookers at Barnes Denim, ready for the first shovel of dirt to be cast. The workers had come outside for the ceremony. Logan stood in a place of honor at the open field. Beside him, a pretty blonde talked animatedly to him.

Gina had heard one of the women in the crowd say, "That's Amy's sister. She came from Amarillo."

Logan settled a hand on the blonde's shoulder and gave it a squeeze, then he faced the crowd. Gina stood in the front row and he smiled at her. Then his focus shifted away.

He said to the group gathered, "As you know, I'm going to name our day-care center the Amy Barnes Day-Care Center in memory of my wife. I'd like her sister Maggie to say a few words."

Amy's sister stepped forward and smiled at everyone. "I just want to tell you how honored I am that Logan is doing this for Amy."

As Maggie spoke, Gina watched Logan's face. There was pain there, and an element of the grief he wouldn't express. The lines across his forehead, the tight set of his jaw, the tension in his stance told Gina this was difficult for him. She wished she could be beside him, but that was impossible. Especially today.

The late afternoon sun was hot, and Gina could feel prickles of perspiration wending their way down her back. She thought about Daniel and how Logan would shape the memory of his mother for him. Did Maggie visit often? Was she involved in Daniel's life?

After Maggie finished speaking, someone handed Logan a shovel and he dug a few heapfuls of ground from the earth. Then he thanked everyone for coming and guided Maggie toward Gina.

As they approached, Gina pasted on her I-can-handle-anything smile.

Logan introduced the two women and then said, "Gina helped Daniel learn to walk. She's a developmental specialist. I'm also using her as a consultant on the day-care center."

Daniel's specialist. A consultant. Gina wondered what other words he could use to describe her.

"I spent the evening with Daniel last night," Maggie

mentioned. "He's growing so fast. I wish I could come to Sagebrush more, but my work is so…sporadic."

"What do you do?" Gina asked.

"I write scripts for children's videos and TV shows. I'm usually on deadline and work late most nights when I'm in the middle of a project."

"That sounds like a great job, though," Gina said, meaning it.

"Oh, it is. I just wish my schedule weren't so crazy. It's either feast or famine. I drove in yesterday morning. I have to leave tomorrow morning. It's a short visit."

"We'll pack as much into it as we can," Logan assured her.

Maggie nodded. "Tonight I want to collect those videos of Amy you were talking about. I'll take them along and have everything digitized. It will be an important memento for Daniel when it's finished."

Gina could see this was going to be an evening for the two of them to remember Amy Barnes and everything she'd meant to both of them.

Logan said to Maggie, "Why don't you go over to the building and get out of the sun. I'll be there in a minute."

After a wave and a goodbye to Gina, Maggie walked away. Logan turned to Gina. "Thank you for coming today."

"I know this must be difficult for you."

"It's bittersweet. I'm glad you suggested naming the day-care center after my wife. It's a solid reminder of what she meant to me and Daniel. Are you going to come in to the social? Punch and cookies for everyone."

"No, I think I'll go now. I brought enough work home to last me all night."

"New clients?"

"Some. And financial projections for Baby Grows, too. I'm not keen on that, but it's part of the job."

Logan looked torn for a moment. "I'd ask you back to the house, but—"

"I understand, Logan. Really I do." She wanted to give him a hug, but didn't know if that would be appropriate here and now. Instead, she said, "Call me if you want to talk. If I don't hear from you, I'll see you at your place Friday at five for Daniel's appointment."

He studied her for a few moments and then nodded. "I'll talk to you later."

As Logan headed back to the factory and Gina went to find her car in the parking lot, she knew he wouldn't be calling.

On Wednesday evening, Gina was still in her office at Baby Grows when her cell phone rang. She picked it up automatically, not even looking at the caller ID. "Yes," she said absently, her mind on the file she was studying.

"Gina?"

Her attention snapped into focus. "Yes, Logan, it's me. Sorry, I was in the middle of something."

The silence between them vibrated with emotion and tension. She could still remember the pain on his face as Maggie had spoken of her sister.

He began, "I want to thank you again for coming to the groundbreaking."

"I wasn't so sure it was a good idea that I attended."

There was a long pause before he asked, "Because the ceremony was about Amy?"

"Because you didn't need your attention divided that day."

"It wasn't divided. Lots of people who were helping with the center were there. You were one of them."

"One of the crowd."

She could hear him swear under his breath. "That didn't come out right, Gina. I have a habit of making a muddle of things with you."

"You called to tell me that?" she teased kindly, wondering why he needed to talk to her. She'd be seeing him Friday night. Unless he was canceling.

"I thought we could do something different Friday night."

"With Daniel? Do you want to bring him to Baby Grows?"

"No, I'd like to take him swimming. I thought maybe you'd have some exercises in your repertoire we could do in the pool. Then afterward, maybe you and I could just swim."

Swimming with Logan. Sitting by the pool. Talking for hours. History repeating itself?

"I have to ask you something, Logan."

"I'm not going to like this question very much, am I?"

"Probably not. Do you want a diversion so you can stop thinking about Amy?"

The complete silence told her exactly what he thought of her question. But then she heard him blow out a breath. Finally, he admitted, "Maggie stirred up all kinds of memories when she was here, especially when we went through the videos. But at the end of all that, by the time I said goodbye to her, I realized naming the day-care center in Amy's honor was the end of something. She's gone. She's never coming back. The center will be the tangible proof of that. I need to see more for my future than what might have been. So, to answer your question, I don't want a diversion. I just want to go on and live my life."

"That's honest," she assured him, thinking he was taking a big step in moving on.

"I'm glad you think so because I don't know how to be anything else but honest with you."

She hadn't been completely honest with him—not where his father was concerned. What good would it do to reveal now what his father had threatened her with?

"So how about swimming?" he asked.

"Does Daniel like the water?"

"He's not particularly fond of getting his face wet."

"I know a few adults who have the same problem," she said with a laugh. "I'll bring a life vest along. I think I'd like to do a land routine with him first, then we'll just do a few exercises in the water."

"Sounds good. Do you think you might be in the mood for steaks on the grill? I can tell Hannah we'll handle our own supper."

"Steak sounds fine. Have you had much experience being a chef?"

"I'm better on the grill than I am in the kitchen. Remember my attempt to make beef stroganoff for you?"

"I remember that very well. You ended up with overdone beef tips, lumpy sauce, sticky noddles. But it tasted wonderful."

"I thought you just said that to be kind."

"No, it *did* taste good. It just wasn't four-star-restaurant presentable."

He chuckled. "I promise I'll do a better job with the steaks tomorrow night."

When Gina closed her phone a few minutes later, she

was smiling. Maybe she and Logan could become friends again…maybe so much more.

"I think we've tired him out."

Logan lifted Daniel from the water and went up the steps to the deck around the pool. He unfastened the Velcro of Daniel's life vest and Gina held a towel ready to wrap the toddler in. Daniel did love the water as long as it wasn't splashing his face. At her encouragement, he'd kicked his legs and arms and had fun with her and his dad.

Now, as she held him and patted him with the fluffy towel, he wrapped his arms around her neck and snuggled his cheek against her shoulder. A lump crowded her throat and for a few moments she dreamt of being his mother.

Then reality struck. He *had* a mother, and Logan wasn't going to forget her. And he shouldn't. But denying the longings in her own heart was impossible. They weren't going to go away.

As she sneaked a peek at Logan—he was toweling his hair—she knew she was falling deeper in love with him. She held Daniel a little tighter, rested her cheek against his wet hair, and wished for everything she'd wished for when she was eighteen…everything that hadn't had to do with college and a career and her family.

Hannah opened the sliding screen of the sunroom, walked across the patio and opened the gate that led into the pool. She brought a tray of hors d'oeuvres with her and set it on the table where Gina's and Logan's bottles of water sat with Daniel's sippy cup.

"Why don't I take this little guy inside, get him a bath and something to eat. You two can swim some more if you want. I'll bet you didn't get much of a chance while you were entertaining *him*."

"That's a good idea," Logan said with a thankful smile to his housekeeper. "Do you want to do some real swimming?" he asked Gina.

Now his gaze was on her bathing suit and her legs. Glad she'd bought a new one—a blue and green flowered maillot—she stood perfectly still, accepting his male appreciation, though she felt a little unsettled by it. For years she'd gone out of her way *not* to be noticed. But today, she liked Logan noticing. She liked the sparkle of hunger she saw in his eyes and his interest in her that she believed was more than friendly.

"Logan to Gina," he teased as he once might have during their summer together.

She quickly smiled. "I'm here."

"I can tell when you're thinking. Smoke puffs out of your ears."

She smacked his arm with a towel.

He caught the edge of it and pulled her toward him.

By this time, Hannah had taken Daniel inside and they were alone. Their gazes held.

Gina was amazingly aware of Logan's bare chest…the tawny hair arrowing down under the waistband of his wet swim trunks. Her heart beat even faster at the thought of being here with him.

"You look terrific in that suit. With your creamy white skin, you look like a princess who's never seen the sun."

"I never consider myself a princess."

"Even *I* remember Cinderella's story. She worked and slaved and then Prince Charming swept her away. The problem was you didn't want to be swept away."

Over the years, she'd had to learn how to express many

emotions that she'd kept hidden. She'd had to learn not to take the backseat, to realize her opinion was important.

She returned, "Modern-day Prince Charmings don't sweep women off their feet. They stand beside them and support them and whisper in their ear at night that they can do anything."

"That's the fairy tale now?" Logan asked with arched brows. "That's not nearly as romantic or life-changing."

"I'll bet it's more life-changing for the man than being swept off her feet ever was for a woman."

Leaning back to study her more thoroughly, he asked, "Are we going to have an argument about this?"

"Not if you agree."

Logan laughed out loud. He put his arm around her, towel and all, and led her to the edge of the pool.

With Logan's arm circling her, she felt protected and not at all afraid. She thought about the security system she'd had installed in every apartment she'd lived in. She hadn't even thought of having one installed at the Victorian.

She knew safety was an illusion. Alarms and locks and self-defense courses couldn't always keep a woman safe. Since her experience in college, she'd been hyper-vigilant, waking up several times during the night just to make sure everything was quiet, and no one was trying to break in. Relaxation exercises helped her fall asleep, but staying asleep—

Yet here with Logan, she felt as if she could let that vigilance slip. She could relax. How crazy was that?

Because you're still in love with him, that tiny voice in her head told her.

And all of a sudden, his arm around her changed from comforting to exciting. As she turned into his chest—

But before the thought could become action, he started down the pool steps and took her towel from around her shoulders, tossing it onto the terra-cotta pavers. The look he gave her now was long and appreciative, and she felt her cheeks getting hot.

"Sorry," he apologized. "I didn't mean to make you feel uncomfortable. But you do look beautiful."

She tried to treat his compliment lightly. Running her fingers through her damp hair, she asked, "Even all wet?"

"Especially all wet."

Her mouth went dry and it was hard to swallow.

"Do compliments like that bother you?"

Now she said something that seemed bold to her. "Not coming from you."

The expression in his eyes changed in the evening light and she realized those green depths were reflecting the passion in her own gaze.

How would she react if he gave in to it? Was she ready for that step? Was *he?*

He took her hand and drew her into the water. "Thoughts are going through your mind at the speed of light."

"More smoke coming out of my ears?" she joked.

"No." He reached out and brushed a finger over her forehead. "But there's a crease here." He touched each corner of her mouth. "And little lines here. I know those lines. They mean you're analyzing. What are you debating so vigorously?"

The water was above their waists now, and she realized she had nothing to lose by being honest. "I'm trying to decide if you're afraid to let an attraction between us go anywhere."

"I don't think *afraid* is the word. Besides a history, we both have baggage. I'm concerned."

"I won't tell you not to be concerned. But that concern won't go away if we act like best friends rather than—"

"Rather than lovers?" he finished, looking at her with an intensity that made every nerve ending tingle. He circled her waist and brought her closer. "Does being close to me like this, without much between us, make you nervous?"

"No," she assured him with all the certainty in her heart, believing all the tingling in her body had to do with arousal, not anxiety.

As he bent his head, she lifted her chin. His lips met hers without hesitation and she was glad of that. Her fingers went to the back of his head and she relished the feel of his hair, the crisp strands, thick and damp under her fingertips. He groaned and his tongue slid into her mouth. She was ready for the intimate play, the chase and retreat, the exploration. She welcomed it and responded to it. Her body sought Logan's like a ship searching for its harbor. Pressed together as they were, she felt his arousal, had one flutter of panic that went up in flames as their passion turned hotter.

Logan's hands caressed her back, slid to her backside, and then gently urged her to wrap her legs around him. When she did, he pushed against her at just the right spot. He kept up the rocking motion until she exploded in his arms. Their lips clung together and the sounds in her throat told Logan of her pleasure. He held her even tighter.

When her body stopped trembling, she whispered into his neck, "Why did you do that? Why did you stop before—"

"I wanted to give you a gift. I wanted to give you

pleasure that had no price tag, no reason to be other than to make you feel good."

She leaned back so she could gaze into his eyes. "What about you?"

"This wasn't about me, Gina. It was about us finding a new direction, searching through the rubble of years ago to find something good."

"Do you think we found it?"

He shook his head and she saw the doubts in his eyes when he said, "I'm not sure. I have to ask you something."

"What?"

She ran through at least ten questions before he asked, "Are you going to stay in Sagebrush?"

That wasn't one she expected. When she didn't answer right away, he let her legs slip down and took a step back from her. "The fact that you can't give me an unqualified 'yes' means you might leave again. You've been hopping around from one place to the next, moving every three or four years. Why?"

She'd faced that question herself before she'd returned to her hometown. "Because I didn't feel safe… because I didn't feel settled. Because I wasn't exactly sure what I should be doing to feel…fulfilled."

"You were always searching for something better." The fact that she'd wanted "better" didn't sound like a compliment.

"Even all those years ago, I was searching for where I belonged. I was hoping when I came home to Sagebrush, I'd feel at home. But life isn't that simple."

"So you're going to move again?"

"I didn't say that."

He sighed and ran his hand over his jaw. "Gina, let's

just say we decided to become involved again. I'm an adult. I know fate strikes blows. I know irreconcilable differences happen and relationships break apart. But Daniel is just a little boy who knows he likes you. He's attaching to you. I don't want him to get hurt. If you decide someplace else will make you more fulfilled...where will that leave him?"

How could she tell him this was all about the two of them and what they worked at and built together? *That* was what would keep her in Sagebrush. *That* was what would make the difference. But Logan wasn't ready to commit to anything. She knew he wasn't just using Daniel as an excuse. His adorable little boy was part of this equation, too. Yet Gina wondered—

She put her thought into words. "Do you want an excuse to hold back...not to try this at all?"

"I don't know," he responded hoarsely. "Maybe I *am* looking for a reason not to get in too deep. Do you blame me?"

No, she couldn't blame him because she had left once before. They should have had this conversation before she'd felt the wonder of intimacy with him again.

He must have seen the regret on her face because he said, "I was going to ask you to help me put Daniel to bed tonight. But maybe it's better if you don't."

"Maybe it's better if I don't," she agreed, heading for the steps and her towel and a life in Sagebrush that possibly didn't include Logan.

Chapter Ten

Gina's heart went out to Lily two weeks later as they sat in the living room of the Victorian. "I'm surprised you came over tonight."

Lily was obviously attempting to keep her spirits up, though it seemed to be tough. "Troy's deployment ceremony is Tuesday. He'll be gone for training, and then he'll be in Afghanistan for a year." She sighed. "I can't think about it. I'm simply going to concentrate on this weekend."

Thunder grumbled outside as a storm moved across Sagebrush. Gina and her friends were waiting until it passed to enjoy their movie night.

In response to Gina's original comment, Lily said, "He had some furniture he wanted to finish in his workshop tonight. But I think he needed a few hours for himself."

Gina knew Troy was a general contractor and did

woodworking as a hobby. The couple had only been married a year and were still settling into married life.

Raina moved from the easy chair to join Lily and Gina on the sofa. "I have a feeling you're going to be celebrating the Fourth of July weekend with fireworks of your own," she teased Lily.

Lily blushed and was about to retort when the phone rang. Raina plucked it up from the side table. "It could be my mother—her regular Saturday night check-in."

Lily remarked wistfully, "It must be nice to have family."

Lily had no family except for Troy. Gina felt compelled to say, "You can call me or Raina whenever you need somebody to talk to."

Raina handed the phone to Gina, her brows drawing together. "It's Hannah Mahoney."

Gina's panic button screamed a warning as she took the phone and put it to her ear. "Hannah?"

"Gina, I know this is Fourth of July weekend and you're probably busy, but Logan's away and Daniel's scared of the thunder. He's calling your name."

"He's saying my name?" He'd started saying "Gee, gee, gee, gee" whenever she was around.

"It seems like it to me. He misses his dad. He's calling for him, too."

"Logan's away?"

"Since Thursday night. He's in Seattle on business, but that's hard to explain to a fifteen-month-old. It's even harder to explain why he hasn't seen *you* for two weeks."

It sounded as if Hannah wanted an explanation, too. "Daniel is doing well on his own now. Dr. Rossi can give him regular assessments and can also recommend a parent group to Logan if he feels like attending."

"Uh-oh. You two had a fight."

Gina remained silent. Sometimes she felt as if Hannah was trying in subtle ways to play matchmaker. She could hear Hannah sigh as Daniel's crying rose in volume. His nanny must have taken the phone over to his crib.

"Well?" Hannah asked when she came back on. "Are you going to come over here and give me a hand? I don't want him to make himself sick."

Gina didn't want that, either. "All right. I'll be there in ten minutes." She settled the phone back on its console and found Raina and Lily watching her expectantly.

"Daniel's crying. Hannah said he's calling for me. Logan's away and she thinks I can help."

"Sounds reasonable to me," Lily said with a shrug. "Kids want what they want when they want it. Maybe all you have to do is hold him for a little while and he'll fall asleep."

Raina's response was a little more tempered. "Daniel will have to get used to not seeing you if you're stopping his sessions."

"I know, but—"

She didn't have to say more because Raina finished for her. "But you've grown attached to him. So go save the day."

Lily assured her, "I'll leave the DVD and you can watch it tomorrow if you'd like."

"I might be back before you're gone."

Shaking her head, Raina said, "I wouldn't count on it. With kids, the unexpected always happens."

Knowing that was true, Gina grabbed a light jacket from the living-room closet to wear over her navy shorts and navy-and-white striped knit top in case she got caught in the rain. After she waved to her friends, she grabbed her purse from the foyer table. "See you later."

"Later," Raina and Lily called in unison.

Gina liked the fact that she had friends who cared about where she was going, where she'd be and when she'd return. She hadn't let anyone get as close as Raina and Lily in many years. Maybe one day soon, she'd confide in Lily the way she'd confided in Raina.

The windshield wipers struggled to keep up with the sudden downpour. Thunder rolled ominously in the distance. She wasn't surprised that it had spooked Daniel. Most kids were afraid of loud bangs, especially at night. She wondered how many business trips Logan took in a year. Maybe as Daniel grew older, he'd take more. Yet Logan was the type of parent who'd want to stay close to his son. A child needed a committed parent, even when they were older. And even then, with a parent's guidance, a son or daughter could make the wrong decisions.

Like your wrong decision? her conscience asked her.

Precisely like that, Gina thought. A teenager might not yet be able to sort out what would make her happy, to sort out her inner voice from all of the voices outside of herself. But Gina wasn't that teenager anymore. She knew what her heart needed.

At the estate, Gina parked at the top of the circle near the front walk. She was going to get wet. She dashed up the stairs to the house and didn't even have to ring the bell. Hannah was there waiting to let her in, holding Daniel, who was red-faced and still crying.

She shook her head as Gina stepped over the threshold. "I know he's heard thunder before, but it never affected him like this."

"Has Logan ever been gone during a storm?"

"That's a good question. This is his first trip in a while, so I suppose not."

Daniel was already leaning over Hannah's arm toward Gina, reaching for her.

"See, I told you he wants you."

As if on cue, Daniel said, "Gee…gee, gee, gee."

Smiling, feeling her heart warm, Gina held the baby close, running her hand over his sweat-dampened hair. His little body was hot from all the pent-up emotion, all the words he couldn't yet say, all the feelings he tried to express with tears and gurgles and the kick of his legs.

She rocked him back and forth and murmured, "You're fine, big boy, just fine. You're safe here and no one's going to hurt you." His tears slowed as he cuddled close to her and expressed a baby sigh of ease.

"Well, look at that," Hannah said, hands on hips. "You'd think I hadn't been taking care of him since before he was born."

"You know it's not you, don't you? He just needed something different tonight, I guess."

"He missed you, and no matter what Logan says, I know it's so."

No matter what Logan says. Apparently they'd discussed it. "Do you think it would be all right if I take him to his room, change him into another set of pj's and wash him up a little?"

"I think you could do anything you want with him," Hannah joked. "While you're doing that, I'll fetch him some milk, then maybe you can rock him to sleep. I'm sorry I called you out like this, but he was just so unhappy."

"This reaction of his worries me, although I imagine if Logan were here this wouldn't have happened."

"Maybe," Hannah said, not sounding sure about that at all. "Pretty soon he'll be able to get your whole name out and Logan will see for sure he wants *you*."

A half hour later, Gina had washed and freshly dressed Daniel for bed. She was sitting in the rocker in his room, holding him and his bottle. He'd fallen asleep while drinking and she couldn't bear to put him down in his crib.

"What are you doing here?"

Gina jumped, startled when she heard Logan's voice. The reflexive action wakened Daniel and he started to cry. She cooed to him, and when he looked into her eyes, his tears stopped. He reached for her, winding his little arms around her neck. She wasn't going to pull away from him because Logan was watching. She was going to give this baby the comfort he needed.

Patting his back, she murmured, "It's okay. There's no more thunder."

Logan crossed to her and crouched down, eager to take his son from her arms. He'd left his tie somewhere and the top buttons of his shirt were open. It was wrinkled and he looked tired...even more tired when Daniel turned away from him, holding on more tightly to Gina.

Daniel mumbled, "Gee," and wouldn't let go.

"What's going on, Gina? Where's Hannah?"

Suddenly Gina was annoyed with his attitude. It wasn't as if she'd planned this. It wasn't as if—

"Hannah's in her room. I told her I'd buzz her after Daniel fell asleep. I didn't come here to steal the silver, Logan. She called me because Daniel was crying, and she couldn't get him quieted. Apparently the thunder scared him. She insisted he was calling my name."

Logan raked his hand through his hair. "I don't get why he'd call your name. It's not as if you—"

"It's not as if I take care of him every day, feed him, bathe him, put him to bed. No, I don't do those things. But over the past weeks, he and I have developed a rapport. He knows he can trust me, even though he doesn't like some of the things I ask him to do. He knows I…I love him."

Their gazes locked and neither of them could turn away. Gina wished she hadn't divulged what she had, but it was the truth. Logan was very big on the truth. What would he say if she said she still loved *him?*

She wasn't going to go there. She couldn't.

Finally, he tore his gaze away and stood, still studying his son as if he didn't understand what had happened.

"I don't think Hannah expected you home tonight, did she?" Gina asked.

"No. I told her I'd be home tomorrow or the next day. I kept thinking about Daniel, this being my first trip away from him for a while. When I called, Hannah said everything was fine."

"It was, until the storm hit."

"Do you want me to take him? I mean, I know you have to get home."

"I'm my own person now, Logan. Raina knows where I am. But if you don't want me here, I can leave."

He looked torn between what was best for his son and what was best for him. Finally he suggested, "When he falls asleep, lay him in his crib. I'll take over from there. I have to take a shower. I've been in meetings for the past forty-eight hours, then storms delayed us in Chicago."

Again he studied her with Daniel, but his gaze lingered on her face. She saw those sparks in his eyes, the same sparks that had been there when she was eighteen.

Daniel stirred and her attention shifted to him.

When she looked up again, Logan had left the room.

Logan stood in the shower, letting the stinging cold water hit his body. He willed it to chase away the desire for Gina, the need he struggled to hide. Damn it, but he wanted her and there were so many reasons why he shouldn't, not the least of which was Daniel.

He switched the water from cold to hot but the warmth did nothing to ease the tension in his neck and shoulders from too many meetings and too much negotiation. He'd packed a week's worth of work into two days so he could return to his son.

And his son had turned away from him—toward Gina.

Was it simply the fact that he was a man and Daniel needed a woman's touch? Apparently Hannah's hadn't worked.

He soaped with a vigor that was almost abrasive and he toweled off with the same vehemence. He'd never in a thousand years expected Gina to be here when he got home. What had Hannah been thinking?

She'd been thinking about Daniel.

With a sigh, Logan admitted he couldn't be upset with Hannah. She always did what was best for his son. He wished he knew exactly what that was at this point.

Maybe Gina would be gone by the time he returned to Daniel's room.

Avoidance? That's your strategy? his common sense asked him.

He thought that avoidance might be a good thing right about now as he slid into a pair of gray jogging shorts, still aroused. The air-conditioning in the house sent drafts across his wet back, but he hardly noticed as he pulled on a T-shirt, forgot about shoes, ran his fingers through his still-wet hair, and with some reluctance went to Daniel's bedroom.

Gina had switched off all the lamps except for the Winnie the Pooh nightlight that glowed like a beacon in the corner of the room. She stood at the crib, patting his son on the back. Her profile was backlit, limned in the golden light. Her soft curls lay along her cheek, down her neck to her shoulder. Her nose was straight except for that tiny little bump. Her small chin was defined and the outline of her lips—

She apparently sensed him watching her because she dropped her hands to her sides and turned his way. "He's asleep. He's tuckered out from all that crying."

As she walked toward him, Logan stood perfectly still. She stopped in front of him. "I'll be on my way now." She didn't even take a breath before she walked into the hall.

Swiftly, he went after her and caught her hand. "Gina, wait."

She looked up at him with those big brown eyes that had captivated him when he was twenty-two. "This is difficult for both of us, Logan. I didn't know whether to come or not. I didn't mean to overstep—"

Before he could even think about what he was doing, he swore, brought her close, then held on to her as if she were a vision who might disappear. She didn't push away. Not wanting to scare her or panic her or let any demon from her past raise its head, he gently pushed her hair back from her ears and kissed her. It was a soft tender kiss that told her he remembered everything they'd once had.

She wrapped her arms around him tighter and buried her head in his chest. "Logan."

He didn't know what she was trying to tell him. He was aroused and he knew she could feel it.

"Gina," he murmured. "There's a connection between us that's been there from the moment I met you. And it's still there."

After she pushed away from him, she gazed up at him and took his face between her hands. "I know."

"Do you want to come to my bedroom with me?" He nodded to the door down the hall.

"Is that where you and your wife slept?"

He shook his head. "No. We took a suite upstairs. This one was a guest room. I had it and Daniel's room redone before he came home from the hospital."

Gina's voice was soft, as if she was afraid to say the words out loud. "I want to come to your bedroom with you."

Unable to help himself, Logan swept her up into his arms. His bare feet made no sound on the carpeted hallway and when he pushed open the door to the bedroom, it creaked. The hall light spilled inside, but Gina wasn't looking around at the decor. She was looking at him.

After he set her by the side of the bed, he tossed back the covers, then hesitated. He'd heard of rape victims having flashbacks. He didn't want to trigger anything that would cause her panic.

"Logan, don't look so worried. Try to forget about my past, please."

"I want you to understand something, Gina. I haven't been with a woman since before Amy died. I'll try my best to hold back with you, to do whatever you need. I *will* stop if you ask me to. I want to make that clear. But I want you with a need that's been building for weeks. You have to understand that, too."

"Undress me, Logan," she said shakily. "Let's just start with that."

He was heading into troubled waters. Once they started getting swept away, how difficult would it be to turn back?

When he looked into her eyes, he didn't care. When he let himself feel the heat between them, nothing else mattered. That was what concerned him most.

Still he went ahead, slid his fingers under her top, and slowly pulled it up and over her head. Standing before him in her bra, she smiled at him, a sweet, encouraging smile that told him she definitely wanted to go ahead with this.

As she reached for his T-shirt, she said, "Maybe we can do this at the same time." She lifted his T-shirt up, stood on tiptoe to drag it up over his chin and his head.

He mumbled, "Maybe we can."

When she slid her hand over his chest, his breath hitched.

"Your skin is still damp."

To talk, he *had* to breathe. "It was still wet when I dragged on my T-shirt."

"Do you often dress without drying off?"

He laughed. "Only when I'm in a hurry."

"No hurry now," she said, leaning forward, kissing his chest.

He slid his hands into her hair and gently tugged her

away from him. "This is about *you,* too. You don't have to prove anything to me. I know it's probably easier for you to focus on my pleasure than yours, but I want you to be *here,* Gina, really *here* while we do this."

He saw her chest rise and fall as she closed her eyes for a few seconds and then opened them again. "I'm here."

Her vulnerability awed him. She trusted him completely. That was the responsibility he had to handle like a treasure.

Bending forward, he kissed her while his hands caressed her back and unhooked her bra. His mouth told her in a hundred ways how much he desired her. She didn't hesitate to stroke his tongue with hers, to put her hands on his body, to rub down his spine until all he wanted was to bury himself deep inside her. When he broke off the kiss, her fingers went to the drawstring at his waist and his went to the button on her shorts. They stripped each other quickly and crawled into bed together, eager and short of breath.

They lay face-to-face for a while, touching and kissing. Logan wanted to make sure Gina was ready for him…wanted to make sure she didn't doubt what they were doing…wanted to make sure he didn't do anything to make her afraid.

Finally, when he didn't think he could hold back any longer, he asked, "Are you on birth control?"

She shook her head. "No, I didn't even think about it. I never thought we'd—"

"I have condoms in the drawer."

Her eyes asked him what her lips wouldn't.

"The box has never been opened," he said with a wry chuckle. "I was saving them for the day I was ready."

"Are you ready?"

He nodded. "All I know is that at this moment, I want you, and I need you."

As Gina caressed him, he groaned, wondering at the same time what was going through her head.

But she didn't say. She just whispered, "Get the box and I'll put one on you."

He slid over to the nightstand, searched in the drawer and found the box in the back. Quickly he took out a packet and handed it to her. He was a man who usually took control of any situation he was in, but he knew tonight he couldn't. He had to let Gina take the lead.

He lay back and watched Gina tear open the packet. She was beautiful as she sat up and slid out the condom.

He'd turned on the bedside lamp and now he asked, "Do you want me to turn that off?"

"No. I want to see you, and I want you to see me."

He knew exactly what she meant. She didn't want him to get confused and imagine his wife's face in his mind.

"Gina—" He had to keep her focused on him, in the now, right here.

She didn't roll the condom on right away, she teased him first with her fingers. His jaw locked. His hands clenched into fists. He had to last for her. He had to do whatever was necessary to make this good for her.

After she'd finished, he exhaled and reached for her. "On top of me, Gina. You set the pace."

Now she looked a little rattled, as if the extent of what they were going to do had hit her.

"We can stop," he forced out when it was the last thing he wanted to say.

Instead of answering directly, she stretched out on top of him and requested, "Kiss me again."

Logan gladly fulfilled her request, alert for any nuance of change. Soon, however, he was absorbed in their passion, aroused to a limit he'd never experienced…using willpower in a way he never thought possible.

She must have realized he was at the end of his control. As she broke the kiss, she sat up and straddled him.

Logan's aim was to give her mindless pleasure. He stroked her breasts and thumbed her nipples until she moaned and murmured his name.

The next thing he knew, she was allowing him to slowly enter her. He gazed into her eyes and saw only pleasure as she began to move. He held her hips as they both began to glisten with passion, as her soft cries mingled with his groans. When she moved faster, he rocked with her. Seconds later she cried out, calling his name.

He knew everything was all right. He knew she'd stayed *here* and had allowed herself to fly with him. She kept moving, her body tightening around him until his climax hit, too, and his need was satisfied in a shuddering release.

It was a long time until they could both catch their breaths. After they had, he gathered her into his arms.

"Are you okay?" He leaned away slightly to study her face.

She smiled at him. "I'm more than okay. How about you?"

"More than okay."

The problem was he didn't know where they should go from here.

* * *

Gina was still floating in a sensually induced haze when Logan returned from the bathroom. Everything about tonight had been unplanned and surprising. She didn't know what was going to happen next.

Is that so bad? she asked herself, knowing organizing and compartmentalizing and planning had become defense mechanisms over the years. If she knew what was in a room before she walked into it, she could stay safe. If she dotted every *i* and crossed every *t,* nothing would surprise her. If she ate the right foods, exercised enough and took self-defense courses, she could defend herself no matter who came after her. She'd lived her life without any deviation from her carefully chosen path.

Until she'd impulsively decided to return to Sage-brush. Until destiny or serendipity had put Daniel's chart on her desk. Maybe fate wasn't that mysterious. She'd moved into the Victorian with Francesca, become friends with Tessa—

The Victorian. The rumor. Any woman who resided there would find true love. She'd found true love once with Logan and turned her back on it. But now…

When he climbed into bed beside her, she didn't know what to expect. Did he have regrets? Had tonight been physical rather than emotional for him? What would he want now? What would he do next?

"Do you want something to drink?" he asked.

She shook her head. She didn't need something to drink. She needed to know what was in Logan's head.

"That really was good for you?"

She knew he meant their lovemaking. He couldn't bring himself to use the words, she supposed. She knew tonight might not have been possible with anyone but Logan. She'd known he'd never hurt her. With each kiss and each touch, he'd respect who she was and what she'd been through. She trusted him implicitly, at least where a physical intimate connection was concerned. She wasn't sure about their emotional one. Was he really ready to move on? Had he truly forgiven her? Would he trust her to put a commitment to him and Daniel first above all else?

"Logan, I'm more than okay. Tonight was wonderful. This couldn't have happened with anyone but you."

"I didn't intend for anything to happen."

"I know."

They both looked toward the monitor and Daniel sleeping soundly in his crib. "We're getting to know each other all over again," he murmured.

"Is that something you want?"

"I thought I didn't. I thought Daniel and I would be better off going it alone. But tonight, when I came home and saw you with him, I began to doubt that decision."

"For your sake or his?"

"For *both* our sakes." Now he brushed his thumb across her cheek and laced his fingers in her curls. "Maybe we should try being friends, try being lovers, and see where it goes. We won't rush headlong into anything."

So he could hang on to his wife's memory? Or was he protecting himself in case she turned her back again? She wouldn't do that. She couldn't.

"I'm not sure I understand what you want," she admitted. "A weekend together, now and then? Should I stay in or out of Daniel's life? Do you want me here to help put Daniel to bed? Do you want to go riding together, be seen in public, have dinner at my mom's house?" She hadn't intended for all the questions to spill out, but they just had.

"I don't have the answers, Gina, but I do have a suggestion."

"What?" She liked the sense of anticipation in his voice.

"Next weekend, I have to go to Houston. How would you like to come with me?"

She didn't hesitate. "I'd love to go with you."

"I'm having a full day of meetings with the people who run my foundation," he explained. "They're going to catch me up on the research, explore ways to help pregnant women with cancer. If you'd like, you can sit in on the sessions with me. There's a dinner and dance Saturday evening to raise money. We'd have Friday night together and Saturday night after the dance. I'm thinking about asking Hannah to go along with Daniel. I don't want to leave him again after what happened tonight. That way I can spend time with him on and off while we're there. What do you think?"

From the sounds of it, he would be incorporating her into his life. And not just his life, but Daniel's, too. "I think it's a terrific idea. I can help with Daniel."

Logan slipped his arms around her and brought her close to him. "I'm not asking you to go along for that reason."

"I know."

"Do you think he'll handle a plane ride okay?" Logan wondered.

"We'll make it okay. With you, me and Hannah, he won't be bored."

Logan laughed, an honest-to-goodness, genuine laugh. "You're right about that." He lifted her chin and kissed her deeply. Afterward, he said, "I guess we should get some sleep."

She'd like nothing better than to sleep all night in his arms.

She suddenly realized that wasn't exactly true. She'd like nothing better than to spend *every* night in his arms.

Chapter Eleven

Gina sat quietly beside Logan at the dinner-dance Saturday evening, taking in the conversations swirling around her at the long table.

"The guide who led the white-water rafting trip was exceptional," Logan commented as he continued his discussion with the fundraising guru on Saturday evening.

Then Logan glanced at Gina, their gazes lingered and she felt anticipation building between them.

Last evening hadn't gone as planned. After they'd landed in Houston in the late afternoon, Daniel had to be acclimated and settled in. Logan had reserved a suite for Daniel and Hannah and an adjoining room for Gina and himself…to enjoy more privacy. But last night Daniel hadn't wanted to go to sleep, so they'd ended up playing with him and watching TV until it was time to turn in. Even then, however, he'd wanted his father. So Logan had wheeled the crib into his room and he and Gina had just snuggled while his son slept.

Now happy excitement danced in her stomach as she looked forward to her time with Logan tonight… dancing…and making love later.

Dr. Katz, the guru, targeted Gina now. "Have you ever been white-water rafting on the Colorado River?"

"I've never been white-water rafting," she had to admit, considering the fact that being with Logan now was so different from when they were teenagers and she'd worried about fitting in with his crowd.

"Gina has skied in Vermont, though," Logan interjected, giving her arm a squeeze.

"What part of Vermont?" Katz questioned her.

"Killington."

"Did you enjoy it?"

He was in his fifties and his heavy brows almost came together in the middle of his forehead. She was beginning to realize his gruffness was just part of who he was and didn't reflect on her. "I did enjoy it, but I like horseback riding more."

The gentleman across from Gina, Dr. Silverstein, pushed his silver-rimmed glasses higher on his nose and addressed her. "Logan mentioned you worked with his son."

Meetings all day had involved PowerPoint presentations on the effectiveness of certain treatments and the difficulty of treating a pregnant woman. Introductions had been made, but Gina had listened more than she'd interacted with anyone there. But Logan had been involved in several private conversations.

It pleased her that Logan had spoken about her time

with Daniel. "I work with babies who have developmental issues," she explained.

"You have a degree in child development?" Dr. Silverstein asked with interest.

"I have a master's in pediatric physical therapy as well as a Ph.D. in infant and toddler development."

"Who do you work for?" Silverstein wanted to know.

"I work for myself. I have a practice called Baby Grows in Lubbock."

"That's very interesting." The doctor looked thoughtful. "There's such a need for that kind of practice with all kinds of children—children with Downs, with epilepsy. Children who have been in accidents."

"She's published articles," Logan said proudly. "If you search the Internet, you'll find them." He folded his napkin, laid it on the table and pushed his chair back. Standing, he said, "I think I'm going to ask my beautiful companion to dance with me before the band stops playing."

Logan's gaze lingered on her as if he'd been waiting for this dance all night. Whenever he looked at her like that, she felt so special…so pretty. She'd worn a black dress with a white bow on her left shoulder, no sleeve on the right. Sterling jewelry sparkled at her ears and around her neck. She'd never felt more self-confident…or appreciated.

Logan helped her with her chair and then swept her away to the dance floor. There he pulled her close.

"I'm not ready to sacrifice any more time for mingling and conversation. Last night should have been different. We should have had some time to ourselves."

"Logan, when a child is involved every situation is in flux."

His green eyes were gentle as he studied her face. "You can understand that with your head, but do you understand it with your heart?"

"I do," she assured him, her lips almost touching his jaw. "I loved you holding me last night. That was enough."

"Tonight will be different. Hannah took Daniel down to the kids' area before supper. I looked in on him while you were getting dressed. His eyes were almost closing over his dinner."

"We're good as long as we don't get any storms," she teased.

"No storms tonight. I checked the weather report."

The weather outside might be perfectly calm, but she could see the hunger building inside Logan. The simmering intensity in his eyes told her he wanted to give way to it. She wished he would. She wished he wouldn't continue to hold back with her. But she sensed he wasn't just holding back his passion, he was holding back part of his soul, too. Tonight she wanted to give herself to Logan completely. She wanted him to realize that he could depend on her and trust her, that she wouldn't turn her back on him again.

The music was smooth and dreamy. They gazed into each other's eyes, searching for answers that maybe they could find tonight.

Logan moved his hand to the small of her back. When he did, her breasts pressed into his chest. As she laid her face against the lapel of his suit jacket, she inhaled his cologne, anticipated what was to come and felt the excitement heat her whole body.

Logan's lips were close to her ear. "Do you feel it, too?"

"The music?" she teased, looking up at him.

"Gina," he murmured in part exasperation and part amusement.

She knew she had to be the one to say it because he wasn't going to push her into feelings or into physical pleasure if she didn't want to go there. "Yes, I feel it. I feel you. I'm ready to get naked if you are."

He laughed.

She realized she could be provocative with him as well as share pleasure with him. She could be the girl she'd been at eighteen.

Bending to her, he kissed the shell of her ear and she felt his tongue on her earlobe. Shivers danced up and down her arms. She wanted to kiss him long and hard, but not in the middle of the dance floor, not with these people who respected and admired him and expected propriety.

She leaned back and warned with mock sternness, "If you don't want me to undress you right here, you'd better stop teasing."

"No, what I'd better do is take you up to our room." With that he stopped the pretense of dancing, wrapped his arm around her and guided her back to their table. Fortunately everyone was mingling, talking or dancing, so they didn't have to make excuses. They just slipped out of the room and headed for the elevator.

The sounds of the hotel lobby were background noise as they stood at the bank of elevators glancing at each other. Gina's heart was racing and she wondered if Logan's was, too. But it was impossible to read him. He was so good now at hiding what he was feeling.

She just wished he'd talk to her about what was ahead of them…about the future. They hadn't had much time together this past week. Both had had full schedules. Logan had called her mid-week before bed, but it had been a short call and she'd wondered if he wanted to avoid talking about the future.

When the elevator doors opened, they stepped inside. Alone now, Logan enfolded her into his arms. She forgot about the future, caught up in right now. Logan kissed her. His mouth was more demanding, more possessive than it had been before. He broke off the kiss to look at her, checking if she was okay.

"Don't treat me as if I'm going to break," she pleaded. "I want you, Logan. I want *us*."

His expression was tender as he said, "I'm afraid I'll trigger something."

She knew what he meant and she didn't know how to reassure him except to say, "*You* are not that man. My mind, my heart, my body and my soul know that. Please, don't hold back with me tonight." She hoped he understood she wanted to give herself to him completely, and she wanted him to do the same in return.

At their floor he curled his arm around her as if he didn't want to let her go. After he opened the room door with his key card, he brushed his hand down her cheek and said, "I'll be right back. I'm going to check on Daniel."

Gina had barely had enough time to undress when he returned from the adjoining suite. "He's sound asleep."

Logan shed his suit jacket and tie and began unbuttoning the buttons on his shirt, his gaze focused on her.

She'd donned a satiny nightgown in swirls of pink and yellow. As she moved toward the bed, she could feel the spaghetti straps slipping slightly, the material molding to her.

His hands stilled on the placket of his shirt and he watched her as if she were a mirage which might disappear in the blink of the eye. "You're beautiful," he said hoarsely. "I want you so much my hands are shaking."

Crossing to him, she took his hands in hers, opened one and kissed his palm.

When her lips touched his skin, tension rippled from him to her. Their gazes locked. Not hesitating, she pulled his shirt from his trousers. Logan tugged her close for a impetuously erotic kiss that told her exactly how much he wanted her. Excited, thrilled to be with him again, she kissed him back, needing him to know how much she wanted him, how much she *loved* him.

The feelings welling up in her heart were no surprise. Logan had been there all these years. He was the man she'd always envisioned spending her life with. He was the man who could put the past truly in the past.

When he broke off the kiss, he ran lighter kisses down her neck to the pulse at her throat. His hands caressed her back and he began to lift her nightgown in handfuls. After he slid it over her head and tossed it aside, a ruddy flush darkened his cheekbones.

He mumbled, "I've got to get out of these clothes."

Moments later they were lying in bed. Logan stroked her face, gently kissed her lips and lingered on her breasts. His tongue teased her nipples until she was pulling at his shoulders, almost begging him to enter her. But he didn't. His hand gently reached between her thighs, his fingers sliding in and out of her, doing wonderful fluttery things that made her feel as if she were going to fly apart.

"Do you want to be on top?" he asked when she was practically senseless with desire.

"No. I want *you* on top, all over me, inside me." She closed her eyes.

But his deep voice coaxed them open again. "Look at me, Gina. Look at me and know I only want to give you pleasure."

Tears came to her eyes—because she was so sure of that, so absolutely sure Logan would never hurt her.

He rose above her, his gaze locked to hers. When he entered her, all the pleasure in the world seemed to be theirs. It filled her heart. It filled her body. And it filled the room. Logan and the sensual sensations rippling through her burned away the past and healed any part of her that still held pain. She felt whole again. She let go of herself and flew to the stars with Logan.

His release came as the tremors of her orgasm still washed through her, as she held on to him and murmured his name.

Stretched out on top of her, he dropped his head to her shoulder. When he rolled them onto their sides, still joined, she snuggled into his chest as he kissed her temple. They fell asleep holding on to each other.

A few hours later, still tucked into Logan's arms, Gina awakened. She relived making love with Logan— every detail, every wonderful sensation. Suddenly, however, her breath caught. She realized something she hadn't given any consideration to a few hours before. They hadn't used birth control! They'd been so caught up in each other and the moment that it hadn't even entered their minds.

The hush of night was veiled by the hum of the air conditioner. Logan's chest hair brushed her cheek, his scent surrounded her and she felt as if she'd been born to be held in his arms. What if they'd made a baby last night?

What if she was carrying his child?

Gina closed her eyes again, embracing the idea, perhaps even hoping for it.

But would Logan feel the same?

The sun was just peeking through the draperies when Gina opened her eyes the following morning. Logan had moved away from her during the night. She reached out a hand before she turned and felt his muscled arm. Then she shifted to her side to look at him.

He was lying on his back, one arm tucked under his head as he stared at the ceiling. Something was different and she suspected what it was. After all, Logan was as pragmatic as he was passionate.

"Good morning," she said lightly, hoping he'd come to the same conclusion she had about a pregnancy.

"I'm not sure about that," he said, sitting up, pushing pillows behind him and hiking himself up against the headboard.

He was out of reach now and she felt the distance emotionally as well as physically.

"My condoms are still in the suitcase," he said wryly.

"I know."

"You mean you thought of them and you didn't say anything?"

Now she quickly sat up, too. "No, of course not. I woke up in the middle of the night and that's when I realized it. Logan, why would you think I wouldn't say anything?"

"I shouldn't have said that," he muttered. "Of course you wouldn't. You wouldn't want to be pregnant any more than I'd want you to be pregnant. You've got a career, a practice."

"Yes, I do. But I wouldn't look on a baby as an awful thing happening. I mean, a child would be something wonderful, wouldn't it?"

His silence wasn't the answer she wanted, and she realized that last night might have been something different to her than to him.

Finally he said, "You really sound as if you might want a baby."

Not any baby. Your baby. But she decided to keep that comment to herself.

Looking troubled, he assured her, "If you were to get pregnant, you don't have to worry. I'll support you."

He would support her. She was afraid to ask what that meant. Did he mean monetarily? Did he mean emotionally?

She simply said, "I appreciate that," and slid out of the bed. Without another glance at him, she hurried into the bathroom. She needed to take a few deep breaths before she said something she couldn't take back…before she said something she'd regret almost as much as she regretted leaving him when she was eighteen.

She was brushing her teeth when Logan rapped on the door. "I'm going to check on Daniel."

"Okay," she murmured around her toothbrush.

"Will you be ready to go down to breakfast in about half an hour?"

She took the toothbrush out of her mouth and swallowed. Wiping her mouth with a towel, she said clearly, "I think I'm going to skip breakfast and pack. I'll order something from room service, then we'll meet back here in time to leave for the airport."

He opened the door, then stepped inside.

She'd put on the white, fluffy robe the hotel provided, and right now she was grateful for it.

"Gina, about the birth control—the possibility of you being pregnant just threw me for a loop."

His green eyes were turbulent with emotions she didn't understand or know anything about. "Why?"

He seemed to debate with himself then said, "When Amy told me she was pregnant, I thought it was the happiest moment of my life. But then a few months later everything went to hell. Just thinking about the idea brought it all back."

"I can see how it would," she said softly, grateful he was sharing this with her, thankful he wasn't closing himself off to her.

Logan had pulled on jeans and a snap-button shirt. His tall, hard body seemed to fill the bathroom. She remembered how his body had covered hers, how he'd kissed her, how he'd touched her. And she wanted last night back. She hated this tension between them. She wished he'd hold her.

But he didn't. He just asked again, "Are you sure you don't want breakfast?"

"Positive," she said with a smile she didn't feel.

"All right. I'll meet you back here in a little while."

She stood perfectly still, unable to go to him. He seemed unable to move toward her.

He left the bathroom and closed the door behind him.

Gina gripped the sink, took a couple of deep breaths, then shed the robe and stepped into the shower. The hot water was soothing and she let it wash over her, trying not to think...trying to deny the fact that Logan might not be ready for a new relationship. He might not be ready for her to be an integral part of his life.

Fifteen minutes later, she'd toweled off and dressed when the phone in her room rang. She picked it up, thinking it might be Logan.

"Dr. Rigoletti?" a male voice asked.

"Yes, this is she."

"Good morning. It's Dr. Silverstein. We spoke briefly at dinner last night."

She remembered the man. He had kind eyes and silver wire-rimmed spectacles. "Yes, Dr. Silverstein, I remember. Do you want to speak to Logan?"

"No, actually I'd like to meet with you for a few minutes. Is this a good time?"

She checked her watch. "I have a few minutes."

"My room is down the hall from yours. There's a sitting area at the end of the hall. Shall we meet there?"

Gina's radar had told her she'd have nothing to fear from Dr. Silverstein, so she didn't hesitate to say, "Sure. I'll meet you there in five minutes."

Gina had dressed in white jeans and a navy knit top. Now she quickly slipped into sandals and stopped long enough to dab some gloss on her lips. After picking up her purse, she let the hotel-room door close behind her and went down the hall.

Dr. Silverstein was standing at the windows that looked out over the city. "I'm grateful that you could give me a few minutes."

"What's this about?" she asked, puzzled, as they both took a seat.

"I searched your credentials and work history on the Internet last night. They're very impressive."

"I feel as if I'm interviewing for something," she said, joking.

"Not interviewing exactly, but I did wonder if you do any consultation work…if you do any outside training."

"I did in Connecticut and Massachusetts. But when I set up the Baby Grows practice in Lubbock, I concentrated on that."

"Would you consider doing it again?"

"Where?"

"My company has facilities in Houston, Dallas and Tyler."

The way Logan had acted this morning, she didn't know what the future held for them. Still, she thought about Dr. Silverstein's offer and said, "I'm really flattered by your offer and thank you so much for considering me. But for now I want to concentrate on my practice in Lubbock."

"You won't even discuss a consultation fee?"

She smiled at him. "Not at the present time."

Thoughtfully, he studied her. "Logan told me a little about your sessions with Daniel. You know, don't you, that there's a need for DVDs for parents and more centers like yours? I'd really like you to consider that."

She thought of a business plan she'd developed after she wrote her dissertation. The plan was similar to what Dr. Silverstein was suggesting.

"You *have* considered it, haven't you?" he asked perceptively. "More than one center? In more than one city?"

"Years ago after I worked on my Ph.D., I wrote up a business plan."

"Would you consider letting me see it?"

Something about that idea was exciting. After all, what if Logan decided she had no place in his life? The idea of having a baby with her had definitely unnerved him. For the past hour she'd been thinking about the repercussions of that. She did understand the pain he'd gone through with his wife. But if he really wanted a future with Gina, would he be in as much turmoil as she sensed he was in?

She thought about the future and dreams and she knew she couldn't count on a life with Logan in it. "I'd have to think about it."

"Well…I'd like to see your concept. Our hospital system is large enough to invest in a project like that." Dr. Silverstein slipped his hand into his suit-coat pocket and brought out a card. He handed it to her. "That's my contact information—e-mail, home phone, fax and cell phone."

She slipped the card into a pocket in her purse and stood. "I'll keep it in a safe place."

"On your refrigerator under a magnet would be good. Then it will be front and center and you won't forget about the idea."

She laughed. "I won't forget."

After they shook hands, Dr. Silverstein headed toward the elevator and she hurried toward her room. She had to finish packing for her trip home with Logan.

Home. Maybe soon he would see that the three of them *could* have a home together.

Logan had gone from paradise to hell almost as fast as he could say his name.

As he drove home from the airport Sunday afternoon, he glanced over at Gina in the passenger seat. She went from staring distractingly out the side window to checking on Daniel in the back where he sat in his car seat beside Hannah. His son was oblivious to the tension between him and Gina, but Logan was sure Hannah could feel it.

Last night with Gina had been world-splitting. The first time they'd made love he'd been so concerned about her and her reactions he hadn't gotten lost in the immensity of it. But last night, not using birth control—

The idea of Gina being pregnant unnerved him. Because he wasn't ready for another commitment? Because Amy had died for Daniel? Because Logan had thought sex with Gina would stay in the realm of satisfying physical needs?

If he accepted the fact that Gina had a place in his life, everything would change. Absolutely everything.

He did not want another commitment that could tear his heart out. He'd been through the wringer twice and the bottom line was, Gina had left once before. She could leave again.

Logan's cell phone rang. He checked the readout on his hands-free apparatus and pressed a button, aware that both Gina and Hannah would be able to hear the conversation. "Hi, Maggie. What's up?"

"Hey, Logan. Do you have a minute?"

"Sure. I'm on the way back to Sagebrush from the airport."

"How was the trip? Are the clinical trials from the new cancer drug proceeding on schedule?"

He summed up what he'd learned in his meetings on Saturday. Then he asked, "Is that why you called?"

"Not exactly. I finished digitizing the videos. I have a break between scripts. I had this bright idea that I could drive down this afternoon, spend the week with you and Daniel, and you could see what I've done with the DVD. I think you'll like it."

By *like it* she meant he'd *remember.* He could watch Amy float across the screen, hear her words and think he could go back in time. His chest tightened at the thought. But then he understood this was something he had to do for Daniel. He was sure Maggie had put her best effort into producing the DVD. "Sure, drive on down. It doesn't matter how late it is when you get here."

He had a feeling sleep wasn't going to come easily tonight.

"See you in a few hours," Maggie said and clicked off.

Gina looked over at him and their eyes caught and held for a second—a very intense second. Had she expected him to invite her to stay over at the house tonight? What had *he* expected? That they'd go their separate ways? Entwine their bodies together again?

They entered the outskirts of Sagebrush. "Do you want to come home with us for a while?" he asked Gina, not at all sure what he wanted her to say.

"Just drop me off at my place," she said. "I have cases to look over before tomorrow."

Logan couldn't blame the hollowness in his heart on fate this time. But he had some heavy thinking to do and it would be easier to do without Gina laughing and playing with his son.

On Sunday evening, Gina's heart ached. She thought about Logan, Maggie and Daniel together at the estate. Maggie had most likely re-created the past for Logan with her DVD. Would he even want to think about the future?

Gina understood why he might not want her there during Maggie's visit. But another part of her just didn't understand—not after what she and Logan had shared.

When she climbed the steps to the attic of the Victorian, she hoped to find her business plan right away. She headed toward the seven boxes stacked in one corner, a bit set apart from two trunks, an old wardrobe and a few more cartons. Tessa had told her the wardrobe and trunks had been there when she moved in. They belonged to the landlady.

In spite of herself, Gina flashed back to the expression on Logan's face in bed that morning as they'd talked about the possibility of her being pregnant. *I'll support you,* he'd said and she'd heard the duty in his voice.

If she was pregnant, she'd have to think about her child's future. She would *not* depend on Logan for monetary support, especially if he didn't want to be their child's father.

By the time she'd sorted through box number three, she was almost ready to give up. But at the bottom of the box, she saw the blue folder. She paged through the plan inside the folder, remembering how ardently she'd worked on it. In the pocket in front, she found the disk.

There would be no harm in e-mailing the files to Dr. Silverstein. Would there?

Chapter Twelve

A week and a half later, Logan stood at the day-care center site and swiped the sweat from his brow. He didn't know what he was doing out here in the afternoon sun in a dress shirt and suit slacks, but he couldn't seem to work, couldn't concentrate, needed to be outside. He might as well go home. But he wasn't that kind of CEO. He wasn't that kind of boss…unless Daniel needed him.

Last week Maggie had convinced him to go clothes shopping with her. Daniel was outgrowing everything. Logan had gone, but the whole time all he could think about was that he'd rather be doing it with Gina.

Was she pregnant? Just how soon would she use a pregnancy test?

He should call her, but—

His cell phone beeped and he checked the caller ID,

knowing he had to call Gina but not sure of what he was going to say when he did. It had been ten days since they'd talked. Would she call him if she was pregnant? If she wasn't? He recognized the name on the screen. "Dr. Silverstein. What can I do for you?"

"This time it's much simpler than asking you to raise a million dollars for the foundation."

Logan chuckled. "Well, I'm glad to hear that. What kind of help do you need?"

"I wanted to talk to you about Dr. Rigoletti."

"I see," Logan said, hoping to prompt more information.

"She sent me the business plan for Baby Grows. It's comprehensive and timely. She's going to fly to Houston the first week in August to discuss giving seminars here for our pediatric physical therapists. She'd be a great asset and your endorsement might help her make up her mind—about the seminars *and* the business plan."

"Tell me about the business plan," Logan requested, in turmoil about where this was going.

"Essentially, it proposes setting up Baby Grows practices all over the country. There would be a central headquarters for training personnel who would then be sent to other locations."

Logan considered how Gina had moved around from Connecticut to Massachusetts then back to Connecticut again. He thought she'd returned to Sagebrush to settle in and stay. But maybe that hadn't been her plan. Maybe she wanted to travel all over the country. If she did, what would that mean to him and Daniel? What if *she* was pregnant?

At Logan's silence, Silverstein continued, "Logan, I

think this is a profitable idea in the making for investors and for her. She could make money hand over fist and never have to worry about her future again."

After Logan got off the phone with Silverstein, he had to ask himself if Gina really *did* want to be CEO of her own corporation. Just how would a baby figure into that? He had to talk to her. He had to know.

Logan left work early after all. But instead of going home he headed into Lubbock—to Baby Grows. He needed to have this conversation with Gina *now*.

The drive to Lubbock intensified his concerns. In spite of himself, he found he remembered too well the day Gina had left...the evening she'd returned his mother's locket and rejected his proposal. The old resentment grabbed on to him and held tight. He'd been here before—with Gina putting her future ahead of anything they might have together. How could they spend time together if she was running around the country? What if she decided to move her practice to somewhere more inviting? What if she decided to leave this practice under other management and set up headquarters somewhere else? He knew how that worked. Businesses did it all the time.

One thought after another ran rampant in his head. Daniel would miss her. Maybe she'd never meant to stay.

When the sliding-glass doors opened to give him entrance to the Baby Grows practice, he spotted a therapist working with a group of three babies and their moms. The moms were sitting on the floor and the babies were lying on their tummies.

He knew those exercises. He'd done them with Daniel at Tessa's encouragement.

The door to Gina's office was closed, but the blind

in the door was open. She was working at the computer to the side of her desk.

He rapped on the door.

As she glanced up, she spotted him through the open blind. Rising from her chair, she came around the desk to the open door. She was wearing her smock with babies and rattles printed all over it. She must have been working with infants earlier.

"Logan, this is a surprise! Is Daniel okay?"

"Daniel's fine. I need to talk to you in private."

At the tone of his voice, her forehead creased with concern and she seemed to pale. Then she straightened her spine and looked him straight in the eye. "Come in. We'll talk."

Once he was inside, she closed the door as well as the blind. He'd wanted privacy and they had it. She motioned to the two chairs in front of her desk. "We can sit and—"

"I don't need to sit. I have a question for you. When were you going to tell me your plans for Baby Grows? Silverstein says you're flying to Houston again to talk about consulting…that you'd like to open developmental centers across the country. Was this in your plans when you came to Sagebrush?"

To her credit, she didn't become defensive. "I shared with Dr. Silverstein a business plan I had developed a few years ago. It's a dream, Logan. It's a dream to set up programs where parents can learn how to strengthen their babies and help them grow."

"I thought you returned here to be with your family and settle down."

"And to make peace with you."

He was silent.

"It's never going to happen, is it, Logan? Peace between us? Forgiveness from you?"

"I forgive you," he said tersely, as if that was all she needed to hear. "Last Saturday night I proved that, didn't I? I couldn't have—"

"Made love with me the way you did if you hadn't forgiven me? Can't you say the words, Logan?"

He felt his face flush.

She went on. "Or maybe love didn't enter into it for you. Maybe it was all about physical release and nothing else." She waited, as if she wanted him to deny it.

"All I know, Gina, is that you left once before. How can I trust that you won't leave again?"

She looked upset…in as much turmoil as he was. The corner of her lip quivered. "I want to make sure I understand you. Are you saying you won't give me your love until you're sure I'll make you and Daniel the focus of my life?"

"How can we have a relationship if you don't?"

"*Do* we have a relationship, Logan? I haven't heard from you for over a week."

"Maggie was here and…I've been busy."

She let his words stand between them until she said, "I know Daniel has to be the focus of your life. And you have an empire to run. Do I fit in at all?"

He knew she did; maybe he just didn't want to admit it. "Did you use a pregnancy test?"

She sighed. "Yesterday, I had an appointment with my gynecologist. I'm *not* pregnant. I was going to call you."

He felt relief, yet another part of him was sad at the news, too. "So now you have nothing standing in your way if you want Silverstein to buy into your plan."

She shook her head. "You're using that as an excuse."

"An excuse for what?"

Hesitating for a few moments, she looked down at her hands then back up at him. The emotion in her eyes spilled over into her voice. "An excuse not to love at all, ever again. You're still angry I left when you proposed. You're still angry because Amy chose Daniel over her life with you."

Her words struck him like a physical blow. "How *dare* you say that. I could *never* be angry with Amy for wanting to save our child."

"You wanted her to fight."

"Of course, I wanted her to fight! I wanted it all. I wanted my wife *and* my baby."

"But she didn't see it your way."

No, she hadn't. But he wasn't going to get into that with Gina now. He'd wrestled with all of it when Amy had been diagnosed with cancer and made her decision. He wasn't going to wrestle with it again.

So he tossed a question at Gina. "What about *you?* Can you really love? Sure you were young when you left, but you knew what you wanted. You wanted that Ph.D. You wanted to *be* somebody. Apparently being my wife wouldn't have been enough. That's *why* you left. All the talk about not wanting to let down your parents, putting Angie through college. Those were side issues that coincided with your ambition. You had it then and you have it now."

"My ambition?" Now Gina's cheeks were red, her eyes were wide, dark with something he hadn't figured out yet.

"You think ambition was my main reason for leaving? Let me tell you, Logan, there were a lot of reasons why I left. One you don't even know about."

"And that was?" he prodded.

"That reason was your father telling me he'd disinherit you if I married you."

In the ensuing silence, everything inside Logan went stone-cold. "I don't believe you."

"I have *never* lied to you, Logan, and I won't start now. At first I thought he was bluffing. I thought he'd never do that to you. So I kept seeing you. I kept falling deeper in love with you. Then at the end of the summer, when my mom and dad talked with me about it, about how young we both were—about how we both had futures we shouldn't limit—I kept wondering, what if your father *wasn't* bluffing? You were going to take over the company. You were going to be his protégé. You'd told me how remote your father could be. But the family business was your connection. You'd looked forward all your life to working with him, making him proud, becoming the one in charge someday. I couldn't let him take that away from you. *I* couldn't take that away from you."

Logan felt sweat break out on his brow. When he'd set eyes on Gina again two-and-a-half months ago, the numbness that had been inside of him since Amy died had begun melting. But now it was back. It kept him from feeling too much, from seeing too much, from analyzing too much.

But he still didn't want to believe what Gina had said. "Why didn't you tell me before you left?"

Sinking down on the desk, she took a deep breath. "As you said, I was eighteen and not very sure of myself, especially not with you. Why would Logan Barnes want *me?* I had so many insecurities. Why would I think you'd choose me over the life you'd been born for?"

Yes, he would have had to make a choice—Gina or the legacy his father had promised him.

"Tell me something, Logan. At twenty-two, what *would* you have chosen? A life with me without all the trimmings? Or a future with your father—the man you'd worked your whole life to get to notice you?"

Logan had been hopelessly in love with Gina at twenty-two. If he'd had to choose, he would have chosen his love for her. But then he thought about his father's stroke, his father teaching him everything he knew, his father approving of some of his decisions, disapproving of others, How long had that taken? One year? Two? Three? Would he have stood up to his father if the stroke hadn't happened? He'd never know.

Gina's eyes were shiny with unshed tears. "At least—" Her voice broke. "Fourteen years ago, you told me you loved me and wanted to marry me. I was foolish to walk away. I should have stayed and fought for you, and believed you would fight for me. But now I don't think you're willing to fight for anyone but Daniel. After we made love without protection, you withdrew."

"Gina—"

"Please, let me finish. The idea of a baby with me totally rattled you. I've been sorting through all the reasons why. Because you don't love me and we're together again for old times' sake? Because you felt sorry for me and wanted to make up for the fact you weren't there for me? Why *didn't* you come after me, Logan? I know now your dad had his stroke. But after our conversation, couldn't you tell by my voice that something was wrong? Why didn't you ask? Why didn't you call again? Why didn't you come and see me? If you had…"

A tear rolled down her cheek and her voice caught.

"If you had, maybe we could have held each other. Maybe we would have had each other. I've taken the blame for our breakup all these years, but I'm not sure I should have. Some of that blame was *yours,* too."

"You left," he said almost stubbornly.

"Yes. And I came back."

"So why are you flying to Houston in August?" His tone was still accusatory. He didn't want to see what she was trying to show him. He *did* want all the blame to be on her.

She sighed, a deep, sad sound. "Because I realize deep in my heart that you're going to pull away. When we were in the car and Maggie called, I sensed you didn't want me anywhere near you and her and Daniel. I understand that you want to cherish Amy's memory. But if I were truly going to be part of your life, if you were really going to let me in, wouldn't you want me there, too? And if not, if you thought Maggie might not understand, wouldn't you explain that to me so that I didn't feel as if you were pushing me away? You pushed me away hard, Logan. The dream of my business plan coming to fruition, and the idea of doing consultations was a way for me to pick up myself by my bootstraps, stay in Sagebrush near my family for now, and figure out what comes next. When I learned coping mechanisms, one of them was planning for every possibility. After all, loving you all those years ago brought *me* pain, too."

Looking at Gina's beautiful face, seeing her tears run down her cheek into the black curls there, noticing the way she was holding on to the desk for support, he realized he never should have come here to have this conversation. Her office wasn't private. He should have shown her more respect than to do this at her professional home base.

"You'd better leave, Logan." She swiped the tears from her cheek. "I have a session with a new client in fifteen minutes and I need to pull myself together."

She'd given him a lot to think about. He felt barraged by emotions and feelings and knowledge that he had somehow to shake into place, sort the good from the bad and figure out what he was left with.

Were he and Gina finished? He just didn't know. And because he didn't know, he turned and left her office. After he closed the door behind him, she left the blinds shut.

That about said it all.

Angie gave Gina a ferocious hug the following evening. Both of them were crying. Gina had stopped by Angie's apartment to tell her *everything*. She should have done it a long time ago.

Now she leaned back to study her sister's face. "I shouldn't have waited this long to tell you."

Angie backhanded the tears running down her cheek. "I thought you blamed *me* for your breakup with Logan. I thought that's why you wouldn't talk to me for so long. I thought that's why you didn't come home for Christmas that year."

Gina felt terrible that she had let her sister down. "I had to get myself together. I couldn't let any of you see what had happened."

"So you told Logan everything? How did he take it?"

"He was wonderful. He went really slow with me. But I knew I never had anything to fear from Logan and being with him was wonderful."

"Then why do you look as if you haven't slept for a while?"

"Because he's not ready to love again. I can't just be friends with him. Not when I love him and Daniel so much. He doubted I'd stay in Sagebrush. He was afraid I'd leave again."

"Why?"

She told Angie about the offer Silverstein had made.

"You could be rich and famous!"

"I don't want to be rich and famous. I want to be successful, but I just want to love my work. And I do."

"And what about you and Logan?"

"He'll never forgive me for telling him about his father. I never should have done that. But I was so frustrated and hurt. Oh, Ange, you should have seen the hurt in his eyes. I had no right to cause him that pain."

"You were just defending yourself."

"Maybe, but at what cost?"

"Don't you think he deserved to know the truth?"

Gina shook her head. "I'm not so sure."

"Sis, the truth doesn't hurt us. It might make us re-examine what we think, maybe even who we are. But you can't tuck it away and pretend it doesn't exist. It's like this secret of yours. If we'd known, we could have supported you. We wouldn't have thought *we* had done something wrong."

Gina felt her throat close again and she and her sister shared a heartfelt glance.

"You *are* going to tell Mom and Dad now, aren't you?"

"I don't want to hurt them. I know what I'll see in Mom's eyes—pain for me and what happened. And with Dad, I know I'll see rage—rage that someone could hurt his little girl."

"You're going to have to let them deal with it, just as I have to. In time, maybe we can all put it in the past."

"We *will* put it in the past," Gina said with an assurance she truly felt. Telling Angie, just like telling Logan and Raina, had been freeing. Her parents were a different matter, but she was hoping they'd become even closer than they were now.

"So what are you going to do about Logan?"

"There's nothing I can do." As she said the words her heart felt broken.

"Maybe when you go to Houston you should think seriously about expanding Baby Grows."

"That seems to be the logical thing to do—to throw myself into a new project and let that change my life. But I think I just need to be me for a while. I have plenty of clients, plenty of work to do here. Logan and I certainly don't run in the same circles. With a little luck I won't see him for a very long time."

Just saying the words practically stopped her heart. When she thought about him...when she thought about Daniel...

She rose from the sofa in Angie's living room and nodded toward the kitchen. "Let's get a glass of iced tea. Now I want to know everything about *your* life. I want us to really be sisters again."

Angie rose, too, and gave Gina another hug. "Afterward, do you want me to go with you to Mom and Dad's?"

Gina shook her head. "No. I have to do that alone."

She was used to being alone, but at least now she had her family and Raina and Lily. She'd face each new sunrise and create a life for herself. Without Logan.

* * *

Logan pulled up to the gas pump at a station on the outskirts of Sagebrush Friday night, intending to fill the tank quickly before he headed home. Daniel would be waiting for him.

Gina wouldn't be, though.

With a frustrated sigh Logan took off his Stetson, ran his hand through his hair, then plopped his hat back on his head. The empty feeling in his heart, in his chest, in his stomach hadn't left, not for an instant over the past two days. He wasn't sleeping, he was eating only when he had to, and he was rowing or riding when he wasn't working or playing with Daniel. Being with Daniel was almost painful when he called, "Gee, gee," and Logan's conflicted emotions about Gina seemed more confused than ever.

He filled his gas tank, then went inside the small convenience store to pay. He spotted Raina Gibson right away. Back when he was a teenager and had come home from boarding school in the summers, he'd often admired Raina's beauty as she waitressed at the Yellow Rose. But he'd never tried to date her. Her older brother, Ryder—now a cop on the Lubbock police force—had been more than a little protective. Logan had respected him for it.

Knowing Raina might rebuff him now because of her friendship with Gina, he approached her anyway. After she paid her bill, he tapped her shoulder. When she turned and saw him, she froze.

"I have to pay for my gas," he said. "But I'd like to talk to you for a few minutes after I do. Would that be all right?"

She looked torn between loyalty and—maybe—curiosity. Tucking her wallet into her purse, she nodded to the back of the store near the cold-beverage cases. "I'll wait for you there."

As soon as he paid, he joined her. "How is Gina?"

Raina met his gaze squarely. "Why?"

"Because I care about her. Because—"

Raina didn't make him finish. She tucked her purse under her arm. "She's doing about as well as you from the looks of it. She's not sleeping. She doesn't have an appetite. She works late. Does that about sum up *your* life, too?"

"I shouldn't have stopped you," he muttered. "There's no point." He turned to go.

But Raina called his name. "Logan."

He paused and turned to face her. This friend of Gina's, who probably knew the whole story, would be one hundred percent on her friend's side.

So she surprised him when she said, "I know where you are, Logan. I lost my husband. Going on and fighting for a new life is like climbing Everest without the proper tools, without preparations for the blizzard you know you're going to run into. The difference between you and me is that I didn't have a child to remind me even more deeply every day of what I'd lost."

She really *did* seem to understand, and, more important, she didn't seem to be judging him. "I believe I *am* ready to move on. I think Amy would want me to. But Gina and I— For years I believed one thing. I thought she'd betrayed me. I had doubts. But then Wednesday she dropped a bombshell about my father and I didn't know how to handle it."

"Gina told you the truth."

He nodded. "We always think we want to know the truth, but then when we hear it, we change our minds."

Raina didn't disagree. "Your father attempted to interfere with your relationship with Gina all those years ago. Are you going to let him do it again now?"

That was a punch Logan hadn't been expecting. "You don't beat around the bush, do you?"

"Not usually. And I won't lie to Gina about running into you today. But I probably won't say anything unless she asks, either."

When Raina didn't move away, he realized she wanted to tell him something else but didn't know if she should.

"What?" he asked.

"Putting the past behind is never easy. Gina has struggled with that, too. But maybe you should know… She told her family everything, too. It was time."

"No more secrets. Nothing else kept in the dark."

"Exactly," Raina agreed.

Logan saw a wisdom in Raina's dark eyes that he wished he possessed himself at this moment. "Thanks," he said, meaning it.

"No thanks necessary," she said with a shake of her head, her long black hair falling over her shoulder. "I just wish you and Gina could get on the same page before it's too late."

The words *too late* echoed in his mind as he drove home. The sound of their hum was somewhat muted as he had supper with Daniel, played with him and then put him to bed.

In his crib Daniel's expression when he looked up at Logan and asked, "Gee, gee? Gee, gee?" made Logan's heart feel like a lead weight. The words *too late* rever-berated like a clanging bell as he settled in his office.

Raina's words became louder than the bell. *Your father tried to interfere in your relationship with Gina all those years ago. Are you going to let him do it again?*

Why *hadn't* he gone after Gina after she'd left? Sure, his father's stroke was the easy answer. But there was another answer, deeper and more unsettling. His pride had been hurt. Oh, he'd known it all these years, but he just hadn't admitted it. Until Gina, he could have had any woman he wanted. After all, his father was wealthy and Logan knew he could attract pretty women. But when he'd met Gina, she honestly hadn't seemed to care about his money. All she'd wanted to do was take care of the horses. They'd been a priority for him, too, and the two of them had bonded over the birth of a foal. They'd looked into each other's eyes and known…they were soul mates.

They'd talked for hours on end before they'd gotten physical. And once that had happened, every moment with Gina had been one to be cherished and savored. When he'd asked her to marry him, he hadn't expected her to hesitate. Not for an instant. But she'd not only hesitated, she'd said no. She'd left him. He'd been dumped. That feeling had been new and raw and tearing. So when he'd finally called her and she'd rebuffed him, he'd decided he didn't need that humilia-tion. He was Logan Barnes. He could find another woman easily.

But he hadn't. Not until Amy. Because Gina had never left his mind and he'd compared every woman he'd met to her.

Now she'd turned his world upside down again. The

father he'd thought had loved him had been as cold as everyone had said he was. He had no doubt that Elliot Barnes *would* have disinherited him if Logan had insisted on marrying Gina. Why hadn't he seen his father's hand in everything back then? How could he have believed that the love that he and Gina shared hadn't really been there but had been a figment of his imagination?

And now? Oh, yeah, he still had his pride. Small comfort *that* was. Maybe he'd have to learn how to toss it away.

No—there was no *maybe* about it. If he wanted Gina back—and he now knew down to the soles of his boots that he did—he'd have to trade pride for happiness.

If it wasn't too late.

Chapter Thirteen

On Saturday evening, Gina didn't know what to make of Raina. Or Lily, who had arrived at the house with several containers of Chinese food, as if she and Raina had planned it.

Raina forked lo mein onto a dish. "We thought you'd enjoy something different for a change."

Lily waved at the tallest container. "The lemon chicken's wonderful. You've really got to try it."

Neither of them said anything about her lack of appetite but she knew this dinner was all about that.

"Rice, too," Raina prompted. Then she added, "Lily's going to teach us how to crochet. That way you'll have something to concentrate on instead of staring into space."

"Do you really think I need something else to concentrate on? I picked up three new clients this past week."

"Just think, you can get an early start on Christmas," Lily advised her. "You can make a sweater for everybody in your family. They'll love it."

Gina supposed that was true, but she didn't see crocheting as a real outlet or hobby. She'd still be able to think while she was doing it.

"There's another reason for me to crochet." Lily's cheeks took on more color.

Gina studied her and began to smile—a genuine smile she felt straight from her heart. "Are you—?"

"Pregnant!" The word erupted from Lily in a burst of joy. "Can you believe it? I e-mailed Troy yesterday. He's through-the-roof happy. I can't wait until—"

The doorbell rang.

"Are you two expecting someone?" Gina asked.

A knowing smile crossed Raina's lips. "No, but you are. Why don't you go answer it?"

What had they done? Sent her balloons and a singing clown to cheer her up?

"If this is something that's going to embarrass me," she called over her shoulder as she hurried to the door, "I'll make sure that on your birthdays—"

She never finished the sentence because as she entered the foyer she saw a shadow through the side glass. A tall, very broad-shouldered shadow.

She felt like running back to the kitchen, but she knew she couldn't do that. Not and face life as she should. So she opened the door. Although she'd suspected who that shadow belonged to, she was still shocked to see Logan there.

"You look like you've seen a ghost." His voice was deep and husky and she wondered if she saw a bit of uncertainty in his eyes.

"I never expected to see you at this door again."

"Would you come with me?"

She took a step back. "Where?"

Lily and Raina had appeared now. Raina had brought Gina's purse. Lily was carrying the light shawl Gina used for cooler nights. "What's this?" she asked them.

"We think you should go."

Gina felt a little angry now. "So you know what's going on? Would you please tell me?"

"Logan will tell you if you give him a chance," Raina advised her.

If she'd give him a chance. A chance to do what?

"Go with the flow," Lily whispered in her ear in a fairy-godmother type of way.

Just why was she hesitating? What did she have to lose?

More pieces of her heart. She remembered what Logan had said. *How could I ever trust you'd stay?*

"Don't think, Gina, please." He stretched out his hand for hers. "Just come with me."

She looked down at the sundress she'd put on, simply because it was light and cool. "I'm not dressed for—"

"You're dressed just right." He was still holding out his hand and she was truly afraid to think about what this could mean.

Raina gave her a little nudge and Gina took Logan's hand.

He smiled at the two women behind her. "Thanks. I owe you."

"Count on it," Lily said with a smile.

Then he was leading Gina out the door to his Range Rover. When he helped her inside, she was aware of his face close to hers. But then he stepped away and shut her door.

After he climbed into the driver's seat, he said, "I have something to show you, so just be patient. Okay?"

She sighed and looked out the window. Even though night had fallen, she realized quickly they were headed toward the Barnes estate. "Does Daniel want to see me?"

"He calls for you often."

"That wasn't exactly an answer."

After they drove between the entrance pillars, Logan didn't veer toward the parking circle, but rather to the unpaved side road that led to the lake.

"Where are we going?"

"Trust me, Gina." He glanced over at her.

Could she trust him now? The better question was, did he trust *her?*

She said nothing as they bumped along the potholes and over the ruts. Logan parked and helped her out of the SUV, a large flashlight in his hand. He shone it ahead of them as they walked through a crop of trees to the small dock.

Once they'd cleared the foliage, everything changed. There were candles everywhere…surrounding the dock, along the rim of the lake, even in the rowboat.

"What is this?" she asked, her breath hitching, her voice small with wonder.

He led her to the dock and stood with her surrounded by candles. "It's light in the darkness, Gina. It's you lighting up my life. Will you row out into the middle of the lake with me?"

Hope began to take root in Gina's heart, so much hope her throat closed. She finally murmured, "Yes," and let him lead her to the boat.

He climbed in first and then held up his hands for her. She didn't hesitate to take them after she tossed her purse and shawl to one of the seats.

Once they were positioned in the middle of the lake, sitting next to each other directly under the almost-full moon, they settled their oars in the boat. Logan shifted slightly to face her, and held her hand, his thumb rubbing along her knuckles.

When a tremor went through her, he asked, "Are you cold?"

She shook her head. She was as warm as warm could be, not knowing what to expect, a wash of sensual current running through her.

"Nothing has been easy for us, and that's mostly been my fault," he admitted.

She began shaking her head, but he kept going. "You know it's true. If I'd come after you when you went to college, you would have told me the truth and we could have confronted it together. We could have confronted my father together."

"That's what you would have done? You would have given up your inheritance?"

"I would have given up anything for you. The problem was, I didn't give up what I needed to give up most—my pride. If I hadn't been so damned stubborn and self-absorbed, I would have recognized the change in your voice when I called you. I would have realized something was wrong."

"You were worried about your dad. There was so much on your mind. And I was still in shock."

"You should have told me why you left sooner." There was gentle rebuke in his voice.

"I didn't want to hurt you. Not just as far as the inheritance went, but I knew what your father said would put a wall between you. You were finally beginning to believe he wanted you in his business…that he wanted to be the father he'd never been."

"You shouldn't have to protect me. *I'm* supposed to protect *you*."

"It goes both ways."

"About Houston—"

"We don't have to talk about that," she said, concerned it would tip the happiness she was beginning to believe they'd find together.

"Yes, we do. No more half truths, no more misunderstandings. I want you to succeed, Gina. I want you to go after whatever you feel is going to fulfill you. But that day when Silverstein called me, all I could see was your interest in travel growing, your interest in setting up the centers growing. All I could see was you leaving me and Daniel someday when we weren't enough to hold you in Sagebrush."

She didn't know where this was leading, but she did know she loved Logan. She squeezed his hand. "I would never do that. Not if you want me to stay."

At that, he draped his arm around her, pulled her close and lifted her chin. His mouth was tenderly passionate claiming her, making promises he wanted to keep. "I'm sorry, Gina, that I had so many doubts. I'm sorry that I didn't know how to let go of Amy to concentrate on us."

She wrapped her arms around his chest and held him tight. "She's part of your life, part of your past, and she'll always be Daniel's mother."

"She'll be his mother, but not the one he remembers. *You're* going to be the mother he remembers."

She gazed into Logan's eyes, searching for sadness. But she didn't see any. Suddenly, what he'd said dawned on her. "You want me to be Daniel's mother?"

Instead of answering her, he slipped something from his shirt pocket and held it in the palm of his hand. The gold locket glowed under the moonlight.

"It's your mother's locket—the one I returned to you!"

"Yes, it is. I've kept it in the back of my dresser drawer all these years." He opened it, showing her the picture of the two of them when they were much younger. "I couldn't give it to Amy because it belonged to you."

As she lifted her hair, her heart so full she couldn't speak, he clasped it around her neck. Taking Gina's hand, he asked, "Will you marry me, Gina Rigoletti?"

Somehow she found words, happiness a tangible essence flowing through every fiber of her being. She wrapped her arms around his neck. "Yes, I'll marry you, Logan Barnes. And I'll love you always." Her love for Logan had begun so long ago, and she knew it would live forever.

"For always," he repeated and kissed her under the light of the Texas moon.

* * * * *